ONE MOMENT IN TIME

Sleep would just have to wait. Before she could indulge herself in another thought, just as she poured the water into the coffeemaker he came into the kitchen. Dressed in burgundy silk lounging pajama bottoms and a matching silk T-shirt, he looked sexy and very desirable. Her heart screamed out for his attention.

"Are you hungry?"

"I wouldn't mind something to snack on. What you got good?"

"Depends on what you have a taste for."

His eyes scanned her entire body. "I know you don't want me to go there."

"Maybe I do." Her eyes flirted openly with him. "Why don't you take a stab at trying to find out exactly what I want?"

"What if I said I wanted to snack on you?"

She bit down on her lower lip. It was all she could do to keep from opening the top of her pajamas and offer him her breasts to snack on. "What part of me would you nibble on first?"

Eyeing her intently, he gently snapped the waistband of her pajama bottoms. "You know this is a dangerous game you're playing, don't you?"

"Dangerous? In what way?"

"Don't start that innocent act with me, Tarynton. It won't work. You know you're playing with a blazing fire."

"What if I decided I wouldn't mind getting burned?"

BOOK YOUR PLACE ON OUR WEBSITE AND MAKE THE ARABESQUE ROMANCE CONNECTION!

We've created a customized website just for our very special Arabesque readers, where you can get the inside scoop on everything that's going on with Arabesque romance novels.

When you come online, you'll have the exciting opportunity to:

- View covers of upcoming books

- Learn about our future publishing schedule (listed by publication month and author)

- Find out when your favorite authors will be visiting a city near you

- Search for and order backlist books

- Check out author bios and background information

- Send e-mail to your favorite authors

- Join us in weekly chats with authors, readers and other guests

- Get writing guidelines

- AND MUCH MORE!

Visit our website at
http://www.arabesquebooks.com

ONE MOMENT IN TIME

Linda Hudson-Smith

ARABESQUE

★BET★

BOOKS

BET Publications, LLC

http://www.bet.com

http://www.arabesquebooks.com

ARABESQUE BOOKS are published by

BET Publications, LLC
c/o BET BOOKS
One BET Plaza
1900 W Place NE
Washington, DC 20018-1211

All Kensington Titles, Imprints, and Distributed Lines are available at special quantity discounts for bulk purchases for sales promotions, premiums, fund-raising, and educational or institutional use. Special book excerpts or customized printings can also be created to fit specific needs. For details, write or phone the office of the Kensington special sales manager: Kensington Publishing Corp., 850 Third Avenue, New York, NY 10022, attn: Special Sales Department, Phone: 1-800-221-2647.

First Printing: October 2002
10 9 8 7 6 5 4 3 2 1

Printed in the United States of America

In loving memory of:
Violet Aarons
Sunrise: August 6, 1919
Sunset: November 28, 2001
I'm so happy that you were a part of my life.
I will always miss you. . . .

And to the four very special women in my life:
My big sisters:
Marlene Holmes, Donna Brinson, Candace Chandler, and
Sherry Eddington
I love each of you dearly!

ACKNOWLEDGMENTS

I would like to extend a very special thank you to the following persons and organizations:

Chandra Sparks Taylor, Consulting Editor: Thanks for your kind words, understanding, patience, and for always keeping an open ear and an open mind.

PMG International Ltd.: Robin Schuetz, Stacy English, LaTwanisha Criss, & Michelle Bannister.—Thanks for all that your group did to make my tour to Germany a huge success.

Soulful Journey Book Club—Germany: Thanks for the warm welcome I received from the book club members on my recent tour to Germany. Your support meant a lot to me.

Stephanie Kuykendall: March Air Force Base, CA— Thanks for your continued support.

Tabahani Book Circle: Thanks for all your tremendous support.

Cousins Calvester & Ollie Carter: Thanks for your hospitality on our visit to Germany.

Wallace Allen—Empire Talks Back Radio Host: Thanks for your constant support.

Cousin Herman West, Detroit, Michigan: Thanks for the special hook-ups.

Clay and Linda Robinson—Thanks for being such wonderful and loyal friends and two of my biggest personal and professional supporters. I love you both.

Joe Huwyler and Stephanie Kuykendall, Managers, March AFB Exchange—Thanks for the continuous support and your never-ending kindnesses. You both always make me feel right at home whether I'm signing books or just shopping at your store.

One

Tarynton Batiste closed her softly seductive sable-brown eyes. "Let's savor this for a moment or two. Ah, a weekend in northern California's Solvang, where you'll experience a delectable taste of mystery and an intriguing dessert of uninterrupted madness and endless passion. Let's first fire up the old taste buds with a wine and cheese reception—and then follow it up with a light but very appetizing dinner. The calories can then be worked off by an hour or two of dancing in one of the glitzy nightclubs located right on the premises. The actual murder-mystery event included in the plans won't be completely solved until Sunday morning during breakfast. Prior to that, we can delight in a generous portion of midnight mystery and intrigue in the bedroom of the quaint little bed-and-breakfast, the Victorian Lady. A bit of treasure hunting also comes to mind. How am I doing so far?" Her taupe-brown skin glowed with her excitement.

Lance Simpson grinned. "Sounds divine! I love it. When can you have everything wrapped up?"

"Being that it's Friday, and it's already late in the day, I'm going to go with Tuesday afternoon. I'll make all the final arrangements on Monday. The recommended roses and bottle of champagne should be delivered a short time before you and your guest arrive. Are we using the same credit card number that's on your service order application?"

"One and the same. Tina is going to flip out over this. She's always accused me of having no imagination whatsoever. But she'll see my hiring a professional special event planner, such as you, as very imaginative. Whatever made you consider doing something like this as a business? It's only the most brilliant idea I've ever heard of!"

"Friends always asking my advice on how to make a date special is what actually got me to thinking about it. The idea was also spurred on by my constant thoughts of all the things that I would want to do with someone special in my life." The only person Tarynton had ever loved was her childhood sweetheart of long ago, Drakkar Lomax, the only person she'd ever spent that one moment in time with. "But since I have no special person in my life, I have to live vicariously through my clients." She laughed but crying would've been more appropriate.

He raised an eyebrow. "I find that hard to believe! You mean to tell me you haven't whipped up one of your special dates on some willing brother who's sitting at home alone?"

She nodded. "You heard me right."

"I hear that you're also a freelance writer. What kind of material do you write?"

"I write magazine and newspaper articles for several different popular, major publications. I actually get the opportunity to interview and then write a lot of articles on important people. I also do a bit of entertainment and travel writing."

"Ever thought of writing a novel?"

"Funny you should ask. I'm working on my first full-length book. I've done a few short stories already, but I've never attempted to get them published. I plan to submit this one."

"Good luck. Thanks for all your help. I can't wait to spring this on Tina."

"Just remember that your discount will only apply if you write me a short note about your experience with my service and the services rendered by the other sources we're using. The rating scale is from one to ten, ten being the best. Good luck with everything!"

"You'll definitely hear from me, Tarynton. If you need me to hook you up with a date, I work out at the L.A. Sports Club with a great bunch of professionals, even athletes, single ones. Someone is always asking me if I know any fine sisters that are looking for a great man, a sister that demands respect and love long before the sheets come into play."

Her long-ago relationship with an athlete came to mind. Drakkar had been a bright NFL hopeful until a serious knee injury ended his lifelong dream. That he was employed, as a sportscaster in New Orleans, was the last word she'd heard on him—over a year ago. The loss of Drakkar was something she'd never quite gotten over. Although she had moved on with her life, she'd never met anyone that came close to what Drakkar had and still meant to her.

"I've sworn off athletes," she joked. "But thanks for the offer. Instead of a date, maybe you can hook up one of your athlete friends with my services. I sure would appreciate it. This sister can use all the business she can get."

"That's a given. My friend told me that the special dates you hook up are out of this world. That's why I'm here. Word of mouth is always the best advertisement for any business. At any rate, I've got to run. I'll wait to receive the other documents. Tina's going to think I've lost my mind, but she'll be glad that I did."

Smiling, she watched as he made his way to the door. Lance waved good-bye to her before he shut the office door behind him.

Tarynton sat back in the leather swivel chair behind her desk. As she looked at the stack of folders on her table, she wondered if she should cancel out on her friends and work a few hours more. After perusing a couple of files, she realized there wasn't too much she could do in the way of making special arrangements before Monday. Besides, she was tired and the kinks in her neck were beginning to protest the overuse. At any rate, some fun and great conversation would do wonders for her. She might even be able to gather some good material for her book.

A night out with her girlfriends was always an exciting adventure. Everyone was single and most of them were brokenhearted. That alone made for interesting conversations. She couldn't remember a night out when men didn't start out as or eventually become the main topic of their conversation. Male bashing was discouraged, but it did happen on a rare occasion, usually right after someone experienced a bitter breakup.

Denise Morgan, Tarynton's best friend, was between men at the moment. Even though she was good at maintaining long relationships Denise usually bailed when the M word came up. Marriage wasn't for her, yet she liked the idea of it. It was the reality of it that didn't work for her. Her guys tried to wait her out, but only after three or four years of waiting for her to commit did they finally get the message and take a hike. She'd be depressed for a short time after the breakup, but then she'd just up and find another great guy to get involved with. She was now looking for Mr. Right number four. She had yet to realize that she could just be Miss Wrong. Denise didn't think that three serious relationships, spanning age eighteen up to her present age of twenty-eight, was all that bad of a track record. Tarynton and Denise were the same age.

Refusing to think about her own passionless history with men, Tarynton shut down her computer and turned off all the lights in her office, except the ones on a timer. Her office was conveniently located. The original owners had converted the two-car garage in her lease-with-option-to-purchase, one-story, four-bedroom house into a spacious office. After work, she normally jogged in the park across the street. But when daylight savings came around, like now, she did her jogging at the health club but only during the week.

Upon opening the door that led into the laundry room, Tarynton turned on the subtle lighting fixtures as she made her way down the long hallway. She passed through the living/dining room combination, where the upscale furnishings were done in colors of white and green. Carved from pecan-colored hardwoods was a formal dining room set with six chairs and a beautiful matching china cabinet.

In the master bedroom, beautiful eighteenth-century mahogany furnishings sat atop plush wintergreen carpet. Exquisite white sateen goose-down bedding covered the king-size bed. Loose pillows in various sizes and shapes, done in a variety of shades of soft greens, were propped in between two white king-size shammed ones. Antique-white shutters versus draperies had been the owner's choice in window coverings. The shutters allowed in as much or as little natural light as desired.

They were a great feature for sleeping in late on the weekends.

A brisk, refreshing shower had Tarynton thinking she had superpowers. Instead of her usual choice of basic black, she felt a bright red mood coming on. It seemed that everything decent she owned was in dark colors. Well, that was going to change, she suddenly decided. What she needed was a new attitude—and that called for a new wardrobe. Glad that it was the weekend, she went to work making plans for which fashion boutiques she was going to pop into on Saturday and possibly sometime after church service. She hadn't purchased any new clothes in a while and she was now looking forward to enjoying a fun shopping spree.

"Look out, American Express! Tarynton Cameron Batiste is back. L.A. men, I am now declaring myself single and eligible. I've mourned love long enough. Watch out now!"

A long red clinging skirt with a back slit, complemented by a low-cut red silk shell, made Tarynton feel rather sexy. A pair of red linen backless heels felt good on her small feet, but when she thought about dancing in them she exchanged them for a pair of red pumps. The black linen blazer would keep the chill away, she thought, especially when she wasn't on the dance floor. The nightclubs could get pretty cold from the constant operation of the air conditioner.

While looking in the mirror, she thought that her chestnut-brown hair could use a good cut and perhaps a few dramatic highlights. That would be easy enough to achieve since she had an early morning salon appointment for next Saturday. Her hair stylist, Melanie, fondly referred to as Mel, was dying to fashion her a new cut and style. She made a mental note to call Mel and tell her that she was ready to have her hook her up with a great new look.

Tall, model-slender, with stunningly keen features, gorgeous Denise Morgan was waiting for Tarynton at the entrance to the club. Smiling warmly at each other, the two best friends embraced. They had met during their sophomore year of college. Both had attended the same writing seminar that day. Denise, also a writer, had graduated from UCLA.

Tarynton liked Denise's newly layered and slightly flipped hairstyle. From head to toe, the various styles of the seventies seemed to be back in full-effect, an era that Tarynton's parents had once enjoyed tremendously.

Careful not to mess up her friend's jazzy style, Tarynton patted Denise's hair. "Love the new do. I'm thinking of having some dramatic changes to my own style. A nice cut and a few highlights should do the trick. What do you think about that?"

"I love the idea, Tarynton. But I have to ask. What prompted the change?"

"Just tired of the same old me. I'm searching for something, but I just haven't figured out what yet. Perhaps just a brand-new me." Tarynton shrugged her shoulders. "I guess we'll have to wait and see. Are the others here yet?"

Denise nodded. "Everyone is inside, except Narita. She can't make it because of a bad headache. Chariese, Rayna, and Roxanne just got here a few minutes ago. Ready to party?"

"You bet! But we need to check on Narita during the course of the evening. Is it a migraine? I know she suffers with them."

"It sounds like it, although she didn't come right out and say that. She just said the pain was quite intense."

As the two women made their way to the table, where the other friends awaited them, conversation was halted. Tarynton had become friends with the other women through Denise since they were longtime friends of hers. The music was too loud to talk over it, especially when moving through a throng of party people. Tarynton exchanged hugs and kisses with the three other very attractive women before taking a seat. A quick glance around the room gave her somewhat of an idea of how many people were crowded into the large, popular nightspot.

Tarynton was asked to dance immediately. She followed the medium-height, dark, and handsome brother to the center of the dance floor. She smiled when she looked back and saw her friends also being escorted to the dance arena. The music was fast and stirring, the way Tarynton liked it. She rarely slow-danced with anyone. Being that intimately close to a stranger made her uncomfortable. After several songs, the gentlemen escorted Tarynton back to the table, but no names or comments were exchanged.

While her friends were still dancing, Tarynton slipped into the ladies' room and made a cell phone call to Narita, their ill friend.

"It's Tarynton. We miss you. Feeling any better?"

"Girl, somebody has planted a jackhammer inside my head. I've got all the lights out and I'm lying down. This is one humdinger of a migraine and it might take a while to get over."

"Sorry you're so miserable. I won't hold you. I just wanted to check on you and let you know that we're thinking of you."

"This is so typically you, Tarynton. We both know that those other four Jezebels couldn't care less. I'm sure they're too busy getting their groove on to give any thought to me and my pitiful self.''

Tarynton chuckled. "That's not so. You just get better. We'll talk tomorrow.''

"Okay. Thanks again, Tarynton. I appreciate how considerate you are of me.''

Tarynton used the bathroom and freshened her makeup before returning to the table. Her friends were still on the floor gyrating like mad to the funky rhythms, but it looked like they'd already changed partners. Tarynton laughed when she remembered what Narita had called them.

Tarynton turned around at the soft tap on her shoulder. Her smile nearly froze on her face at the same time her eyes connected with a warm, golden-brown gaze. Drakkar Lomax? It couldn't be. But it was, all six-feet-one of him. No one in the world could make her entire body tremble this way. Afraid that her legs wouldn't work, she just sat there with a bewildered look.

His cool outward appearance belied the chaos he felt inside. He had no idea that Tarynton was the woman he'd been studying the back of for the last half hour from a table across the room. As close as they'd been, he should've known. Perhaps he had. Something that he couldn't explain if his life depended on it had compelled him out of his seat. She was one compelling woman, anyway. It seemed that she hadn't lost her magnetic powers. At least, not where he was concerned. She'd always been able to draw him in or out with ease ever since he'd known her.

Denise came up and discreetly nudged Tarynton in the ribs. "Are you going to get up, or what? You're embarrassing the hell out of the poor guy. He looks ready to bolt.''

At the commanding sound of Denise's voice, Tarynton found the courage to try out her legs. As Drakkar reached for her hand, she smiled nervously. Without uttering a word, he led Tarynton to the dance floor. Although her legs trembled, she was glad they hadn't yet buckled on her. Drakkar's strong athletic physique was enough to make the coldest-hearted woman quiver. It seemed that nothing had changed in six years. Drakkar Lomax still had it going on, still had a way of turning her body into a raging volcano of unbridled passion. Being next to him again made her want to devour every part of his anatomy. How had they gotten so emotionally far away from each other? How had they gotten to the end of forever—and so quickly?

Slowly, almost cautiously, as if touching Tarynton might burn his sienna flesh, he brought her in close to him. The scent of her perfume was familiar, even after all this time: Paul Sebastian's Design. He recalled that it was her favorite scent. He'd actually bought her a gift set, which had included the lotion and shower gel, during one of their Christmas holidays together.

Her hands were practically limp on his waist. She feared holding on to him too tightly, knowing she'd only to have to let go of his warmth at the end of the song. Him holding her felt so surreal. She'd only been thinking of him earlier in the day, which seemed odd in an eerie kind of a way. He came to her mind often, but she never allowed herself to get too deeply into her thoughts about him. It had only been over for six years, during their senior years at college, yet they'd never once discussed the breakup that had been accomplished through the U.S. mail.

She knew it was ego on her part, but she wasn't sure about his reasons. It seemed that they'd both stopped going home during college breaks and other special occasions that last year. She hadn't wanted to run into him. Could that have been his reason, too? When her parents moved out of the state of Pennsylvania, the families eventually lost the close contact.

Tarynton was still a perfect fit in his arms. She smelled sweet as ever, and the urge to push his hands up through the back of her hair, something he loved to do, made him want to totally forget the reason why they were no longer together. Sweet Tarynton. Unlike most girls, who went from dolls to boys, she started in by hanging out with the guys and playing tough, highly competitive sports on the local playground. She had been just one of the fellows. When she turned sixteen, and came to church in what the teen boys had referred to as a grown-up dress, the boys no longer saw her as one of the guys. It was open season on Tarynton Batiste—and every man for himself. As the best man, he had won . . . and they eventually swapped hearts.

The song "Fallin' " by Alicia Keys came to an end much sooner than she would've liked, but it was probably for the best. The song described her feelings about him. And being so close to him made her even hotter than she already was for him. The fact that she hadn't removed her blazer only made matters worse. Having him so near also brought back a flood of memories, good and bad. It was the bad that she had a problem with, simply because she never thought it was bad. The only real bad memory that she had of their relationship was the day of the breakup.

Then a weird question came to mind. Did he even know who she was? Of course he knew. They had only rocked in the cradle together, grown up together, played in the same sandbox, gone to the same schools, and lived on the same street all of their lives. Going to college in different cities had been their first separation ever. But she'd never planned on it becoming a permanent one. Their one moment in time was supposed to go on and on until forever.

Drakkar walked Tarynton back to the table and pulled out her chair. "Thank you, Tarynton. I'm sorry we couldn't talk over the music. It's nice seeing you. It's been a long time."

So the loud music was why he hadn't tried to talk to her, she thought. Then again, she hadn't been very vocal either. She could recall a time when he would've just whispered into her ear to be heard. But that was another moment in time.

She snapped out of her reverie. "It has been nice, Drakkar. Thanks for the dance."

She hadn't expected him just to turn and walk away. When he did, she felt faint. Watching him leave left her with so many questions unanswered. Certain that she'd never see him again, especially since he hadn't asked her for any contact information, she sucked up the incredible pain burning deep in her belly and inside the place where her heart used to reside.

Tarynton couldn't wait to get out of her clothes and hop into the shower. She desperately needed to wash away Drakkar's engaging natural scent mixed with the aroma of Oscar De La Renta. While she'd danced with one person before him, she hadn't done so with anyone after him. It had to be his scent that had her senses reeling since he was the only one that had held her close. The memory of those few moments hurt like the dickens and she didn't need another reminder of what it used to be like. The memories of those times were indelible.

Before hanging up her blazer, Tarynton emptied out the pockets first. Surprised to see a business card among the contents, she took a close look at it. Her heartbeat quickened at the sight of Drakkar's name written in bold black letters. So, he had made contact with her.

Perhaps it was his way of allowing her to call the shots. Even if the way he'd accomplished it was unusual. It was more than unusual. It was downright intriguing. But Drakkar had always intrigued her—and in so many scrumptious ways.

In further examining the card, she saw that Drakkar was still a sports commentator for a major television network. What excited her beyond description was the fact that this particular station was right here in Los Angeles, right in her own backyard.

She and Drakkar were once again living in the same city. Was Cupid behind this intriguing turn of events? Euphoria only lasted for as long as it took her to remember the pain that had been caused. Damaging pain, the kind of agony that incinerated the soul.

Seated in his black Lexus 400, across the street from Tarynton's home, Drakkar was contemplating his next move. He felt bad about following her home, but he thought it was the easiest way to find out where she lived. He'd waited for her and her friends to leave the club and then he'd stayed a safe distance behind Tarynton's car. He hadn't expected them to stop off at an all-night diner, which had left him sitting in his car for nearly two hours. He had convinced himself that he just wanted to make sure that she got home safely, but he knew that was a lie.

If Tarynton didn't find the business card he'd slipped into her jacket pocket, this had been his way of making sure he could contact her again. Knowing Tarynton Batiste as he once did, inside and out, she would have an unlisted phone number. That was the simple truth of the matter. Since her parents had moved, he could no longer call home and get the information from them as to her whereabouts. But after stumbling across her unexpectedly, though he was well aware that she lived in Los Angeles, he hadn't wanted to lose any more time. Six years had already been thrown to the dogs. Now it looked as if fate had taken matters into its own hands.

He looked at the clock on the dashboard. It was practically three A.M. He couldn't believe how the time had gotten away from him. He cursed himself for not going into the diner to seek her out, to ask her if they could talk. Then he missed another grand opportunity by not letting his presence be known when she got out of her car after driving up to her place. He didn't understand why she hadn't put the car in the garage. It was dangerous for her not to have done so. He had decided not to go to the door in case she was living with someone. Women and men involved in serious relationships went out on the town with their friends all the time.

Drakkar started the engine and drove off. Tomorrow was already here, but it would be just another day if he hadn't figured out how to see Tarynton again. They had a bit of unfinished business, so much so that it wouldn't allow him to move on until it was wrapped up. All he could do was pray that she'd find the business card and call him. If she did find it, he hoped she'd turn it over and discover his hotel phone and room numbers written on the back. The moment he'd learned that he'd landed the job in California, all he could do was think about finding her. That could've turned out to be an impossible feat in a metropolis like Los Angeles.

Seated in the center of her bed, with her legs crossed, Tarynton was engrossed in a powwow with her thoughts of the past. She held Drakkar's card in her hand. Both his business and hotel numbers were already seared in her memory. Should she call or shouldn't she? was the million-dollar question. God only knew how much she wanted to talk with him. Was it possible for them to get together again as friends without discussing the past? Although it didn't seem likely, she thought that a slim chance for it to happen might exist.

She didn't really want to talk about the past. What purpose would it serve? They couldn't go back and retrieve it. In fact, their past apart didn't have them in it. Only memories of yesterdays had kept her company. Was it even possible for them to share in another today or even a tomorrow after what had gone down? Did she owe it to herself to find out?

Yes, she did, she concluded. They had truly been best friends as well as lovers.

She reached for the phone but only dialed four digits before hanging up. Tears fringed her lashes. Maybe her confidence was a little too high. She could just be setting herself up for more pain and disappointment. Deciding she needed to think things through a little longer, she got up from the bed and rushed into the bathroom for her morning shower.

More thinking in the shower brought her to the conclusion that since he'd left the card, which obviously meant that he wanted to keep in contact with her, then maybe she would wait for him to come to her. That way she would be sure that he really wanted to see her again. Let him make the first move toward reuniting them. She wasn't convinced that their bumping into each other was just a coincidence. Drakkar was known to go after what he wanted. He wouldn't change his method of operation if he'd decided that he wanted to be back in her company again.

With headphones from her Walkman on her ears, Tarynton listened to Mary Mary's gospel CD. At the health club, where she'd been a member for the past three years, Tarynton took to the indoor jogging track like a hunted woman. She ran hard, as if someone were chasing her. There was no doubt that her past was trying to catch up to her. But she wasn't sure if she wanted to be caught or not. At least, not yet. More thoughts of Drakkar had only brought on more uncertainties. It wasn't a good thing to try and retrieve the past—since it was impossible.

Another shower after exercising had left Tarynton feeling refreshed and her head finally felt clear. As she inserted the key into her front door, she heard a car pull up into her driveway. She looked back at the shiny black Lexus that had no license plate on it, which suggested to her that it was brand-new. Then she saw the driver. Her heart went into stampede mode inside her chest. It didn't take him as long as she thought it would, but she had somehow felt confident that he'd try to find her. How he'd accomplished it so quickly made her delirious with curiosity.

She walked back to meet him as he got out of the car. "You're certainly full of surprises, Mr. Lomax. How did you know how to find me?"

He grinned. "You haven't forgotten how persistent I am, now, have you, Tarynton? But if you'll invite me in for something cold to drink, I'll satisfy your curiosity."

Drakkar had decided just to go for it regarding seeing her. If she did live with someone, a male someone, the fact that they had grown up together should explain him wanting to see her again. What harm was there in that? Who could find harm with someone desiring to see a childhood friend? Of course, they'd been a lot more than friends. Hot and heavy lovers was more like it.

Tarynton hesitated for a moment. She wanted him

to come in, but her sofa was littered with dozens and dozens of pictures of him and her taken when they were together. She'd pulled them out last night. That wasn't something she wanted him to see, for sure. It would only be a dead giveaway of how much she'd thought of him since their encounter the past evening.

He took her hesitation for reluctance. "Maybe this is a bad time. If I'd had your number, I would've called first. Give me a call when you have time. I put my card in your jacket pocket."

"No, no, it's not that. My house is a mess and I wasn't expecting company. If you don't mind waiting in my office until I tidy up a bit, I'd love to offer you something to drink."

Barely able to believe this incredible blessing, he sighed with relief, silently thanking God for answering his prayer. "In your office it is."

Instead of opening the front door, she reached inside her car and hit the remote to the garage. When her office came into plain view, he saw why she'd hadn't parked in the garage last night, rather, early this morning. He followed her inside and she gestured for him to take a seat on the cream-colored leather sofa.

"I should only be a couple of minutes. Citing my house as a mess was a bit of an overstatement. Just need to pick up a few things."

"Take your time, Tarynton Cameron Batiste. I've only waited six years for this moment."

She cut her eyes at him but didn't comment. She didn't like the sound of his remark, which seemed to suggest blame on her part. That couldn't possibly be the case. She left the room a little worried about spending time alone with him.

In one fell swoop she picked up the pictures and shoved them back into the box where she kept them.

After storing the box in the hall closet, she went into her cheerfully decorated kitchen and made sure that everything in there was neat and clean. Her cozy kitchen was as good a place as any to sit down and have a long overdue reunion with a childhood friend and ex-lover.

Two

Tarynton was surprised to find Drakkar looking at the pictures on the wall when she returned. Quietly, she watched him from the doorway. He had a body that wouldn't quit, one that had never failed to satisfy hers. She couldn't help conjuring up past images of her naked body beneath his in bed. Their sexual appetite for each other had been nothing less than voracious.

Drakkar had taken possession of her virginity the night of the senior prom. It hadn't happened in a pay-by-the-hour cheap motel or in the backseat of his car. He had saved up for a year to afford the grand suite at a first-class hotel out near the Pittsburgh Airport. That night had been dubbed their *one moment in time*. Boy, that had been one long moment, one that had lasted several hours. If she hadn't had a curfew, it more than likely would've lasted the entire night.

Their lovemaking was terribly awkward at first. Both of them were fearful, she recalled. She didn't feel anything akin to being on cloud nine until long after the pain had subsided. He was no more experienced with the physical side of a relationship than she was. He didn't know she knew that, which had made for lots of fumbles and quite a few hits and misses. Then the magic moments finally arrived. That first climax had soared them both right up into heaven.

His turning to look in her direction caused her to reshelve those bittersweet memories in the back of her mind, where she kept them neatly tucked away but always close at hand.

"Ready for that drink now?"

He smiled brightly. "More than ready."

"What's your choice in beverages? I have water, coffee, tea—hot or iced—Sprite, or Coke."

"Dare to take a stab at it?"

"At what?"

"My choice?"

Without bothering to respond, she filled a tall glass with ice and removed a can of Sprite from the refrigerator. After dropping several red maraschino cherries into the glass, smiling smugly, she set the items on the table in front of him. "How did I do, Mr. Lomax?"

"Perfect! Nice to know you haven't forgotten."

How could I forget? "Yeah, it's been a while." She took a seat facing him. "Now, I'd like to know how you found me in a city this size."

He chuckled. "Care to guess at that, too? I'd like to see if you still know me as well as you used to."

"No more guessing games. As for knowing you, it turns out that I didn't know you as well as I thought I did." She instantly berated herself for saying something she'd promised not to.

The derisive remark had him puzzled. "I see that you're still direct as ever. But here goes. I followed you home last night."

She didn't look one bit surprised. He was a man who

knew how to get exactly what he was after. But what was he after now? Her heart? If so, she'd already given it away—and it couldn't ever be returned. Taking her heart back from the man who possessed it had already been proved as an impossible feat.

"You don't seem at all surprised by what I just said. Maybe you know me a little better than your previous barb seemed to suggest."

His comment made her realize she'd unintentionally hurt his feelings. Then it suddenly dawned on her that she didn't come straight home. "I stopped last night before coming home—"

"Hal's Soul Food Diner," he interjected.

"You were inside?" That wasn't possible. The diner was so small that everyone could see everyone else. Had he walked through that door she would've been the first to notice.

"In the parking lot. I even nodded off a couple of times during my wait. What were you ladies talking about for over two hours?"

"Men!" *Doggish' men. Players. Cool jerks.* He had her heart skipping more than a couple of beats. That he'd waited out in the parking lot all that time was certainly impressive.

"Did my name happen to come up, Tarynton?"

I said men. She was glad she hadn't said that aloud. That would be too sarcastic, not to mention an outright lie. Drakkar was definitely all man. He'd only mishandled his business once that she knew of, even if he had handled it very badly. It still rankled sorely within her. But no one was perfect. "No, your name didn't come up. And you should be glad about that."

"Why's that?"

"We were talking about dogs, the human variety, and jerks and players."

"Player hating, huh? But thank you. I'll take my name

not being mentioned as a compliment." He grinned, showing the very smile that Tarynton had loved over the past years, the one that had rendered her totally powerless against his powerful physical and personal allure.

"So, what's been going on in the life of Tarynton Batiste? I'd like an account of the past six years." Eager to hear whatever she had to say, he sat back in his chair and got comfortable.

In a thoughtful gesture, she put her forefinger to her chin. "Graduated from SC with a degree in English lit. Worked for a couple of magazines and newspapers for a time. I then opted to freelance while I built up my own business. Besides freelancing, I'm sort of a travel agent."

"Sort of?"

She laughed. "It's like this." She went on to tell him about her knack for booking special, exciting trips for couples that wanted a quick getaway or even a lengthy vacation. She gave him a detailed account of how she'd started out, why, and how much success she'd had thus far.

"Sounds like you landed on a gold mine. Congrats!"

"Thanks. Now it's your turn."

He frowned. "Well, you already know that I blew out my knee before I finished up at Grambling. Even though I'd earned my degree in communications, I started out teaching physical education and coaching football at the high school level. I later went to broadcasting school and I'm now employed as a sportscaster for a major television network here in Los Angeles. But I worked for a short time in Louisiana as a sportscaster before coming out here."

Each had noticed that the other hadn't said a word regarding their personal lives.

His expression grew somber. "We both know that this

isn't what I want to talk to you about. We have some serious unfinished business to discuss, T.C."

T.C. It had been a long time since she'd been called that. In fact, he was the only one who ever called her by her initials. *Help me, Lord.* A few words to "Fallin' " swept through her mind.

Pain crept into her eyes. She couldn't handle all this right now. In fact, she didn't know if she'd ever be able to. The past was something she wasn't willing to explore at the moment, or maybe she'd never be ready. At any rate, it wasn't healthy. "Drakkar, I allowed you to come into my home because we were the best of friends for so many years and I wanted us to try and catch up with each other. But I'll allow you to stay or even to come again only on one condition."

He looked pensive. "Spell it out, Tarynton. Dot every single *i* and cross each *t*. You've always been good at doing that."

"I know. But when you spell things out in no uncertain terms, no one can later accuse you of miscommunication. I don't want to venture into the past, Drakkar. There's nothing back there that I want to conjure up. At least, not the part of the past that I think you're talking about. I like living in the moment so that I can make sure that each second is well represented. I can't change a thing about the past or ever predict the future. I favor present. Can you please respect that?"

He studied her intently for a brief moment, toying with the things he needed to settle with her. But he could clearly see that now wasn't the time. If he pressed her, he knew she'd enforce her conditions. Not being able to see her again was not at all an attractive ultimatum. Though she would never call it an ultimatum, that's what it was. He vowed to tread lightly, but he also swore never to give up on settling the past between them. "For sure. So where do we go from here?"

"We?"

"You and I, Tarynton. We were always close friends. I know we lost contact, but I never stopped thinking of you." *What an understatement.* "When I landed the job here in sunny Cal, I made a vow to find you. It turned out to be easier than I expected. Fate, I guess."

"Fate? You come to the club where you knew I'd be— and then you follow me home. You call that fate?"

"Sorry to disappoint you, sunshine, but I didn't know you would be at that club. I'm just glad that you were. I knew that finding you was going to be like looking for a needle in a haystack in this city, but I was determined to comb through every straw if need be."

This time she *was* surprised, extremely so. Calling her *sunshine,* another of his pet names for her, caused her to will her heart into resuming a calm state. Then she looked for signs that he might be putting her on about not knowing she was in the club. "You're not kidding, are you?"

"Not in the least. Nothing to kid about. Even before I asked you to dance, I didn't know that it was you I'd been checking out. I should've known, but I didn't. Your hair is much longer than I've ever seen you wear it. I was busy staring at the back of your head when something pushed me out of my seat and dragged me to where you were seated." They both laughed. "Something serious had a hold of me in that club, T.C. And it brought me straight over to you."

She gave him her best smile. "Maybe fate did have a hold of your bad butt!"

He chuckled. "Okay! Can we now move on into what you do for fun in L.A.?"

"I don't have a lot of time for extracurricular activities. But when I do hang out, I love to go to Choices, the club we were in last night. I like that it caters to young professionals who are looking to make their mark on the world. I take in a movie now and then, but I prefer live theater, especially gospel plays. But my favorite thing to do is curl up with a good book featuring a positive good-looking man and a striking female who knows exactly who she is. I like a book with lots of spice, a good bit of adventure, a little dash of sass, and lots of—"

"Hot sex," he finished for her.

She blushed but she wasn't about to admit that he was right about the ending of her sentence. She did love her books to be filled with loads of steam. When she'd realized what she was about to say, she'd swallowed the words, but it seemed as if they'd gotten out anyway. He still remembered quite a bit about her. Astonishing but not so hard to believe.

"Still love to take long drives?" In seeing her embarrassment, he decided not to tease her about the hot sex, but there was no doubt in his mind that it was the ending of her sentence.

"I do. Flattered that you remembered. The mountain ranges in California are awesome. My friends and I drive up to Lake Arrowhead and Big Bear a lot in the spring and summer. It's lovely up there. We're not into the hiking and camping thing, just the scenery and hitting all the quaint little retail outlet shops. How long have you been in L.A., and what have you done for fun since arriving in the beautiful City of the Angels?"

"No sarcasm intended, but there are also quite a few ugly devils living in this city. I've only been here a few weeks, but the local news in itself is harrowing. As for fun, I haven't had much of that. Learning the ropes at the studio has been exciting. I love what I do. When I'm not working, I'm apartment hunting. I'm still in a hotel. I came out last night because I thought I needed a break from work and from searching this big city for somewhere decent to live."

"Thought?"

"Well, now it looks like I came out because fate knew that you were out there just waiting to be found by me." Had he been sitting closer, he would've ducked. Tarynton had a mean right hook. The look she now had in her eyes packed the same kind of punch.

She rolled her eyes at him. "I guess! What's your favorite sport to cover?"

"I love them all. But, as you already know, my first heart has always been football. Basketball comes second. Don't know a hell of a lot about the NHL, but I'm learning in case I get the opportunity to cover a game. Baseball, I can take it or leave it, but I can definitely call the game. What project or projects are you currently working on?"

"I have a few special dates to design. I also have several writing assignments with the holidays just around the corner. The most challenging of them is the Kwanzaa project for a major African-American publication. I've been asked to write a story on something that I know zilch about. I'm embarrassed to admit my ignorance on the subject matter, but I'm prepared to get deep into my research. I have several months before my deadline."

He laughed. "Did you tell the magazine what you just told me?"

"Not a chance. I probably would've lost the assignment. It's something I've been curious about but never found the time to pursue. Time isn't exactly one of my strongest allies. It usually works against me these days. I took the assignment because I saw it as a challenge and I really want to learn all about the tradition. It has become a very important celebration among our people. Since you've questioned me on the subject, what do you know about Kwanzaa?"

He shrugged. "Not as much as I should or would like to. I do know that the celebration of family, community, and culture lasts for seven days. Kwanzaa also builds on the five fundamental activities of continental African 'first fruits' celebrations: ingathering, reverence, commemoration, recommitment, and celebration. Maybe you can teach me what else you find out. Then we'll both be well informed on the subject. What do you say to that?"

"I think that can be arranged. I love sharing knowledge, as it *is* power."

"Speaking of arranging, if I don't make some living arrangements pretty quickly, I'm going to go insane. I've gotten to the place that I'm starting to hate hotels."

He instantly thought of one hotel that he could never come to hate. Prom night. That was some hotel and one unforgettable night. The same night he and Tarynton had lost their innocence. She didn't know that he was a virgin then, and he didn't think she knew it now. As many fumbles as he'd made, he couldn't see how she hadn't guessed. But if she had, she would never have fronted him like that. Tarynton had never once made him feel weak or inadequate in anything. He couldn't remember her ever putting anyone down. Still, a breakup had occurred and lots of distance had somehow gotten in between them.

"I'm not that fond of hotels either." She snapped her fingers. "I know of a great complex that just opened. It's not too far from here and this part of the valley is not too far from your job location. I'm sure you know that already since you've been stalking me." She laughed to make sure that he knew she was teasing.

Knowing that he would've gladly stalked the city if it had meant finding her, he smiled broadly in return. "How about riding along with me to show me exactly where this place is?"

"Sure. Just say when."

"What about right now?"

She looked at her watch. "The office may close early

since it's the weekend so we'd better catch the wind at our back this instant. Let me get a jacket. I'll be right back."

The complex was located approximately five and six-tenths of a mile from her place. Drakkar liked that. He also liked the idea of security gates with a twenty-four-hour-patrolled guard shack at the entrance. Another feature that excited him was the fully equipped physical fitness center. Even though he was a member of a fitness center, having one on the property where he lived would be convenient for those times when he couldn't get to the health club.

Seated in the leasing office, having completed the tour of the complex, Drakkar and Tarynton looked over the colorful and very informative complex brochures while waiting for the leasing agent to finish up with another client.

"What do you think of this place? Is it somewhere you'd actually consider living?"

"This place is absolutely great! The location is also superb. Close to the freeway entrances is a major attraction for me. How do you feel about me living so close to you? Does it pose a problem for you?"

She looked amazed. "If it was an issue, I don't think I would've told you about the complex. Drakkar, if nothing else, we are still dear friends. I know we've been away from each other for a very long time, but our friendship is important enough to me to try and maintain it. I hope you feel the same way." *We should never have let our friendship end in the first place.*

His heart fluttered. "I do." He also hoped that they could get back what they once had as lovers, but he was content to let her set the rules and the pace. He wasn't going to force any romantic notions on her, not at this point. Having her back in his life was what was most important to him. With both of them being twenty-eight, time was running out on his desire to have a family. Tarynton was the woman he wanted as his wife and the mother of his children. He'd decided on that at eighteen years of age—and nothing about his decision had changed.

"It's extremely important to me. . . ."

The appearance of the leasing agent kept him from responding further. He was glad because his response would've been an emotional one. Tarynton was one of those rare beauties, inside and out, the type that often went unnoticed by others. Never looking for praise or any recognition for her good deeds or sincere kindness, she did almost everything in a very quiet, humbling way.

The leasing agent extended her hand and then gave each of them a business card. She smiled when Drakkar introduced himself and Tarynton. "My name is Patricia Gallaway. It's nice to have you visit Mount Vista Courts." The agent joined Drakkar and Tarynton at the table set up for interviewing potential residents. "What did you think of the complex?"

"It's wonderful. We both love it. I'd like to know what you have available," Drakkar said.

"What are you needing in the way of apartment accommodations? Oh, by the way, do you have children?" she asked, quickly scanning the application for pertinent information.

"No, we don't. We're not even married." Knowing that they'd always talked of marrying each other, Drakkar and Tarynton exchanged uncomfortable, painful glances. "I'm the one looking for an apartment. Tarynton and I are lifelong best friends. She's here to support me."

"I see. I asked about children because this is an adult complex. We have other family properties that I could've recommended if you had a family. Why don't you tell me what you're looking for, Mr. Lomax?"

"I need at least two bedrooms but three would be ideal. I need an office and I'd really like to have a guest room. In fact, I'm not sure I want to settle for anything less than three."

"Unfortunately the three-bedrooms won't be finished for approximately another month. They're also very few in number. If that's not something you can wait on, I can offer you a two-bedroom apartment and put your name on the waiting list for the three."

Drakkar frowned. "The thought of moving twice in such a short period of time doesn't excite me in the least. Since I hate to pack and unpack anything, I'd like to go ahead and fill out an application for the three-bedroom. Are you sure it's not going to be more than a month or possibly a little over that? The thought of another month in a hotel isn't too appealing either."

"The project is right on schedule, but I'm afraid I can't guarantee the time frame. I'm sorry. I wish that I could. Unforeseen things have a way of happening in this business. Do you still want to fill out an application? I highly recommend that you at least put your name on the waiting list. The complex is filling up rather quickly."

Drakkar smiled. "That sounds like a winner."

Out in front of her house, but still seated in Drakkar's car, Tarynton toyed with the idea of asking him if he would like to stay in one of her guest rooms until his apartment was ready. Like him, she hated living in hotels and out of a suitcase for long periods of time. But their living together under the same roof could be playing with a blazing fire, she thought. Maybe it wasn't such a good idea, after all. Seeing him every day for a month could get under her skin, especially knowing that she still loved him so deeply. That scared her more than anything.

"Hey, what about you renting me out one of your guest rooms until my apartment is ready?" He had asked the question as if he'd read her mind. "I promise to pay top dollar. And I promise not to get in your hair or in your way. I work long hours and I know I have at least one weeklong trip coming up before the month is up. What do you think?"

Wow! What could she say to that? That they thought a lot alike wasn't so unusual to her. It had always been that way with them. That was why forever for them hadn't been far-fetched.

"I'm only leasing with an option to buy, but I guess I could let you stay here since it's only for a short period of time. The house also has a private entrance in the back, which will allow you to come and go as you please. I wouldn't think of charging you rent because you wouldn't be a guest then. My lease prohibits me from subleasing." Instantly wishing she had given herself more time to think about it, she groaned inwardly.

"And I wouldn't think of staying here for nothing. So, we have to come up with something that we can both live with."

"Okay, but why don't we first start with you taking a look at one of the guest rooms before we decide on anything? You may not even like the accommodations."

"Great idea." Drakkar got out of the car and rushed around to open Tarynton's door. Always the gentleman, she thought, smiling up at him.

After entering the house, Tarynton took Drakkar on a quick tour. She showed him both guest rooms and he seemed partial to the one that gave him a great view of the mountains. This particular room was also designed similar to a master suite, as it had an adjoining bathroom. He'd have to use the one in the hallway if he took the other one.

"I think you just got yourself a roommate. Sure you're okay with me moving in? By the way, how's your man going to take another dude living here with you?" He held his breath.

"I'm okay with it and he'll be just fine with everything. I can assure you of that." She didn't have a man. At least, not a special one, but it might be better if he thought she did. She didn't like lying about it, but in this instance it was probably best for both of them.

But how are you going to handle him bringing another woman into your house if he has one? came the annoying little voice inside her head. "But are you going to be okay not being able to have overnight guests? I can fudge on having one guest staying over for an extended period, but I'm not sure of any more guests than that since I haven't actually exercised my option to purchase this place." That restriction should nip that little dilemma right in the bud, she mused.

He looked nonplussed. "I wouldn't think of doing something like that. I consider this a genuine courtesy that you've extended to me. If I need to spend the night with a woman, I'd just get a hotel." *As for your man, that's what I don't know if I'm going to be okay with.* He had asked the question because he just had to know if she was romantically involved with someone or not. Now that he had the answer, he wished he hadn't asked the question. It hurt like hell.

He remembered how relieved he felt when one of their mutual friends had told him that Tarynton hadn't gotten married, after Drakkar had asked about her wedding plans. In fact, no one but him seemed to know anything about her plans to get married. It was still all a mystery.

"I didn't think you would, but you know my philosophy on communication. If you don't talk openly about it, you can't ever hope to reach an understanding."

"I've always admired that about you. For someone who's degreed in the art of communication, I sometimes fall short in that department, especially when it comes down to my personal life. There are instances when I have a hard time communicating my intentions and my feelings to others outside of the workplace. That's the one thing I'd like to change about myself. But I do work on it constantly. And I have gotten somewhat better at it."

"Thank you for the compliment, Drakkar. Communication *is* important."

"With all that out of the way, when can I move in?"

"That's up to you."

"What about today?"

She hadn't expected to have it happen that quickly, but she had said it was up to him. "That's fine with me." *If it's really fine, why are you suddenly feeling so apprehensive?*

"Would you like to ride to the hotel with me and help me gather up my things? As you can probably tell by the sound of my voice, I can't wait to get out of there."

"I feel you. But if you don't mind, I think I'll stay here and get the room ready for you. I noticed that it was a little dusty when we were in there. I also need to stock the linen closet in your bathroom and add a few other touches to make you feel right at home."

"Okay. It shouldn't take me that long to toss everything into my suitcases. On my way back here, I'd like to stop and pick up something for us to eat. What do you have a taste for?"

"Why don't I just cook? I've already taken some meat out of the freezer for dinner. There's more than enough for two. I usually cook enough to have leftovers for the next day."

"Only if I can cook the next time." She nodded her approval to his suggestion. "You need me to stop and get anything?" he added.

"I think I've got everything covered."

He pulled a card from his wallet and handed it to her. "My cell number is on there should you find that you need something from the store." Without the slightest hesitation, he brought her to him and kissed her innocently on the forehead. "Thanks for doing this for me, T.C. I promise you won't regret it." *As for me, I know that I won't have a single regret.*

I already do. Only because I know what it's going to cost me emotionally. I haven't come close to getting over you, Drakkar Lomax. I've already tried to retrieve my heart from your possession, time and time again. But I have failed miserably at each attempt. The one thing that she didn't know how to pull off was presenting a nonexistent boyfriend. But she'd have to worry about that later. The agreement made between them was already a done deal.

"Let me get you a set of keys to the back entrance." By giving him keys to just the back entryway, she thought she could maintain some semblance of privacy. It would also allow him to have his privacy, too—and it would keep him from seeing who came and went. This way, she might not need to try and present a love interest.

Tarynton had dashed into the guest room the moment she closed the door behind her newly acquired roommate. She took inventory of all that she needed to do to make the room more presentable. Even though no one had slept in the queen-size sleigh bed since she last changed it, over a month ago, she stripped it down and redressed it in fresh linens.

Vacuuming and dusting the furniture came next and then the installation of new electrical-outlet air fresheners. She thought that Drakkar might like the ocean breeze scent, which was more of a manly odor, versus a perfumed or a flowery aroma. In stocking the linen closet, she provided him with several sets of bed linens, towels, soaps, and several rolls of toilet tissue.

Finished with the bedroom, she washed up and then went into the kitchen to cook. Instead of fixing the chicken breasts she'd taken out to thaw, she decided to make a curried shrimp, rice, and stir-fry vegetable delight. Both she and Drakkar loved anything with curry in it.

In less than two hours she had her curried dish all prepared and had set a lovely table. She had also taken a shower to freshen up. She always kept chilled bottles of both white and red wines, which she thought would go well with the meal. As she opened the refrigerator to pull out one of the bottles, she felt warm air on her neck. When she turned around and saw a man standing there, startled, she screamed.

He held her briefly. "I can see that you're really going to have to get used to someone being in your space. Sorry, I should've called your name first. I wasn't thinking."

She took a moment to regain composure. He had only scared her half to death. "How'd you get in here?"

He raised an eyebrow. "With the keys you gave me. I'm going to be living here for a minute. Remember?"

She laughed. "I do now. It's not even that I forgot. I'm just not used to having someone appear without the least bit of noise. You must have padded feet, brother."

"No, sister, you have plush carpet." He sniffed the air. "Is that curry I smell, T.C.?"

"Your smeller is definitely in working order. Have a seat. Everything is ready."

"You have a seat. You cooked, so I'll serve."

"You get no argument here. I still love to be waited on, Lomax."

He grinned. "I figured as much. Hand and foot, if I recall correctly."

"You show me a woman that doesn't like to be pampered and I'll show you a woman that doesn't think she's worthy of it, or one who doesn't know the meaning of the word."

"I'm feeling you."

Before sitting down to Tarynton's special feast, he poured both of them a glass of white wine. She nearly fell out of her chair when he turned off the dining room light and lit the candles situated in the center of the table.

Old feelings and singeing heat raced against one another up her spine and shot clear through her. She had a hard time calming her heart. Sitting across the table from Drakkar in such a romantic setting was a little more than she had bargained for. It seemed that he had a little more in mind than just being her temporary roommate.

The question for her was this: how much more than that did he have in mind?

Three

Tarynton had lain awake most of the night thinking about her very gratifying evening with Drakkar. It seemed like old times as they watched a couple of movies. She'd even made a big bowl of popcorn drizzled with melted butter. They talked late into the evening but stayed clear of discussing the past, as agreed upon. She was saddened when he told her that his grandmother had died a little over a year ago. His Grandma Liza had been very special to her. She didn't object to him holding her close to him when she'd tearfully showed her obvious grief. He'd even kissed a few of her tears away, stroking her back in hopes of bringing her comfort.

When he'd walked her to the door of her bedroom, they'd warmly embraced before she went inside to prepare for bed. No matter how innocent the embrace was it had stirred up powerful feelings. It had also touched a place deep down inside her soul.

She felt tired as she dragged herself out of bed and

trudged into the bathroom. Uncertain of the nature of the noises she could hear, she listened intently before recognizing the sound of water running. Then she remembered that she now had a roommate, a very handsome one. A generous smile formed on her lips as she once again thought about the previous evening.

Closing her eyes, she willfully and wantonly conjured up an image of the tall, dark, handsome brother in her guest bathroom, an enticingly nude one. Remembering the firm, sweet, rounded buns that she once loved to squeeze made her moan with pleasure. Thinking of the many times she'd run her fingers through his curly chest hair caused her to groan. The lower she went on his anatomy, the louder her moans came. Breathing deeply now, her eyes glazed with lust, she could actually envision the long, dark, thick majestic maleness that had been responsible for bringing her hours and countless hours of unadulterated gratification. Her body trembled as she recalled the late nights featuring sensuous foreplay, which later turned into a frenzy of wet, passion-filled kisses, deep thrusts, and maniacal gyrations that had left them both soaked in lust.

After turning the cold water on in the shower, she practically leaped under the rushing flow hoping to cool the burning fever attacking her flesh with a vengeance. How was she going to get through the next month if this kept happening? Her body was already on fire for him.

Out in the kitchen Drakkar was busy preparing a simple breakfast for himself and Tarynton. While the eggs finished boiling, he popped two slices of whole wheat bread into the toaster. He wouldn't actually toast it until she appeared. After finding some Canadian bacon in the refrigerator, he cut several thick slices and then heated it in the skillet he'd placed on top of the stove. He had already started the coffeemaker, so he took a minute to run out the front door to see if she subscribed to the Sunday newspaper. Picking up the *Los Angeles Times* from the front porch, he carried it inside and laid it out on the kitchen table for her to see.

Looking well rested despite her sleepless night Tarynton ventured into the hallway and followed her nose into the kitchen. Her eyes went straight to his attire, astonished that he wore the same Los Angeles Lakers warm-up that she had on, only his was in black, purple, and gold. Hers was purple, gold, and white. It certainly hadn't taken him long to get into the Laker spirit.

He grinned. "Look at us! Were you spying on me as I got dressed?"

She snorted. "You wish! But I could ask you the same question."

"Oh, I definitely thought about it, but I didn't want to get kicked out of here before I could get settled in good." She laughed heartily. "Hungry?" he asked.

"Yeah. It was the delicious smells that drew me out here in the first place. What you got going on inside them pots and pans?" The fact that he seemed so comfortable in her space made her feel extremely happy.

"Good breakfast foods, girl. Check out the newspaper while I put the meal on the table." On his way across the room to pour her a cup of coffee, he pressed down the lever on the toaster.

In the next several minutes Drakkar had all the food on the table, impressing the heck out of his old girlfriend. He closed his eyes to pass the blessing and she followed suit. When he thanked God for bringing them together again, she felt immediate joy leap to her heart.

Tarynton shelled her boiled egg and then sprinkled it with salt and pepper. Once she spread strawberry preserves on her toast, she fixed her coffee to suit her taste, wishing she had thought to buy some oranges to squeeze for fresh juice.

As if they'd never lost contact with each other, Tarynton and Drakkar fell into an easy comradeship while consuming the meal. Between bites she read the headlines to him and he read to her some of the cartoons and then each of their horoscopes. He was a Capricorn and she was an Aquarius. Their birthdays were just shy of being a month apart. His was at the end of December and hers was at the end of January.

After biting into a slice of Canadian bacon, Drakkar took a sip of coffee and placed the cup back down on the saucer. "What do you have planned for the day, Miss Batiste?"

"When I get back from the nine o'clock church service, I'm going to do some research on my Kwanzaa assignment. I want to know my subject thoroughly. I also plan to work up a few special dates just in case I get some of the usual last-minute frantic calls. I have several outings already planned for a few clients, but I can't finish up the arrangements until tomorrow."

"Who *are* these people that can't think up something fun and unique to do?"

"Most of my clients are men with no imagination even though they have a strong desire to please their women. Females call also but they have a tendency to give me some idea of what their men might like. The women usually cite the lack of time in planning a special outing as their reason for calling on me to do it for them. The impression that I get is that some of the guys that call seem to have no clue about anything to do with romance or purchasing personal gifts."

"Really?" He sounded as if he found her statement hard to believe.

"Oh, yeah! But it's all good. I give out a lot of wonderful tips whether they come on as a client or not."

"What kind of tips?"

"The type of things that a lot of women like."

"For example?"

"Hot oil massages, bubble baths, candlelight dinners, an evening of dancing, you know." *If you don't, you should.* She could think of them indulging in everything she'd mentioned and much, much more. Drakkar was one extremely romantic brother, one who loved to surprise her.

"You're right, I do know, all too well." He couldn't help thinking about all of the romantic dates they'd had. All planned by him. "I guess everybody can't have it going on in the romance department. I wish you weren't bent on working today. I could use your help."

"With what?"

"Shopping for furniture. I have none. Both of my apartments in Louisiana came furnished. It'll be nice to own my own things for the first time ever. I'll actually get to see the place come to life with the kinds of decor that really appeal to me."

That was somewhat of a white lie about both of his apartments being furnished, since he'd borrowed one set of the furniture from a woman he was briefly involved with. Tamara Lyndon was a woman that had nearly driven him insane with her obsessive, possessive behavior toward him. He had gotten involved with her at a time when he really needed someone badly. His heart had been badly broken and she was there to help him pick up the tiny fragments that had gotten scattered all over the place. In fact, she'd been all over him from the first day he'd stepped onto the Grambling University campus. She was nonexistent to him at that time.

Tarynton should've been the one that was there for him, but she'd had another agenda back then. Bitter feelings toward her crept into his soul every now and then, but it was hard for him to blame her for his broken heart. He should've protected his own heart, as he was the only one responsible for it. But the truth was this: he hadn't thought he'd ever have to safeguard it from someone that he thought truly loved him.

"Well, I could probably help you out, but I have to go to church first. This girlfriend doesn't miss church for nothing or no one. I can't make it through the week without my spiritual food. I am a sinner, boy. I do need Jesus. And I don't mind letting people know it."

He laughed at her comments. "I know the feeling. Mind if I tag along? I haven't gone to church since I got here. Grandma Liza wouldn't be too happy about that if she were alive."

"That's one request I couldn't deny anyone. Help me clean up the kitchen?"

"Not a problem. How was your food?"

She looked abashed. "I'm so sorry that I didn't thank you for preparing such a nice breakfast. It was very good." She licked her lips to show him how good. Not a wise choice in demonstrations, she thought, when she saw the wanton look in his eyes. "Can you forgive your childhood friend for not saying so about an hour or more ago?"

"If I can get a hug."

She stood and went straight into his outstretched arms. In the same moment their eyes met in a heated embrace, her heart practically shut down on her. Quickly, she put a safe distance between them to keep herself cool. "I'm going to get dressed for church. There's no particular dress code for the church I attend, but I go dressed the way I was taught by my parents."

His eyes lit up. "I can remember the first dress you wore to church. The first real one you ever wore, period, the one that changed your life. Girl, your little, young, tender body was wearing that dress out. Your body was talking loud and saying everything that teenage boys wanted to hear. The guys talked about how sexy you looked in that dress for the next two years."

"And I still know how to wear the hell out of one." With that said, smiling smugly, she left the kitchen.

Thunderstruck by her awesome figure, he watched after her as she walked out the room. His sex grew hard as a rock and began to throb as he thought about all the times that she'd taken him up to heaven, with him locked securely deep inside her hot, tight, and moist feminine secrets. Tarynton used to put him on cloud nine with just a whisper against his lips. Back then she didn't have eyes for anyone but him. He had felt the same about her. He missed the days when they'd simply been high on each other as well as seriously addicted to each other.

Beautifully dressed in a plum-colored wool suit, a lavender blouse, wearing matching plum shoes and carrying the same color handbag, Tarynton left her bedroom. Drakkar came out of his room just as she came into the hallway. Dressed to the nines, Drakkar looked scrumptious in an expensive-looking navy blue pinstriped suit, a baby-blue silk shirt, and a navy-blue-and-white Swiss-dotted tie. Tarynton thought the brother looked as if he were employed on Wall Street. Men didn't come any finer than this one.

Hello, her heart cried out with joy.

She could barely take her eyes off of him as they made their way out to the driveway. Drakkar still walked with a proud strut. One that said: *I know who I am.*

Tarynton insisted on driving her car to the church, but Drakkar put up only minimal resistance because he didn't want to have to explain his reasons. He didn't like the way most women drove cars and he could only imagine that Tarynton's driving skills weren't any differ-

ent from her female comrades'. However, he wouldn't
think of telling her that. If he dared to, he knew she'd
throw up at him how he flunked his first driver's test
twice because he'd failed at making a proper U-turn.
She had passed hers with flying colors on the very first
attempt. Then again, Tarynton probably wouldn't have
thrown that back in his face.

She simply wasn't that type of person to point out a
person's weaknesses, as she was always mindful of others'
feelings. Tarynton was the kind of woman who tried to
spiritually lift up everyone she came into contact with.
She fought for what she wanted and for those things
she thought to be right, but she always tried to do it
with diplomacy and tact and in a nonthreatening way.
Tarynton had a few flaws, but intentionally hurting
other people wasn't among them.

One of her biggest flaws was taking to heart every
bad thing that someone did or said to her. It always
caused her to do self-examination. She rarely considered that the other person was the one with the problem—and not she. She got hurt a lot by doing that.
Another flaw was her inability to allow others to help
her accomplish her goals. She thought she had to do
it all in order for her to maintain independence. Highly
competitive, she also hated to lose at anything. She used
to sulk for days over a lost game of Yahtzee, Sorry,
Monopoly, or checkers. It wasn't so much that someone
beat her as it was that she didn't think she should've
allowed herself to get beaten. Tarynton was always much
too hard on herself.

He wasn't sure if she'd corrected any of those flaws
over the years, but he was now in a position to find out.
The fact that she'd let him prepare breakfast for her
had signaled a significant change in past behavior. Her
insisting on driving didn't show much growth in the
area of not allowing others to do too much for her. She

really did love being waited on and pampered, but only as it pertained to romantic situations. It was the major helping-hand things that she had a tendency to thwart. Borrowing money from someone was out of the question, in dire need or not.

Being back in Tarynton's life was a dream come true, but he worried about how long she'd let him stay there. Her having a special man in her life complicated things for him. But he was a patient man. Six years of waiting and wondering about her had finally paid off. He had yet to determine how high or low the dividends might be. But he'd continue to exercise patience. It was the only way to approach a complicated situation.

Light conversation and some friendly bantering had taken place on the drive to the church. After she parked in the church parking lot, she and Drakkar walked up to the entrance of the building and entered. Inside the sanctuary, they took seats in one of the pews located near the center aisle. He made it a point to sit close enough to her for their shoulders to touch.

Tarynton looked around for her girlfriends, but she didn't see any of them. Drats, she thought. She wanted them to meet Drakkar. Denise was the only one that knew what had happened between them. Because of all the pictures she'd seen of him over the years, Denise told Tarynton that she was embarrassed that she hadn't recognized him as the man who'd asked Tarynton to dance at the club.

Tarynton had chalked Denise's experience up to the dim lighting in the place. Besides that, Drakkar looked ten times better than he did in any of those pictures. He had matured nicely, physically, mentally, and socially. He had surely come into his own. Even though they hadn't gotten home until nearly three A.M., the two friends had stayed on the phone talking about Drakkar for two hours. That hadn't left them too much time for sleep.

So engrossed in her thoughts about Drakkar, she had missed most of the songs sung by the praise team. Pastor Arthur Lemoyne was a soul-shaking speaker and a dynamic teacher. Tarynton really enjoyed his services. She was pretty sure that Drakkar would like them too. Tarynton turned her full attention on the minister as he began to speak.

"Church, please follow along in your Bibles as I read from the thirteenth chapter of First Corinthians, versus one through thirteen. 'Though I speak with the tongues of men and of angels, and have not charity, I am become as sounding brass, or a tinkling cymbal. And though I have the gift of prophecy, and understand all mysteries, and all knowledge; and though I have all faith, so that I could remove mountains, and have not charity, I am nothing.' "

The minister took a sip of water. "Please indulge me as I use the word *love* as a substitute for charity. My service today is about love and all the things that it is and those that it isn't. . . ."

As he paid close attention to the sermon, Drakkar found that he related most to verse eleven in First Corinthians chapter thirteen. "When I was a child, I spake as a child, I understood as a child, I thought as a child: but when I became a man, I put away childish things."

He was a man now, a man who also believed that love was the greatest of all the things mentioned in this particular chapter of the Bible. The look in Tarynton's eyes told him that she believed in the same truth. These truths didn't just apply to a chosen few, or even just to romantic liaisons; they were applicable to all of mankind and in every situation.

* * *

Out in the church parking lot Tarynton couldn't stop smiling as she introduced Drakkar to Denise Morgan, Roxanne Wilson, Chariese Barton, Rayna Edwards, and Narita Mason. Roxanne, a five-foot-nine siren, lovingly referred to as Roxy, was nearly drooling as she looked into Drakkar's beautiful eyes. The three-inch heels Roxy wore brought her nearly up to his height. Denise had to bump Roxy to keep her from staring so hard into his gorgeous face.

"It was a pleasure meeting you five ladies. I guess you already know that your friend, Tarynton, and I go back a long way—"

"No, we didn't know," Chariese interjected. "Just how far back *do* you go?" Chariese was only two inches shorter than Roxanne but was much smaller in the bosom area. She loved to bat her long lashes at men, especially good-looking ones. She loved to play the role of femme fatale, but she was quite the intellectual. The girl could throw down an in-depth hard rap on most subjects. Chariese was one knowledgeable sister.

"Childhood," Drakkar responded.

Chariese looked perplexed. "Really now. Funny that she's never mentioned you."

"Oh, she's mentioned him all right, Chariese. But since you only hear the sound of your own voice, we're sure that that's the reason you've missed the conversations about Tarynton's childhood friend." Denise felt she had to protect Tarynton's secrets. She was the only one of the five women who knew everything about Drakkar and Tarynton's sizzling love affair.

Narita nudged Tarynton with her hip. "We've got some catching up to do, girlfriend. Despite Denise's attempt to rescue you I think you've been holding out

on more than a little dab of info here. We need to talk."
Naturally redheaded, Narita had one of those sexy, sultry types of voices. She was five-five with an hourglass shape and a sharp wit. Men had a tendency to hang on to her every word. Drakkar was no exception, Tarynton noticed.

"Well, all I want to know is, are you and Drakkar romantically linked?" Roxy asked Tarynton in no uncertain terms. Everyone could clearly see that Roxanne had a definite romantic interest in him.

"What business would it be of yours if they are?" Denise asked Roxanne.

"It's really none of my business. But I'm a little like Tarynton inasmuch as I like to spell things out and also have them spelled out for me. I just want to know if you're involved so I can cool down over here if you are. If you're not an item, I'm all for turning up the heat another notch. And you *are* my kind of man, Mr. Lomax."

"To answer your question, Roxy, I'm already very much involved with a beautiful woman. And I don't cheat. But I'm extremely flattered."

All eyes fell on Tarynton after Drakkar's moment of true confessions. Embarrassed by all that was going on about her, Tarynton looked as if somebody had just thrown her into a lake of fire-breathing female dragons. Hearing that Drakkar was involved with another woman crushed her, but it didn't surprise her. Men that looked as good as Drakkar always had a woman in their life— and one or more was usually waiting in the wings. The Drakkar she once knew had been a one-woman man. That was to his credit. If that still rang true or not, she didn't know. But his remark of not being a cheater didn't seem to support the facts that she had later learned.

"Ladies, we need to move on and let these two old

friends get on with their day. Unless you two would like to join us for our usual after-church brunch?'' Narita inquired.

Drakkar smiled. ''Perhaps we can do it another time. Tarynton and I have already made plans for the rest of day. Thanks for the generous offer.''

Tarynton was glad Drakkar had taken control of the situation. After what she'd just witnessed, getting through brunch with those five sisters would've been too much. She liked her peace on the day of rest. She really didn't blame them for reacting the way they did, but she didn't want it to go on for the rest of the day. A lot of women had the tendency to act totally out of character when in the company of an exceptionally good-looking man, including her.

Her phone was going to start ringing off the hook. Her and Drakkar's relationship was definitely a stimulus to their curiosity. Her other four friends weren't going to stop until they had all the information on her relationship with him. But they'd have a long wait, because she wasn't about to take that long, hurtful journey into the past. Telling Denise, which had occurred a long time ago, had been hard enough on her.

As for Roxanne, Tarynton couldn't fault her for being up front about her heated interest in Drakkar. She only wished that Roxanne had gone about it with a little more discretion. But had she known that Tarynton had once had deep feelings for Drakkar she wouldn't have come off like that. Unlike some women, Roxanne wasn't the type to go after the men her friends were with, or had once been involved with. She didn't want any woman's leftovers.

Tarynton's mind locked in on Drakkar's statement about being involved with a beautiful woman. Her heart sank deeper into depression each time she turned over in her mind his provocative confession. Could she compete with this beautiful woman? Better yet, did she even want to enter into such a competition? Although she'd convinced herself that he'd actually gotten married, especially with not hearing from him ever again after their breakup, she knew now that Drakkar was still a single man. That not only made him eligible, he was also fair game.

Did she want to capture him and recapture his heart again? Most definitely!

In thinking of delectable ways to set her loving trap for him, she giggled out loud. Seeing him again had her positive that he was still the only one for her. In reality, she'd always known that. Drakkar was her one and only, her tried and true one moment in time.

"What are you giggling about over there?"

"Just had a few devilish thoughts about how I'm finally going to land the man that I'm crazy about."

His heart trembled with grief. "Land him? If he has to be landed, he's not worthy of you. He should be begging you to be with him. Don't sell yourself short, T.C. You deserve only the very best that life has to offer."

"He *is* the best. That's why he's worth fighting for."

He gave her a hard look. "I don't like these terms you're using. Landing, fighting. It all sounds so ominous. Why do you think you have to fight for him?"

"Because he's involved with another woman, a beautiful one, according to him."

He looked at her as if she had three eyes, with one being right in the center of her forehead. "Married?"

"No, just involved."

Pointing at her head, he shook his own. "This doesn't sound like you, T.C. You need your head examined. There's one too many personalities going on up in there. I'm stunned to hear you talking like this. I don't know this side of you. Not sure I want to, either."

"Drakkar, you always did think I was perfect. I'm not. Far from it."

"No, Tarynton, not perfect, just the closest thing to perfection that I've ever had in my life. Outside of my mother, of course. But that's like comparing men and women."

His remarks sent her heart reeling. "Do you mean that?"

"Have you ever known me to say something I didn't mean?"

At least once. "I'm sorry. I shouldn't have asked that question."

"And you didn't answer mine."

"You noticed, huh?"

"I notice everything you say and do, everything about you, Tarynton. Why did we—"

"Drakkar! Don't go there. You promised."

He looked highly perturbed at her cutting him off in midsentence. "Whatever. We just got out of church. Now I'm angry as hell and you're talking about an adulterous affair. Is there something sinfully wrong with this picture, or is it just my imagination?"

"One of us would have to be married for it to be adultery. Neither of us are that. Don't go blowing this all out of proportion. And what are you so mad about, anyway?"

"If you have to ask, I guess that you've forgotten a lot of things I haven't been able to. Anyway, I promised." He sighed with discontent. "You want to go home and change before we go furniture hunting?" Changing the subject seemed the best course of action at this juncture.

"That, and eat, too."

"We just ate breakfast, Tarynton."

"Just enough food to make me mad. I usually go to brunch with my friends, so my stomach knows the drill.

It's protesting my not going. If you listen closely, you'll hear the vulgar names it's calling me."

He chuckled. "You're still so crazy. What do you want to eat?"

"Everything. We'll just go to a different buffet from the one the girls went to. Have you even been to a Hometown Buffet?"

"I've never even heard of it before now."

"It serves the best home-style meals. They have a wide variety of choices on the buffet. I love the food there, especially the mashed potatoes, gravy, the liver and onions, and spaghetti."

"Where do you put it all?"

She held up her purse for him to see. "Sometimes in here, but this one's not big enough."

Drakkar howled. "Your mother would throw a fit if she knew you were stealing food, of all things. Woman, that takes the cake."

"Is it stealing when you pay for something that advertises 'all you can eat'?"

"All you can eat while you're there."

"Oh, is that what it means? I didn't know," she said, feigning innocence.

He had to laugh. "I don't know about you, T.C. How far away are we from this place?"

"Three minutes."

"Think you can wait that long?"

"Don't think I have a choice, smarty-pants."

As Tarynton turned the corner and pulled into the restaurant parking lot, she frowned. The line was practically wrapped around the building. "Ugh, do you see what I see?"

"The food must be as good as you say it is. But are you going to brave that line?"

"Not only good, cheap too. I could be starving, which I am, but I wouldn't get caught up in that line unless

I was dying of food deprivation. I still have the boneless chicken breasts that I thawed out yesterday. I'll just cook those. It'll only take a few minutes on the grill."

"There's no place else you'd like to eat?"

"It's the weekend. All the places are going to be like this. One of the reasons we go to the early service is so we can get ahead of the crowds. Also, earlier is better for me. I'm still a morning person."

"And I'm still a breast man." He laughed at his own joke. "Home, T.C."

Yeah, he was definitely that! Her body tingled at just the thought of him suckling her breasts so tenderly. He loved to see her nipples erect, loved to see them pucker up right before his eyes. It was a turn-on for him. But it turned her on even more. Everything about him had turned her on, and still did. But this woman of his was certainly a turn-off. If only she knew the history that the competition had had with her man, Drakkar's woman would insist that he move out of Tarynton's house immediately. Perhaps a month wasn't long enough to catch him in the careful snares she planned to lay down for him, but it was a real nice start.

Comfortably dressed in the Laker warm-up she'd worn earlier, Tarynton seasoned the chicken breasts and placed them on the indoor grill. She also planned on serving the leftover stir-fry vegetables and curried shrimp and rice. After pulling from the refrigerator the ingredients to make a salad, she washed the greens, shredded them, and sliced up the other fresh vegetables.

Coming up behind her, Drakkar wrapped his arms around her waist and nuzzled her neck. Her libido immediately responded to his warm embrace. "Can I do anything to help you out?"

You can take me into the bedroom and undress me all the

way down. Then you can use your thick, lengthy fire hose to put out this four-alarm fire burning between my legs by making love to me until you completely run out of steam. "You can set the table. The plates are—"

"Uh-uh," he interjected, "you don't have to tell me. I found almost everything in here this morning when I fixed breakfast. Let me continue to find the rest for myself. I like to familiarize myself with my surroundings through exploration." *And, baby, I plan to once again familiarize myself with that sweet, sexy body of yours. In case you've forgotten, I'm going to remind you of how well I used to explore your innermost secrets. But I'm a patient man.*

His having backed her buttocks up against his manhood had him wanting her in the worst way. It had started out innocent enough, but it hadn't ended up that way. How he was going to get his lovemaker to go back down was his real dilemma—since he couldn't just run into the bathroom and take a cold shower. *Just wing it, brother. You can't let her know she's getting to you. Not yet.*

Drakkar showed Tarynton that he indeed knew where almost everything in her kitchen was. After setting the table, he made a large pitcher of cherry Kool-Aid, a favorite for them, from the several packs he'd discovered on his earlier expedition of her pantry.

This time Tarynton passed the blessing. Prayer was important to them. They'd grown up on it. Her dad, Steven, used to say a family that prays together stays together. But it hadn't worked for her and Drakkar, and they'd prayed together often. Perhaps youth had played a part in their separation. They were way more mature now. Maybe things would be different for them if they did happen to get back together. But she'd thought everything was already perfect between them. Then that damned letter was written.

Turning her thoughts off, she looked over at Drakkar, wondering if he was thinking the same sort of things that she'd been entertaining. Probably not. He was more than likely involved with thoughts of his woman. Did she live in Los Angeles or was it someone back in Louisiana?

Well, whoever she was, she was in for the fight of her life. Tarynton Batiste hated to lose at anything—and she wasn't about to lose Drakkar a second time. She planned to give his woman a run for all she was worth. And she was going to do everything in her power to hand the other woman a resounding defeat and then walk away with the grand prize.

Drakkar was a prize catch.

Four

It didn't take Drakkar long to make up his mind on the type of furnishings he wanted in his apartment. He loved the saddleback look in Italian black leather. A two-piece set was on sale at a good price. To go with the sofa and love seat he had his choice of a free chair with an ottoman or a recliner. He let Tarynton decide. She chose the chair and ottoman because he would get two pieces that cost more when combined than what the recliner did. After thinking it over a bit, he decided he wanted the recliner too, making the salesman a very happy camper.

"Do you want to look at coffee and end tables or you want to save it for another day?"

"Thanks for asking, Tarynton. I think I'll get everything today just to get it over with, all except my office furniture. What do you think?"

She shrugged. "The sale prices are fantastic. Do you want wood or glass tables?"

"I think a blend of both would be nice. That's a

nice set right there," he said, pointing at a very strong looking ebony table with smoked glass. "Does that seem like too much black?"

"Not really. We can brighten the room with lighter-color accents. A light rug would do."

"That's a nice thought."

Drakkar turned to the salesman. "I didn't think to ask if these purchases can be kept at the store until my apartment is ready in about a month from now."

"You can only do that if you put the items on layaway."

"Layaway? Now that's a word I haven't heard in some time." He turned to Tarynton. "I remember when our moms put everything on layaway. Can I still get them at the sale prices?"

The salesman nodded. "Sure you can. But you'll have to pay fees for the layaway."

Drakkar threw up his hands. "Catch-Twenty-two. Maybe I should come back when the apartment is ready to be moved into."

"The sale may be over by then, my friend," the salesman remarked.

"You can have it delivered to my house. I'm sure we can find some space, but not all in the same room. Then you'll have to move it again. You know how you hate moving, Drakkar."

"I'll tell you what. We'll just waive the layaway fees on this purchase. Does that meet with your approval?" the salesman asked Drakkar.

Pretty sure that the salesmen's change of heart had to do with the thought that this sale was starting to get away from him, Drakkar chuckled under his breath. "You sure you can do that? Don't want you to get in any trouble with the owners."

"Very much so. We try hard to please our customers. I'll even throw in free delivery."

Drakkar extended his hand. "Now that's one of the

ways I like to be pleased." While thinking of other ways he liked to derive at pleasure, he let his eyes travel heatedly over Tarynton. She was the one woman who knew how to please him in every way.

Drakkar opened his wallet. "Let's wrap up the deal! Here's my American Express card."

"That was easy," Tarynton interjected. "I wish I could make up my mind so quickly."

"Sir, do you already have a dining room set?" the salesman inquired.

Drakkar looked at Tarynton. "You're supposed to be helping, T.C. Why didn't you think of that?" He nudged her playfully.

She nudged him back. "I can't think of everything. Besides, you once loved to eat on nothing but TV trays so you could watch all the sports telecasts. With that in mind, are you even going to use a dinette set if you get one?"

He jerked his head back. "If I don't have a table and chairs, I can't invite my beautiful woman over for a romantic candlelight dinner. And recollection has it that you hate eating on TV trays." He turned to the salesman. "Show me what you have on sale for the dining area."

Tarynton looked spellbound. She didn't know if he was referring to her as the beautiful woman or if he was talking about the other woman in his life, or both. And she wasn't about to ask him for clarification. At any rate, it was just a matter of time before she was going to be the only woman in his life. Drakkar Lomax wasn't going to get away a second time.

It took Drakkar even less time to choose a dinette set than it did on the other items. He decided on a round black lacquered smoked-glass table with four chairs and a matching china hutch. Tarynton mentally arranged the beautiful furnishings as she thought of the apartment floor plan he'd chosen. Then it suddenly dawned on her that he hadn't purchased a bed. A bed was a must. She had every intention of helping him pick that out, especially since she planned on sleeping in it, with him, at some appointed time in the near future.

Smiling, she took hold of his hand. "Are you going to sleep on the sofa or the floor?"

He hit the side of his head with an open palm. That she was the one who thought of the bed intrigued him. It also made him wonder what she'd been thinking of before she'd voiced her thoughts. A bed was one of the most important pieces of furniture in a man's home. If a brother had nothing else in his place, he had a bed, or some other sort of comfortable sleeping apparatus.

"I don't know how the need for a bed escaped me, but I thank you for reminding me, Miss T.C. A bed is an absolute essential in a man's pad." He smiled knowingly at Tarynton. She turned away so he couldn't see the color she felt rising in her face.

"My man, you are making out like a bandit today," Drakkar told the salesman. "This sale alone might garner you a salesman of the month award."

The salesman cracked up. "You got a point there. If you come up with some other furnishing needs, please don't hesitate to let me know. Now let me show you what we have in the way of bedding. On sale, of course." The three of them laughed. "We also have washers, dryers, stoves, and refrigerators."

Drakkar shook his head. "Won't be needing any of those. The apartment comes equipped with them. But I'll come back and see you when I'm ready to purchase that dream home."

The salesman grinned. "I certainly would appreciate more of your business, sir."

A dream home, Tarynton considered.

How many times over the past years had she and

Drakkar sat down together and designed their dream home? Many, many times. He wanted a pool and a spa and she wanted gardens with both vegetables and flowers. His dream room would have state-of-the-art audio and visual equipment, a couple of sofas, and several comfortable reclining chairs, a pool table, and a wet bar. She dreamed of a music room with a piano in it, though she didn't know how to play. A Jacuzzi tub and a massive walk-in closet were essential for her bathroom. Last but not least, she desired an office where she could bring her writing creations to life in sheer comfort, with all the latest in both office furnishings and the best in electronic equipment.

Drakkar had to nudge Tarynton to get her attention. "Where were you? I've been calling your name for the last few seconds."

"When you mentioned dream home, I guess I was thinking about my man and the plans we've made for ours."

"Sorry I asked." His irritation with her response was apparent in his voice and in his body language. "What do you think of this brass bed? That is, if you can get your head out the clouds and off of Romeo for a moment or two to take a look at it."

In seeing and hearing his agitated reaction Tarynton decided it was best not to provoke him any further by talking about the man she was crazy about. He had no way of knowing that she was talking about him. She had no desire to hurt him or flaunt the idea of an affair with a man that only existed in her fantasies: him. It was all about the way things used to be for them. She'd have to find another way to win him back. Making him jealous was not her intent, nor was it the answer. But it seemed to her that she still mattered more to him than just as a dear friend.

But then again, his irritation with her could simply

be a result of his concern about her being romantically interested in a man involved with another woman. She had to admit that it was totally out of character for her even if she was now pursuing him knowing he was involved with someone else. He didn't know of her plans either, but it wasn't going to be too long before everyone knew of her desire to recapture his heart.

Tarynton had had every intention of using the weekend to shop for new clothes, but Drakkar had changed that. She still planned to accomplish her goal, but it would have to wait until the next weekend. Drakkar had asked her if she wanted to shop for anything for herself, but she'd been eager to start on her Kwanzaa assignment. As soon as they'd arrived back home, he'd gone into his room, right after she'd told him she was going into her office to work. They planned to watch a movie together later in the evening.

After logging on to the Internet, Tarynton began her search. Several items on Kwanzaa came up and she checked out the first one on the list. She read the content of the first file and then printed out the information. It excited her to learn so much in just one reading. It was interesting to know that Kwanzaa was a cultural holiday, not a religious one, created to reaffirm and restore the people's roots in African culture. It was also created to serve as a regular communal celebration to reaffirm and reinforce the bonds among Africans as a people, designed as an ingathering to strengthen community and reaffirm common identity, purpose, and direction as a people and a world community. Kwanzaa also introduced and reinforced the *Nguzo Saba,* known as the seven principles.

In her opinion, the Internet was an amazing research tool.

* * *

Tarynton stretched her arms high over her head as she looked at the clock. She couldn't believe her eyes. Three hours had already flown the coop. Often she set the timer to keep time spent on the Internet from mushrooming into an unreasonable number of hours. The subject matter had taken her through many files and had linked her to numerous Web sites featuring information on Kwanzaa's origin and the ways in which it was celebrated. Happily, she had followed the trail that had led up to so much pleasurable reading. Another forty-five minutes passed before she shut down the computer and turned off the office lights.

It was awfully quiet when she went inside the house and down the hallway toward the bedrooms. It was just as it was before Drakkar had moved in. It seemed as if no one else was in the house but her, but she knew different. Stopping outside his bedroom door, she listened for any sounds of movement. None came. The urge to open the door and peek inside niggled at her, but she won out in the end. She then moved into her bedroom where she stretched out on the bed to think about the time she'd later spend with her childhood buddy and ex-lover.

Drakkar stood outside Tarynton's door and knocked several times. He grew concerned when she didn't answer. Thinking she might still be in her office, he went through the laundry room and opened up the door leading into her work space. When he saw that she wasn't there, he went back to her bedroom door.

Unsure of what to do next, he stood there for a couple of minutes. Then he opened the bedroom door and stepped inside. Immediately, seeing her lying there asleep, he knew he'd done the wrong thing. Intruding on her privacy was dead wrong. She could've been in here with someone. He groaned inwardly as he turned to walk back out.

Before he could vacate her room, Tarynton awakened, startled at seeing him there. Her recovery was instantaneous, but she felt cold and her limbs had cramped up. Slowly, she sat up in bed, wishing she'd draped her body in a revealing piece of black silk or satin. Lying there totally nude would've worked even better. She scolded herself for thinking such sinful thoughts.

"I'm sorry for being in here. This shouldn't have happened. I got concerned after you didn't answer the insistent knocks on your door." He backed up toward the exit. "Now that I know you're okay, I'm out of here."

"Hey, no apology necessary. I was out cold. Didn't hear a thing. Thanks for caring."

"I do care. But I shouldn't have compromised your privacy. Your dude could've been in here with you. That would've been embarrassing to all of us." He was glad she wasn't angry.

"I'd never entertain a man in my bedroom with someone else living under the same roof with me. The same rules regarding overnight guests of the opposite sex applies to both of us as long as we're roommates. Okay?"

"Okay." Grateful for that bit of news, he smiled. "It's time for our movie date. Do you want to cancel out and do it another time? You look pretty tired."

She moaned. "Never tell a woman she looks tired even if she does. We instantly imagine black and blue lines and puffy bags under our eyes, not to mention ugly crow's-feet at the corners." As Drakkar laughed heartily, she added, "I'm awake now. After I splash some water on my face, I'll be as good as new. You can get the DVD player ready, the one in the family room."

"Why don't we watch the movie in here? These barrel chairs look pretty comfy to me. And you can just stretch back out on the bed. I'm sure you'll be more comfortable in here."

She scowled. "That might not be such a good idea."

"Why not? Afraid you might get the desire to jump my bones? Never knew you to be a chicken, T.C." He loved seeing her expressive features when he taunted her.

"Boy, if I wanted to jump your bones, fear wouldn't ever come into the mix. I've already been there and done that. Recall?" *And, oh, how I'd love to do it again and again . . .*

"Totally. So, if you're not afraid, then what's the problem?"

She gave him an incinerating look. "I can see that you're not going to let his go. Get the movie so you can see for yourself that I'm totally immune to you and your bones."

"Girl, you're still lying to yourself." He laughed as she pulled a face. "Be right back. I'll make sure I don't pick anything with skin games in it. Don't want your complexion to start peeling from the sexual heat when you watch an R-rated film with adult content."

"I can see that I'm not the only one that needs prayer around here. Brother, I promise to pray extra hard for you on a daily basis."

Laughing, Drakkar left the room.

So she wouldn't have to do it later, Tarynton went into the bathroom and scrubbed her face and then lathered it with moisturizer. After pulling out of the drawer a pair of baggy gray-, black-, and white-checkered flannel pajamas, she put them on and then donned a terry bathrobe.

She then chose her attire for the next day. Undecided as to whether she should pull the covers back and get in bed, or just lie across it, Tarynton decided she'd be better off just sitting up in one of the barrel chairs. Just as Drakkar had suggested, they were very comfortable.

Drakkar not only came back with the DVD movie *Two Can Play That Game,* he had also popped some microwave popcorn. The type of popcorn she kept in stock only took two minutes in the high-powered microwave oven that she owned.

The DVD movie Drakkar had chosen had never been opened. The feature had been out over a year and had come out on video and DVD several months later. Tarynton belonged to Columbia House, a music and video club. She'd ordered the movie months ago, but she hadn't watched it. She had numerous movies that she hadn't had the opportunity to view because of her extremely busy schedule, as of late, since her business had begun to boom.

"Okay, you ready for me to get this thing rolling?"

She nodded. "Ready."

He eyed her curiously as she came across the room and sat down in one of the chairs. "I thought you were going to lie down in bed?"

"That was your suggestion, not mine. I'll be fine right here."

"Cool. As soon as I polish off some of this great smelling corn, I'll lie down over there. That is, if you don't mind."

She shrugged. "Whatever turns you on."

"Are you sure about that? Maybe you should clarify that statement."

She frowned with intolerance. "Drakkar, can we just watch the movie, please?"

Smiling devilishly, he took the clear wrapping off the disc and popped it into the DVD. With the popcorn bowl situated on the round mahogany table between the two chairs, Tarynton and Drakkar ate as they watched the previews of future films to be released on video.

Although Tarynton maintained the appearance of being intent on the movie, she was engrossed in thoughts of Drakkar. So much of what had gone on with him over the past six years was still a mystery. He could probably say the same about her. She somewhat regretted the conditions she'd placed on him about discussing the past. There were a lot of things she wanted to know, but she feared opening Pandora's box, as well as exposing herself to more pain.

Drakkar had been one of the most considerate people she'd ever met, and she'd been just as considerate toward him. But apparently something along the way had changed both of them. Perhaps their living in separate cities was the culprit, but they'd maintained a wonderful relationship the first three years of college. It was in their senior year that the emotional separation had occurred. In all her wildest nightmares she could never have imagined that something so terribly hurtful would've happened to them. Who was to blame was the question she'd never figured out the answer to. From all indications, it appeared to her that he didn't have the answers either.

Drakkar's laughter cut into her thoughts. She looked at the television screen but she had no idea what was going on in the movie. She was too embarrassed to ask—and she hoped Drakkar didn't ask her what she thought about the film when it was over, especially if she couldn't get into it before then. Feeling the need to stretch out her limbs, still cramped from her earlier nap, Tarynton moved over to the bed and lay down across the foot of it.

As she finally got into the movie, she thought it would be much better without the narration from one of the actresses. It really took away from the story. Then she began to critique it from a writer's standpoint, which completely took away the entertainment value.

Tarynton fought the urge to fall asleep for the next forty-five minutes, but she lost the battle just before the movie ended. When Drakkar got up to turn the television off, he looked back at the bed. His breath caught. The woman he adored looked peaceful enough, but she didn't look comfortable. Her body seemed rather twisted at an awkward angle. With the thought of waking her and having her get into the bed properly, he went over to where she lay.

As he looked down upon her, his expression was soft, filled with longing. What would she do if he dared to lie down beside her? He knew it wasn't the right thing to do under the current circumstances, but he wanted to be with her so badly. He didn't necessarily want to make love to her, but he did want to hold her all through the night. After taking the time to reason things out, he found his common sense finally prevailing.

When he lifted her up to place her at the head of the bed, her arms immediately went around his neck and her head fell forward against his chest. He nearly stopped breathing. What was he to do now? In the past he would've just placed her comfortably in bed and then settled himself in alongside her. But this wasn't the past and he wasn't sure if there was even a future for them as a couple. She had given no indication that she might still be in love with him. But he'd never stopped loving her, not for a second. He'd wanted to tell her that from the moment he laid eyes on her in the club. But things were even more complicated than before, now that he'd moved in with her. Smiling, he reminded himself that he was a patient man; good things came to those who had the sense to wait on all that was worth waiting for.

She didn't move another muscle as he laid her down

in the bed and covered her up. Bending over, he kissed her forehead. The desire to kiss her sweet mouth was almost his undoing. Quickly, he headed for the door.

"Thank you, Drakkar. Good night." The drowsiness in her voice made it sound sultry and seductive. "See you in the morning."

He turned on his heels and went back to the bed. Bending over her, he lifted her head up and kissed her full on the mouth. "Good night, T.C." Without breathing another word, he hastened from the room.

Buckets of rain ushered in the morning hours. Tarynton loved rainy days but she was not too crazy about the timing. She had tons of things to do that required her to leave the house. Picking up from the jeweler a special anniversary gift for one of her clients, and then taking it to his office, was high on her top-priority list. Purchasing a roll of stamps at the post office was a must for today. And she'd also promised Chariese she'd meet her at a restaurant close to her job so they could have lunch together. Chariese worked for Pacific Bank as an account manager.

Out in the kitchen, already dressed for the day in heather-gray slacks and a white tunic sweater, Tarynton put a slice of bread into the toaster. It was only six A.M., but she was sure that Drakkar was already gone. She'd heard him say that he had an early day and that it was to be a very long one. Before her next thought of him came, he was there before her. Thinking about the sweet but a little more than friendly kiss he'd given her last night made her blush.

"Morning, sunshine! You must've forgotten to cast your beautiful smile upon the clouds this morning. I'm sure that's why they're crying."

She smiled and blushed at the same time. "Cutesy but so sweet. I thought you'd be gone by now, Drakkar."

"Is that why you didn't fix enough breakfast for me?"

"I guess you could say that. You can have what I cooked already. I'll just fix more for me. I don't have anywhere to go quite this early."

His expression softened and his smile danced in his eyes. "You're what's so cute and sweet." Unable to stop himself, he brought her to him and gave her an endearing hug. Stepping slightly back from her, he rested both hands on her shoulders. "Do you have any idea of how much I've missed you? It feels so good being around you like this again. I hope we stay friends forever, without any more long absences. Deal?"

Boldly, she reached up and slid the back of her hand down the side of his clean-shaven face. It took everything in him to keep from holding her soft, gentle hand in place against his skin. "You got a deal, Drakkar. I've missed you, too." *Your sexy smile, the warm hugs, the sweet, lingering kisses, and everything else about you. Especially our delicious lovemaking.*

"Thanks for offering me your breakfast. Wish I had time to sit down to share your meal with you, but I've got to hit the freeway. I'll just grab something quick at a McDonald's near the studio. Monday night football tonight! Will you tune in to the network and watch me do my thing on the air?"

"I wouldn't miss it for the world. I cook practically every night during the week, but only 'cause it's cheaper than eating out. I'll make enough food to put aside for you to eat when you get home. Have a great day."

"If it's not too terribly late when I get back home, do you think I can have your company while I eat? Promise to rave about your cooking."

"We'll see how late it is. I'm an early-to-bed, early-to-rise person. Maybe I'll take a short nap so I can hang out with you for a few minutes tonight." She gave him an awesome smile.

This was so surreal for him. Wouldn't it be so nice if she were the loving wife seeing her dear husband off to work? It was the very scenario they'd planned on for most of their lives.

Then something that neither of them had ever attempted to talk about had upset their once peaceful existence. Now stupid promises had been made never even to bring up the subject. Promises he wasn't sure he could keep. Shattered was beyond an understatement for what he'd felt that rainy winter evening. And he was getting the strangest feeling that Tarynton had been no less affected by the events in the winter of six years ago. An extremely painful letter had destroyed their chance for love and happiness.

She walked him to the door. "Be careful now, Drakkar. California drivers have no respect for people that don't drive like they do. They will run you over, literally. Road rage is at an all-time high in this state. You're no longer in Louisiana."

"Boy, do I know it! Staying aggressive is the key. See you later, sunshine. Don't forget to smile up at those clouds. We don't want them crying all day and into the night."

Lowering her lashes, she gave him a bewildered smile. "See you later, Mr. Lomax."

"Count on it, Miss Batiste."

Tarynton stood at the window looking out at him as he made his way to his car. She didn't like seeing him get the least bit wet, wishing she had thought to offer him her spare umbrella. If he hadn't already backed the car from the driveway, she would've tried to catch him.

Where was this all going? She had to wonder if they'd ever get back what they'd lost. It was anyone's guess, but she wasn't going to let a perfect opportunity to get him back slip through her fingers. She didn't want to see his girlfriend get hurt, but if she didn't find out if there was another chance for them she'd end up seriously hating herself for the rest of her life. All she could do was try. If it wasn't meant to be, she'd have to live with that hurt. Unlike before, at least she'd know that she'd given it her best shot.

"This is exquiste! Look at all the fine detail." Mr. Chamberlain held up the solid-gold unicorn pendant with encrusted diamonds. The eyes of the figure were fashioned in sapphires, his wife's birthstone. "Trish is going to love this. She's not going to believe I picked this out, so I'm not even going to try and lie to her about it. Thanks, Tarynton. You've been a godsend. I commend the jeweler you chose to design this magnificent pendant."

"He *is* excellent." She handed him a large brown envelope. "All of your documents are in there. At mid-morning I have you and your wife booked for full body massages, facials, body wraps, and mineral baths at the spa in your hotel, the Palm Desert Resort. A five-course meal will be served in your suite in the early evening. I suggested formal attire. The three-piece combo will arrive to sing happy birthday to your wife, right after the delivery of the cake. The musicians have been hired to stay on and play for a full hour for your dancing pleasure. I didn't think you'd want them there much longer than that. You're on your own when it comes to your very personal and private celebration."

"That part of the evening I've got under control. Are we all squared away as far as your bill is concerned, Tarynton?"

"All squared away. I hope you and your wife, Trish,

have a wonderful three days up in Palm Springs. I've been there but I haven't had the pleasure of staying overnight. Let me know how it goes. And please don't forget to claim your discount by writing an overview."

"I'll write an overview, but you keep the discount. You earned every cent of your fee. I'll be calling on you in a couple of months. Anniversary time."

"Thanks. Something I'll look forward to. Good-bye for now."

The long line at the post office was infuriating to Tarynton. The place was equipped with eight cashier booths but only three were open for business. This wouldn't happen in Beverly Hills. Every single station would be manned. In checking out the contents of her wallet, she found that she had enough cash to put in the vending machine for a roll of one hundred stamps. Then she thought about the receipt she'd need for tax purposes. Groaning under her breath with utter dismay, she settled herself in line for the long wait.

Surprised but pleased when all the other windows began to open up, Tarynton called Chariese on her cell and told her that she could get there earlier than originally planned. Chariese was glad to hear that since she was super hungry.

Tarynton smiled at Roger Graves, the postal clerk, as they indulged in their usual mild flirting with each other. Roger always seemed to look forward to her weekly visits to his window. Most of the time she waited until he could serve her, but he'd later tell her that he was disappointed when she didn't have the time to wait for him to become available. Though he was involved in a serious relationship, he'd once told Tarynton that she deeply intrigued him. He was always telling her that he loved having her as a casual friend, that their witty conversations always made his day complete.

"So, what's been happening, my beautiful African queen bee?"

"Not much. Oh, that's not true. I have a roommate now."

"Really. What's her name?"

"It's a he."

Roger looked shocked. "A roommate or a live-in boyfriend?"

"Roommate. It's all very innocent. He's a childhood friend. Only a temporary arrangement until his own apartment is ready."

"So that means I still have a chance with you." He grinned.

"Yeah, right. I've seen you at Choices with that Amazon, Monica. She doesn't look like she takes stuff from anyone, especially no man. That's probably why you haven't introduced her and me. Are you feeling what I'm saying?"

"She is a little jealous." He laughed at the skeptical look on her face. "Okay, so she's unreasonably jealous. You know how you women are about your men being friends with other women. You all don't think it's possible for men and women to be friends without lusting after one another. And that's usually the way it is."

"If I didn't care about holding up this line, I'd really like to get into that very interesting topic with you. But the line is long and I've also got to meet my girl, Chariese, for lunch."

"Where you ladies going to eat?"

"The food court in the Sherman Oaks Mall, down from Woodman on Riverside Drive."

He looked at his watch to see how close it was to his lunch break. "I might run over there and join you ladies. That is, if you don't mind." They'd eaten together a couple of times, but only when he'd run into her at one of the local fast food places. They'd never had a scheduled luncheon date. He was either committed to Monica, just plain scared of her, or both.

"That is, if Monica won't mind."

Knowing where she'd gone with that remark, he laughed softly. "If I don't show up, have a good one, Tarynton."

"Thanks, Roger. But I hope to see you later." She had a pretty good idea that she wouldn't. Roger was all talk with no way to execute his walk, not without Monica. In her opinion, commitment was a very good thing to practice in any personal relationship. If one mate was uncomfortable with a set of circumstances, the other mate should try and understand things from the other person's perspective.

Five

Chariese stretched her eyes. "Girl, I can't believe he's living with you! Why haven't you said anything to us girls before now?"

"I had decided not to discuss this with you guys, but then I thought that maybe I should. It happened all of a sudden. I was thinking of asking him if he wanted to stay in one of the spare rooms, but then I changed my mind. It wasn't two seconds after I thought about it that he asked me about letting him rent a room from me. I still haven't told Denise all of it. We've both been very busy. I'll talk to her on the phone later this evening."

"That's too much. I know you're childhood friends and all, but damn, that brother is too fine for someone not to want to get it on with him. Besides, I got the impression that you and he are more than just friends or childhood, hometown homeys. I think you two were lovers at one time. Am I right?"

"Were he and I that obvious?"

"Girl, you two should've just gone on and put the

handwriting on the wall for all the good it's done you in trying to hide your burning desires for each other. Those sappy looks passing between you two had love affair written all over them. But that didn't stop Miss Roxanne from being all up in his grill, a beautiful grill to boot. He has the prettiest teeth. So, do you think you two will get back together?''

"I didn't hear anyone say we were trying to get back together. Here you go with all the freaking drama. Drakkar and I are just friends who are merely trying to catch up on old times."

"Does that include catching up on the booty calls? I would've had him the first night he slept under my roof. He would not have escaped my feminine wiles. That is, if he were someone other than your ex-lover.''

"To tell the truth, we were sure that we would marry each other one day. It was never about booty calls. Then college happened. And then some other major drama followed.''

Tarynton went on to tell Chariese a few more details, surprising herself since she'd promised never to go there with the others. It had been painful enough sharing it with Denise.

"Whew! I see why you haven't said much about this. What are you going to do since you still have such deep feelings for him?''

"Try to go on like it never happened. He wants to get into a discussion about it. I don't. We've agreed not to, ever. But I know it's going to come up again. I just keep thinking that what happened was a lack of maturity on both of our parts. All I know is that I've never stopped loving him and I don't think I ever will.''

"So, what's the problem?''

"He's involved with someone. I have never gone after another woman's man, but this situation is different. He was my man first.''

Chariese laughed. "Girl, this doesn't even sound like you. But I'm loving it. If he comes back to you, she didn't have him on lockdown, nor does she have his love. Go for it, sister."

Tarynton bit down on her lower lip. "Do I just come right out in front with it? Or do I settle for practicing subtlety? I absolutely burn for that man. Even before, and especially since he moved in, there are times when I wake up at night thinking I'm in hell. Knowing heaven is now occupying a bed right down the hall makes my situation doubly hard. I won't make a physical move on him while we're living under the same roof, but when he moves out . . . it's on!"

"Fire, boom, boom, boom, fire! What's one of those real old dance songs say? Burn the roof off the sucker, or something like that?"

"Chariese, you're too crazy."

"Insane is more like it. Hey, you're doing that Kwanzaa article, right?"

"Yeah, why do you ask?"

"Well, Rayna, a few other friends, and I are thinking of pulling together a Kwanzaa celebration. We'd like to have something on a grand scale. Since we all belong to some sort of social clubs and sororities, I was wondering if you'd be interested in inviting some of your other friends and clients. We could pull off a really wonderful celebration."

"I love the idea. Since I'm just learning about the principles of Kwanzaa and all, it would be nice to get involved on another level. It could make my story real interesting. Have you and Rayna talked to Denise, Narita, and Roxy to get their input?"

"Yeah, we have. You know Roxy belongs to Black Women Are, which is about two hundred women strong. Denise is going to try to get her book club, the Tabahani Book Circle, involved. We already know how the Tabahani girls throw down a great celebration. Those are some awesome women. Denise is also going to talk to several other black women's groups and organizations to get some input."

"Where's the seed money going to come from?"

"I thought we'd all pitch in and do a couple of fundraisers. Church bake sales always work pretty well. There are numerous ways to raise funds until the ticket sales take off."

"Raffle tickets for a special date for two might be a good draw." Tarynton didn't like the idea of selling tickets for this particular event, but before voicing her opinion she'd wait to see what the others had to say on the subject when they discussed it as a whole.

"Girl, we both know that everything Denise and the Tabahani Book Circle put their touch on turns to gold. But we do have to get cracking on this. With it being the beginning of September, we've got a little less than four months to pull it together. A lot of organizations that do these types of celebrations start planning a year or more in advance."

"We should definitely have a meeting as soon as possible, Chariese."

"I agree. Now let's get back to the sexy male animal living in one of your spare bedrooms. Namely, the handsome sportscaster, Drakkar Lomax. What a powerful name!"

"Let's not. I get all worked up just thinking about him. He's on the air tonight for the post-game telecast. I promised to watch him wow the audience and I also promised to stay up until he comes home this evening. Peep this. I saw him off to work this morning, as if he were my husband. It felt real good. He's such a sweetie."

"Sounds like you got it bad."

"Really bad. He is still such a sweetheart. We were inseparable while growing up. The guys used to tease him about hanging out with me so much, after we'd hang out all day playing sports and such. As you've heard before, I was a tomboy. He would tell the guys that one day they were going to envy him for spending so much time with me. When I turned sixteen, all his partners were trying to hit on yours truly. But by then Drakkar was the one that held my heart in his hands.''

Chariese shivered. ''That last statement gave me goose bumps. You just have to pursue this relationship. There are stars floating all up in your eyes as you talk about him. Yeah, you have to do this, Miss T.''

''I'm feeling you. I'm already over here trying to think of what I can cook for a special dinner tonight. Can you believe that?''

''I definitely believe it. What's his favorite?''

''Curried shrimp and rice. Cooked that the other night.''

''Hello! Miss Batiste, I see that you *are* already working that brother.''

''I'm not working him quite yet. But I'm gradually going to turn the heat up a notch or two. Other woman or not, Drakkar's feelings for me are still running pretty deep. I can feel it.'' Tarynton snapped her fingers. ''He also loves braised curried lamb. I'll stop and get some lamb shanks on the way home. Macaroni and cheese goes well with mutton. I'm going to make it real special for him. Hope he's not too late. You know how hard it is for me to stay awake after ten.''

''Speaking of late, girl, I'm that. I've run way over on my lunchtime. Got to get back to the bank.'' Chariese stood up. ''As for making a special dinner for him, we both know that good food is not the only popular or the most prevalent way into a man's heart. I'll say no more, but I think you get my drift. Be a love and pay the check. I'll square with you later.''

''Well, good meals are certainly a start. Not a problem

with the check. See you later. And don't forget to schedule the meeting to talk about the Kwanzaa celebration."

"I won't. Tell Drakkar hello for me," Chariese shouted in parting.

Mesmerized by the aura of mystique surrounding him and the deepness of his sexy voice, Tarynton listened intently to Drakkar's postgame commentary. The brother looked as good as he sounded. The blue iridescent tie was striking against the deep yellow shirt and the navy blazer that he wore. The left pocket of the jacket was embroidered with the network's colorful logo. As it was football season, he was commentating on the end results of the Monday night football game with the Oakland Raiders and the San Francisco Forty-niners. Good thing she was a football fan. If she hadn't been, she would've watched the postgame show just to get another glance at the man that flipped her world upside down. The mere sound of his voice had a way of melting her entire being.

Drakkar looked so professional, but his genuine smile seemed to put at ease the others around him. He possessed loads of personality. No one could say that he didn't know the game of football. The boy was right on it. It made her happy to see that he was such a great commentator. Drakkar had always known how to sell himself and his ideas. He could even sell ice to the Eskimos. He was that good at it.

A short time into the postgame Tarynton found herself getting sleepy. Thank God she had prepared the meal as soon as she'd gotten home. The lamb was being kept warm in the oven, though the gas had been turned off. Covered with aluminum foil, the macaroni and cheese was stored in the toaster oven. She had put the stir-fried sugar peas in a Tupperware container.

But how was she going to pull off a special dinner if she couldn't stay awake? She feared a quick nap at this late an hour simply because she probably wouldn't wake up from it until morning. Wishing she had napped earlier, she went off to take a quick shower and dress herself for bed in very presentable but attractive nightwear. The kind of loungewear Drakkar liked.

Drakkar's moist mouth brushing softly against hers was what awakened her. She opened her eyes and smiled up at him. Stretched out across the bottom of the bed, she yawned and then raised her body into a sitting position. Tarynton looked at the clock on the radio. It was after midnight. She had blown it, just as she'd feared.

"Couldn't wait up for me, huh?"

She smiled sheepishly. "I tried. I really did."

"It's okay. That was one hell of a meal that you set aside for me."

Her heart fell. "You've eaten already?" When he nodded, she looked so disappointed. She immediately noticed that he had already changed into comfortable attire. She couldn't help wondering if he still wore silk boxers. The boy's body looked good in them, she recalled.

"Just got through eating. That's how I know it was so good. You wouldn't be trying to seduce me by preparing all my favorites, would you?"

She swallowed hard. "Hardly. But I had planned on eating with you. Sorry."

Deciding not to pursue that line of questioning, he bent down and kissed her on the forehead. "It's the thought that counts most. I know what a sleepyhead you are. I also know how early you get up. Personally,

I don't know why you do it since you don't have a real job."

Offended by his remarks, she rolled her eyes at him. "A real job? Maybe not, but I get paid *real* well for what I do—and with *real* money, lots of it. Thank you."

He threw up his hands. "No malice intended. I just meant that you're not on anyone's clock but your own, yet you get up every morning before five A.M."

"It's called discipline, Jack. I was taught that the early bird gets the worm. My clock is the most important tool of all. If I don't get up and get to work, I don't get paid. It's up to me to make sure that my financial future is bright and prosperous. You feeling me yet?"

"I definitely see your point. I'm glad for your success, T.C. I meant no harm."

She grinned. "I know you didn't."

"Did you catch my Los Angeles Monday night postgame debut? If so, how'd I do?"

"I did—and you were just great! You talk rings around your colleagues. I was so proud of you. You come off as the very educated man that you are, and you are extremely well informed about your assignment. You seem to know all the important stuff there is to know about the different players."

He dropped down on the bed. As he stretched out his full length alongside her, his quick moves came as a surprise. Taking a tendril of her hair, he twirled it around his finger. "Did you watch the entire postgame show?"

"I'm afraid not, Drakkar."

He looked disenchanted. "So you missed my special interview with Joshua Lewis, the superstar running back."

"Yeah, I'm afraid so. But I got up and taped the rest of the show when I couldn't seem to keep my eyes open. If you'd like to, we can watch the interview now."

"Think you can stay awake?"

"I can promise to try."

"That's honest enough. Let me rewind the tape."

After rewinding the tape back to where his interview began, Drakkar pressed PLAY. He then came back to the bed and reclaimed his spot. Tarynton instantly thought of all the times they'd lain across each other's beds watching cartoons or some other favorite show. For many years it had been innocent. Then the day came when they could barely keep their hands off of each other. Those were the times and the kinds of memories that had kept him so close to her.

In total silence they watched his special interview. Tarynton thought that he was even better at interviewing than he was at commentating. His friendly persona seemed to reach out and draw the heralded football player into his genuine warmth. She hung on to his every word, so much so that she didn't know he had fallen asleep sometime during the telecast—and at the bottom of her bed. Her heart became full at the sight of him. Should she wake him up or not? was the question floating around inside her head.

Careful not to awaken him, Tarynton covered up Drakkar before moving to the top of the bed and settling herself in. She wasn't tall enough for her feet to disturb where he lay at the bottom of the bed. She felt totally unthreatened by his presence in her bed; no sooner did her head hit the pillow than the sweet embrace of sleep took her over.

Drakkar awakened, surprised to find that he'd fallen asleep on Tarynton's bed. He looked over at the clock. Three thirty-three A.M. Thirty-three had been his football jersey number in college. Tarynton had had that number embroidered on a lot of her wearing apparel, including the ball caps she loved to wear back then. Her nightshirt had been one of the most appealing of all. He laughed inwardly at the very intriguing situation he was in.

After six long years away from her, he was now lying at the foot of the bed belonging to the girl he'd adored practically all of his life. He could only pray that this reunion with Tarynton wouldn't end like his football career and their past love affair had ended, abruptly, painfully.

Using extreme caution, he got up and went to his own room, carrying with him erotic thoughts of her and him entangled in the sheets of her bed. Then the old apple orchard came to mind. That was where they'd made love the second time. Afterward, they'd cooled down their burning bodies in the bubbling brook that ran alongside the grove of trees. The cool waters hadn't been deep enough for them to completely emerge their bodies into, but it had served the intended purpose.

She was as sweet as those green apples had been tart, but not quite as ripe. Her breasts had puckered with innocence, the same breasts that only his mouth had known. Sweet and creamy with the dewdrops of love, her gentle flower had always opened to him with eagerness. As if he owned a permanent place inside her, they'd always fit to each other like a hand to a glove. How many times had they made love until fatigue took them over? Numerous times.

Had anyone else touched her in that way? While he thought it was a dumb question—and he shouldn't expect that she'd remained untouched by another during all these years, deep down inside he hoped that she had. But she did have a man, one that she was crazy about. Although those very words had come out of her mouth, he found them to have been said without any conviction behind them whatsoever. Man or no man, he'd come back to claim his only heart.

Drakkar had only been involved with one woman since the devastating breakup with Tarynton, but his heart was never in it. He couldn't even bring himself to dwell on that volatile, highly manipulative relationship with Tamara Lyndon. Thoughts of her were bitter and cold. On the flip side, thoughts of Tarynton were purer, sweeter than any nectar he'd ever tasted.

Just before he slid into his bed, he turned around and hurried back to Tarynton's side. Standing over her, he watched her sleep. There was even eroticism in that, yet he wasn't looking to score with her. The sunshine of his life simply took his breath away. Beautiful couldn't completely define her. She had such an inner glow, one that spoke of pureness of heart.

Taking what he thought of as one of the biggest risks of his life, he climbed into bed alongside her. As if she'd been expecting him, she curled into him and laid her head upon his hairy chest. Instantly, his arms tightened around her. He thought there might be hell to pay later, but he was going to thoroughly enjoy the here and now. Like times of old, with no burning desire other than his need to hold her, Drakkar fell asleep with Tarynton wrapped up tightly in his arms.

Tarynton awakened to find herself locked up in Drakkar's strong arms. She would've been blown away had this been anyone else. Being in his arms thrilled her senseless. Dangerous ground? It was more than perilous. It was downright insane, but less dangerous than anyone could ever think was possible. Despite his six-year absence, this scenario was as familiar to her as the features on her face when she looked into a mirror. Having him around was a constant reminder of the way things used to be. It would be a dream come true if they could make it like it was. Her dreams of something like this happening between them hadn't come true so far. But then again, maybe they were coming true right now. After all, he *was* asleep in her bed.

Not wanting to make things awkward for him should he awaken, she slipped out of bed and pulled on a bathrobe. She had to admit to herself that awkwardness wasn't her only reason for getting up. A sleeping body lying next to her was an altogether different story from a fully aroused one. Drakkar's sex was already stiff beneath the sheets. She'd felt it against her stomach when she'd first awakened. If she'd stayed in that bed with him a second longer, instead of feeling his sex beneath the sheets, she'd find herself beneath him and his sex buried deep inside her. Of that, there was no doubt in her mind. Tarynton Batiste was a woman who knew her limitations. The problem was this: she had none when it came to Drakkar Lomax.

Instead of showering in the master bathroom, so as not to disturb him, Tarynton trudged down the hall and went into the third bathroom. Her body was in a frenzied state as she installed herself under the brisk flow of hot water. Closing her eyes, she imagined Drakkar's hands and mouth all over her body.

Remembering how he used to lift her over his head to taste her sweetness from within left her weak in the knees. He had such powerful hands, but his tongue possessed no lesser skills than his hands in the art of seduction. There were times when it seemed as if they were everywhere on her entire anatomy—and all at once. It had taken her quite a bit of time before she'd taken him into her mouth intimately. But once she'd grown comfortable with doing so, she became like a newborn to its mother's breasts. Drakkar nearly lost his mind the first time she'd dared to taste all of him.

The intense throbbing between her legs caused her to turn on the cold water full-steam. Her thoughts of Drakkar making love to her with his tongue and hands had set fire to her flesh. It took everything she had within her not to run back to her bed in hopes of finding him still there.

Although Tarynton had tried to avoid the awkwardness it appeared to have settled in between them anyway. Drakkar could barely make eye contact with her as they sat at the table over the hot breakfast of sausage, eggs, toast, and orange juice prepared by him. She wasn't afraid to look him in the eye, nor was she afraid of what had happened between them. As far as she was concerned, last night was no different from any other night they'd shared in the past even though she understood that this was the present. They had slept in each other's arms, an awesome experience for her. Perhaps he was feeling guilty because of his romantic involvement with the other woman. It wasn't as if anything had happened, but she had a darn good inkling that it could've gone quite far had they both been awake at the same time.

"You seem awfully quiet. Are you okay, Drakkar?"

He looked up at her, making direct eye contact with her for the first time. "I could ask you that same question." He sounded testy to her but she didn't understand that.

"I'm fine, but that wasn't the question I asked. Does it bear repeating?"

Pushing his hands through his hair, as if he was frustrated, he sighed. "I'm fine. Thanks for asking." He sighed again, only harder. "I don't know how you can sit over there with that devil-may-care attitude of yours, especially after what happened last night."

"Are you speaking of the fact that I didn't watch your interview? I apologized for that."

"Damn you, Tarynton, you know that's not what I'm talking about."

"Instead of huffing and puffing ovals of steam over there, why don't you tell me what you're talking about? I'm not a mind reader, you know."

"I remember a time when you read mine pretty well, but I've been forbidden to go there. What I'm talking about is what happened between us last night—and you already know that."

She raised a questioning eyebrow. "Did something out of the ordinary happen between us last night? If so, what do you think that something was? I must've missed out on it."

He looked exasperated. "Tarynton, we're not teenagers anymore so don't play childish games with me. You've always been good at toying with me like this. I can't believe you still like to do crap like this, especially for someone who likes everything spelled out for her."

"Drakkar, because I do like everything made plain, why don't you just do that and stop beating around the dang bush?"

The intolerant look she tossed him made him wish he hadn't started this with her. It didn't look like he was going to be the victor of this little battle of wills.

"We slept in the same bed and you're acting like nothing happened."

"Nothing did happen, Drakkar. You fell asleep in my bed and I covered you up. I don't know how you ended up at the top with me, other than under your own steam, but you did. Do you have a problem with that, because I don't?"

He was stunned that what he'd done hadn't bothered her. But he wasn't so sure she'd tell him if it did. The Tarynton that he knew would desire to spare his feelings even when she hated something someone had done to cause her discomfort, including him.

"Well, even if you don't have a problem with me sleeping in your bed, with you wrapped up in my arms, maybe your man would."

"Are you going to be the one to tell him?" Awaiting his answer, she raised an eyebrow.

Another response he hadn't expected. "What are you really saying?"

"It's not about what I'm saying, brother. You're the one that seems to have the problem with it. Maybe your woman is the one that would mind. Perhaps it's the guilt over your relationship with her that's at work here. In case your memory fails you, I didn't get into bed with you. Quite the contrary."

"So it's like that, huh?"

"That's exactly how it is! Furthermore, I've had enough of this one-sided interrogation. I've got important stuff on my mind. And what you're talking is nothing but plain bullshit."

The instant she jumped up from the table he got to his feet too, pulling her into his arms. His mouth claimed hers in one of the most feverish kisses they'd ever shared. The kiss went on and on, without any objection on her part whatsoever. Her heart did a perfect swan dive.

When they finally pulled apart, not knowing what to say or do next, she took off running. He caught up to her before she could reach her bedroom. "Tarynton, I'm sorry. I'm taking advantage of your wonderful hospitality. That's unfair of me. If you think I'm only trying to get you into bed, you're dead wrong. Anyway, I promise not to make intimate advances like that toward you again, for as long as I'm under your roof."

"And after you've moved out?"

Seeing the mischief in her eyes, he grinned. It was

her way of putting him at ease, the Tarynton way. "Now that's another matter to consider. Don't say you weren't forewarned."

Laughing with a delicious sound that thrilled him, she went into her bedroom and closed herself in. With her back against the shut door, she slid down to the floor. "Yes," she cried quietly, "he still wants me every bit as much as I want him. Oh, how blessed we both are."

But what would taking advantage of their desires cost her in the way of emotions?

Drakkar popped his head into Tarynton's office door. "I'm about to leave. Is there anything you need me to do for you before I go?"

Take me to bed. She shook her head in the negative. "I hope you have a good day."

He smiled endearingly at her. "Knowing you're okay with everything, I'm sure I'm going to have a great one. You have my cell number." He headed out but turned back abruptly. "Are we having dinner together tonight? I should be home early, around five-thirty."

"If you're cooking."

"I cooked breakfast."

She shrugged. "And?"

"Girl, if I don't start cooking until after I get home, we won't eat until late." He scratched the side of his face. "I'll just take you out to dinner. How's that?"

Her smile came bright. "Now we're talking. I'll be ready when you get home."

"There's a great restaurant near the studio. The food is divine. Why don't you just meet me there? We can have an early dinner and then take in a movie. If you like, we can even stop by Choices for a drink and listen to some good music."

"What's the name of the restaurant?"

"Good question. I just know where it is. I'll call you back with a name and specific address after I get to work. If you're not here, I'll leave a message. I'll also shoot you an e-mail."

"I love a man who knows how to cover all his bases. I'll look forward to our evening."

His heart told him to give her a gentle kiss to seal their plans, but his head told him to hightail it out of there before he got himself into more trouble. He followed his heart.

Moved by his delicate display of affection, Tarynton stared after him as he retreated. That sweet, tight behind of his had her wanting to run after him for just one good squeeze. She flexed her fingers, as though she had a handful of his beautiful derriere. Drakkar presented her with a captivating challenge, one that she was definitely up to. She was only sorry that neither of them had seriously challenged the breakup. It seemed that talking it through might have kept them together. The whole thing had been strange.

Jumping right into her work, Tarynton called several clients and gave them the final rundown on their getaway plans, promising to send their travel documents out that day. There were a couple of plane tickets that she had to send FedEx and she had one client that had requested her to use UPS for his travel documents. Both courier services picked the packages up from her office whenever she called in and placed a pickup request. She kept in stock a variety of mailers from each courier service, including those used by the regular post office.

The house phone rang, which had a different sound from the office lines. When she picked up, the caller clicked off. Probably a wrong number, she guessed. As it rang again, she looked puzzled since it was rare for her house phone to ring during business hours.

Then she thought of Drakkar. He did say he'd call. But when he normally called her, he had reached her at the office number. He knew that's where she was until six in the evening even though she sometimes stayed later than that. She picked up the phone, only to have the caller hang up again. It almost seemed intentional to her since they hung up after she answered. She dismissed it as strange but nothing to worry about.

Tarynton worked nonstop throughout the day. Knowing she had a date with Drakkar kept her upbeat even to the point of humming her favorite tunes. Having gathered a lot of pertinent information for her magazine article, she felt confident that she could deliver a wonderful, very informative story. Should the proposed Kwanzaa celebration come off the way she and her friends hoped, she desired to do a follow-up article to include the highlights.

To meet Drakkar at five-thirty she had to shut down early. Besides, she needed to administer a little self-pampering, desiring plenty of time for primping in front of the mirror. Wanting to look extra good for Drakkar, as well as for herself, she thought about what she would wear. He liked to see her in red. But his number-one preference was basic black, in something clinging, something that hugged her curvaceous figure like a body glove. She thought of the perfect dress, a sexy black spandex number, with a low-scooped neck and three-quarter-length sleeves. It was nothing short of elegant and it was very sexy.

Her excitement grew as she tried to decide how to wear her hair. A soft, sophisticated style would work best for her. She didn't want to wear it up because Drakkar liked it down. Perhaps a nice style pulled back with a decorative hair ornament might do the trick. A few loose hanging tendrils would also complement such a style.

For the next hour Tarynton worked on a quick get-away for a couple who'd only known each other for a short time. He wanted to take her away for the weekend, but he'd asked Tarynton to book separate but adjoining rooms for them. Tarynton smiled when she thought of her conversation with her client. He'd told her that he wanted to take things slow with his lady friend, that she was indeed a special one. Separate rooms were her only condition for the trip, and he had readily agreed to it, he'd told Tarynton.

Her client had talked of Vegas, but Tarynton didn't think Sin City was the appropriate first weekend for a couple just getting to know each other. Something intimate and more private seemed in order for this couple. With that in mind, she booked them into a quaint little inn up at Lake Arrowhead, California. It would really be nice up there just before the snow was due to arrive, but it was already fireplace weather at that high an altitude. The lake was gorgeous and they could take a boat ride across it. With numerous shopping venues and cozy restaurants for them to enjoy, they could stay plenty busy if they desired. If they chose just to kick back, Lake Arrowhead was still the appropriate weekend getaway. Lots of picturesque scenery could be enjoyed on both the ride up the mountain as well as from the beautiful panoramas at the top.

The office phone rang and she picked it up on the second ring. It was Drakkar calling to inform her of the name to Gladstones 4 Fish up at Universal City Walk. She laughed about Drakkar's not knowing the name since it was such a popular restaurant. But she understood. Drakkar was new to southern California. She would enjoy showing him around her adopted city should he ask her to do so.

He surprised her when he told her he was leaving the studio early in order to pick her up. He didn't want them in separate cars since they planned to go out after dinner for some fun and relaxation. When it finally dawned on Tarynton that they were actually going on a real date, she squealed with delight. She didn't want to read too much into it, but she couldn't help being thrilled silly at spending an entire evening with the one man she truly loved. Tarynton somehow felt that she was in for a real treat. But then again, so was Drakkar. She was by no means a slouch. He should feel as blessed about her as a date as she did him.

Six

The meal had been superb, not to mention the wonderful company they had rediscovered in each other. Although it was a chilly night, they'd opted to sit outdoors on the terrace where they could people-watch. All through dinner, as they sat next to each other on the same booth, rather than opposite, Drakkar's warmth had had her wanting him to heat up her body all over. He was certainly a warm-blooded specimen, through and through. Being seated so close to Drakkar was like sitting inside a warm oven.

They were now at Choices, seated at an intimate, cozy table for two, the club where they'd first reunited. They had decided to take in a movie another evening. Drakkar kept Tarynton laughing and smiling with his effervescent style of communication. She could tell by their various topics of conversation that they still had a lot in common.

His mood was exuberant as he told her about some of his wonderful experiences in Louisiana, expounding greatly on the many attractions of the city of New Orleans. Though she'd gone to Grambling for his homecoming three years in a row, they hadn't made it to the Big Easy. He had promised to take her there, telling her she would love it as much as he did.

"Louisiana now has casinos on land rather than over water, which had once been mandated by law. Harrods has a major presence in New Orleans. It's located downtown near the French Quarter. Do you ever go to Vegas?"

"Been a time or two. I like to play the slots, but I'm stingy. I don't like giving my money away. My friends tease me about cashing in my winnings as soon as I get ahead. I'm totally through with gambling once I hit a nice jackpot. I've been lucky so far. And I do know when to walk away from it. Twenty dollars is about all I'm willing to lose. If nothing happens with that initial twenty, I'm gone."

"You've always been tight with the mean green. Girl, back in the day you were known for squeezing the buffalo until it popped off the back of the nickel. You gave the store clerks a fit when you went inside to buy candy. You certainly got the most out of your pennies in buying only those items that were two for one. Your favorite thing then was five shoelaces of red licorice for a dime."

She turned up her nose. "Was I that bad?"

"Worse! Remember when we shopped at the outdoor markets? You used to haggle over the price of every little thing. Merchants often gave you your price just to get rid of you."

She smiled. "Yeah, I do remember. I guess I *was* pretty bad. I recall how embarrassed you got when I went on and on about the prices being way too high. You would slink away until I finished up. But it was my money and I loved to stretch it as far as it would go. I still do."

"I'm sure of that. Do you want another white wine?"

"Thanks but no thanks. Coffee would be nice. I'm starting to get sleepy. I'd already be in bed if I were at home."

Home, he thought. That's exactly what her place had become to him.

"Okay, sleepyhead, one coffee coming right up." As he excused himself, he smiled at her. He preferred to go to the bar and order the coffee rather than wait for a waitress to appear since the club was pretty crowded. He didn't want Tarynton to have to wait, but he wanted to get back to her as soon as possible.

Tarynton watched after his confident stride as he made his way across the crowded room to the bar. Smiling, she took in the more than admiring glances in his direction coming from several of the women patrons. He *was* quite a looker. His being a born leader came across in spades, especially in the way he held his head high, his chest out, and in the squaring of his shoulders. It also showed up in the graceful way he moved. Drakkar's self-assured movements had a way of making a very positive statement about the type of human being he might be.

More than anything Drakkar had a real heart of gold. He was kind and gentle and he loved his mom like crazy. He used to hate that his father was so strict, up until he realized his dad, Eddington—fondly referred to as simply Ed—had only been teaching Drakkar to be a man and how one should treat a woman.

Drakkar had two older brothers, Ellison and Jordan, but he only got along with one sibling, Jordan. Ellison was always strung out on something or other and he usually had a beef with everybody. His choice in drugs was anything he could get his hands on.

It was Ellison's serious issues and troubled life that made Drakkar really see what his dad had tried to get across in their strict upbringing. He then began to appreciate and understand the things that his dad had taught them, though it didn't seem that Ellison had ever gotten a grasp on the valuable lessons. Drakkar had told her that Ellison was in rehab for the sixth or seventh time.

Tarynton recalled how strong a black man Drakkar's father was. Father and son had grown extremely close, but only after Drakkar got heavy into sports during his freshman year of high school. Eddington Lomax had never missed a single game that his son played in even if it meant taking a day off from work. Mr. Lomax had been very disappointed when Drakkar's knee injury had occurred, but it was the encouragement and spiritual guidance from him that had gotten his youngest son through the worst of times of his career-ending injury.

Both sets of their parents had great marriages. She couldn't wait to see her mother and father over the Thanksgiving holiday, less than a couple of months away. She had one brother, Camden, whom she adored. She could hardly wait to see him since he always came home for the holidays, too. She and Camden were thick as thieves.

Drakkar glanced over at Tarynton. She looked delectable in that little black number. Had she worn black just for him? She knew he loved to see her in simple black elegance. The dress she wore was all of that and more. He still couldn't get over the fact that she didn't have a problem with him sleeping in her bed last night. But he understood it. When two people had been as close as they'd been, he could see why it hadn't disturbed her in the least. But this wasn't back then. This was now. Just one of the many intriguing ways of Miss Tarynton Batiste was her ability to accept people and things for exactly who and what they were.

He and Tarynton had started out like sister and brother while growing up. And over the years they'd had many major scraps and squabbles, as most siblings sometimes do. Tarynton was the type who always took her marbles and went home when things weren't going her way. But as she blossomed into a lovely teenager, she remained competitive, but it was no longer an *I must win or I will die* scenario. Tarynton loved to win—for keeps. She'd certainly won his heart for all eternity, the way he'd thought he'd had hers. For all his joy over their reunion, the man in her life was an issue for him. How to win her heart away from her guy was an even bigger one.

Like Tarynton Batiste, Drakkar Lomax also liked to win. Tarynton was the grand prize.

Only for a second did he allow thoughts of Tamara Lyndon, the Grambling campus fatal attraction. To have escaped her obsessive, possessive, stalkerlike nature was one of his greatest accomplishments to date. She hadn't been too happy when she'd heard he was moving to California. That was something he hadn't wanted her to know. But somehow she'd found out. He still didn't know how she'd obtained the information. Because she worked on the production side of the house for the same television station that he'd once been employed with, he figured that it was probably her source of information.

Although it had been over with them for a very long time, she had a way of popping up all over the place in order to disrupt his life. In actuality it had never really begun for him. He had only turned to Tamara after the breakup with Tarynton. That situation had kept him with her longer because he feared her unpredictable behaviors. Whenever Tamara learned that he was dating someone new, she showed up to bring about further confusion. It had gotten to the point where he just stopped dating for fear of her finding out and causing him more grief. While she hadn't got physical with anyone, he feared that the potential for such an occurrence was great.

California was a fresh start for him all the way around.

He settled in back at the table, watching Tarynton as she took a sip of the hot drink. "How's your coffee, sunshine?"

"Thanks, Drakkar. It tastes as good as it smells."

He looked at his watch. "In about another hour or so the glass slipper comes off and your beautiful outfit will turn into rags."

His reference to her as Cinderella caused her to laugh heartily. "You remember, huh?"

"Remember! That was a night that I don't think anyone at the winter costume ball will ever forget. You have a way of coming up with the darnedest, most intriguing ideas."

At exactly midnight Tarynton had emerged from the ladies' bathroom wearing raggedy, threadbare clothes and an ugly pair of old, worn-down shoes, he recalled. No one could believe their eyes. "Just minutes before you came out of that bathroom, you were looking so stunningly beautiful in your white satin Cinderella ball gown. Lady T, you took the whole dang show that night. But then again, you always did."

"It was a costume ball, Drakkar. I was Cinderella. In order to make it real, I thought that I had to act out the entire story."

"That was some plan you cooked up. You also made it some special night."

"Yeah, what was even more special is when you came to my house the next day with a plastic replica of the glass slipper with clear acrylic heels, asking me to try it on to see if it fit the lovely woman's foot that had run away from the ball. Now that was what I couldn't believe!

My parents still talk about that extremely romantic, imaginative incident."

"I guess I have somewhat of a great imagination too!" His look seemed to ask, where had those days gone, how had they let them end, and all so abruptly. He missed those days more than he could adequately express. He quickly snatched his mind away from the anguished thoughts. "Speaking of your parents, how are they? It's been a minute since I last spoke with them."

"You know that Pamela and Steven Batiste don't let any grass grow under their feet. I'm going home for Thanksgiving. It's nice traveling to Atlanta for the holidays. But you know something? I don't feel the same warm things that I felt in our home in PA. It's a beautiful place, but I guess the memories just aren't there for me. They bought the Atlanta house while I was still in college. How are your mom and dad?"

"Still going strong, though Dad had to slow down a bit. He had a mild stroke last summer. He lost use of his left side for a short period of time, but he has now regained full mobility. It took a while, but he finally recovered."

"Sorry to hear about his illness but glad to know that he's fully recovered. Whatever happened to the other part of our partners in crime, the three stooges, Larry, Curly, and Moe?"

"They're now deputy dogs. Ronnie, Ricky, and Bill are all cops. Can you believe that?"

"It's a stretch. Them boys used to steal the sugar out of candy, not to mention as much candy as they could stuff in their pockets. Cops! Who would ever have thought it? Those were your boys back in the day."

"Our boys! You were as much a part of our little group as any one of us was. Then you up and grew those round things."

She looked puzzled. "What round things?"

His eyes went straight to her breasts. "Those two sweet rounded mounds that I used to feast off of every chance I got."

Her cheeks flushed hotly. "Our communication was going great up until now. You had to go there, didn't you? Couldn't help yourself, could you?"

"I can't help myself period when it comes to you. When you came to the playground wearing that training bra, we couldn't play ball for eyeing you. You could see that bra right through the thin white T-shirt you wore. I think you were so proud of wearing it that you wanted us to see it. That's the first day my feelings for you began to change. The grown-up dress came a couple of years later, but there were subtle visual changes to your body that didn't go unnoticed."

Her smile was soft and sentimental. She looked as if she'd just stepped into a delicious dream. He studied her, noticing the moisture pooling in her lovely eyes. Sentiment could be hard on the emotions, especially when you had the world at your fingertips, only to discover that you'd let it slip right through your fingers. How had they slipped through each other's fingers? It was the one question that probably neither one of them could answer. Drakkar knew for sure that he couldn't. Perhaps that was how it was meant to be. Nothing happened without a reason. Their being together like this was no coincidence. Divine intervention and destiny had a hand in this reunion. Of that, he was sure.

Although she'd had a cup of coffee at the club, Tarynton wanted another one. Coffee kept her awake—and tonight she had plenty to stay awake for. Although she'd pay for it in the morning, that was okay with her. She had in-depth plans to think and rethink about her lovely evening with Drakkar. Sleep would just have to wait. Before she could indulge herself in another thought, he came into the kitchen, just as she poured the water into the coffeemaker. Dressed in burgundy silk lounging pajama bottoms and a matching silk T-shirt, he looked sexy and very desirable. Her heart screamed out for his attention.

"Did you make enough brew for me to have a cup?"

"I did even though I wasn't sure you wanted any. Are you hungry?"

"I wouldn't mind something to snack on. What you got good?"

"Depends on what you have a taste for."

His eyes scanned her entire body. "I know you don't want me to go there."

"Maybe I do." Her eyes flirted openly with him. "Why don't you take a stab at trying to find out exactly what I want?" Her eyes went straight to his crotch.

Taking her comment for the challenge it was, he came and stood right in front of her. "What if I said I wanted to snack on you?"

She bit down on her lower lip. It was all she could do to keep from opening the top of her pajamas and offer him her breasts to snack on. "What part of me would you nibble on first?"

His insides trembled with desire. As if he'd read her mind, he stared at her breasts. "You already know that I'm a breast man, so I'd probably start with that delicacy first."

"Hmm, sounds intriguing. What would your appetite desire next?"

Eyeing her intently, he gently snapped the waistband of her pajama bottom. "You know this is a dangerous game you're playing, don't you?"

"Dangerous? In what way?"

"Don't start that innocent act with me, Tarynton. It

won't work. You know you're playing with a blazing fire."

"What if I decided I wouldn't mind getting burned?"

His hand automatically went to the crotch of his pajama bottom. If she kept talking like that, he wasn't going to be able to hide the sudden new growth beneath the silk of his attire.

Sauntering up to him, she put her arms around his neck. "Can you even handle all this?"

He eyed her curiously. "I can, but I won't. You're letting your libido do the talking for you. Besides, I don't think you're ready for me, or ready for us to come together in that way."

While trying to cool down her out-of-control desires for him, she poked out her lower lip. "Are you rejecting me?"

"I wouldn't call it rejection. Just practicing a little caution here. I also made a promise not to make any intimate advances on you while I'm living under your roof. I know you recall that."

"Why don't we pretend that you've moved out and that you're just an overnight visitor?"

He shook his head from side to side. "Tarynton, Tarynton, if you only knew what was going on down inside these pajamas you'd behave yourself. The fire is getting out of control."

The thought to touch him down there to feel what was going on occurred to her, but then she realized it was too bold of a move for now. She'd certainly find more than just a handful of sweet, hardened flesh if she were to intimately explore his more than adequate sexual endowment. Her memory served her well. "What exactly *is* going on down there?"

"Something big, long, and throbbing is mighty interested in reacquainting itself with your sweet inner treasures. But I've learned patience. Let me drink my coffee and then go to bed before we suddenly find ourselves butt naked and sprawled out here on this kitchen floor." Stepping around her, he poured himself a cup of coffee and then took a seat at the table. She had him so hot that sweat seemed to pour from within him.

Fighting the urge to drop down into his lap to further excite him, she somehow managed to sit in the chair closest to his. Hot and bothered by their erotic verbal foreplay, Tarynton even considered handcuffing him to his bed in order to have her way with him. She laughed inwardly knowing it was such a ludicrous thought, especially since she didn't own any handcuffs. But then silk stockings might work just as well, more so if he was willing. Tarynton wanted Drakkar more now than she ever had before, but she desired more than just a night of hot sex. She wanted his heart and she needed his love. Her one desire was to have him back in her life forever.

After getting to her feet, Tarynton leaned over him and kissed his smooth cheek. "Good night, Drakkar. Sleep well."

He instantly got to his feet. "Can I get a real kiss good night? Let me say this before you answer. I want to kiss you as if you were my lover, not just my best friend. I want my tongue and my mouth to indulge in a seductive slow dance of passion with yours. Is that asking too much?"

Immediately her arms went around his neck. Ready and waiting for the seductive slow dance to begin, she wasted not a second in offering him her lips. Feeling the rigidity of his lengthy sex made her crazy with longing. Rubbing herself against him, without a thought of later regret, Tarynton meshed her body into his, hoping he would eventually give in to the madness of their beyond heated desire for each other.

Though she felt his body trembling with need, she

could clearly see that their coming together intimately wasn't going to happen when he held her slightly away from him. "Good night, sweetheart. This has been some wild evening. Though we haven't discussed it, I'm getting the impression that we're on the same page as far as wanting to get our loving relationship back on track, as well as reviving the intimate parts of it. *Are* we on the same page?"

Time for payback. "I know you don't want me to go there. Your libido is doing the talking for you. Besides, I don't think you're ready for me, or ready for us to come together in that way. Just practicing a little caution here. I've learned patience. Good night, Drakkar."

His exact words of earlier tumbled recklessly through his head. Was she the most intriguing woman on the planet or what? Tarynton Batiste was too fascinating for her own good. Or for his, for that matter. All he could do was laugh as he watched her walk away without so much as a backward glance in his direction.

It was going to be a very long night. Knowing that Tarynton was sleeping in her bed right down the hall from his room was going to challenge him in ways he didn't want to imagine. This was one test of strength that he wasn't sure he was up for.

For the next couple of weeks Tarynton and Drakkar went about the days and nights as if there were nothing between them but friendship. Though each of them knew better than that, fear of the unknown made them extremely cautious, especially him. Because he was so reserved around her, Tarynton feared that she'd come on too strong with him. Still, they ate their meals together practically every morning and evening that Drakkar didn't have to leave for the studio super early or get back home unusually late.

Tarynton added liquid Cheer and color-safe bleach under the heavy flow of hot water filling the washing machine. After loading her unmentionables into the washer, she turned the dial to the delicate cycle, closed the lid, and then went into the kitchen.

Seeing Drakkar seated at the table reading the newspaper warmed her heart. "Good morning, sir. How are you?"

He looked up from the paper and smiled. "Morning, T.C. Doing just great on this lovely Saturday morning. What about you?"

She blew out a steady stream of breath. "Not bad at all. Since I'm washing clothes this morning, do you have anything that needs washed? If you do, I can put them in the washer after I put mine in the dryer."

His eyes softened. "Thank you, but I can do it. I don't want to add to your workload. But it was such a nice gesture. How about if we pull together this morning and do the chores? I can run the vacuum in all the rooms and you can follow behind me and dust."

"I like your plan. The beds need to be stripped and the linens changed. I can do that."

"Okay, and I'll clean all the bathrooms." A thoughtful looked crossed his features. "Is it going to be a problem for you to have me cleaning in your private space? If so, I understand."

She frowned. "Of course it isn't a problem. I'll take all the help I can get. There are times when I think of hiring someone to clean this entire place, but then I feel guilty about having someone to come in and tidy up my mess. I try to keep all the rooms in good condition."

He laughed. "Girl, you're probably the only person on the planet that thinks this way."

"No, I'm not. My dad is like that. After many years of doing everything himself, he finally hired someone to do the yard work. But then he'd do most of the work before the gardener ever got there. My mom used to complain about that all the time. But as an adult, I know where he's coming from. Although I'm not as bad as I used to be, I still struggle with asking or considering paying someone to do for me what I can do for myself. Maybe I'll feel differently if my schedule gets even crazier than it already is."

"I can see that you've gotten better about letting people help you out. I wasn't sure how you were going to respond when I asked about assisting with the chores. I'm glad you're okay with me helping out around here. It's the least I can do."

"I might have a problem with it if you weren't living here. I'd probably feel guilty about you cleaning up something you didn't mess up. It's not that I mind someone helping me out, I just don't want to appear too needy. Doing it all myself is hard at times, but the fact is I'm the only one here to do it. I have the option to purchase this place, but I may need something smaller. This is a lot of square footage for just one person."

He looked around him. "You seem to have the majority of the spaces filled. If you get something smaller, you're going to have to rent storage. Also, your big office would be gone."

"I see what you mean. I actually leased this place because of the amount of space it had. I probably went wrong when I started purchasing things to fill up those areas. I didn't own half of these furnishings when I moved in here. Should I decide to move into a smaller place, I can always sell some of my things."

"That's certainly an option to consider. I'm sure you'll make the right decision when the time comes. Ready to start on the chores?"

"What about breakfast?"

"Hadn't even thought about it." He put a finger to

his temple. "Whose turn is it to cook? If my memory serves me correctly, I think it's yours, T.C."

"I think you're right. What about a fresh vegetable omelet?"

"You're on to something. I can fix the coffee if you don't mind."

"Have at it. I'll have the omelets ready in just a short time."

As Tarynton chopped up the raw onions and fresh tomatoes, she stole covert glances at Drakkar while he did his part in getting things ready for breakfast. After removing the sliced fresh mushrooms from the store container, she washed them and then mixed all the vegetables together. Using a whisk, she blended some milk and several eggs. She then sprinkled the mixture with three types of shredded cheese. Once the omelet-maker heated to the desired temperature, she poured the mixture into the pan and folded in the fresh vegetables.

Seated back at the table, Drakkar watched her as she made her way around the room. In thinking of their moments of flirtation, he regretted that they now seemed to be in a different frame of mind with each other. The state of their relationship no longer felt natural. He had gotten used to them joking and kidding around in a playful manner. It didn't seem so long ago that she had him hotter than a firecracker. He thought about what she'd said about taking the risk of getting burned. Then he'd made the stupid statements about her not being ready for them to come together in that way. The moment she'd thrown his idiotic remarks back in his face was when he realized he'd made a big mistake. Up until that point Tarynton's comments had suggested to him that she was ready for anything that would bring them closer together.

He was no longer sure of what she wanted to happen

between them. At that very moment, he decided that he'd soon find out if they could get back on the same page. His eyes looked up at her when she leaned over his shoulders to place a plate in front of him. She could've placed the dish down without leaning over him, but she had come so close to him that he'd caught her delicately perfumed scent. He had to wonder what her motive had been. If her intent was to physically arouse him, she had succeeded.

She stood still while he passed the blessing. Before taking a seat, she grabbed the butter dish and jelly out of the refrigerator to use on the toast. The curious look on his face caused her to wonder what he was thinking, but she wasn't concerned enough about it to ask him. She'd seen Drakkar looking pensive plenty of times. Like she used to do, she'd wait until he told her what was on his mind.

"Are you doing anything special today, Tarynton?"

"I'm going to the health spa for a brief spell, after the chores are done. When I come back, I'm just going to relax. This feels like one of those do-nothing Saturdays. So that's what I'm going to do, nothing."

"Sounds boring, but I'd like to do nothing with you. Is that okay with you, T.C.?"

"That's up to you, Drakkar. I don't ever mind being in your company. We're never at a loss for great conversation. I have lots of video movies to catch up on if you want to join me. I also plan to order in pizza. That's why I'm going to work out for a minute, so I won't feel guilty when I gorge myself later."

"Black olives, lots of cheese, and extra tomato sauce, right?"

"The exact toppings that I love on my pizza. And for you, the works, right?"

"You got it. It doesn't look like much has changed."

Yes, it has. In fact, too much has changed. And I'm not

sure that I like any of the changes. I want things the way they used to be. She didn't think that it could ever be precisely the way it was for them, but she wasn't going to stop praying. Something was telling her that she and Drakkar still had a future. Not to explore that possibility would be a tragic mistake, one that she wasn't willing to make. Enough mistakes had already been made by both of them.

"How's your omelet?"

"It's divine, girl. Light and fluffy, just the way I like it. I might hire you as my chef when I move into my place. Is that a position you might be interested in? I pay very well."

Only if my last name changes to yours. "Do any fringe benefits come along with the job? If so, what can I expect?"

He rocked back in the chair. "Well, let me see here. I can offer tons of compliments, and I can highly recommend you to others. What other benefits do you have in mind?"

"None, 'cause I don't want the job. It doesn't sound permanent enough."

His questioning eyes met with hers. There seemed to be a hidden message in her pointed comment. Did he dare ask her what she meant? He decided not to ask, but he wasn't going to let it go unchallenged. "The job can become as permanent as you want it to be. It's up to you."

She pushed her chair back from the table. "I think I'll pass. I prefer working for myself. But any time you want me to prepare one of your favorite dishes of mine, I'll be happy to oblige, but only if you agree to do the same for me. No one in this world can barbecue ribs like you do." She closed her eyes and licked her lips. "I wish I had a slab right before me. This girl has been known to hurt herself feasting on your delicious bones, not to mention your heavenly sauce."

He laughed. "Girl, you better watch your choice of words. But you always did like my rib bones. I owe that skill to my dad since he taught me how to cook them so well. You have a deal, T.C. And I won't hesitate to ask you to cook any one of your great dishes for me. I may do wonders with the rib bones, but you can throw down on all those curry dishes you prepare." He got to his feet. "I guess we'd better get the chores done if we're going to get on with our day."

Our day. She liked the sound of that. "I think you're right."

Drakkar began his household chores by putting the kitchen back in order since she had cooked. Tarynton went off to change his linens first and then she'd take care of hers. She wouldn't dust all the rooms until after he vacuumed. Despite his voiced concerns she had no problem leaving all three of the bathrooms for him to take care of, which included hers.

Seeing that she'd forgotten to transfer her clothes from the washer to the dryer, he went into the laundry room to take care of it for her. That way, the washer would be clear when she got ready to wash the next load.

His breath caught as he emptied the washer of her very personal items. Imagining her wearing each intimate article, he gently fingered the delicate lacy and satin items as he made the transfer. A black lace teddy caused him to sweat. Then jealousy set in on him when he began to wonder if her current man had ever seen her in it. The thought of another man getting next to her physically made his blood boil. The only person Tarynton had ever given herself to should've been him. When he'd first made love to her, he'd told her that he wanted to be her first, last, and only lover, forever. She had vowed to him that he would be the only one.

Finished with all the chores, Tarynton was dressed for the health club as she waited for Drakkar to come into the living room. When he did appear, she saw that he wore the same clothes he had on earlier. "When are you getting ready for the spa?"

"I hope you don't mind, but I decided to stay here and work on a couple of things that I've been neglecting. I'm sorry if I've held you up."

She was bitterly disappointed, but she didn't let it show. But she had to wonder if he was opting out of all the plans they'd made for the day and into the evening. "No harm has been done. I just finished getting ready a couple of minutes ago. I guess I'll see you when I see you."

"What's that supposed to mean? We're still hanging out together when you get back, aren't we?"

Inwardly, she gave a sigh of relief. "I'll admit that I wasn't sure if you still wanted to go forward with our plans or not. Glad to know that you do."

He came over to where she stood. "Just a little delay in getting things started. That's all. See you shortly, okay?" In an innocent display of affection, he kissed her forehead.

Drakkar rushed to put the finishing touches on the dinner he'd prepared. He'd opted out of going to the spa so that he could fix Tarynton's favorites, his barbecued ribs. He couldn't wait to see the pleasurable look on her face. To go along with the meat, he'd fixed baked beans and spiced up some frozen collard greens. Drakkar had also purchased a pound and a half of fresh potato salad from the grocery store's deli. Because he'd started so late he didn't think he'd have everything done by the time she got back home. But when she'd called to say that she'd run into her girlfriends at the spa, and would be gone a little longer than planned, he thanked his Creator for the extra time to get everything done.

No sooner did he finish trimming the candlewicks for lighting than Tarynton entered the dining room. She seemed surprised to see the table all set since they had talked of ordering in pizza. She couldn't read the expression on Drakkar's face, but it appeared to her that he looked a little guilty. "What are you up to in here? I can't believe you set the table for pizza."

He pulled out a chair in response to her question. "Just have a seat. I promise to let you in on my little surprise within the next few seconds."

Wondering what he was up to, Tarynton looked dazed as he left the room. Then her nose caught the delicious food scents permeating the room. Drakkar had cooked dinner for them despite their plans to order takeout. She smiled at his thoughtfulness.

Before bringing in the main event, he carried all the other dishes in. With the meat hidden under a covered platter, he finally brought it to the table and set it down. When he saw that he held her rapt attention, he removed the lid.

Her eyes lit up with the brilliant facets of a hundred flawless diamonds. "Ribs!" She jumped up from her seat and planted a juicy kiss on his lips. Realizing what she'd done, she backed away from him. That one kiss had each of them desiring a couple hundred more. "You are too wonderful. This is so thoughtful of you. Thank you. It looks like you lied to me about your reason for not going to the spa. That's one lie I can forgive. Thank you so much." Without wasting another minute, she grabbed a rib bone from the platter.

As if he were chastising a small child, he took the rib from her hand before she could bite into it. "Think we should pass a blessing first?"

Looking abashed and a tad annoyed for the interruption, she fought the urge to smear the sauce from her fingertips all over his smiling face. Instead, she looked up toward heaven. "Sorry for that." She then bowed her head and closed her eyes.

Tarynton was stretched out fully in bed as she revisited the entire morning, afternoon, and evening with Drakkar. In the latter part of the evening she and Drakkar had watched three different movies. If someone had asked her to name each of them, she honestly couldn't do it. All evening long she'd sat in eager anticipation of something beautiful happening between them. Drakkar never made so much as a joking pass at her. There were so many times that she wanted to take the initiative in getting him aroused, but she chickened out each time. She may as well have been watching movies with her brother, Camden, for that matter, because that's exactly how Drakkar treated her, as if she were his sister.

More than ever before, she was convinced that her earlier come-ons to Drakkar had completely turned him off. Wishing that she had never acted in such a brazen way with him, never to have had it happen like that, she turned out the bedside lamp.

Seven

This morning had certainly come in brighter than it had for the past several days. The rain had come to stay, or so it had seemed. But now the sun was shining brightly, typical southern California in the early fall season.

Despite the sunshiny day Tarynton felt gloomy as she sat at her desk pondering Drakkar's sudden absences. She hadn't seen hide or hair of him since the barbecue dinner he'd prepared for her over a week ago. He hadn't appeared at any of her breakfasts or dinners and she hadn't encountered him at any other time before retiring at night.

She feared the worst.

Her open flirtations of a few weeks back *had* scared him off. He had said she wasn't ready for them to come together intimately, but it seemed that he was the one that wasn't ready. She'd simply played the wrong cards that night, and had gotten stuck with the Old Maid— what she was probably doomed to be for the rest of her life. She had toyed with the idea of calling his cell phone, but she hadn't been able to bring herself to do so. It didn't make sense that he wouldn't call and at least let her know that he was okay. He had to know she'd be worried.

An eerie feeling hit her all of a sudden, a really weird one. Getting up from behind her desk, she went through the laundry room and down the hallway toward Drakkar's bedroom. The thought that he might be in there sick had hit her like a lightning bolt. She knocked softly. Then she hit the door harder with the side of her fist. Thinking only of his well-being, she opened the door and went inside. The room looked as if it had never been lived in. With the closet door standing open, she saw that it was empty. Her heart rate went berserk as she tried to make sense of what she saw. Her thoughts turned to the night when she'd made a bold play for him.

It appeared that Drakkar had moved out without so much as breathing a single word to her regarding his plans. How ungrateful was that even if it was all her fault? Her bold moves had sent him packing. She had run him off. To make sure that she was correct in her assessment of the situation, she checked all the drawers. Not even a piece of lint occupied the spaces. Tears came hard and furious. Drakkar's sudden disappearance broke her heart yet again.

Feeling used, abused, and regretful, Tarynton decided to go to bed and hide herself and the shame she felt beneath the blankets. She plainly felt worn out. She also felt stupid for coming on to Drakkar the way she had. He was probably laughing at how big a fool she'd made of herself with him. She must've been stone out of her mind to think that she could win back his heart like that. While Tarynton made her way down the hall toward her bedroom, she saw movement, nearly fainting dead away at seeing Drakkar only a few feet away from her.

Smiling, he held a large bouquet of flowers, which he handed to her. "Hi, sunshine. How are you doing?"

She was too stunned to speak. Where were his clothes if he hadn't moved out? She couldn't even find her voice to tell him how beautiful the colorful flowers were. All she could do was stand there and stare at him. Although she burned with anger, she couldn't voice it.

He looked concerned for her. "What's wrong, T.C.?" When he put his arms around her shoulders, she had to fight hard to keep from falling apart. Drakkar lifted Tarynton's chin with two fingers. "What's going on? You're acting weird. And it looks like you've been crying."

Brushing away her tears, she did her best to give him a convincing smile. "I'm sorry for acting so strange. I just have a lot on my mind. Where have you been the last several days? I've been worried since I haven't seen you at all." *How dare you come in here and tell me I'm acting weird! You're the one that flew out of here without so much as a so-long.*

He held up a key ring with a couple of shiny keys on it. They looked brand-new. "I've been moving into my new place and getting it all fixed up. I wanted to wait until I had it all ready so that I could surprise you. I see now that I should've said something to you even if I didn't tell you exactly what I was doing. I was also out of town on an assignment for a couple of days."

Though totally annoyed with him, she only looked puzzled. "That might have worked. They have your apartment finished already?"

"No, not yet. I took the two-bedroom until the three is completed."

"But why? I thought you were happy living here."

Taking her into his arms, he nibbled at her lower lip.

That caused her pulse to race. Then he kissed her full on the mouth, kissing her until he took her breath away. His tongue flicked at her ear as his hands took liberty with her firm breasts. Finally, he released her.

Looking into her eyes, he smiled. "I promised not to make advances to you while I was under your roof. And I'm sure you remember your flirtatious taunts to me. Well, I've moved out so that we can take our verbal foreplay to another level. Are you up to us? Or were you just talking your usual trash?"

Her heart danced with glee. Wasting no time on explanations, she went into his arms and kissed him breathless. Her hands entwined in his hair as she lost herself in their kiss.

He held her slightly away from him. "How can I convince you to come and see my place? Right now."

"You already have. Let me get a sweater. I can't wait to see what you've done with your apartment. I feel a little put out that you didn't solicit my help, but I understand your mission."

"I'm glad you're so understanding, T.C. I can't wait for you to see my place."

Tarynton was surprised to see that all the furniture had been delivered. The placed looked beautiful but definitely manly. His choices in furnishing were all very masculine. What blew her mind was that he'd arranged the furniture in the very same way she'd mentally placed it when the purchases were being made. While she was happy enough for him, the selfish part of her wished that he'd stayed on with her until the three-bedroom apartment was made available. They'd had fun getting reacquainted, among other intriguing developments.

It seemed to her that Drakkar wanted to take things a step further, as he had suggested back at her place.

According to him, his reasons for moving out had every-thing to do with the possibility of changing the nature of their relationship. That made her heart very happy, indeed.

"Come on into the kitchen, Tarynton. In hoping that I could persuade you to come home with me, I picked up some Chinese takeout before I came over. If you didn't agree to come, I still had to eat. Just need to warm it up. You are my first dinner guest, so to speak."

Well, that's one I got up on your beautiful woman friend. Let her put that in her pipe and smoke it. As far as his apartment was concerned, she planned to be the first in everything, including spending the night, eventually. That is, if she had her way.

"Yeah, I am. How nice. That makes me feel extra special. I love your place. Thanks for bringing me over here to see it."

"Thanks. I'm glad you like it. And you don't have to thank me for bringing you here. I'm honored to have you as a guest."

Delighted with his comments, Tarynton sat at the dining room table while he warmed the food. Just as he'd done at her house, after he turned out all the lights, he lit several candles. Once he settled himself down at the table, they chatted amicably while enjoying the chop suey. He had also purchased both teriyaki and sweet-and-sour chicken, fried rice, stir-fried noodles, and crunchy vegetables.

After the meal, they cleaned up the kitchen and then moved into the living room.

Drakkar turned on some mellow music before joining Tarynton on the sofa. Lifting her legs, he placed them across his lap. "Sorry for not telling you I was moving. As I said, I wanted to surprise you. You look somewhat . . . uh-oh, you told me never to tell a woman that. You don't look so much tired as you do sleepy. Want to try out my new bed? You can just lie there while we have our talk."

"Are you going to lie down with me?"

"Wouldn't think of disappointing you if that's your desire. There are speakers in there, so we can still listen to the music. If you fall asleep, I'll make sure to wake you up before it gets too late so I can take you home."

"If I fall asleep, you'd better leave me alone until morning. I'm horribly cranky if I'm awakened before I get my sleep out. That's if you don't mind me spending the night."

He grinned. "Don't mind at all."

They immediately moved into the bedroom. Drakkar lit several candles situated in candleholders on the dresser and the nightstands. "Do you want to change into something comfortable? I remember that you used to love to wear my shirts to bed."

"I've come to be most comfortable in nothing at all, but I realize I'm not home. It would be nice to change into something comfy. What about one of your large sweatshirts? It should cover everything quite nicely."

He pulled a face, wishing she'd asked for a T-shirt instead. It would leave a lot more of her delicious-looking body exposed for him to enjoy. Once Drakkar gave her the sweatshirt, she went into the bathroom to change, with thoughts of a wonderful evening dancing in her head.

After neatly folding her slacks and sweater, she carried them back into the bedroom and placed them on the leather recliner. She thought it was interesting that he'd chosen to put the chair in the bedroom, the same exact spot she'd imagined it. The piped-in instrumental music was nice, soft, and sweet. Drakkar was a jazz buff, owning an extensive collection that included a variety of popular artists.

He lay down on the bed and opened his arms to her.

She moved in close to him and rested her head in the well of his arm. Candlelight and music, a perfect combination, she thought.

Perfect for what?

As if she didn't know the answer. She smiled. A serious romantic liaison might not come this evening, but she was sure that it would arrive and eventually take them both by storm. Whether he knew it or not, he was hers for keeps this time around.

Drakkar gently kissed her on the mouth. "It feels good being here with you. Are you okay with everything?"

"Very much so."

To show him how much she was in tune with it, she allowed her tongue to tease his own. The kiss deepened and the burning between her legs intensified. Mindlessly, her hand went inside the waistband of his sweat pants. As her hand made contact with his already aroused maleness, she shuddered. His flesh was rigid beneath her fingers as she stroked him tenderly.

In response to her heated caresses, his hand reached under the sweatshirt and touched the fleshy crease at each side of her treasures. His fingers then massaged her through the silk of her briefs. While stroking the exposed flesh on each side of her panties, he lowered his head and his lips followed the trail that his fingers had taken earlier.

Half crazed with desire, Tarynton arced upward, desiring to take every hard inch of him into her mouth. But she thought it to be too soon for that, yet was in no doubt that the time for such an intimate act would come. That type of sweet intimacy belonged to committed couples. But she wasn't going to try and stop him if he desired to relieve her with the tenderness of his mouth. Making her desire increase tenfold, his lips kissed and his tongue flicked at her flower through the silk of her panties. Tarynton didn't know how much more she could stand before she begged him to enter her and take her to heaven.

Turning her over on her stomach, Drakkar traced each side of her buttocks with his lips and then covered every inch of her bare legs. Moving back upward, toward her buttocks, he kneaded them gently. In one gentle motion, he turned her over on her back again. This time he feasted off each of her swollen breasts, hungrily, greedily. She moaned with pleasure as he suckled each with tender care. Tarynton desperately wanted him inside her but she wasn't sure if she should let it go that far this soon, as if it hadn't gone too far already.

As his hands feverishly worked her panties down over her hips, she lost all thought of what was or wasn't too soon. Using tender fingers, he carefully parted the flesh leading to her inner core. While she held her breath in utter anticipation, his tongue slowly wrapped itself around her moist flesh.

Drakkar didn't stop seducing Tarynton's inner secrets with his tongue until he felt her spasmodic eruptions. Satisfied that he'd physically completed her, he moved upward alongside her in the bed and drew her into his arms, kissing her deeply. Tasting her own flesh on his lips made her tremble with the need to do the same intimate act for him as he'd so expertly done for her. Thoroughly, he kissed her until her wild trembling lessened.

Peace had encompassed Tarynton all through the night. Upon awakening, she saw that Drakkar had already gotten up. As though he'd felt that she was no longer asleep, he came out of the bathroom and sat on the side of the bed. She tasted the mint freshness of the toothpaste he'd used as he kissed her.

"Morning. How'd you sleep, sunshine?"

"So good. How about you? How is it sleeping in your very own place?"

"With you by my side, I slept very well. I love sleeping in my own place, but I have to admit that it's more pleasurable with you being here to share the bed with me. Ready for something to eat?"

She looked over at the clock on the dresser. "I've got to get home and do some work. This is not like me to let things go. But being here with you has all been worth it."

His face took on a serious expression. "Some time ago, before I moved into your place, I told you that I had to go out of town for a week. Do you remember?" She nodded. "I leave late this morning. With that in mind, will you please stay and have breakfast with me?"

Although her heart was saddened by the thought of him leaving, especially when things were starting to look up for them, she smiled. "I'd love to. Work can wait a little longer."

"Thanks, baby." He kissed her forehead. "Oh, by the way, I have something to ask you. Would you mind me going home with you for Thanksgiving? I'd love to see your parents again."

Her heart flip-flopped inside her chest with happiness. "I would love that. But you can cut the bull about your wanting to see my parents. You know you just want to keep a close eye on me. You never did like to have me out of your sight for very long."

Then, foolishly, they had decided to go to separate colleges, never dreaming that distance would pull them apart. All of their dreams and aspirations had at one time included each other.

He chuckled. "I can't even debate that, but I really would like to see your parents, too. I'd also like you to go home with me for Christmas. I know that's planning far ahead, but sometimes that's what you have to do to achieve the outcome you desire. Christmas with me in PA?"

She took a minute to think about Christmas. "It sounds appealing, but I have to be back by December twenty-sixth. Kwanzaa starts on the same day. The girls and I are planning a special celebration. If I can get a flight out late Christmas evening, I'd love to go home with you. But the thought of not spending Christmas with my parents makes me a little sad. I've always gone home for both holidays."

"Well, take some time to think about it. Just know that I'd love to have you with me. My parents would love it, too." Suddenly he scowled hard, eyeing her curiously. "T.C., what about this man of yours? What are you going to do about him?"

She wrinkled her nose. "What man? The only man I have is sitting right here next to me." She kissed him to show that she was committed only to him. "My one and only man."

That statement caused him to grin broadly. Although he had expected her to go into more detail regarding the now ex-man in her life, he decided to leave it alone. Her claiming him as her only man was good enough for him. "Girl, you just made me one happy brother. In fact, I'm one of the happiest men on this planet. Now I don't have to go through all the trouble of kicking his butt out of your life. I'll leave it up to you to kick his behind to the curb. Welcome back into my arms, Tarynton Cameron Batiste. Welcome back into my life. It's been terribly lonely without you. Welcome home, sweetheart."

She kissed the back of his hand. "Thank you. I'm just glad to be back. Now that we have my personal issues settled, what about your involvement with this beautiful woman that you told my friends about after church?"

He kissed her tenderly on the mouth. "Woman, are you dense, or what? I was talking about you. You're the only woman I'm interested in. A lot of things have gone down in my life, and a lot of them have gone wrong, T.C., but I've never stopped loving you for a second. I've only had one relationship since you. I want things back the way they were for us."

Unfortunately the relationship hadn't been serious on his part. Fear had kept him with the woman he'd gotten involved with, serious fear. It had kept him stuck there long after he'd realized they weren't good for each other. Tamara Lyndon's Dr. Jekyll and Mr. Hyde personalities had caused him grave concern. He prayed hard that she wouldn't find out any time soon that Tarynton was back in his life. He was in no doubt that she'd eventually do so. She still had this crazy notion that they were still together as a couple. That alone was scary.

Moving away from Louisiana was due largely to his wanting to escape the insane ways of the woman who refused to accept that she was not the one that he eventually wanted to settle down with. Tamara simply refused to get over it.

His finger lazed across Tarynton's lower lip. "I know we have to work out a lot of things between us, but do you seriously want to give our relationship another try? Do you want us to have an exclusive relationship? I won't settle for anything less than that."

She laid her head against his chest. "I want the same as you do, Drakkar. But I don't want it to go back to six years ago. It's painful there. I want what we have now. I've made my peace with the past. A lot of hurt occurred back then, but I'm over that. I'm simply ecstatic to have my old man back. Can you agree for us to live in the here and now?"

He held her head back to look into her eyes. "When

I first came here, I was determined to see you and settle the past, thought it was imperative to do so. The present and the future are what are most important to me now. You're right about the past having no place in this moment, or in the recovery of our one moment in time. I want to live in the moment with you. As you've mentioned, it's living in the moment that counts. I'm okay without us settling the past, T.C. When I get back from Phoenix, we'll have a dinner celebration in honor of us getting back together. You and I together like this is what I've lived and hoped for, for a very long time now."

Placing his hands on both sides of her face, he brought her head forward and kissed her passionately. His tongue mingled with hers, causing excitement to well in her breasts.

Beside herself with joy, she giggled. "What about that breakfast you promised? It's getting late—and you have a plane to catch."

"There's a McDonald's right across the street. Let me guess at this. Egg McMuffin, hash browns, and O.J., right?"

Her eyes twinkled with merriment. "You got the famous order down pat. Are you going to get coffee or do you want me to make some?"

"I've got a shiny new coffeemaker just waiting for you to break it in. I'll be right back, sunshine. I'm going to wash up and then quickly slip into a pair of jeans and a T-shirt."

"I'll have the coffee ready and waiting when you return."

As if she were in her very own home, Tarynton had showered and then put on the same clothes she'd worn the previous night. It was hard to believe that she and

Drakkar were back together again. That they still loved each other was somehow easier to accept as true. Their love had sprouted out from the sandbox, had burst forth onto the playground, and had then blossomed into a loving intimate relationship on prom night. It seemed that love had been theirs forever. He'd confessed to never having stopped loving her. She hadn't ever stopped loving him either.

In Drakkar's kitchen Tarynton made the coffee. She laughed at seeing that the coffeemaker was just like the one she had at home. Making the coffee was going to be a snap for her. There were no newfangled buttons for her to try and figure out.

While she pulled two coffee mugs from the cabinet, her heart rate soared into another zone. She looked closely at the two mugs that had her and Drakkar's names written on them in cursive. That he still had them brought tears to her eyes. They had purchased them in Louisiana, at a county fair, in their second year of college, right after a summer break. This was just too impressive but so puzzling. Why had he kept them after they'd split up? It didn't make sense. Then she thought of all the memorable things that she'd kept. Still, a lot of things regarding their past relationship wasn't making sense.

"Hey, girl," he shouted as he made his way into the kitchen. Seeing the mugs affected him the same way in which they had Tarynton even though he'd run across them a few days ago while unpacking his things.

She picked up the mug with her name on it. "I can't believe you kept these all this time."

His eyes were moist. "Found them when I was unpacking some boxes that I've been carrying around for years. They still look brand-new to me. Maybe they're a good omen, T.C. Just as I've washed them up to make them look and shine like new again, that should give us high hopes to do the same with our relationship. We can have a brand-new start. I'm glad that I found them, glad that I found you."

Tears fell from her eyes. "Me too, Drakkar. Me too."

He had her in his arms before she could take her next breath. His mouth set fire to hers in a delicious, passion-filled kiss. Her hands inched under the navy blue sweater he wore. The feel of his bare flesh made her shudder with desire. The soft flesh between her thighs quivered with desperate need.

She looked into his eyes. "I can't wait a week, Drakkar. If I get any wetter betwixt my legs, you'll need to loan me a pair of your boxer shorts."

His heart leaped into his mouth. The thought of her wet and hot for him made his sex instantly stiffen. Leave it to up to Tarynton to spell everything out in no uncertain terms. She never did have a problem telling it like it was.

Neither of them knew or cared how they'd gotten from the kitchen to the bedroom—and so quickly—but the bed seemed to welcome them. Not wanting to rush things, Drakkar slowly peeled away Tarynton's attire. Before removing her wet panties, he put his mouth to the areas he'd already traced with his fingers. Unable to wait any longer, Tarynton pushed him back on the bed and unbuckled his belt and removed his sex through his fly. Lowering her head, she kissed the crown of his penis, teasing him relentlessly before taking him fully into her mouth.

The gasp from his lips was loud as her mouth and tongue worked their sheer white magic all over his trembling body. Drakkar moaned with undeniable pleasure. Fearful that he might explode before they physically reunited for the first time in six long years, he shook all over as Tarynton straddled him. After she gave him enough time to protect them, she lowered herself onto him, guiding his throbbing organ into the forest fire raging between her legs.

As if they were trying to make up for lost time, Tarynton and Drakkar made love in every way imaginable. They'd climax, rest, and then start the fiery journey all over again. Both were completely drained of energy before they finally fell asleep in each other's arms.

Drakkar awakened an hour later. When he looked over at the clock, he realized he'd missed his plane. There wasn't enough time for him to make it to the airport to catch his scheduled flight. As Tarynton slept, he placed a call to the airlines and was fortunate enough to book a later flight. As for Phoenix, he didn't have to be in place until the next day; therefore he would arrive in plenty of time. The flight was a short one.

The woman lying next to him meant the absolute world to him; had always been the special woman in his life. He loved her so much and he had cause to fear for her safety. If past incidents were any indication of how Tamara Lyndon would react if she found out that he was back with Tarynton, he was right to be fearful, not only for Tarynton but also for himself. He'd told Tamara a lot about Tarynton and had also expressed to her how much he had loved her.

Tamara had seen Tarynton on the numerous times she'd come to Grambling for homecomings. She would know exactly what Tarynton looked like. Anyway, Drakkar had hundreds of pictures of her. The eleven-by-seventeen senior picture of Tarynton was the one he'd kept on the wall in his dormitory room. Tamara making trouble for him and Tarynton was a big concern for him. But he would protect Tarynton Cameron Batiste with his life. So that she might not be harmed, he was willing to go through the fires of hell for the woman he loved.

Turning up on his side, he took Tarynton into his arms. "Hey, sleepyhead, it's time for us to get up."

She yawned as she put her arms around his neck. "Hey, back to you. What time is your flight?" She ran the back of her hand down his cheek

"Missed it already."

Her mouth fell open. "I'm sorry. Were you able to book another one?"

"Yeah, I leave in a few hours. Will you drive my car to the airport and see me off?"

"That sounds like a good plan, but what will I do with my car?"

"Come back here and get it after you drop me off. Then you can pick me up when I return home next week."

She frowned. "That sounds a little complicated. Let's do this. I'll follow you to the airport and we'll both park our cars. I'll go into the terminal and see you off. That way, you'll have your car at the airport for easy access and I'll have mine. You can come over to my place as soon as you get back. I'll cook dinner for us."

He kissed her on the mouth. "You always did have a good head on your shoulders. Your plans work for me, especially the dinner part. I love your cooking. Something curried would be nice. But I'll eat whatever you decide on."

"Drakkar, you know I'm not going to be able to come up to the gate. The events of September eleventh changed all that. There are a few coffee shops at the lower level. We'll sit there and visit for a short time and then I'll take off."

"That's great. I just want you with me up until the last possible second."

She grinned. "I know the feeling. Enough time has already been wasted."

His expression got serious. "T.C., do you still love me the way you used to do? Before you answer let me tell you this. I love you. Have always loved you. Never stopped for a second."

"Drakkar, I wish you didn't think you had to ask me that. I thought it was obvious, but since you've asked, the answer is yes. Like you, I've never stopped. If you keep this sentimental verbiage up, we're going to end up back in bed."

His heart felt elated. "We've got a few minutes to indulge ourselves before I have to get moving. It's only seven-thirty and my plane doesn't leave until eleven forty-five." With that said, he set out to seduce her once again.

Drakkar had had to rush to get ready. He and Tarynton had lost all sense of time for the second time that morning, and they'd also had to warm up the breakfast before they ate. Tarynton had packed his last-minute items while he'd run around the apartment making sure that he had everything needed for his business trip.

Tarynton fought her tears as they reached the airport's security checkpoint.

He brought her in close to him. "We'll talk six or seven times a day. Okay?" That made her laugh. "I'm going to blow your home and cell phones up," he continued. His eyes filled with moisture. "You have no idea how happy I am to have you back in my life. I never want us to be apart ever again. You are my dream girl, my dream come true, Tarynton."

"I *do* have an idea since I feel the same way about you. Have a safe flight, Drakkar. And remember that God is always in control."

"You bet *He* is." He kissed her passionately before getting into the security-point check line. Silently, he promised to tell her all about Tamara Lyndon when he got back home.

She waved good-bye to him before making her way out of the terminal. After hopping a parking lot shuttle, she settled back in the seat to daydream. Drakkar Lomax would play heavily into her daydreams. Drakkar was her dream, her dream come true.

Tarynton's fingers shook from excited anticipation as she dialed her parents' home phone number. *Please be home, Mom,* she prayed. *Don't be out shopping.*

"Hello!" came the cheerful female voice on the other line.

"Mom, I'm so glad you're home." Emotionally full, Tarynton began to cry.

"Tarynton, what's wrong? Are you ill, baby?"

Tarynton started to laugh and cry at the same time. "No, Mom, I've just been bitten very hard? Very hard indeed."

"A dog bite?"

"No, Mom, I've been bitten by the love bug. I'm seriously in love, Mom."

Pamela Batiste sighed in relief. "What else is knew, Tarynton? You've been in love your entire life. Are you telling me that there's a new man in your heart?"

"Exactly. Mom, I want to bring him home for Thanksgiving. Is that okay with you?"

"Of course it is. I'm thrilled for you. But you know I've got to have some answers from you. Are you finally over Drakkar? Can you really move on with your life this time?"

"I'll never be over Drakkar, Mom. But I've got a new chance at a life of happiness. You know I'm not one to stay stuck in the past, especially for too long. Will you get one of the guest rooms ready for my new boyfriend?"

"Sure, but tell me a little bit about this guy. His name would be nice for a start."

"I'm not going to tell you a thing about him, Mom. I want everything to be a surprise. Can you please let me play this act out? You and Dad are positively going to love him. He's a wonderful human being and he really loves me."

"Okay, my little drama queen. You always did like to act out the stories you write. You should've been an actress, too. Let me warn you, though, Auntie Cleopatra is also coming for the holiday. You know she's going to be all up in you and your man's personal business."

"No, she's not. 'Cause you're going to check her real hard. She's your baby sister. You're going to tell her that if she embarrasses your only daughter she has to go. She'll listen to that. She never messes with you, especially when you tell her how it's going to be up front. Besides, for a fact, I know that Auntie Cleo is going to absolutely love my man. Everyone will."

Her Auntie Cleo thought the world of Drakkar. She was nearly as brokenhearted as Tarynton when she learned of the breakup. Cleo had also cried over it, for weeks.

"The downstairs guest room will be ready, Tarynton, but I'm going to have to work real hard to get your daddy ready for the new man in your life. After all these years, he still prays nightly for you and Drakkar to get back together. He loves that boy like a son. Speaking of sons, Camden is bringing a special woman home. For a minute there we were afraid that he didn't even like women." Pamela laughed. "But we'd accept any choice he made in a partner, the same as it is with you. You two are our bright stars, the brightest spots in our life.

I can hardly wait to give Mommy's grown-up girl lots of big hugs and kisses.''

"Mommy, Camden has always been about education. He has always taken his studies seriously. He's a full-fledged doctor now, so he has a little time to play. He's done well for himself. Give my brother his props. Got to run now because I'm already behind in my work."

"You're great at articulating the facts, Tarynton."

"Okay, Mommy. It's a couple of months yet, but I'm so excited about seeing you, Dad, and Camden. I really do have to go. I've got tons of work to finish up."

Tarynton's brother, Camden, was all about education, but he wasn't a so-called nerd. Her brother was downright fine. At six-two, sexy, smart as a whip, with a beautiful complexion the same color as a Hershey's bar, Camden was every woman's dream man. Four years older than Tarynton, Camden was the big brother in every sense of the meaning. Fiercely so, he protected his sister like a black gladiator. No one messed with his little sister even though he knew she was quite capable of defending herself. Tarynton would take on any boy as quickly as she would battle anyone else that treaded in her private space.

Tarynton couldn't wait to see Camden. Although they talked on the phone every week, she hadn't seen him in a few months. The fact that he was bringing a woman home for the holidays excited her. It was about time that the boy had some real fun. She was happy for him.

By the time Tarynton had settled down in bed for the night, she was all tuckered out. Her schedule had been hectic. Several new clients had come on board and most of them were the usual last-minute scenarios, which meant that she'd had to work hard to achieve wonderful accommodations to make dates extra special and unique. She also missed Drakkar like crazy, missed him being around the house. But she was glad that he'd moved out, especially under the circumstances. Living under the same roof with him as his lover didn't appeal to her, but she was sure they'd spend many nights at each other's residences.

Although they'd practically been inseparable, they'd never lived together the entire time they were a couple. She had thoroughly enjoyed spending the night in Drakkar's apartment. It had felt like being right at home.

As Tarynton reached over to turn the bedside light off, the phone rang.

"Hey, baby, did I wake you?"

Upon hearing Drakkar's sexy voice, she smiled. "No, but I was just about to call out the sleep brigade. It has been one busy day. You know me, got to have my beauty rest."

"No matter how much sleep you get, you couldn't be more beautiful. Besides being busy at work, how did the rest of your day go?"

"Fine. I had lots of things to do around the house. Talked to my mom today. I told her that I was bringing a guest home for the holidays, but I didn't tell her it was you. I want to surprise them. Is that okay with you?"

"I like the idea. It'll be fun to see their faces and their reactions when they find out we're finally back together again. Is Camden going to be there?"

She chuckled. "Yeah, so is Auntie Cleo. You know she's going to have a conniption fit when she sees you. She hated our breakup. I can't wait for us to go to Atlanta."

"I'm also looking forward to it. Miss you."

"Miss you, too. Five more days, and I *am* counting."

"Me, too. Girl, that intimate going-away party we had was off the hook. It was the best lovemaking we've had yet. It was just like I dreamed it would be over the past six years. We're still so good together, in every way. You still got it going on."

"Can't wait until you get back home. I've been aching for you all day. But I'm so happy that we have more than the physical side going for us. Our history together is awesome. It's not like we're strangers getting it on for the first time. We're still very familiar with each other."

Drakkar laughed. "T.C., strangers we're not. What you got on?"

"Nothing," she purposely taunted, though she had on pajamas. "I've been lying here thinking of how you freaked when I got extremely intimate with you. You were so excited."

Conjuring up the earlier erotic image of her mouth on him, he blew out a shaky, ragged breath. "Please don't go there, T.C. At least not until I get back home. Then you can have carte blanche with my body. I couldn't concentrate on my meeting for thinking of your lips and mouth wrapped around me. It felt so good. Girl, I'm getting worked up just thinking about what you did to me. I can't wait for us to be together again— and I'm not just talking sexually. I miss being in your company. We have so many things we enjoy doing together. Still, I can't wait for us to come together again physically. Thinking about those erotic acts makes it even harder to wait."

"Now you already know that you're not getting that type of lovemaking every time. Don't want to spoil you. The extreme erotica will remain a special treat."

"We'll see about that. I plan on having you for breakfast, lunch, and dinner. You taste that good."

Her libido responded to his promises of things to come. "Okay, now. You're going to get into trouble. You are too far away to be talking like that."

"I feel you. To change the subject to something more benign, I need a favor from you."

"Anything, Drakkar. What do you need me to do?"

"I left some important papers on my dresser. I need you to get them and fax them to me here in Phoenix. I need them for an afternoon meeting tomorrow. Can you do that for me? I would appreciate it."

"I can do it, but there's one little problem. How do I get into your place?"

"In anticipating that you'd agree to do the favor, I've already called the front office. They would be more than happy to let you in. With what's happening now, I have to make sure you have keys to my place."

She didn't think she should have keys to his private space, but now wasn't the time to debate it. He still had hers, but she planned on getting them back. They should both maintain their privacy. Not that they had anything to hide, everything would just be better that way.

"I'll get the papers first thing in the morning. Is that okay with you?"

"Perfect. Thank you." He gave her the fax number in his hotel room before ringing off.

Tarynton felt weird being in Drakkar's apartment without him being there. It seemed somewhat intrusive even if he had asked her to be there. She located the papers with ease. They were on his dresser, right where he'd said they'd be. As she turned to leave the bedroom, the phone rang. Wondering if it was him trying to reach her, she stared at it, unsure as to whether she should answer it or not. Then the answering machine came on, the antiquated type of machine. She laughed, thinking Drakkar should subscribe to the local phone company's message center services. An important man like himself should have a modern answering service.

"Hello, darling, this is your boo. Thought I could catch you before you left for Phoenix, but I got all caught up in an important last-minute production project," a sultry voice came from the answering machine. "You have been a bad boy for not calling me right away and telling me that you've already moved into your new apartment. You know you're going to have to pay for that. I'm leaving for Phoenix late this afternoon. Looking forward to us making it real hot. See you real soon. Love you, boo bear."

Tarynton nearly gagged on the adrenaline pumping wildly through her. That must've been his beautiful woman on the line, the one he'd obviously lied to her about. Was she the real reason he'd moved out of her house? This woman was also going to meet him in Phoenix. Now that was the real kicker. He had her doing a favor for him knowing all the while that he was betraying her. Then she had to wonder why he had waited to tell his woman that he was moving into his own place. When had he called her to give her his new phone number? After he'd had the night and morning of hot sex with her? Tarynton just couldn't stomach that revelation.

The entire situation with this woman was downright puzzling. It seemed that Drakkar was the only one that could explain it, the only one with the answers. But he was nowhere around. The thought occurred to her to leave the papers right where they were, on the dresser. But she couldn't be that vindictive since he really needed them for an important meeting.

Tarynton grabbed the papers she needed to fax to Drakkar, wishing she hadn't come there. Everything suddenly felt wrong. Their getting back together made her feel the worst. It had all been based on lies. What was she to do now? She began to cry when she thought about their Thanksgiving plans. How could she back out of that now that she'd told her parents that she was bringing someone special home? Could they fake a happy relationship for a couple of days? She only knew that she had to try, but that would only happen if Drakkar was willing to front.

Then she would kick Drakkar Lomax's behind to the curb, once and for all.

This was not the man she'd fallen in love with. Her Drakkar wouldn't think of toying with two women at the same time. He had never been that kind of a man. Had time changed him? When she got through with him, he was going to know exactly what *change* meant. All the changes she planned to put him through would leave him reeling for years to come.

Even in all the anguish she'd gone through over the other woman Drakkar's time away from her had flown by with lightning speed. The broiled steak and baked potatoes were almost ready. His request for curry had been ignored on purpose. Drakkar should come through the door any minute. She was still stuck with the dilemma of whether or not to tell him about the phone call she'd overheard at his place. The fact that the other woman had been with him in Phoenix hurt her more than she could express. His lying to her about everything hurt the worst.

If he was seeing them both at the same time, he was going to catch more hell from her than he could stand, more hell than anyone could raise within a twenty-four-hour period of time.

But cheating didn't at all fit Drakkar's personality. He'd told her that he still loved her. One woman at a time for him was the way he'd always conducted his personal affairs. If that was the case, then how did she explain the phone call? It wasn't going to just up and go away. The other woman wasn't a figment of her imagination. She'd heard that damn phone call, loud and clear. "I'm leaving for Phoenix late this afternoon," was the one sentence that kept ringing in her ears.

If he hadn't told her his plans, how had she known exactly where he was going to be? Drakkar had some tall explaining to do, but she didn't even know how to begin to broach the subject with him. She trusted Drakkar, had always trusted him.

Then she thought of the letter for the umpteenth time. The letter she could recite word for word without ever having to look at it. Now it seemed that her and Drakkar getting back together again had been far too easy. Nothing in life came easy—and it now looked as if her and Drakkar's relationship was in for some real hard times.

Eight

Kneeling down in front of Tarynton's car, Drakkar felt like crying. Every window, including the windshield, had been smeared with dozens of raw eggs. He was in no doubt as to who was responsible. He thanked God that Tarynton hadn't come outside while this was happening. The message on his answering machine was enough to convince him that Tamara was up to no good again. Her knowing about his scheduled trip to Phoenix didn't surprise him one bit, but her attack on Tarynton's car did. That meant that she'd possibly been in California within the last twenty-four hours. She seemed to know where he was twenty-four-seven, but he was a public figure, so there was no great mystery in someone knowing of his whereabouts.

But now his precious Tarynton had been dragged into his messy relationship with Tamara Lyndon. But there was one big difference involved in this situation. Tamara had no idea of what he was physically capable of when it came down to protecting Tarynton. He didn't believe a man should ever hit a woman, but he would do more than that to Tamara if she ever dared to come near Tarynton again. That was a message that he somehow had to relay to Tamara, immediately.

Tarynton didn't know whether to go into Drakkar's arms or not as he appeared in her kitchen. God only knew how much she wanted to hold him, to have him hold her, but something had somehow gotten in between them again. It seemed that it was yet another woman, or perhaps the same woman of six years ago. He looked so sad, so lost. Was he feeling guilty about being in Phoenix with the other woman? She'd never seen him look like this before. Had something happened to devastate him? His face appeared drained of most of its sienna color.

Regardless of what she thought he'd done to cause her pain, she went to him and threw her arms around his neck. "What's wrong with you? The look on your face is scaring me."

He held her tightly. "I *am* the one that's scared, Tarynton, more scared than I've ever been in my entire life. We've got to talk. First I need to take you outside and show you something. Then I need you to sit down and listen to what I have to say."

Tarynton's limbs trembled as he guided her outside. A scream escaped her lips when she saw the condition of all her car windows. She knew that this was a criminal act. No one smeared eggs everywhere without criminal intent. This was an act of pure malice. The other woman immediately came to her mind. Then she dismissed her thought, since it seemed unreasonable.

He held her in his arms. "Let's go back inside so I can tell you how and why I think this happened. I'm sorry that you've become yet another target of one psycho bitch. I hate to talk about someone like that, or call someone out of their name in a disrespectful manner, but that's what she is. She's been disrupting my life for a long time now. But it's time for it to stop. I won't let her harm you in any way. I will kill her first.''

Tarynton's eyes widened with fear. "Kill her! Drakkar, I don't want to hear you talking like that. Hearing you say something like that scares me more than anything someone might do to me. Baby, please don't talk like that.''

As they entered the house, he hugged her. "I'm sorry, sunshine. I shouldn't have said that." *Even if I meant it.* "I can't stand the thought of you being hurt.''

Tarynton had Drakkar sit down in the kitchen while she put the food on the table. This wasn't necessarily a time for eating, but it would give them something to do to keep from going insane over the incident with her car.

While eating the great meal Tarynton had prepared, he told her everything there was to tell her about one Tamara Lyndon, except for when he started seeing her and why. That was a part of the past that Tarynton didn't want to know about, though he still thought that she should. Especially now that Tamara had gone on the attack against her.

"She sounds like an awful woman. I can't believe the things she's done to disrupt your life. How do you stop someone like her?''

He looked heartbroken. "I'm afraid we're going to have to put our relationship on hold. I can't have anything happen to you. Her hurting you would destroy me. I was concerned for the other women I dated, so I just stopped seeing them. But I'm in love with you. And Tamara knows that, has always known that. You are her biggest threat. Now that we're back together, she may come at you with everything evil that she has in her, all of it. Though she has never attacked anyone physically, make no mistake about it, this woman is sick. The first thing we have to do is file a police report regarding the windows and then we'll both need to get restraining orders against her."

He knew that an order of protection wouldn't stop Tamara, but he didn't want to frighten Tarynton further. She already looked scared to death.

Tarynton threw her fork down on the table. "We are not going to do anything to disrupt our relationship. We can't give her our power. I'm stronger than you think. She obviously hasn't run up against anyone like me yet. Don't you dare entertain the idea of us breaking up to satisfy some little twit that doesn't even know the meaning of love. We are in this together."

He couldn't help smiling. Tarynton was still as feisty as she was when they were growing up. She didn't take any crap from anyone back then—and it appeared that nothing had changed. Still, he feared for her safety. Tamara was obviously unbalanced, something that Tarynton had never had to deal with before. The fact that she had gone through the trouble to find out where Tarynton lived was of grave concern to him, especially her actually finding Tarynton in a city the size of Los Angeles.

The thought that someone was helping her in her criminal activities was in the back of his mind since Tamara lived and worked in Louisiana. She couldn't be in two places at once. Through a reliable source, he knew for a fact that Tamara was at work this morning. He'd checked on her whereabouts after he'd checked his messages from Phoenix.

As for what she'd said on his answering machine, she left messages like that all the time. She'd made an art form out of getting his phone numbers, so he didn't even bother to have them unlisted anymore. The messages had more to do with her keeping him on edge than anything else. It wasn't that she hadn't shown up at the places where he was, because she had, on numerous occasions. She just called and said that she was coming more often than she came.

Now that she knew for sure that Tarynton was back in his life, he shuddered to think of what her next move might be.

He looked at Tarynton with concern. "Are you sure about what you're saying? This woman is no joke."

"Neither is this one. I carry a gun and I have a permit to do so. I go to the target range once a week to practice. I don't ever want to have to use my gun on a human being, but I will. If this woman is going to come after me, she'd better come with a guarantee that she can take me down. Otherwise, there'll be a slab at the city morgue with her name on it."

His eyes widened with disbelief. "You just told me not to talk about killing someone; now listen to you."

"I said that to you before I knew all the facts. As you've said, we're dealing with a psycho bitch. Not long ago I asked the question about what would stop someone like her. I now have the answer to my own inquiry. Nothing less than a bullet, perhaps a couple of bullets. If she dares to come onto my property again, the body-bag people will be scooping her up and hauling her behind off to a drawer in the city morgue. If you know how to warn her, you should do so."

"Tarynton, this doesn't sound like you talking. I know this is a frightening situation, but we've got to think this through reasonably. We can't go crazy over this."

"You do what you want, Drakkar. This has gone way past reasonable. But if she physically comes after me, I'm not going to just sit by and let her take her best shot at me. If it comes down to her or me, she's history. Are we staying at my place tonight or at yours?"

Amazed by her tough resolve, he laughed. "I'm already here. But we need to call the police department and have them come out and take a report before we can even think of getting any sleep. I'm going to rinse the windows off tonight, but we'll take the car and have it detailed first thing tomorrow morning."

"Sleep isn't what I had in mind. I have some physical aggression to work off. Let's call the police now and get it over with. We have to try and keep the things in our lives as normal as possible. We can't let her win. This is our party and we'll be the ones to decide on the games to be played. We have to take control. It's a must."

Tarynton was so happy to know that Drakkar hadn't lied to her, thrilled that he wasn't romantically involved with someone else. Even though she may've doubted him for a minute, she'd still found it hard to believe that Drakkar's moral codes had changed that much.

Glad that they didn't have to change any of their holiday plans, she thought about all the things they were going to do rather than keep her mind on the horrible things Tamara Lyndon was capable of. That was one person she didn't care to waste any time or energy on unless she was forced to do so.

The two Los Angeles police officers gathered from both Tarynton and Drakkar all the pertinent information on the criminal incident involving the windows on her car. Pictures were taken and then the exterior of the car was dusted for fingerprints. The couple were told to stay alert and that they'd be contacted immediately if the fingerprints matched any of those that were already on file. The officers also promised to alert and confer with the local police in the Louisiana city of New Orleans where Tamara Lyndon resided. Once the police finished, Drakkar was given the okay to rinse the windows off.

* * *

Tarynton got into bed naked. She didn't want Drakkar to waste any time on disrobing her. Time enough for him to put on the condom was the only timely thing that really mattered. Her body craved his. There would be no fumbling around and no lingering foreplay tonight. Him inside her was the outcome she desired, the sooner, the better. Her body was on fire just from thinking about him inside her. It was going to be hot, hot, hot up in her bedroom tonight.

As he slid into bed next to her, she handed him the unopened condom packet. "I guess you know what I want. If not, I have no problem telling you."

He smiled broadly. "I think I've got it. Come here, baby. Let me relieve you of all that pent-up physical aggression you talked about earlier. Hold on tight, T.C., 'cause I'm ready to rock your world and have you blow up mine at the same time. It's on!"

Tarynton had slept in Drakkar's arms the entire night. He had gone home early that morning only because he was due at the television studio by seven A.M. Before going out into her office, Tarynton made herself a slice of toast. She would use the coffeemaker in her office to brew up a fresh pot of coffee. She'd been using the one in the kitchen only since Drakkar had come there to live. Now that he was living in his own place, she'd go back to using the extra one.

She picked up the house phone on the first ring but heard nothing on the other end. This silly heifer wanted to play childish games that she just wasn't up for this morning. Tarynton hung up and hit star-sixty-nine, which rang the caller back. This woman didn't even have enough sense to block the number she was calling from, she thought. Then Tarynton realized that the number belonged to a pay phone that didn't accept calls. Maybe Tamara wasn't as dumb as she was acting. Or perhaps she was even crazier than Drakkar thought she might be. Fear wasn't something she gave in to easily, but what Tarynton felt right now couldn't be defined in any better terms. Still, she wasn't going to become a willing victim.

Drakkar unhooked his microphone and headed for his office in the back of the studio. At the same moment he sat down behind the oak desk, he reached for the phone. Knowing Tamara's work number by heart, he dialed the digits in haste. With Louisiana being two hours ahead of California in time, he wanted to catch Tamara before she took a break for lunch. He cringed when her voice came across the line, soft and mellow. If only she was as soft and loving as her voice, these horrible things wouldn't be happening.

"Tamara, are you free to talk candidly?"

"Drakkar," she moaned sweetly, "I'm so excited to hear your voice. How are you, boo?"

"Don't start that with me, Tamara. This is not a social call—and you know it. I just called to give you a stern warning, one that you should seriously consider heeding. You've disrupted my life for the last time. What you did last night, or possibly had done, is unconscionable. I don't understand why you can't get it through your head that we're not meant to be. I've moved out of New Orleans, Tamara, hoping to move on into the rest of my life. I don't want to get ugly with you, but if you come back to California and try to cause any more trouble for me, you may not travel back to Louisiana in the same mode of comfortable transportation you arrived in. Do I need to say more?"

"What are you going on and on about? You sound like a crazy person. Or have you been smoking crack again? I thought you were still in recovery. I hope you haven't relapsed. But if you want to explain to me what you're talking about, I promise to listen."

Her mention of him smoking crack caused his blood to boil. That was what she'd threatened to tell one of his supervisors some time ago, when he first tried to pull away from her. There was always some insane lie she'd threaten him with, but a brother didn't always get the benefit of the doubt when someone made a serious accusation about him. The studio heads probably would've believed her and he would've no doubt lost his job behind her pack of lies. She was the crazy person, but she hadn't been able to figure that out thus far.

"My friend's car was smeared with eggs last night. And then there's that crazy message you left about meeting me in Phoenix. I guess that wasn't your voice on my service. My bad!"

"Your friend? What friend? I don't have a clue as to what you're talking about, Drakkar."

"You know what friend I'm talking about, but I don't have time for these silly-ass games. I called to warn you. Since I've done that, I'm terminating this conversation."

"Drakkar, I haven't done anything to anyone's car. Have you considered that it might be your friend's man that did this to her car? If you haven't, maybe you should."

Her question stunned him. He hadn't thought of that possibility, but neither had he said that his friend was a woman. But Tamara certainly had just done so. And it wasn't a man who'd left that message on his service. "Good-bye, Tamara." He hung up without uttering another word.

After putting his feet up on his desk, he lost himself

in some deep thinking. Tamara's question was definitely a provocative one. He hadn't given any thought to Tarynton's man being the culprit. Maybe Tamara hadn't been the one who had vandalized the car, after all.

There was no doubt in his mind that Tarynton had broken it off with the guy. She was not the type of woman to have two men on a string. And she certainly wouldn't be sleeping with both of them at the same time. It seemed to him that Tarynton hadn't slept with anyone in a while, a long while, boyfriend or no. The girl had been starving for a night of hot, passionate lovemaking—and he loved being the one feeding her damn near insatiable hunger.

The six women were seated around the worktable in Tarynton's office. They had come together after getting off of work to discuss the Kwanzaa celebration. But after hearing about Tarynton's car windows and learning of Drakkar's crazy ex-girlfriend, the celebratory plans were all but forgotten for the moment.

"What are you going to do if she comes up in here on you?" Denise asked.

"Shoot her," Tarynton responded.

"Then you're going to have to go to jail," Rayna exclaimed.

"Not for defending myself. This woman has already smeared my car up. Am I just supposed to wait around and see if she's going to slash my throat next? I don't think so."

"Tarynton, we're all going to need to come over here and stay with you, or you need to come and stay with one of us. This is some dangerous stuff going on over here," Chariese stated.

"I'm not leaving my home and no one needs to leave theirs. I have a gun and God will cover all of what a bullet won't. Besides, this woman is in Louisiana. That's where she called from this morning."

"How do you know she's not here in California and is simply having someone calling you from Louisiana to make you think she's there? This witch sounds crazy as hell. Girl, you need to be extra careful, gun or no gun," Denise said, sounding off.

"I know what you're saying and I do appreciate your concern and caring. But I just can't let this psycho case disrupt my life. Drakkar and I are in love, have always been in love with each other, and she's going to have to accept that. There are two of us in this relationship and we're not making any room for three. Tamara Lyndon has just got to get over it!"

"She hasn't gotten over it yet," Denise interjected. "In fact, it sounds like she can't seem to get over it, period. It sounds like she'll go to great lengths to destroy any relationship that Drakkar involves himself in. Are you willing to put up with that from now until she's somehow stopped? That's a tough way to have to live."

Tarynton shook her head. "I hear you. It's a lot for me to deal with, but I can be just as persistent as she is. Drakkar and I are back together. That's how we're going to stay. I think it's time for us to get back to our celebration planning. Drakkar and I have a date tonight."

Everyone had to admire Tarynton's courage and fighting spirit, but that didn't mean there wasn't concern for her. Each of her friends was very concerned for her safety. But they knew her, knew that her mind was already made up about how she could best handle this situation.

Denise pulled a sheet of paper from her briefcase. "You all felt pretty confident that my book club, Tabahani Book Circle, was going to come through for us. They haven't disappointed us yet. They loved the idea that I presented to them and have already voted to become very much a part of our celebration. Once we touch it, it turns to gold. I've been thinking of some of the ideas that our book club has discussed on prior occasions, which I plan to share with you today. For starters, each table will have a love or other special date theme. Tarynton, you and your wonderful ideas will go a long way with this one."

"Please explain," Chariese requested.

"We'll decorate each table with a special theme that has to do with love or a special date. What don't you get about what I've said?" Denise asked Chariese.

Looking thoroughly annoyed, Chariese rolled her eyes at Denise. "More details, please."

"Okay, okay. Anniversary, wedding, Valentine's Day, and others. Since our country is in such a crisis right now, we can also do a 'We Love USA' theme table as well as a Fourth of July one. While the holiday season will still be in full effect, we talked about doing a Christmas and a New Year's table. And the most important one of all will be done with a Kwanzaa theme. Do you get it now, Chariese?" Denise inquired with a hint of reproach in her tone.

"I do," Chariese shouted. "I really do. It's a fabulous idea. I believe you're saying that we're going to formally set each table to reflect a theme of each of these special dates."

Denise clapped her hands. "She's got it. This celebration is going to be so special. No one will be able to top this one but I'm sure many will try to duplicate it. I'm even going to have a special outfit designed from fine African fabrics for this event, but I have to find a new designer. My old one moved without leaving a forwarding address."

"Really! That sounds interesting. I'd like to do that, too. I don't own a thing in African print. And I've never seen anything that appealed to me in the retail stores,'' Tarynton offered.

"Madame Julia is a fabulous black female designer. She owns a lovely shop, Vintage Africana, in the Crenshaw District. She creates all of her own designs and orders her rich fabrics from all over the world. Her creations are so regal, fit for royalty. Maybe we should all get her to design our outfits for the celebration,'' Roxanne suggested. "What do you guys say to that?"

"That's a wonderful idea,'' Tarynton remarked. "I can't wait to get started. Is everyone free to go and see her on Saturday?"

"The question should be, are you free, Miss Batiste? You've been pretty tied up lately,'' Narita interjected. "Tied up tight.''

Tarynton laughed. "Don't be a hater. I'm the one who's always been sitting at home or working on some project during the weekends—while you all are out on romantic dates or single excursions of some sort. Let me have my time at some romance and hot passion. It's been a while for me, you know. Since the question's been posed regarding my freedom, I'm free after I get my hair done on Saturday morning. I could meet you guys there around eleven.''

"I'll e-mail everyone the shop address, but it's not too far from the Crenshaw Mall. I just hope she'll have enough time to do our creations. This woman stays busy. Her orders come in way in advance of a special event. We'll be lucky if she can take us on,'' Roxanne said. "While we're out, we can also look at the china patterns for our tables.''

"The book club has most of that covered. That's an expense we don't even want to entertain. Everyone has a formal set of china they can lend to the celebration. One of the women even has a set of dishes in an African design. It'll be all the festive trimmings that we add to the tables that'll complete our theme. I'm going to donate my Christmas china. Tarynton, you have that lovely china pattern with the gold rims. They would make an exquisite statement for an anniversary or wedding table."

Tarynton felt a twinge of anguish at the mention of her china. She'd collected over the years the beautiful china place settings for the home that she'd hoped to share with Drakkar, once they were married. That her plans hadn't turned out the way she'd thought still hurt deeply.

"I also think that would be nice. I've had the china for many years and it's never been used. I'd love to loan it to the celebration. Furthermore, I'd like to do the design for that particular table. I think I'd like to do the anniversary theme, a golden anniversary, which is what I hope one day to achieve. That is, if I don't reach senior citizen status before I even get married. You all need to know this. Even though he doesn't, I'm still hoping to marry Drakkar in the not so distant future."

"He hopes for the very same thing, to one day marry the beautiful and sassy Tarynton Cameron Batiste."

Tarynton turned around at the sound of his voice. Her cheeks were nearly the color of fire. That he'd heard her embarrassed her to no end. The thought to get her keys back as soon as possible popped into her head. She couldn't have him keep showing up like this without any warning whatsoever. Not that she minded him coming over whenever he wanted to, but she'd like just a little advance notice now that he'd officially moved out.

The five women jumped up at the same time, grabbing up their personal items.

"Ladies, please don't run on my account. I'd love to get to know Tarynton's close friends. Please stay and join us for dinner. I'm doing the cooking."

"We don't want to intrude. Besides, Tarynton said you all were going out tonight," Denise responded to Drakkar.

"Tarynton said that she had a date with Drakkar tonight," Tarynton said, correcting Denise. "She didn't say what the date entailed. I'd love for you all to stay for dinner. But only if you help clean up the kitchen afterward."

"By all means," Roxanne offered. "It's not often that we get a man to cook for us. And, Drakkar, though I still think you're one hot brother, I've truly cooled my heels where you're concerned. More so, now that I know for sure you really are my girl's man."

"And how do you know that?" he asked Roxanne, smiling.

Roxanne laughed. "Please! All you have to do is look at her face when you're around. The same goes for your handsome mug. Your names are clearly written upon each other's hearts. Your feelings for each other are apparent. And didn't I just hear someone mention the *marriage* word a time or two?"

Drakkar pulled Tarynton into him. "Did you hear that, T.C.? Looks like our not so little secret is out. Not that we were ever trying to hide it." He kissed Tarynton full on the lips. "I'm going to go and get that dinner started. It'll be quick and easy 'cause I'm getting into grilling everything, the California way. I hope everyone likes lamb kabobs, grilled zucchini, onions, and butternut squash."

"Do you need some help?" Tarynton called after him.

He looked back at her. "I can handle it, sunshine. Just come to the table with a healthy appetite and be willing to give a brother his props. You know how I love to be complimented on my cooking skills." With that said, he winked at her and moved on into the house.

Denise bumped Tarynton with her hip. "I can see

why you're willing to fight to the death for that one. Girl, you're not just lucky, you've been blessed with a fine, black angel.''

"If my memory serves me correctly, I think you've let a couple of blessings get away.''

"Maybe so. But it just never felt like the right one to me. I think I'll know when that special blessing comes along. Until then, I just have to keep myself in the dating game. Marriage is not always the greatest thing that can happen for a woman these days. But it's going to be the most wonderful thing that can occur for you two. I see how you feel about each other. I don't know how you all made it for six years without each other, but something tells me it wasn't easy for either of you. I wish you the best.'' Denise hugged Tarynton as the others looked on.

"Hey, you two,'' Chariese called out, "you're breaking our hearts over here. You know how sentimental we are. What about going inside and turning on some good music?''

"I'm all for that,'' Rayna chimed in.

"Narita, you and Denise set the dining room table while Chariese and Rayna set the mood with music. Roxanne and I are going to go inside and harass Drakkar until he lets us help him out.'' Tarynton smiled devilishly. "I think we can persuade him to let us do something.''

Roxanne gave Tarynton a high five. "Now that's an assignment I won't mind at all. But I promise not to flirt with your man. I've got nothing but respect for you, sister.''

Tarynton smiled. "In that case, I won't have to put your bad butt in check. Let's get this dinner party started.''

They all laughed.

* * *

Drakkar had everything under control when Tarynton and Roxanne popped into the kitchen to see if they could help. Instead of using the indoor grill, he had the lamb kabobs and the fresh vegetables grilling on the gas grill outside on the patio. He hadn't mentioned a rice dish, but the rice cooker was turned on and the temperature dial set on steam, Tarynton noticed.

"Looks like he doesn't need us," Tarynton said to Roxanne.

Drakkar tossed Tarynton an engaging smile. "Oh, I need you all right, just not in the kitchen. But since you're already in here, how about making the Kool-Aid? Red, of course."

Tarynton cracked up. "I'll make some for you, but we ladies are drinking wine tonight. We're trying to get a mellow groove going on up in here. Najee is also in the house, along with some vintage Grover Washington Jr. This is how we do it when we girls get together for dinner and an evening of fun and great conversation. Still want the Kool-Aid?"

Drakkar grinned. "I think I'll have what you ladies are having. Sounds like you all have something really good going on for yourselves this Thursday night. Count me in."

Roxanne took a bottle of both red and white wine out of the refrigerator and held the bottles up for Drakkar to choose from. "What will go best with the lamb?"

"The red," Drakkar suggested, "but it really doesn't matter. It's all about an individual's choice. Different strokes for different folks."

"We can get real crazy and mix them," Roxanne said, laughing. "I can make a wine punch that throws a mean jab. Instead of going mellow, we'll be rocking the house with some cool hip-hop and a little rhythm and blues.''

Tarynton rolled her eyes dramatically. ''Mellow is what's going on during the meal tonight. You want to go hip-hop, we'll go out to one of the livelier clubs after dinner. Club Mahogany's plays a little of every kind of music. That's one of the reasons it's so popular with all age groups. We'll wait and see what everyone wants to do after we've eaten.''

''Sounds fine to me,'' Roxanne said. ''We've only got one more day of work this week.''

''Okay, ladies, let's gather up everything and take it to the dining room table. The food is done! And this man is ready to eat.''

The women made Drakkar feel like the man of the hour when they asked him to pass the blessing. In turn, he made the six women feel like cherished treasures as he served each of them, before sitting down to his own meal. Tarynton insisted on serving him even though he mildly protested. After filling his plate and setting it in front of him, she kissed him on the mouth and thanked him for preparing such a lovely dinner.

No one felt like going out to dance, not after an enjoyable couple of hours of eating, wine tasting, and listening to great music. Through great conversation Tarynton's friends had learned a lot about Drakkar during the evening, and they were each impressed by his personal and professional credentials. No one brought Tamara Lyndon into the conversation, but Drakkar and Tarynton momentarily thought of her off and on throughout the evening. Both of them had to wonder when her next assault would come. As promised, before taking their leave, the women helped out in putting the kitchen back in order.

Drakkar held Tarynton's head in his lap as they sat on the sofa listening to music. Her eyes were closed, as he looked down on her, watching as her lips silently mouthed the words to "Just the Two of Us," the timeless love song, playing on one of the digital cable music channels.

He stroked her cheek with his forefinger. "I need to ask you something. Can I have your attention for a second?"

She opened her eyes and looked up at him. "You've had it all evening, but I don't mind giving you as much attention as you need from me. What's on your mind?"

"Your man."

She sat up and craned her neck back. "What is it about *you* that's on your mind?"

"I guess I should've said your ex-man?"

"Maybe so, but I thought I made it clear to you that you're the only man in my life."

"The only one in your life now, but someone else was here before I arrived. I'm wondering if maybe he's the one who did the damage to your window. Do you think he's capable of doing something like that?"

Disturbed by the line of questioning, Tarynton laid her head back in Drakkar's lap. "No one in my life, past or present, is capable of being so malicious as to smear eggs all over the windows of my car." She hoped her answer would satisfy him. To tell him that she didn't have a man in her life before him wasn't something she wanted to confess. But she might have to reveal the truth if he pressed the issue. How embarrassing would that be? "What made you think that someone I knew could do this? You seemed sure that the Lyndon woman was responsible. What has suddenly changed your mind?"

"I talked with her today. She denied doing it but suggested that someone you were involved with may have done so. I hadn't given that aspect any thought, but I began to after she brought it up."

She sat straight up, annoyed by his remarks. "Let me make sure I have this right. You talked to the woman who you claim is nothing but a liar, a woman who has harassed you repeatedly, and a person who has no respect for you or your feelings. This same woman with all these defects of character suddenly decides to tell the truth—and you now believe her?"

"You're upset—"

"Damn skippy, I'm upset! I don't know what makes you think that you can believe her all of a sudden. Care to enlighten me?"

"I didn't mean to upset you. I was just curious. We should take everyone in our lives into consideration in this matter. It was your car that got trashed, not mine. I thought we should at least discuss the possibility of there being someone else."

"As far as I'm concerned, we have discussed it. Trust me when I say that no one in my life would do something this horrible to me. If I thought there was any reason to believe that there was, I would've told you that right away. I've never had any fatal attractions in my life."

"Up until now! Why didn't you just go ahead and say it since you were thinking it?"

"Oh, you can read my mind now? If that's the case, before you started questioning me you should've known that I was thinking about how I couldn't wait for you to make love to me again tonight. So much for your mind-reading skills!"

He pulled her into his arms and kissed her forehead. "I'm sorry, sunshine. Maybe we should forget about this conversation and begin concentrating on what you were thinking before I opened up my big mouth and ruined the mellow mood we've been working up all evening. Think we can do that, T.C.?"

As Silly Putty came to mind, which was what she felt like in his hands, she caught his earlobe between her teeth and bit down gently. "I think so, but only if we can swap sexual fantasies first. I want to hear one of yours before I tell you one of mine."

"That's a great idea, but I'd like to act mine out, with you. Since I didn't get the pleasure of stripping your sweet body bare last night, I'll start my fantasy there." Without giving her the chance to respond, his mouth claimed hers and his hands went to work on the buttons of her blouse. Looking into her eyes, he smiled. "My fantasy includes whipped cream and maraschino cherries. I know you have the cherries, but what about the whipped cream?"

Tarynton giggled out loud. "I use Cool Whip! You'll find it in the refrigerator."

Nine

Drakkar's fantasy was coming to an end with him giving Tarynton a sponge bath at bedside. While washing clean all the body parts he'd spread Cool Whip on, he'd periodically dab her nose and mouth with the white cream and then lick it off.

He kissed the center of her forehead. "Are you too tired for your fantasy?"

She could barely keep her eyes open. "No, but I'll have to tell you about it since we can't act mine out, not in here. There's not enough room."

He raised an eyebrow. "Sounds intriguing. Let's hear it."

"My fantasy includes a horse."

Both of his eyebrows shot up. "A horse?"

"Yeah, a black stallion."

He hurried into the bathroom, emptied the water from the metal washbasin, and rushed back into the bedroom. To listen intently, he settled himself comfortably in the bed, eager to hear of her flight of the imagination.

"I've often imagined us both stark naked while riding on the back of a mighty black stallion." He winced, thinking of how hard that would be on the family jewels. She went on, "With my arms wrapped tightly around your waist, you'd guide the horse's graceful movements by using his long, beautiful mane. After taking a long ride through the countryside, we'd find a field of wild-flowers to make love in. With the blanket from off the horse's back, we'd spread it out over the flowers. Once we've completed each other, that is, over and over again, we'd cover ourselves up with the blanket and then sleep in the field the entire night." Sighing with content, she smiled up at Drakkar.

"That *is* some fantasy! It may be very hard indeed to act that one out, especially when I think of the pressure to certain tender places on our bodies," he said. She laughed softly. He continued, "But I promise you this. If there's a way, and I already know that we have the will, we can certainly try it. I'll keep my eyes open for a black steed and a beautiful field of wildflowers."

She giggled. "Thank you, Sir Galahad. I'm ready to go to sleep now. What about you?"

He smoothed her hair back. "Don't you think I should go home?"

"Tired of me already?"

He kissed Tarynton on the nose. "I could never tire of you. I'd love to stay all night with you, but I'm going to have to start sleeping regularly at my place at some point."

She smiled and then yawned. "Okay. You can sleep at your place tomorrow. Alone."

He pulled a face. "In giving it more thought, that doesn't sound so hot to me." He kissed her gently on the mouth. "May I sleep in your arms tonight?"

"That'll be a nice change since I've slept in yours every night we've spent together. Come here, Drakkar, so I can cuddle you in my arms."

Before resting his head between her breasts, he reached up and turned out the light. "Good night, Tarynton." *I love you,* his heart whispered into the stillness of the night.

"Sweet dreams, Drakkar."

Awakened by the ringing phone, Tarynton looked over at the clock. Three A.M. Moaning, she reached for the receiver, wishing she could sleep as soundly as Drakkar. He hadn't moved a muscle. Upon putting the phone to her ear, she heard soft music. Puzzled by the sound of music at this hour, she listened closely to the lyrics. The message from "You're Still My Man" by Whitney Houston came in loud and clear for Tarynton. This was obviously Tamara's way of declaring that Drakkar was still her man. *Not,* Tarynton mused, bored stiff by the childish games a so-called fully grown woman wanted to play.

"Girlfriend, it's obvious that you're delusional. If he's still your man, someone forgot to inform him of that fact," Tarynton said softly into the phone. "I guess you've made this call as a reminder to him, since he seems to have forgotten that you even exist. Sorry, but you have dialed the wrong number. This phone doesn't accept calls from pay phones or strangers."

Several loud expletives assaulted Tarynton's ear. Then the loud slamming down of the receiver resounded in her head.

Tarynton laughed out loud, which awakened Drakkar. She had bested this little witch at her own silly game. It seemed as if Tamara hadn't expected Tarynton to fight back. But Tarynton had bad news for her. She could hang with the best of the harassers. Tamara wasn't going to take over her life with threats and scare tactics, the way it seemed she'd taken over Drakkar's. Tarynton didn't see this battle with Tamara as fighting over a man. She was simply fighting for her right to live in her home in peace, without someone trying to intimidate and cause her fear.

Rubbing his eyes, he sat up in the bed. "What's going on? Who are you on the phone with at this hour?"

She pulled his head into her arms. "Just a wrong number, Drakkar. Try to go back to sleep now."

He raised his head, eyeing her suspiciously. "Why don't I believe that it was a wrong number, Tarynton?"

"Why would you believe otherwise?"

He rolled his eyes. "Here we go again. Why do you always respond to a question with another question? Don't you think I know when you're trying to hide something from me?"

"It looks like I have two questions to answer now. Which one should I answer first?"

"Why don't you try answering the first one I asked?"

"Could you repeat it? I've forgotten what it was." She didn't care that she was annoying him, because the way in which he was questioning her was just as exasperating.

"I *am not* going there with you at this time of morning. It's okay if your ex-man hasn't quite got the message that you've gotten another one. But you don't have to lie to me about being on the phone with him at such an odd hour."

Dumfounded by his comments, she stared at him in disbelief. "Drakkar, you are so far offside that you'd never make it back to the line of scrimmage without incurring a penalty. I think we should just go back to sleep and let this ride."

"I'm tired of letting things ride, Tarynton. If you need me to enlighten this brother on the nature of our relationship, I'd be happy to do so. But don't expect me to sleep next to you while you engage in late night conversations with him." He got up and began putting his clothes on to leave. "You can have all the privacy you want, when you decide to call him back. I'm sure that's what you're going to do the minute I step."

It was too late for him to duck. The pillow was already in his face by the time he spotted it sailing toward him. Tossing the pillow aside, he glared at her. "What was that all about?"

"Drakkar, in trying to save you grief, I'm only making matters worse for us. That was not my ex-man on the phone. It just so happens that it was your ex-woman calling to remind you that you're still her man." She was still not ready to declare that there was no ex-man in her life, at least not in her recent past. Yet she hated the deep pain and utter confusion that she saw there in his eyes. She instantly berated herself for not handling things a little more delicately. She hadn't meant to blurt the truth out that way. It had only hurt him more.

Desiring to ease his hurt, she tossed him an arresting smile. "If you apologize to me, I'll be more than happy to accept it."

After making his way across the room, he sat down on the side of the bed and took her in his arms. "You'd be more than within your rights if you didn't accept my apology. But I am so sorry about the things I said to you. I need to do more than just ask for your forgiveness. I need to beg for it. Will you please forgive me, T.C.?"

With hunger, her lips sought out his, as she unbuttoned the few buttons he'd managed to close on his shirt before the pillow nearly knocked him silly. Since he hadn't pulled his pants on yet, she felt free to touch him in all the right places. As her eyes filled with lust, she looked up at him. "I won't make you beg if you won't make me beg for it."

His tongue slowly teased hers and then he kissed her deeply. While pressing her head back into the pillow, his mouth continued to have its way with hers. As he succumbed to her wickedly vivacious charms, his hands sought out the warmth between her legs, massaging her inner core until she squirmed beneath his vigorous caresses. Putting on the condom came next, quickly.

Drakkar entered her in a way that nearly brought her to an instant climax, slowly, provocatively. Her legs wrapped around his waist as his thickened maleness rhythmically plunged in and out of the pooling moisture inside her rapturous treasures. While her nails bit into his back, he gently raised her up and placed his hands tenderly beneath her buttocks, bringing her in even closer to him.

Wildly, she flailed her body about beneath his, barely able to contain her tempestuous emotions. As he'd done on so many other occasions, he filled her up until she felt as if his body had overflowed into hers. Audibly panting his name, Tarynton tightened her legs around him as her world began to spin and blur. Closing her eyes, she rode the delicious waves crashing against her inner core. Blissfully weak, Tarynton felt her entire body become as limp as a wet noodle.

Having felt her coming unraveled on the inside, he had feverishly joined her on the maniacally cresting surges of indescribable fulfillment. Rocking back and forth inside her, breathless, Drakkar barely breathed her name as she screamed out his.

Exhausted, he fell over to the side and brought her head to his chest. The smile on his face told her of the deep pleasures she'd given him. For several minutes he savored the moment.

Grinning, he turned up on his side, not daring to touch her again. Tarynton's raging fires had never been easy ones to put out, but she now seemed to require more of a generous dousing of flame retardant. "Why are you so horny, so often?"

Perhaps because I haven't made love to anyone in this millennium. "That's another of those questions that you should never ask a woman. But to finally answer one of your questions, I'm only this way for you. You make me hot. Does that answer satisfy your curiosity?"

He wanted to bring up the subject of sex with her ex-man, but he thought better of it. Even if he did bring it up, there was no guarantee that she'd answer him. It was obvious to him that the other guy hadn't been able to satisfy her physically. Tarynton was more than just plain horny. The girl's sexual appetite was darn near neurotic.

Well, he thought, he did have major skills in that area. But it was really no different for him if he was honest with himself. No other woman had ever satisfied him like Tarynton did—and not just physically. Tarynton satisfied him in every way that a man desired satisfaction from the woman he loved.

"What are you thinking about, Drakkar?"

Her question interrupted his flammable thoughts. "*You.* It's as honest an answer as I can give without incriminating myself."

"What is it about me that you were thinking of?"

"That you rarely answer a direct question. I was also still thinking of how hot you've been. I had a couple of questions in my mind to ask you but decided against asking them. Besides, you probably wouldn't answer, anyway."

"You're probably right." She turned over. Lying on her stomach, she rested her chin on his bare abdomen. "As usual, you're going to think I'm crazy, but I have a craving for vanilla ice cream drizzled with hot chocolate sauce and crumpled-up Fritos, topped off with a handful of Gummy Bears."

His hearty laughter rang out. "You still get those late night cravings, huh? In this case, it's an early morning one. Remember all those times I thought you were pregnant because of the things you wanted to eat late at night?"

"Yeah, you used to live in fear of that, until you got used to my strange, after-midnight desires." She looked puzzled. "Out of all the questions you've asked tonight, I find it interesting that you didn't ask me what Tamara said on the phone."

He shrugged. "You already told me." As she gave him a cagey look, he continued, "Okay, I'll indulge you. What did she say?"

"After I said a few choice words to her, she called me a dirty name. Then she slammed the receiver down in my ear."

"What filthy name did she call you?"

"Rhymes with witch. The same name we called her but only with psycho in front of it."

"What's up with your suddenly reformed mouth?" he asked, without expecting an answer. "But that figures. That's one of her favorite words for all my female friends, whether she thinks I'm romantically involved with them or not. To risk having you not answer again, what did you say to her?"

"That's not fair for you to say about me. I've been answering most of your questions."

"Yeah, within the last few minutes. But I can think of dozens that you haven't answered. Even some from years ago."

"Whatever!" Dramatically so, she told him the remarks she'd made to Tamara. He howled at the top of his lungs, until he caught a cramp in his side. "Was it really that amusing, Drakkar?" His jovial laughter almost made her laugh, too, even though she didn't think any of it was very funny.

"It was funny as hell. She must think you're as crazy as she is. As far as I know, no one has ever stood up to her. Her scare tactics aren't working with you—and I'm sure she hates that. Still, I don't want you to aggravate her any further. I'm sure she's capable of so much more than what I've already seen. Inciting her even more could cause her already fragile mind to snap like a dry twig. It might be easier if you just got your number changed and have it unlisted." He didn't know why he'd suggested that to Tarynton since it hadn't worked for him yet.

She bristled. "I'll do no such thing, Mr. Man! I've had the same number for the past four years. There are so many people that know this number, some that I haven't been in contact with in a long while. If I change my number, they won't know how to get ahold of me. Perhaps she should learn some new numbers to dial. She should be getting tired of punching in these same old digits about now."

He was tired of talking about Tamara. Nothing the girl did ever made sense to him—and talking about it wasn't going to make things any clearer. Insanity was rarely explainable.

"Still want that ice cream, T.C.?"

Aware of his desire to change the subject, she nodded. "Do you want some, too?"

He laughed. "No, T.C., I don't want any ice cream . . ." He paused to look at the clock. "At five o'clock in the morning."

"Dang," she yelped. "I can't believe what time it is already. I'm not going to change my number, but I might consider taking it off the hook, especially when you spend the night over here. Just so I can get some sleep." She put her forefinger to her temple. "On second thought, to ensure that I get my proper rest, I may not let you spend the night ever again."

By the time her remark registered with him, she had already left the room to make her way into the kitchen. Nearly falling out of bed, he grabbed the top sheet and followed after her.

As she stood at the refrigerator pulling the ice cream out of the freezer, he tried to wrap her up in the sheet. Much to his surprise, she pulled away from him.

"That's like closing the barn door after the horse has already gotten out. You've seen me naked enough times to be used to it, even with the six-year separation. Don't need the sheet, Drakkar. But thanks for being so considerate of me."

"Whatever fuels your jets."

She turned around and gave him a bold, sassy look. "You fuel my jets, you alone."

Grinning widely, he came over and sat down at the table, where she'd already set up her ice cream parlor. "I love how you love to flatter me." He kissed her right temple.

She put a spoonful of ice cream up to his mouth. "This is so good. You should try some."

He gently pushed her hand away. "Don't want any, Tarynton. Ice cream this early in the morning just doesn't do it for me. I'm going to go and take a shower. I don't have to be at the studio until late this afternoon, but I'm got some home chores to do and a few personal errands to run. What's on your schedule for today?"

She rolled her eyes. "You mean after I get some more sleep?" He shrugged his shoulders and nodded. "Tying up some loose ends on a couple of special outings for my clients. I also have to input some data into my computer for the Kwanzaa article. I may even find some time to work on the novel that I'm in the process of writing."

"How's the Kwanzaa story coming along?"

"It's doing very well, thank you. I was able to get a lot more valuable information off the Web. It seems that Kwanzaa is an exciting time for our people. The Kwanzaa colors are black, red, and green: black for the people, red for their struggle, and green for the future that comes from their struggle. Seven candles, referred to as the *mishuma saba,* are lit during the ceremony. The candles represent the seven principles. One black, three red, and three green."

"That's different from what the colors stood for in the sixties and seventies. Black was for the people, red was for the bloodshed, and green stood for the land."

"I thought that also. Oh, Drakkar, I forgot to tell you. I'm meeting with my girlfriends tomorrow after my salon appointment. We're each going to have unique custom-designed outfits for the Kwanzaa celebration we're planning. The one I told you about. However, it looks like we're going to have to change our plans for decorating the place. According to what I've read, you shouldn't combine any other celebration or celebratory themes with Kwanzaa. Still, I'm excited about it."

"I can see that you're really excited about this whole celebration idea. Sorry, though, about the changes. Do you have an escort for this special event?"

She shook her head. "Think you can turn me on to someone nice?"

"Yeah, for sure, a real nice someone. What's the date of this exciting event and at what time should I pick you up?"

She leaned across the table and kissed him sweetly on the mouth. "New Year's Eve, the next to the last day of Kwanzaa. The girls and I plan to honor the other six days on our own. Now that you're armed with the exact date, do I still have you as an escort for the event?"

"I have to cover a game on New Year's Day, but I'm all yours for the prior evening. What do you think about us getting matching outfits? An African king and his

African queen matching from head to toe. Just imagine it!''

The thought of it warmed her heart as she rolled with laughter. "I love the idea, but I don't think you want us to match from head to toe. I can't see you in a dress or heels." He had to laugh too. "But we can have our attire made from the very same fabrics, Drakkar. Are you sure you want to do that?"

"Of course I want us to do it. I'll just order the male version of whatever you decide on. I think we make a striking couple already. But when we're costumed in beautiful African attire, whew, we're going to turn a lot of heads."

"Are you going to be able to meet us at the designer's shop tomorrow around eleven?"

He scratched his head. "I have to look at my schedule, but I think we may have a conflict with studio time. If so, I can make sure you have my measurements before then. I can always go there on my own for the necessary fittings."

"That's probably best since we're not sure yet if the designer can take us on as clients. If she can do it, and there's enough time, I'll ask her if I can bring a few fabric swatches home so we can pick them out together. What do you think?"

"I'm all for it. As for this novel you're writing, how close are you to finishing it?"

"Pretty close. I'm nearing the end."

"I'll be rooting for you. We'll celebrate when you're done, since it's your first one. Any chance of a brother getting a sneak preview?"

"Oh, I've already sent several chapters to Camden. He loves it."

"I said *a* brother, not *your* brother. And I was talking about me. But you already know that, don't you? You love to push my buttons. One day you're going to push the wrong one."

"I didn't know you had any wrong buttons, Drakkar, since everything about you is so righteous. You're also pretty even-tempered, most of the time. I'd love for you to take a peek at my novel, but I want to wait until I'm finished with it. You can read it when I'm done. Okay?"

"Sure." Taking her eating utensil away from her, he dipped it into the melted ice cream and chocolate and came up with a scoop. Making a visual connection with her, he drizzled the ice cream over her breasts and then licked it off. "What's your read on that move, sunshine?"

"It seems to me that someone is just as horny as he excused me of being." Boldly, she licked the remaining ice cream from the corners of his mouth. "Care for me to drizzle some of this ice cream on one of my favorite parts of your anatomy—and then lick it off?"

Groaning inwardly, he looked at the kitchen clock. "I'll make the time—and if you can withstand what might come after the drizzling and the licking, I think your stimulating idea is an excellent one."

While lying in bed, unable to go back to sleep, Tarynton looked over her unfinished novel. She thought about the question Drakkar had asked about how she was coming along with it. She hadn't wanted to tell him that all she needed to complete it was the ending. But that had yet to be played out. The novel was somewhat based on their past relationship.

His and her future in their present relationship would write the ending. The end results of their current love affair, such as a proposal of marriage, or another split, God forbid, was what would end up in print. She hoped she didn't have too long to wait to find out. Though she prayed for a happy ending, she knew from experience that those things hoped for didn't always come about the expected way.

A lifetime and a fulfilling marriage with Drakkar was her heart's desire. While her heart hadn't let her down yet, circumstances in life had. Six years ago no one could ever have made her believe that she and Drakkar weren't destined. For them to end up split apart had never even occurred to her, at least not until the letter was sent. Even with all the unexpected things that had occurred she still believed in their one moment in time, their one moment in time together, a moment in time to last a lifetime.

Tarynton was beginning to think that this crazy situation with Tamara Lyndon would add a new spicy twist to her unfinished novel, though she'd rather not have this woman in her life period, let alone in her love story. But the extra added megadrama would make the book a more interesting read. If the truth were known, Tamara might have more to do with their past situation than she could probably guess at. Drakkar had said he'd only been involved in one other relationship—and Tamara was the only other woman he'd ever mentioned to her so far.

As her head became filled with new possibilities for her story, Tarynton pulled out her notebook from the nightstand drawer and began to write. Realizing the ending wasn't as near as she thought, she let her mind take her down paths she hadn't dared to venture on before now. Excited at all the new prospects for her story line, she let her creative mind fly free.

When the phone rang, Tarynton paused, eyeing her newly acquired enemy suspiciously. Upon looking at her recently purchased caller ID box, she smiled. It was Drakkar calling from his office. The clock revealed to her that she'd been working on her book a lot longer than she had intended. It was already early evening. It suddenly dawned on her that she hadn't even ventured out into her office the entire day. Yet she felt that she had accomplished a lot.

"Hey, you," she answered with enthusiasm.

"Hey back to you, baby. You seem upbeat. I'm glad to hear you sounding so cheerful. What are you doing?"

"Winding down. I'm getting ready to fix a bite to eat. I haven't touched so much as a cracker all day. The truth is I've been in bed since you left this morning, except for a couple of trips to the bathroom. What are you up to?"

"I'm up to nothing. On a downer sounds more like it. I'm finished here at the studio, much earlier than I had anticipated. And I'm finding myself at loose ends. My gig is so unpredictable timewise. I had expected to be working until late tonight. I also miss you much. As for your being in bed, is that a result of all the physical energy we expended earlier this morning? In no-nonsense words, did I wear your sweet butt out, T.C.?"

"In your dreams! You're the one that looked like you didn't know how you were going to make it to your car without passing out from sheer exhaustion. I've not just been lying in bed, either. I've also been working but from here in the bedroom. There, now you have it."

"You sure know how to bring a brother crashing down to his knees. Don't you know any humility?" Her thrilling laughter made him miss her all the more. "Let me take you out to eat. I haven't eaten in hours myself."

"Where do you have in mind?"

"There's a Subway next door to the Barnes and Noble bookstore near here. I need to pick up a couple of reference books. I'm thinking we can kill two birds with one stone. I can be there by the time you get dressed."

"Please, let's not kill *any* birds," she joked. "They're God's children, too. Why don't I just meet you there?

It doesn't make sense for you to come all the way here just to go back to where you already are."

"Sure you don't mind?"

"Give me about forty-five minutes?"

"Sure thing. I'll see you at Subway, T.C."

Drakkar looked extremely pleased with Tarynton's appearance. Dressed only in a pair of simple dark blue denim jeans and a plain white T-shirt, with the sleeves of a red sweater tied around her shoulders, she looked fresh and full of vitality. He couldn't help thinking of all the vim and vigor she'd shown him in the bedroom earlier that morning. For a woman who hadn't gotten a full night's sleep, she looked well rested, not to mention stunning.

Taking her in his arms, he kissed her full on the mouth. "Hi, baby." He inhaled deeply of her scent. "Mm, you smell so good. Shower-fresh."

She ran the pad of her thumb across the bottom of his chin. "Oscar still smells good on you, too, even after you've worked all day. Ready to go inside?"

He kissed her again. "Now I am."

Inside the Subway store, at the counter, Drakkar ordered a foot-long turkey sub for himself and a Mediterranean salad for Tarynton. Both had decided on Citrus Hill pink lemonade. A bag of classic Lay's potato chips was Tarynton's choice while he chose the oil-and-vinegar-flavored ones.

Seated at a window booth that looked out onto the strip mall, Tarynton bowed her head to pass the blessing. She also voiced thankfulness for her safe journey.

Before digging into her salad, she opened her bag of chips and then took a sip of her drink. She laughed as she watched Drakkar take a huge first bite of his sandwich. "Looks like someone is hungry."

His eyes danced with desire. "Just a man's appetite, girl. I also have to keep my strength up so I can continue making you happy in the bedroom."

She suddenly looked so chagrined. "Have I been coming on a bit too strong in our physical relationship? If so, I'm sorry."

His expression was soft and tender. "Do you really think that?"

She sunk her top teeth into her lower lip. "That maybe I'm overdoing it a tad? Yes."

He eyed her intently. "I have to ask you this. Are you using sex as a way to hold on to me and to keep me now that I'm back in your life?"

His question shocked her, but only because she thought he might be right. Had she been doing that? She quietly pondered her question to herself. Then Tarynton thought that maybe she should be offended by his inquiry. But she wasn't, not in the least.

"What would you think of me if I *were* using sex in the way that you questioned?"

"Another question answered with a question, I see." He looked her right in the eye. "To be honest, I don't know what I would think. But I hope you know that you don't have to use sex to hold on to me. I'm yours, plain and simple. Besides, you and I make love. We don't just have sex. Understand what I'm saying here?"

Smiling, she nodded. "Thanks for that. But maybe I need to check myself and my motives, anyway." She lowered her lashes, lifted them, and then looked directly at him. "Do I have a reason to worry about this Tamara person?"

"T.C., not only do you not have to concern yourself with her, you don't have anyone else to worry about. Are you having second thoughts about us?"

She quickly shook her head. "No, but your sex question made me stop and think. I don't want to believe

I'm that kind of a woman, but I did have to do a bit of probing. The fact that I'm not having second thoughts should probably be a little puzzling for me, but it's not. I believe in you and me, in us. Have always known you were the one for me. And I only want to celebrate our reunion, not second-guess it. Having you back is a gift from God.''

He grinned. ''Speaking of gifts, I have something for you—and I haven't forgotten that I promised us a celebratory dinner. It's forthcoming.'' He stood up. ''Got to get something out of my car. Be right back.'' Bending over, he kissed her on the cheek.

The moment he departed, Tarynton's mind immediately took her back to the question he'd asked of her. Was she using sex as a way to keep him in her life? She hoped not. But for sure, Drakkar's expert lovemaking was what kept her wanting more and more of him. The man was a master in the bedroom. And out of it as well, she thought, smiling.

The deep heart-shaped box that he set down in front of her filled her with excitement. ''What's this, Drakkar?''

He sat back down across from her. ''Open it and see.''

''You don't have to tell me twice. Say no more.'' She removed the wide purple ribbon and opened the lid. ''Oh, you remembered another of my favorites!'' Hundreds of red-, silver-, and green-foiled Hershey's Kisses filled the deep box nearly to the brim.

''Now you have enough chocolate to melt down for at least several dozen more of your seductively imaginative drizzling sessions.''

She smiled sweetly. ''Thank you, Mr. Lomax. We'll consider this three-pound box of Hershey's Kisses as our private stash. I won't be putting these in any of the candy dishes in the house. We probably should keep them in the bedroom in a cool place.''

He couldn't help laughing. "I don't think there's a cool spot in your bedroom, at least not when we're in there together."

Smiling smugly, he opened one of the chocolate kisses and held it up to her mouth. Her tongue slowly came out and caressed the piece of candy before she sucked it completely into her mouth. She closed her eyes as the chocolate melted beneath her tongue.

His loins ached as he imagined himself melting inside her. "Baby, you look like you're having one terrific orgasm."

"I am. All over you."

He closed his eyes to conjure up an erotic image of such a moment.

Minutes later, when she took another bite of her salad, he frowned. "Chocolate and salad. Girl, you do have one strange appetite."

She rolled her eyes at him. "You put the chocolate kiss in my mouth knowing I wasn't finished eating. So what are you talking about?"

He grinned. "I guess I had an urge to see you suck on it." His intentional choice of words made her feel a little warm all over. "I wasn't disappointed."

"That's nice to hear. Are you satisfied now that you've already annihilated your meal, Drakkar?" Wishing a fan would appear out of thin air, she had the urge to pour one of the glasses of cold water down inside her T-shirt just to cool herself off.

In one quick motion he moved to the other side of the booth and sat down next to her. Without a moment's hesitation, he took possession of her mouth in one long, lingering kiss. "I'm satisfied. Now that I've had my dessert."

Her heart trembled at his warm, loving expression. Not wanting this moment to end, she opened another candy kiss and shared it with him via her mouth. As they swapped the chocolate back and forth between each other's mouths, Tarynton felt yet another firestorm rising up inside her inner core. Only this time it couldn't be corralled and then sedated by him making love to her. After all, they were in a public place.

After an hour and a half of having fun reading some questionable risqué literature to each other in Barnes and Noble, while enjoying a couple of cups of coffee, Tarynton and Drakkar had finally made it back to where Tarynton's car was parked. Leaning up against the passenger door, he held her in his arms.

She smoothed his eyebrows. "It's getting late so I should be going. Thanks for asking me out to eat. I've had mucho fun. We should read to each other more often. I really enjoyed it."

"Me, too. What would your answer be if I asked you to come home with me?"

She turned up her nose. "You're starting to sound like me. That might not be a good thing, especially since you hate me to question you in that way."

He tilted his head to the side. "You're still true to form when it comes to not answering the questions you don't want to. I'm not going to ask again, because I think I already know the answer." He looked all around him. "I know we're in public, but can I get a really passionate kiss before you go? More passionate than the ones in Subway."

She responded with her lips coming together with his in a deeply riveting kiss.

"Good night, Drakkar. Thanks again."

"You can say good night to me at your house."

She looked puzzled. "I thought we decided not to stay together tonight."

"Correction, you decided. At any rate, I'm just following you home to make sure you get there safely. It's well after ten o'clock."

"I'm not going to argue with you on it, Drakkar, because I know it won't do any good. But I will admit that I still like the idea of you looking out for me, very much so. Along with Camden, you took great pleasure in being my protective shadow as we grew up. Even when you knew that I could probably take care of myself. Let's get moving. I'm ready to call it a night. This has been one long day."

He kissed her again before she got into her car.

Ten

While drinking a cup of coffee, Drakkar sat at the table in his kitchen, wishing he hadn't moved out of Tarynton's place as soon as he had. He missed the closeness that they'd shared while living under the same roof. In thinking about calling her, he looked at the clock. Then he remembered that she had a salon appointment this morning and then planned to meet her friends before noon. He would call her later from the studio.

When he looked at the clock again, he realized that he'd better get himself moving at a bit faster pace if he was going to arrive at work on time. But it was a Saturday, an overcast day, and he'd love to be spending a lazy morning in bed with Tarynton. Not making love, just watching cartoons and old westerns on television like old times.

Tarynton had really grown up on him. Six years had brought her quite a long way in her attitude about things. The sex question he'd asked her would've had her wanting to knock his block off back in the day.

An important message from the ARABESQUE Editor

Dear Arabesque Reader,

Because you've chosen to read one of our Arabesque romance novels, we'd like to say "thank you"! And, as a special way to thank you, we've selected four more of the books you love so well to send you for FREE!

Please enjoy them with our compliments, and thank you for continuing to enjoy Arabesque...the soul of romance.

Karen Thomas
Senior Editor,
Arabesque Romance Novels

Check out our website at
www.arabesquebooks.com

SPECIAL OFFER!
4 FREE BOOKS

ARABESQUE ®
A PRODUCT OF
★BET BOOKS

3 QUICK STEPS
TO RECEIVE YOUR "THANK YOU" GIFT
FROM THE EDITOR

Send this card back and you'll receive 4 FREE Arabesque novels! The introductory shipment of 4 Arabesque novels – a $23.96 value – is yours absolutely FREE!

There's no catch. You're under no obligation to buy anything. You'll receive your introductory shipment of 4 Arabesque novels absolutely FREE (plus $1.99 to offset the costs of shipping & handling). And you don't have to make any minimum number of purchases—not even one!

We hope that after receiving your books you'll want to remain an Arabesque subscriber. But the choice is yours to continue or cancel, anytime at all! So why not take us up on our invitation to receive 4 Arabesque Romance Novels, with no risk of any kind. You'll be glad you did!

Call us
TOLL-FREE
at 1-800-770-1963

THE EDITOR'S "THANK YOU" GIFT INCLUDES:

- 4 books absolutely FREE (plus $1.99 for shipping and handling)
- A FREE newsletter, *Arabesque Romance News*, filled with author interviews, book previews, special offers, and more!
- No risks or obligations. You're free to cancel whenever you wish... with no questions asked.

BOOK CERTIFICATE

Yes! Please send me 4 FREE Arabesque novels (plus $1.99 for shipping & handling). I am under no obligation to purchase any books, as explained on the back of this card.

Name _____

Address _____ Apt. _____

City _____ State _____ Zip _____

Telephone ( ) _____

Signature _____

Offer limited to one per household and not valid to current subscribers. All orders subject to approval. Terms, offer, & price subject to change. Offer valid only in the U.S.

ANHL2A

Thank you!

Accepting the four introductory books for FREE (plus $1.99 to offset the cost of shipping & handling) places you under no obligation to buy anything. You may keep the books and return the shipping statement marked "cancelled". If you do not cancel, about a month later we will send 4 additional Arabesque novels, and you will be billed the preferred subscriber's price of just $4.00 per title. That's $16.00 for all 4 books for a savings of 33% off the cover price (Plus $1.99 for shipping and handling). You may cancel at any time, but if you choose to continue, every month we'll send you 4 more books, which you may either purchase at the preferred discount price. . . or return to us and cancel your subscription.

ARABESQUE ROMANCE BOOK CLUB
P.O. Box 5214
Clifton NJ 07015-5214

PLACE
STAMP
HERE

For certain, she would've drenched him with her pink lemonade. Instead, she'd handled everything in a very mature way. The fact that she darn near admitted that she might be using sex to hold on to him was what had impressed him the most. Tarynton was never a liar. She just didn't readily admit to things, especially her shortcomings. Yes, a lot of things had changed about them. But the one thing that had remained steadfast and true was their love for each other. He didn't think that would ever change even though circumstances had.

Upon hearing the phone ringing, he jumped up to answer it. Perching himself on a stool near the wall phone, he picked up the receiver. "Hello."

"Good morning, Drakkar! Getting ready to hit the bricks?"

He felt his eyes light up from the joyous feelings inside him. "I was just thinking about you. I didn't call because I thought you'd already be gone. Are you still at home?"

"I'm sitting in my car outside the hair salon. I just wanted to say hi to you before I went inside. I hope you have a wonderful day."

"Wishing the very same for your, baby. What about tonight?"

She laughed. "What about it?"

"You want to hook up this evening? I'd love to have you over here. It's kind of lonely around here without you. I missed you something terrible after I came home alone last night."

"I missed you, too. Consider it a date. What time do you want me there?"

"I'll pick you up at seven. We'll stop to pick up some groceries and then see what scrumptious morsels we can cook up together."

"I'll be ready and waiting, Drakkar. See you later, then."

"Listen for my messages of love to you in the whispers of the wind. Love you, baby."

"Love you, too."

Tarynton floated into the beauty salon on cloud nine. Drakkar Lomax still loved her. "Oh, what a feeling," she sang out.

Melanie, Tarynton's stylist, looked at her rather strangely. "What's going on with you this morning? You look like you know something that the rest of us couldn't even imagine."

"Child, if I told you, I'd have to put a hex on you to make sure you keep my delicious secrets, the curse of silence."

"Girl, you're gonna tell me something," Melanie challenged. "Don't come in here looking like that while singing—and then try to keep it all to yourself. You look like you just got some—and that it was real good."

Tarynton threw back her head and laughed. "Better than some. Would you believe practically every night?"

Melanie waved Tarynton into the chair at her styling station. "You got a new man, T? Who is the lucky guy?"

"The same one I talk you to death about practically every time I come here."

"The one with the spicy name? Drakkar? Girl, no! When did all this happen?"

"He literally danced his way back into my life. He asked me to dance at Choices, but he didn't know that it was me until I turned around in my chair. But I think he knew the back of my head whether he was aware of it or not." Tarynton could see that Melanie had another battery of questions ready for her, so she went on and explained everything that had transpired between herself and Drakkar since his return to her life.

"So he's back in your life. That's so nice. I'm very happy for you, Tarynton."

"I just hope he's here to stay."

"Why wouldn't he be?"

Tarynton sighed hard. "Unfortunately he brought a little excess baggage with him."

"What?"

"Another woman."

"When you were talking about him, I didn't pick up on that at all. I assumed everything was fine when you told me that he still loved you."

"He did and he still does. But he seems to have one of those ex-girlfriends who doesn't know when it's over, can't accept it if she does, or both. The girl isn't playing with a full deck either. All of my car windows got smeared with eggs."

"Say what? How do you know it was his ex-girlfriend?"

"You know that I've never had this type of drama in my life before now. I often prayed for some excitement, but this certainly isn't what I had in mind. It's getting crazy around here."

"Let's go to the shampoo bowl. You can tell me the rest back there."

Melanie was only one of a handful of people that Tarynton ever confided in. She was someone Tarynton could really trust. While walking to the back room, Tarynton thought of how Melanie had become a cosmetologist, purely by accident, according to her. After getting out of the military, Melanie started cosmetology school just to use her GI bill money. She had worked full time in the electronics field and gone to school at night. After graduation, she had a lot of people asking her to come and work for them. That's when she began seriously to consider opening her own salon. Once her shop was up and running, Melanie never worked in any business other than her own. Tarynton admired her for having the guts to open her own shop.

Tarynton told Melanie a little more about her situation before she fell under the spell of Melanie's magical fingers-massaging technique, which relaxed her and made her want to cut loose any concerns or negativity. Melanie was good at knowing and understanding what her clients needed. She knew that Tarynton loved peace and quiet while getting her hair washed and conditioned. Tarynton used to fall asleep under the hair dryer, until she began writing her first novel. She had recently gotten into the habit of bringing it to the shop with her to work on.

Tarynton and Melanie chatted off and on during the styling process. After paying her bill with a personal check, Tarynton rushed off to meet her friends for an afternoon of shopping and girl talk. The conversations would come during the get-together luncheon planned for later.

Tarynton was surprised to learn that she was the last to arrive at the shop, Vintage Africana, since she was normally the first one to make it to their planned outings. Her friends seemed excited as they all gave her enthusiastic hugs. Roxanne then directed the girls into the shop and introduced them to the extremely beautiful Madame Julia. Roxanne immediately shared the group's need with the designer. After the group of friends held their breath for several seconds, everyone was elated to learn that Madame Julia did indeed have time to fashion the outfits. The girls clapped their hands and jumped up and down like small children.

Soon after that, when Madame Julia began taking measurements, Tarynton realized that Drakkar had forgotten to call her with his. Hoping that she could catch him in his office, she slipped away from the others to place a call to him.

She laughed softly upon hearing his sweet voice. "Glad I caught you in—"

"I was just getting ready to call you on your cell," he interjected. "I forgot to give you my measurements."

"That's what I was calling you about. I can write them down if you're ready."

"Ready as I'll ever be."

Just writing down his measurements made her all hot and bothered. The brother was packing the ideal physique, the type women loved to see on a man: tall with broad chest and shoulders, tapered waist, and thick muscled thighs and legs. She moaned out loud.

Drakkar chuckled. "Sounds that good to you, huh?"

"Darn good!"

"Thanks, baby. You always know how to make me feel great. I'm looking forward to our evening together."

"You're not alone in that. Got to run. Talk to you later."

Drakkar rocked back in the leather swivel chair. *Tarynton my love, my one and only*, he thought, feeling warm on the inside. She was one of the most real people in his life, also the sweetest. Having her back by his side was a miracle, one he'd prayed for so often. Within his heart, an everyday occurrence for him, he thanked God for bringing their reunion about.

But the one thing that bothered him was Tarynton's lack of using terms of endearment with him. She used to call him all sorts of sweet, loving names, but he couldn't remember her calling him by those kinds of names very often since they'd gotten back together. When they were teenagers, she had called him baby love. She'd later graduated to honey and sweetheart. Then one day he became her darling. Baby love had been his very favorite. It was the sweetest one.

Maybe he'd ask her about it tonight. Then, on second thought, he decided against it. Tarynton didn't like to be questioned about too much of anything, but she didn't have a problem when it came down to her doing the asking. His crystal-clear laughter rang out as he left his office and headed back to the studio.

It hadn't taken long for the six women to choose rich, colorful fabrics and unique designs for their special creations in African evening attire. Madame Julia had made available to them a wide range of beautiful solids and daring prints in an array of different materials. Everyone had left the little shop happy and satisfied with the outcome of the meeting with Madame Julia.

Now seated in the Crenshaw Mall's food court, the girls discussed their choices over the variety of delicious seafood dishes purchased from the Hawthorne Fish franchise.

"I love the fabric and the design you chose, Tarynton," Denise said. "Purple, red, and royal blue are great color combinations. Each of them are colors often seen worn by royalty. Drakkar is going to look like a fine African king all decked out in his royal robes."

"With his superfine queen on the end of his arm," Rayna chimed in.

Tarynton closed her eyes expressively. "I can already envision him in his royal attire. I still intend to show him the fabric swatches even though I went on and chose for us." Tarynton frowned, before taking a sip of lemonade through a straw. "I have a bit of bad news to share—"

"About Drakkar?" Narita cut in.

Tarynton shook her head. "Oh, no, nothing like that. It's about the celebration. According to Kwanzaa tradition, we shouldn't celebrate anything else at the same time. The theme tables we've planned for are symbolic of other special holidays and commemorative dates. It looks like we have to can that idea."

Denise folded her hands and put them on the table. "Don't look so forlorn, ladies. All is not lost. You may feel that Tarynton busted the bubble, but we can blow it up again. Although she mentioned it first, I was going to bring it up also. We just got so caught up in the idea of theme tables that we completely overlooked the traditional way to celebrate. But the book club came up with another idea. We will simply celebrate the last day of Kwanzaa late in the afternoon and then have a New Year's celebration to follow later in the evening since they both fall on the thirty-first of December. We can use the tables for the New Year's Eve dinner and gala."

"Isn't that going to be very expensive?" Tarynton asked. "Two celebrations in one day?"

Denise shrugged. "I don't think so, Tarynton. Even though I suggested it, I've not been too fond of charging for the Kwanzaa event. We can up the ante quite a bit on the ticket price if we just do a New Year's Eve event. For people that don't want to attend both, they can just come to whichever one they want. But what makes you think it'll be expensive?"

"Well, first off, I'm thinking of having to buy another outfit. I wouldn't want to wear the same attire to both events."

"Why not?" Roxanne queried. "There will be a few hours in between events. Who's going to care what you wear, anyway?"

Tarynton laughed. "Listen to the woman who has said that she can't possibly conceive of anyone wearing the same outfit to work twice in the same month. Girl, you need to get real. As for caring about what anyone thinks of what I wear, I really don't. But I just have to ask this, don't all of you beautiful divas sweat?"

Everyone laughed at Tarynton's hilarious comment.

"I see your point, Tarynton," Chariese remarked, "but I still love the idea. December is the last chance of the year to have great party celebrations. Let's go for both ideas."

Tarynton grinned. "I agree with you, Chariese. I'm sure that I can dig into my closet and pull out one of my old dresses to wear to the New Year's Eve gig. I was also thinking of the expense that others might have to incur. If people have to buy two tickets and two outfits, they might not be so eager to come. Denise's idea of giving them a choice is a good one. I must admit that I didn't like the idea of charging for the Kwanzaa event either. I've constantly been thinking of other ways to raise the funds. This is a time for us to come together as a people and I don't think we can put a price on that. But charging for the later event is quite acceptable. Potluck is one way to keep the food costs down for Kwanzaa. What do you all think of that idea?"

Narita cleared her throat. "It's funny that you all are saying these things. I never really gave much thought to us charging for the event. But I can certainly understand it now that it's been brought up. Potluck is a great solution. We'll have a varied menu that way. Soul food prepared by many hands and cooked in various ways is the traditional way, anyhow."

"I'm glad we can still do all that we planned," Chariese announced. "The new changes should make it an even more exciting challenge for us."

Denise held up her hand. "With that settled, I've got some other good news. I met a wonderful guy at the library last evening. He's a science professor at USC, really handsome, too. Wilson Mitchell seems to have a lot going for him. He also plays the jazz circuit in a band on the weekends, the trumpet. He claims to be real good at it. If things click between us, I'm thinking of inviting him to both of our celebrations."

Roxanne sucked her teeth. "It'll click for as long as you want it to. You're just a restless soul when it comes down to personal relationships. Face it, Denise, there's no such animal as Mr. Right for you, and it has nothing to do with the man. You're the problem."

Denise sighed hard. "I know you don't think you're telling me something I don't already know, Roxanne. Like I've said many times before, when the right one comes along I'll know."

Rayna cracked up. "Good! 'Cause we've had enough of your Mr. Wrong versus Mr. Right drama to last us a lifetime."

After asking if she could have it, Rayna took a discarded dill pickle chip from Tarynton's plate and popped it into her mouth. "Just like this pickle, Denise, you turn sour on your men quicker than anyone I've ever known."

"With the exception of Tarynton, even though she's going through it now, we've all had our share of drama in our relationships," Denise protested. "What about you and that Tommy Tuna guy?" Denise asked Rayna.

Rayna rolled her eyes to the ceiling. "Here we go! His name was not Tommy Tuna. That's the name you and your sad self dubbed him with. Thomas J. Turner was the name."

"Whatever! Same difference. He had an ego the size of a whale but the physical attributes of a tuna. Besides, you had that boy whipped. You'd say jump and he'd ask, off of which high-rise building would you prefer?" Denise charged. "At any rate, I'm glad to know that you and scary Stephen King don't have any drama going on, currently, that is."

Tarynton pretended to hold Rayna back when she looked ready to pounce on Denise for calling her boyfriend by the wrong last name. Rayna and Stephen Keene had been together off and on for the past year and a half, but back on for the past week or so.

"Speaking of drama," Narita interjected, "how *are* things going with all the latest high drama in your life, Tarynton?"

Tarynton looked disinterested. "I don't give that situation any more thought than I have to. Drakkar and I are doing fine. And that is what's important. I'm going to his place later this evening. We're going to cook up something delicious to eat, but we have to shop for it first."

Chariese nudged Tarynton in the ribs. "Got that domestic thing going, huh? I can't see why he moved out in the first place. You two were already playing house over there. It certainly would've been cheaper for the two of you to live together."

Tarynton blinked hard. "It's better this way. Believe me. I miss him being around, but it's more exciting with us being apart. While I don't think we would've tired of each other, I just feel that we'll do much better living in our separate spaces. The day we begin living together, I'll already be his wife. I'm holding out for the ring, the official title, and all that comes with it."

"Okay now," Narita sang out.

Tarynton stood up and began to clean off the table. "I don't know about you all, but I've got a couple of personal items that I need to pick up, especially the one I plan to model for Drakkar this evening. It's time to shop until we drop."

Denise gathered up her trash. "Looks like it's going to be on, up in Victoria's Secret! I might purchase a few filmy things for my *looking so bright* future with the new man in my going-nowhere personal life. He's playing tonight at the Paris Lounge. We've all been invited."

* * *

Looking into the mirror, Tarynton held up the siren-
red teddy she'd purchased in the mall. The lacy see-
through piece of material would hide enough to get his
imagination really going, just the way Drakkar liked it.
Moving over to the bed, she picked up the tamer of the
two lingerie items she'd purchased, a pair of brushed-
cotton pajamas in baby pink. In thinking about the
possibility of her using sex as a weapon, she decided to
save the teddy for a much later occasion, like the night
of the wedding. For the umpteenth time, she scolded
herself for even thinking of marriage. Although it was
what she wanted more than anything, she had to keep
a cool head. She couldn't help reminding herself of
what her wishful thinking had gotten her before. A
broken heart. Well, that wasn't going to happen this
time. Not if she had anything to do with it. Marriage
was the one pressure tactic that she wasn't going to put
on either herself or the man she loved, she told herself
for the third or fourth time this week. If they were ever
to be married, God would have to be the one to ordain
it.

Just in case she ended up spending the night with
Drakkar, she packed the pajamas. Ugh, she thought,
tossing them into her oversize purse, wondering what
she'd been thinking of when she'd made such an unattractive purchase. Keeping her promise of toning down
the sexual come-ons was the real reason she'd bought
the pajamas, she finally admitted to herself.

Drakkar stacked the groceries on the kitchen counter.
"Buttermilk pancakes and sausage isn't the delicious
meal I had in mind for dinner, but I'm happy that

you're getting what you want, T.C. Are you any better at making pancakes than you used to be?"

She picked up the box of pancake mix. "I follow directions quite nicely, thank you."

He scowled. "I can't believe you do what it says on the back of that box. The recipe doesn't even call for milk and eggs. Just the thought of using nothing but water makes me feel ill. I'll handle the pancakes and you take care of cooking the sausage. Okay?"

"Okay, if you insist." She tried to hide her smile of triumph but failed at it.

He nodded. "Oh, I see how it is! You just set me up real good. You intended for me to cook the pancakes all along, didn't you?" She burst into laughter. "It's all good. At least with me cooking them, we both know they'll be great."

"I can't argue with that. Where are the pots and pans? Nix that question. I'm going to find everything in your kitchen just the way you found things in mine. Is that okay, Mr. Lomax?"

He walked over to Tarynton and put his arms around her. "A-okay." He kissed her passionately and then made his way over to the stove. "On the way to the grocery store you said when we got here that you wanted to discuss some plans with me for later tonight. What did you have in mind?"

"Checking out this band at the Dunbar Hotel's Paris Lounge. A guy that Denise met invited her and all of her friends to come and listen to the band he plays the trumpet for."

"What kind of music?"

"Jazz. Interested?"

"Sounds good to me, but I had something quiet in mind for our evening. However, you know I'm a jazz buff. What time do you want to get there?"

She looked regretful. "No, we can go to the club

another time. You've already given in to me on dinner choices. I wouldn't think of asking you to give up the rest of your plans for the evening. I'm sorry. I should've asked you what you had planned before even bringing the club up. That was inconsiderate of me."

"Don't go building a mountain, Tarynton. It's not even close to being a molehill. But I will compromise with you." She smiled, knowing his idea of compromise would be exciting. "We eat first and then we go listen to some jazz. But first you have to promise to spend the entire night with me—"

"Not a problem—"

"Hold on now, Tarynton. I'm not finished. I also want you to come to the studio with me tomorrow as part of the compromise. When I'm on the air, you can watch from the greenroom."

Trying to hide her euphoria, she snorted. "You don't ask for much, do you?"

"That's my compromise. Take it or leave it. It's all up to you."

"I'm sold, but you sure drive a hard bargain. Now I'm going to drive one. I need to go by the house and get my laptop so I can get some work done while I'm at the studio with you. I need to get a change of clothes, too. Can't go around your colleagues without dressing to impress. Think you can handle that?"

He nodded. "That's an easy bargain to purchase, girl. If you want, though, you can use my laptop. Mine is the same model as yours. About the clothes, you look great in what you have on. Your very nice charcoal-gray tailored pantsuit works for most occasions. The white silk blouse is a nice complement. And those bad black leather boots make you the finest-dressed sister in all of southern Cal."

"I could do that and just use a floppy to save my work on. You have MS Word, don't you? Thanks for your approval of my carefully selected attire, selected with your particular taste in mind. And I guess it won't hurt for me to wear the same outfit tomorrow, too."

"You're welcome, sunshine. And I do have MS Word on my laptop. Let's get this evening under way. Hand me a couple of eggs while you're there in the refrigerator. This batter is going to be smooth and creamy when I get through with it. A couple dozen silver-dollar-size pancakes coming right up for my baby."

Tarynton smiled at Drakkar as she placed the sausage patties on a cookie sheet. After setting the desired temperature, she put the meat in the oven. Glad that Drakkar hadn't seen the buttermilk biscuits she'd slipped into the shopping basket, she took out a baking pan to arrange his favorites in. With his back to her, she could pull off the surprise without him knowing it.

"Hey, Tarynton, when are you planning on baking the biscuits we bought at the store?"

"You just blew my surprise. I didn't think you saw me get the Hungry Jack biscuits."

"I'm sorry, baby, I didn't have any idea you wanted to surprise me. But you know I have the eyes of a hawk. I see everything. Even though I didn't know it was you at the time, I spotted the back of your beautiful head from way across a darkened room. Even you have mentioned that fact on a few occasions."

"So I have."

In less than a quarter of an hour later, delighted to dine on pancakes and sausage by candlelight, Drakkar and his beautiful dinner guest were seated in the dining room. While holding hands beneath the table, they recited in unison the Lord's Prayer.

Minutes later, after smacking her lips together, Tarynton licked the thick maple syrup from her mouth. "Boy, these little hotcakes are as light as a feather. You still got it, I see. I'm so glad your mother taught you how to cook like this. You know what they say. The way into a woman's heart is through her stomach. This meal is delicious."

Drakkar laughed heartily. "You already know that my father taught me how to make the pancakes, not my mother. And that's not how the saying goes. You love to turn things around, upside down, and inside out. That's one of the many things about you that intrigues me so."

"I'm glad that I still intrigue you. Who else would dare to have you eating breakfast foods at seven o'clock in the evening?"

"I must admit that eating breakfast so late and by candlelight wasn't my idea of a romantic dinner, but it is rather intriguing. I have to contribute this romantic aura to my lovely guest. I'm glad you whined and complained until you finally got your way about the pancakes."

"Whined? I don't think so." She looked at her watch. "Do you mind if I change into something comfortable since we're not going out for a couple of hours? I really don't want my clothes to be all wrinkled before we get to the club. I also have to wear them tomorrow."

"You can have a pair of my sweats, but they're probably going to be way too big for you. They're in the chest of drawers in the bedroom. You want me to help you undress?"

She got up from the table, retrieved her bag, and pulled out the pajamas for him to see. "I always come prepared. I should've changed into these before we started cooking."

He eyed her suspiciously. "Why do I feel like I've been set up again?"

She hunched her shoulders. "Set up how?"

"Regarding spending the night. Since you brought

your PJs along, I'd say that you already had intentions of spending the night with me. Tell me if I'm wrong."

"I tried to tell you of my plans when you cut me off to tell me the rest of your compromise conditions. It seems to me that you set yourself up."

He stood. "What else is new? The fact that you didn't answer the question about needing any help getting undressed is old hat, but it still gets to me when you ignore most of my inquiries. I guess I'd better get used to it again since it's not likely to change."

She reached up and ruffled his hair. "Get over it already. Coming into the bedroom with me? I just might need your help after all."

He looked at the kitchen mess. "I better clean up in here first. Work now so I can play later." He winked at her. "Think you can stand to be in those clothes for another fifteen minutes or so?"

Lifting his hand, she kissed the center of his right palm. "Not only will I give you the time, I'm going to help with the cleanup. We're a team."

"I appreciate the gesture, sweet thing, but I don't want that pretty silk blouse to get a speck of anything on it. Why don't you just sit on the stool, look pretty, and keep me company while I make light work of things in here?" He kissed the tip of her nose.

She propped herself on a bar stool facing the sink. "Are you getting into the groove of your new job pretty easily?"

He looked up. "So far it's been a snap. Everyone has been really helpful and nice. There's not a lot of snipping off noses and cutting throats at the studio here in L.A. That was surprising. I've only been there a minute, so things could change, but everyone seems to get along well. I'm one of those people that stay completely out of the office politics. I do a lot of listening but make very few comments. When I do speak on something, it is usually necessary. Even then I choose my words very carefully."

"Very wise, dear brother. That's what I like about working from home. I don't have to worry about any of that messy stuff that can go on in an office environment. I know you don't think I have a real job, but it's more than just that. I'm an entrepreneur. In owning a business, I get to set my own hours and own rules and operating procedures. I have no employees to stress me out and no costly overhead. However, I put way more into my business than I would at any nine-to-five gig. I love being my own boss, although in freelancing I have deadlines to meet and I do have to thoroughly satisfy my own clients. But that's the easiest part for me. Real job or not, I love what I do. I love all the opportunities it affords me." She grinned. "Did I mention loving the money?"

He came over to her and perched his elbows on the counter. "I thought we had the issue of you having a real job settled. But I can see that it's still a sore spot for you. I'm proud of what you're doing, extremely proud. I've been thinking about becoming an entrepreneur myself, after seeing how successful you've been at running your own business. I can't imagine anything being more rewarding than owning a business and being successful at it. You've inspired me, T.C."

She looked surprised. "Thanks. That feels real good. What kind of business are you interested in starting up?"

He went back to the sink. "I've had a few ideas pop into my head, but nothing that has set me on fire yet. Believe it or not, I love the idea of Web site design. There's good money there, but more than that, I love working with the computer. I've also given thought to becoming an agent. After watching and studying my agent for years now, as well as much reading up on and researching contract law, I think I'm capable of negotiating a darn good deal. But those are things that I'd start out with on a part-time basis so that I can build up my business while I still have a steady income. I may even have to take a couple of college courses to prepare myself for the things that I'm interested in doing, but I don't have an aversion to going back to school. Whatever I take on, I'm going to be one hundred percent committed to it, just like you are."

She smiled gently. "I do know that about you. Let me know if there's anything I can do to keep you inspired. Starting my own business is the smartest thing I've ever done. The rewards are boundless."

After seeing that everything was back in its place, he walked over to where she sat, pulled her off the stool, and took her in his arms. "It's only *one* of the smartest things you've ever done, because you've done some pretty wise things over the years. Getting back with me was one hell of an intelligent move." His lips grazed her cheeks. "Do you agree?"

She looked up at him. "Maybe, maybe not, since the outcome is still to be determined."

His expression grew serious. "What is the outcome that you most desire for us, Tarynton?"

The unexpected question caught her off guard. Forming a steeple with her hands, she put them up to her mouth. She definitely knew the outcome she desired, but she wasn't sure if it matched his own. She'd be a fool to expose her heart's desires to him not knowing his own. She couldn't let that happen ever again. So that he wouldn't see her pain, she turned away from him, only to have him bring her back into his arms.

Taking her hands away from her mouth, he lifted her chin with two fingers. "Why did that question upset you?"

She fought the urge to find comfort in pressing her

head against his broad chest. "It didn't. It's just not something I want to discuss."

"Why not, Tarynton?"

She grew agitated. "I don't want to discuss it, period. I don't need any other reason than that. I think we've already visited this a time or two. Can you please accept that, Drakkar?"

"For now." He pressed his lips into her forehead. "Let's go into the bedroom and get you changed into something comfortable."

Eleven

Caught up in the popular television program, *The District*, Tarynton and Drakkar had lost track of time. Tarynton noticed that it was already eleven o'clock when she finally looked up from the TV. Dressed in her comfortable flannel pajamas, she was curled up on the sofa.

Tarynton yawned as she turned to face Drakkar. "I guess we'd better start getting ready for the club. It's later than I thought."

With an eye closed, he looked at her out of his other one. "You don't sound too enthusiastic about going out. In fact, you sound really tired. Am I right?"

She scowled slightly. "Yeah, you are. I'm suddenly very sleepy. But if I don't go, Denise will be so disappointed. She wants all of her friends to meet this new guy. We all try to support one another whenever possible. I'm afraid I don't have a good enough reason not to go. If the shoe were on the other foot, Denise would at least make an appearance."

He got to his feet. "Then, that's what we're going to

do." He helped her up from the sofa. A kiss from his lips to hers made her smile. "I can think of a dozen reasons for us not to go, but I know how loyal a friend you are. I just happen to love that particular quality in you, so I won't try to tamper with perfection, T.C. You are darn near perfect, you know."

"So are you, Drakkar. Even your imperfections are somewhat adorable." *All except for that one very large imperfection that wasn't visible to my naked eye,* she thought with deep sadness as they moved toward the bedroom.

Laughing, he gently palmed her rear end. "I'm not going to go so far as to say that same thing about you. The few flaws you have are quite glaring, my dear."

She chuckled. "I'm not going to take that personally, baby love."

Thunderstruck, he stared at her in utter amazement. "What did you call me?"

She suddenly looked unsure of herself. Something in his tone had frightened her. "By the sound of your voice, I'm not sure I should repeat it. Did I offend you somehow?"

His arms came around her and squeezed her tightly. "Baby, no offense, not at all. It was only this morning that I was thinking of how I missed the endearing names you used to call me by. Baby love was the very first and my favorite. To hear you say it just now blew me away. Think I can get more of the same, often?"

"Most definitely."

Tarynton quickly redressed in her charcoal-gray pantsuit and white silk blouse. Drakkar had dressed himself in all black. His bold, sexy look had Tarynton resorting to catcalls and shrill whistles. He couldn't keep himself from smiling at her flattering gestures, vocal and otherwise.

Dashing into the bathroom, she put on Drakkar's bathrobe so she could brush her teeth. Since she always managed to get toothpaste on her clothes, she was using the robe as protection. Finished with her teeth, she sprayed on some perfume from the purse-size bottle of scent.

The usual greetings of warmth and love passed among the six women as Tarynton and Drakkar joined them at the reserved table situated in front of the bandstand. Each woman also gave Drakkar a gentle hug. After introducing her trumpet-playing friend, Wilson, to Drakkar and Tarynton, Denise explained that he was on a short break. Wilson then went off to order drinks for the late arrivals. Tarynton took a minute to introduce Drakkar to the people he didn't know.

"He's rather cute," Tarynton told Denise. "But he looks mighty young. Are you pulling a Stella on us? But then again, you've never lost your groove."

"I beg your pardon. The man is five years older than me. He's just got that great genes thing going on. His mocha skin is free of razor bumps and that slightly shaven look is gorgeous."

"Or he's lying to you about his age," Roxanne broke in.

"He doesn't look like any professor either," Narita said, putting her two cents in.

"Wait a minute! What are all you divas talking about? You know I don't go out with anybody that I haven't first checked out. The man's age and his credentials are definitely on the up and up. Once we get a little cozier, he'll be asked to have that AIDS test that's required before any real intimacy can occur. Is there anything else you all want to say?"

Stephen Keene, Rayna's boyfriend, laughed. "You chicks are too much. My man," he said to Drakkar, "you better watch your back around these sisters. They don't play."

"I've managed so far to stay on their good side. I don't plan to give them any reason to go for my back." Drakkar's mouth suddenly fell open. Everyone looked in the direction of where his eyes had zeroed in on. Before Tarynton could ask him what was wrong, he took off running.

Tarynton looked after Drakkar as he raced through the club and disappeared beyond the exit sign. Looking totally baffled, she turned to Denise and shrugged. "Don't ask me what that was all about. No clue. But I am concerned for him. Maybe I should go out there and see what's up with him. He could be sick or something."

Denise draped her arm around Tarynton's shoulders. "I think you should, but please don't go any farther than the hotel's lobby area. You shouldn't even think of venturing outside if Drakkar's not inside the building. With all the strange recent happenings, that could be dangerous. But we've got your back, as we'll be watching out for you. Proceed with caution."

Tarynton nodded. "I'll be careful."

Tarynton felt her insides trembling as she exited the club. It could be nothing, she thought. But in recalling the horrified look on Drakkar's face before he'd run off, she knew that something had to be wrong.

With his shoulders slumping forward, Tarynton found Drakkar seated in a chair inside the lobby area. Quietly, she approached him. Kneeling down in front of him, she took both his hands. "Are you okay?"

He moved forward in the seat until their foreheads touched. "I'm fine, baby." He sighed. "I thought I saw Tamara standing there at the entrance to the club. It seemed to me that she ran off at the same moment our eyes connected. By the time I got out here, the person I saw was gone. I didn't go outside because I didn't think it was safe to do so." He shrugged, looking uncertain. "It may not have been her at all. I just don't know." Drakkar helped Tarynton get up off her knees. She then sat in the chair next to his.

"I didn't know you were so worried, Drakkar. Is there something about her that you haven't told me yet?"

He took Tarynton's hand. "In my opinion, she's unstable. But I don't think she would physically harm anyone. But she's damn good at emotional terrorism. Your windows being smeared with eggs may not be the worst of it. That's what has me so worried. The harassing phone calls to me and my female friends, the continuous threats, and her unexpectedly showing up wherever I am, are her most frequently used scare tactics. I have to admit that I am a little fearful of her damaging your property. These acts of intimidation are escalating."

"Is there anything in her background that might suggest mental instability? What about her family ties?"

"Funny you should ask that. Before you came out here, I was thinking of how very little I really know about her. I simply don't know very much about her background, other than that she was born and raised in Louisiana. She's never mentioned anything about her family. But I also must say that I never asked her too much about her family history, after she gave me the impression that she had very little to do with them."

She wanted so much to ask Drakkar if Tamara was the other woman in his life, the one that may've come between them six years ago. Even in the light of these recent events, she still couldn't bring herself to do it. This strange woman was an occupant of his past. Tarynton Batiste was a resident in his present and hopefully a permanent one of his future. The thought sounded really nice to her ears but the problems in their personal relationship seemed to be mounting.

"Look, T.C., let's go back inside and try to have a

good time. My eyes probably deceived me. And we're not going to have any fun by just sitting out here dwelling on this craziness.''

"If you're sure you want to go back inside. Now that we've made an appearance, Denise will understand if we leave. Everyone was concerned when you zipped out of the club like that.''

"Thanks, baby, but having a good time will take our minds off all this bad stuff.'' He stood up. "Come on, T.C., let's go back inside and get our groove on.''

Taking her by the hand, Drakkar led her back inside the club and over to the table where her friends anxiously awaited her return. When Tarynton told them that everything was okay, the other women breathed a deep sigh of relief.

The band resumed playing only minutes after Tarynton and Drakkar's return. A few minutes into the set, Tarynton could see that Drakkar appreciated the band's style. He had a great ear for all kinds of music, but he loved jazz with a passion. Tarynton did her best to have a good time, but her mind kept taking her back to the disturbing events that had come into her life.

On the ride to his place Tarynton had been extremely quiet. Drakkar watched her with concern as she readied herself for bed. Walking up behind her, he wrapped his arms around her waist and splayed his fingers across the flat of her abdomen. "Are you feeling all right?''

She covered his hands with hers. "Just tired, I guess. Nothing that a good night's rest won't cure. What about you? Are you doing okay?''

He led her over to the bed. After pulling the linens back, he gestured for her to climb in. He then got in right behind her and lowered her head against his chest. "I'm worried about you, baby. I know you're not used to having these dramatic kinds of episodes in your life. It seems that I've come here and totally upset your lifestyle. That wasn't my intent. If you think we should cool things down until my past issues are resolved, I won't like it, but I'll understand."

She lifted her head and looked down at him. "It sounds to me like you think that might be best for us. Is that the case?"

He reached up and brushed her cheek with the back of his hand. "T.C., you know that's not what I want. But I don't want to see you upset either. This is happening because of me." *Even though I also hold you in part responsible. You weren't there for me then.* He fought the bitter feelings rising within as the content of the letter swept into his mind.

While he hadn't voiced his thoughts, she still got the feeling that he might somehow think she was also to blame for this situation. But that wasn't even close to the truth. She had goaded Tamara on the phone, but that had only come after the madness began. "Are you upset with me, Drakkar? I get a sense that you are."

He smoothed her hair back. "I'm just thinking of how things used to be for us. Rarely was there this kind of tension between you and me. We were able to settle troubling things with ease. We never stayed mad at each other for too long." He propped himself up on one elbow. "I think that one of the reasons we feel so tense is that there are still so many unanswered questions about the past six years, with so many gaps yet to be filled in. Because you've made it forbidden ground for us, there's a lot of frustration, on both of our parts. I'd still like us to explore what happened even if it was a long time ago. Do you think we'll ever be able to do that?"

Unhappy with his question, she stared at him for several seconds. "It's not a place I like to visit. It's not at all a very nice place for me to find myself stuck in. If you insist on doing so, I'll do it, but you might not like the outcome. It seems to me that you're going back on your word, which is your bond. That's not like you." She blew out a ragged breath. "Okay, I'm going to admit that there are some questions that I'd like to have answered, and some things I'd like to share with you, but I'm just too damn afraid of the answers. I've been taught never to ask a question that I didn't know the answer to, or one that I wasn't sure of how I'd react to the response. So, with that in mind, what would you like us to discuss first?"

Drakkar studied her intently. "Now you have me afraid. As much as I want to settle the past, I don't want to lose you in the process. I had no idea you were so fearful. Still, I see the past coming between us in a big way. One moment I think I can move on without settling the things that happened between us. But then it starts to get to me, especially when I don't know what happened back then. I don't know how we got to where we were and there are times when I want to know more than anything, at all cost. Then the thought of losing you overrides my desire to have things brought out into the open. I think it's a Catch-22 for both of us."

She laid her head back against his chest. "Drakkar, were you ever in love with Tamara?"

He closed his eyes. "How do you expect me to answer that without going into the past?"

"By simply saying yes or no."

He ran his hand across his forehead. "If I answer it one way or the other, can you really leave it at just that?"

"Yes, I can."

"No!"

The emphatic *no* pleased her, but it was hard just to leave it at that. If he didn't love her, why Tamara was acting as if he did would've been her next question. In the worst way, she also wanted to know if she was the same woman that had pulled them apart. That was just another question that she wasn't going to ask. There were some things she was better off not knowing.

Turning her body into his, she brought his face close to hers. Their eyes connected and closed at the same time her mouth hungrily sought out his. Eager to shut out the unsavory memories of the last couple of hours, Tarynton turned all her pent-up frustration into passion. Her burning body gyrated against his with the intentions of tantalizing and seducing him into submission. It didn't take much physical prompting from her to have Drakkar submit to her wantonness. She was hot and his body responded ardently and with urgency to her torrid heat. His sweet lips grazed, his teeth nipped, and his tongue tasted all the flesh from the top of her shoulders down to the indention of her belly button. As his long, slender fingers gravitated toward the wet, delicate flesh between her legs, she moaned in eager anticipation of his sweet, stimulating caresses. She gasped as his gentle fingers worked to bring her divine pleasure.

Slowly, he moved on top of her, looking down into her lust-glazed eyes. "You ready for me to take you all the way there, baby?"

"All the way," she moaned.

Huddled together in the center of his bed, holding each other close, Tarynton and Drakkar listened to the incessant ringing of the phone. He had already picked it up several times only to have the caller hang up on him. It was more than annoying, it was frightening. Tarynton was trembling but she didn't think Drakkar was aware of it, though he felt every single tremor, even the ones in her heart.

If this was a nightmare for him, he could only imagine what it must be like for her. In order to bring this madness to a halt, he thought he might have to back away from his relationship with Tarynton. At least, until he could reason with Tamara. This had to stop. The restraining orders that they hadn't yet attempted to file came to mind. But would the courts issue an order against someone living in another state? It was certainly something worth looking into.

The phone rang without cessation for the next twenty minutes. He wouldn't be surprised if the call was made from a pay phone and that the caller had purposely left the phone without hanging up the receiver. Tamara had already pulled that on him a time or two.

With her head against his chest, Tarynton looked up at him. "If this is any indication of what you've been going through with this woman, I feel really bad for you. I can't imagine anyone doing this to another person. I don't think this woman is crazy, though. I think she's been badly hurt and totally disillusioned by love. These are learned behaviors."

"T.C., I know what you must be thinking, but I didn't intentionally hurt her. It wasn't like that between us. I can't begin to explain my relationship with her, but there was never any mention of love in it. If Tamara's been hurt badly, I'm not the guilty party."

"Maybe we should try to get some sleep. We have an early wake-up call. We're both too tired to make any sense of this tonight." She kissed his chest. "I hope your sleep will be a peaceful one. Good night, Drakkar."

His desire to make love to her until the tension within him had dissipated was strong, but he decided against it. Turning up on his side, he pulled her body into his. "With you by my side, I will sleep just fine. Good night, sweetheart."

* * *

Seated in the greenroom, as she waited for Drakkar to go on the air, Tarynton listed several upscale and reasonably priced places that she'd like to consider when planning future dates for her clients. California had so many wonderful attractions to offer. In arranging special dates, she had the ocean, the desert, and the mountains to choose from. There were even times when the sun shone in one place and the snow fell in another area, at the same time of the year. She listed a couple of popular Lake Tahoe resorts and several areas in and around San Francisco. Journeying south, she entered numerous frequented attractions in San Diego and across the border into Mexico. The possibilities were practically endless in entertainment venues.

At the sound of Drakkar's voice, she saved the information on a floppy disk, and then turned off the laptop. Looking up at the large television monitor, she smiled. He looked so good on the huge screen. Drakkar was a man of many talents.

As he interviewed another popular football player, she hung on to his every word. Drakkar was talk-show host material, she thought, wondering if he'd ever considered his own show. He would be wonderful at it. He had a way of putting his guests at ease. She'd seen the allure the first time she'd watched him do an interview, but now his charismatic ways seemed to leap right out at her. She could only imagine how other women watching the interview might respond to his good looks, strong physique, and powerful presence.

No woman had a ghost of a chance against his handsome face, unfathomable sincerity, and indelible charms. Drakkar had happened to Tamara the same way he'd happened to Tarynton so many years ago. Tamara had fallen under his magical spell, just as she herself had done. That Tamara must love him too wasn't hard for Tarynton to understand.

Drakkar Lomax was simply irresistible.

Tarynton smiled beautifully as Drakkar introduced her to all of his colleagues. After a few minutes of small talk with the television crew, Drakkar showed her all around the studio. Once the tour was completed, he guided her to the commissary where they could sit down and have a bite to eat. Tarynton saw how well Drakkar was liked. Constantly other people stopped him as they made the brief journey from the studio to the commissary.

With so many choices on the grand buffet, Tarynton had a hard time making up her mind. She finally decided on a thick wedge of lasagna, a fresh garden salad, and a slice of lemon meringue pie for dessert. Instead of a soft drink, she chose a bottle of sparkling water.

Seated alongside Drakkar at a long table, Tarynton took a peek at his meal choices. "That baked chicken looks scrumptious. I see that you went pretty heavy on the vegetables. All of those green items on your plate look so healthy. But you know me. I had to go for a meal high in calories. I just couldn't pass on the lasagna. It looked and smelled so good."

"Don't worry about it. You're not overdoing it. You also take great care of your body by jogging and exercising. You know that I've always been a vegetable lover. I especially like the way they cook them here, nice and crunchy."

She smiled. "Yeah, even as a kid. I remember how we used to tease you about eating so much spinach, broccoli, and cauliflower, raw or cooked. Then you would have the nerve to roll up your shirtsleeves and show us your nonexistent muscles. Those times were too funny.''

He cracked up. "Give me a break, T.C., we were only six or seven years old.''

She snorted. "Boy, you were still showing us your muscles in our teen years. But I have to admit that you had some by then. I can think of a few big ones.''

"Okay, don't get started over there. Watch your mouth, girl. So, how do you think I did with today's interview? Your opinion is important to me, you know.''

"I told you on the way over here how great I thought you were. You should be a talk-show host. It would be nice for you to have a sports show. You'd be wonderful at that.''

"You think so?''

"I know so. You should take the idea to your producer.''

He shook his head. "I can't do that. It might seem a little vain.''

"Suit yourself. You'll never know what they think if you don't talk to them about it. What would it hurt for you to at least discuss it with your producer?''

He laughed. "Yeah, and then have him choose someone else to be the host of my idea.''

"This doesn't sound like the Drakkar I know, the one that goes after everything he wants, without hesitation.''

"The way I came after you, 'cause I wanted you?''

"I guess you could say that. But in my opinion, you were a little tardy on the arrival of such a conclusion. When did you decide that you wanted me back?''

Her question puzzled him since he'd never stopped wanting her. "Tarynton, if I'm not mistaken, you're the one who decided . . .'' He threw up his hands. "Sorry, I'm not supposed to go there. If you're through eating, I need to get you home. I'm sure you're tired by now.''

He seemed angry to her as she studied the dark,

brooding cloud settling in his eyes. Her pointed question had certainly ruined the mood. She wished she could read his mind. Perhaps it was all of the things that were happening with Tamara that had him so darn edgy.

Deciding to leave it alone, she got to her feet. "I'm ready if you are."

He felt guilty when he saw that she hadn't even touched her pie. He instantly reached for her hand. "I'm sorry for my drastic change in mood, sorry if I hurt your feelings. Please sit back down and eat your pie. I promise to be nicer to you."

Her head told her to tell him to go to hell, but her heart demanded that she sit back down and accept her man's apology. She smiled to put him at ease. "This pie looks too good to throw in the trash, so I guess I can tolerate your company long enough for me to eat my dessert."

He flashed her a charming smile. "I deserved that. So I will have some dessert also. A nice, thick slice of humble pie."

She laughed. "Eating the whole pie might do it for you. Lots of prayer can't hurt either."

The smashed eggs on her windows didn't bother her nearly as much as the damages she was looking at now. The only thing it had cost her before was the price of a good car wash and waxing, but this incident was an extremely costly one—and in many ways.

All four of her tires had been slashed with some kind of sharp object.

The other incident had come out of the blue, but it was possible that she had provoked this recent attack by taunting Tamara over the phone. It was time for her to get to the bottom of this. She knew where Tamara worked, so getting the number to the studio wasn't a problem. But she wanted more than a phone number. She wanted to know everything there was to know about her archrival.

Rival wasn't the proper term. A rival was someone to compete with. No competition existed in this instance, not as far as she was concerned. Drakkar had declared Tarynton Batiste as the woman he loved, had always loved. Tamara Lyndon was just going to have to cut her losses and get over it.

Her next thought was to call Drakkar and tell him what had happened and ask him to come back and stay with her. Then she decided to give more thought to this serious situation. It was time to take matters into her own hands, time for her to put her mind to work. She would report this incident to the police, as well, but there were some things she had to do on her own to insure her safety. But before she could have the tires replaced, she would call in the report to both the police and her insurance company. On her way inside the house, she made a mental note to make arrangements with AAA to tow her car to the garage she frequented.

Too emotionally exhausted to take her clothes off, Tarynton fell across the bed. She was glad that Drakkar hadn't seen her car when he'd dropped her off. She hadn't seen it either, until she got right up on it. He hadn't pulled into the driveway since he wasn't coming in. However, he was coming back later in the evening, and he would see the damages then. No matter how much she would like to shield him from this latest incident, she realized that that wouldn't be fair to him. He also needed to stay on high alert.

While thinking about the things that had transpired between herself and Tamara Lyndon, Tarynton realized she had to be the one to take the high road. This desperate woman needed compassion, not censure. It was obvious to her that Tamara was hurting badly. Tarynton quickly decided that she didn't want to add to that pain.

Too often women and men alike put all the blame on the other woman or man that their loved one was having an illicit affair with. But it wasn't the other man's or woman's job to protect the heart of a husband, a wife, or a lover. The responsibility for a loved one belonged solely to the partner. There were many instances when the intruding party didn't even know that the person he or she got involved with had a mate at home. Lies like that were often told when cheating occurred. It was an extremely painful experience, no matter who was to blame.

How many women, if any, had Drakkar lied to? Did she even know whom Drakkar was after all these years? He didn't seem any different to her, but neither did she to him, and she had definitely changed over the years. He had yet to see how much she had transformed.

The more she thought about it, the more she realized that she didn't want to hurt the other woman in Drakkar's life. She didn't want to be hurt either. But what could she do to put a stop to the maddening hurricane brewing up between the two of them? Maybe she could try and talk this out with Tamara. How was she to achieve that? Tamara wasn't going to just up and agree to talk with her on the phone. Traveling to Louisiana came to mind, but she'd have to do that without Drakkar's knowledge. He wouldn't want to have any part of something like that. She'd never receive his blessing on it. Besides, the idea was a crazy one no matter how you looked at it.

While things were fresh in her mind, Tarynton decided to make several inquiries about Tamara. Tarynton had friends who had friends that worked for the telephone company. Before she was through, she would have both Tamara's office number and home number, unlisted or not, and her home address. She planned to learn everything about this woman that she could: from her birth date to her dress size. Before this was over, she might even know what type of toothpaste and deodorant Tamara used. To mount a good defense, she had to be armed with the power of knowledge.

Drakkar looked like a man who had just received a death sentence. The tremors in his hands were visible as he brought Tarynton into his arms. Without uttering a word, he held on to her in desperation. Her tears scalded her cheeks as they ran down her face. The unyielding hurt in Drakkar's eyes was what had made her consider not telling him about her slashed tires. She hadn't wanted to see him this devastated. He hadn't said a single word since he first looked at her car, but the expression on his face clearly addressed his anger and turmoil.

Wanting to talk with him, she tried to release herself from his embrace, but his arms tightened around her even more. Her hands went up to his back to massage the tension in his muscles. It was rather frightening to her that he hadn't said a single word, but she had to let him work this through in his own way. All she could do right now was be there to support him. Her car could be easily repaired, but she didn't know how to fix the permanent damage that might have been done to his soul. Drakkar hated conflicts but now he was right in the middle of one that was bigger than the both of them.

For several more minutes they just held each other. Then Drakkar directed her over to the sofa, keeping one of his arms around her waist. His steps were slow and unsure. The confident stride was no longer there. The one thing that concerned her the most was that he might decide to break it off with her, thinking it was for her own good. That, she would fight tooth and nail. There would be no slinking away to lick the deeply inflicted wounds of love's battles this time. Tarynton Batiste had already devised a failsafe plan, one that worked every single time. God had never failed her yet.

He turned her face to him. "I don't know what to say. I don't know what to feel or think. . . ."

She brushed his lips with her own. "You don't have to say anything, baby love. I know you never intended for this to happen. It's all going to work out. I promise you that."

He looked curious. "How can you say that after what happened to your car this time? Although she's never gone after anyone physically, the potential for that to occur is increasing. The vandalism is escalating. What's next?"

She kissed him again. "It's okay for us to be concerned, but we can't give in to fear, and we sure can't give her our power. I don't think this woman is as dangerous as she's trying to make us believe. Do you know who can best handle a woman?"

"Don't have a clue. I sure haven't been able to handle that one."

"Another woman is the only person to handle her; namely, me."

He looked worried. "Baby, I know that you've always been able to handle yourself, but you've never had to deal with something like this. You have to be realistic here. If the woman can get to your car that easily, she's only a couple of steps away from you. To be more specific, she's hanging out right outside your front door. She knows your comings and goings. And I know for a fact that she knows mine. This woman has been to your house on two occasions that we know of. I don't know how she does it. But the only way I can think of is that she takes the red-eye out of here after completing each of her dirty deeds."

"I've been thinking about that. Personally, I think she has hired someone here in Los Angeles to commit these vandalizing acts. That many flights in such a short period of time would be too easy to track down. You thought you saw her in the club a short time ago, so that would make three round trips from New Orleans to Los Angeles in a little over a month. But you aren't sure that it was really her that you saw. So we can count that one out. Drakkar, if you can just trust me for a short period of time, I can get this all figured out. Can you do that?"

He shook his head. "I can't promise you that, but I also know I can't stop you either. When you get some crazy idea into that thick head of yours, no one can reason with you. I just can't stress how much I need you to be careful. Don't try to play the heroine in this story. In fact, T.C., there may be another surefire way to bring this to a close. We should stop seeing each other until she's caught red-handed and then put behind bars. I don't want to see you get hurt."

Her anger caught fire. "If you walk out of my life again, consider it a permanent move. You won't be welcomed back a second time."

He grabbed her shoulders roughly. "What the hell are you talking about? I can't believe you said that. You must be suffering from amnesia—"

Her hand leaped up and covered his mouth. "I don't want to hear anything about that from you. Just know that I won't be here for you if you decide to let this woman win again."

Win again? He had no idea what Tarynton was talking about, but he could certainly recognize denial when he heard it. He could see that she was never going to face the facts of the past, but it was hard for him to let go of it. Unless he wanted to lose her forever, he'd better get over the fact that she may never want to discuss what had happened between them. How to do that hadn't come to him yet. He wasn't even sure that there was a way to accomplish it.

A full week had passed without incident. It seemed to Tarynton that Drakkar's visits with her weren't as frequent as before, although he was coming over later on. If he was staying away for safety issues, she thought she'd made it clear that she didn't want that. He didn't have to stay away from her in order to protect her. If that was the case, it wasn't doing much good. She was also receiving harassing phone calls all through the day and night. She had to admit that it was worse when they were at either place together, as if someone kept tabs on their every move.

Still, it made her sick to think that he was purposely avoiding her, especially after the warning she'd given him. She didn't want to resort to threatening him, but she just couldn't handle going back into the past. She was so sure that Tamara had played a large part in their breakup. Knowing exactly the part she played was what Tarynton couldn't deal with. To know positively that this was the woman involved in their breakup would hurt her beyond repair. If she and Drakkar were to have any kind of future, she didn't want that issue as a constant reminder.

Tarynton had already written several different endings for her novel, yet she was writing another one. Their relationship could go either way. If they didn't find a way to overcome the threats to their love affair, she wasn't sure what might happen.

It was these horrific incidents of the present that were pulling them apart, not so much the events of the past.

Their love for each other was very strong. Even so, there were times when this alien force seemed stronger than their combined strengths. She could only pray for the will of God to be done.

Twelve

Tarynton looked up from her work when someone knocked on her office door. Normally clients could just walk in, but Drakkar had insisted that she keep the door locked. Glad to see Denise standing outside, she got up and let her in.

Tarynton smiled broadly. "Hey, girl, what brings you way out here at the end of your busy workday? You're in the opposite direction of home."

The two friends embraced before taking a seat at the office worktable.

Denise handed Tarynton a couple of newspapers. "You better brace yourself against shock before you read the papers."

Tarynton looked anxious. "Bad news, Denise?"

"Real bad."

Taking Denise's advice, Tarynton took a deep breath. Each paper was already opened to the pages that Denise wanted Tarynton to see. The exact articles for perusal were also marked with yellow Post-It notes.

The woman in the color picture was beauty personi-
fied. Her smile was extremely radiant.

The caption under the photo read BRIDE TO BE,
TAMARA LYNDON. Then Tarynton read the associated
article: "Tamara Lyndon, a longtime resident of the
city of New Orleans, and a graduate of Grambling University, announces her engagement to television sportscaster, Drakkar Lomax. Miss Lyndon is employed as
Executive Producer for TRC Television Station, Chan-
nel Two. Mr. Lomax is employed by the same television
station and is also a resident of New Orleans and a
Grambling University graduate. The happy couple will
exchange vows in June. A honeymoon to the Caribbean
will follow the wedding ceremony."

The announcements appeared in both the *New Orleans Examiner* and the *Los Angeles Times*. The *Times* cited
Drakkar as a new resident in the city of Los Angeles.
Tarynton was floored. "These announcements are outright lies. Where did these papers come from?"

"One of them was sent to me from New Orleans.
When my friend sees something in an out-of-state paper
that I might be interested in, she mails the entire paper
to me. The article she wanted me to see was about
Wilson Mitchell, my current male interest, and the band
he's in. It seems that they make quite an impression
wherever they play. I ran across the other announcement at work, when I was reading the L.A. *Times*. When
you didn't call me about it, I figured you hadn't seen
it. It was by design that I saw these papers, divine intervention."

"Your girlfriend lives in New Orleans?"

"No, New York. She was attending a conference in
New Orleans."

"Drakkar is going to go ballistic over this when he
sees it. This situation is devastating us. Thanks for bringing the articles by. I guess Tamara submitted these arti-

cles after she trashed my tires, or had them trashed. Want something cold to drink, Denise?"

"No, thanks. What if it's all true?"

Tarynton's mouth fell open. "I can't believe you asked me that question. How could you think that these engagement articles are true? You've met Drakkar and you said you liked him."

"Tarynton, have you forgotten that I know the whole story? You can't keep pretending."

Tarynton blinked hard. Picking up the article from the New Orleans paper, she looked at the top for a date. It was printed just last week. The *Times* article had run in today's paper. "I know exactly what you know, Denise, but you don't know Drakkar the way I do. He's not like that. Drakkar isn't playing me now and he didn't play me back then. He was honest and up front about everything."

"Maybe you should be concerned with his method of telling you and his reasons for it. Don't you think? You should also find out if she's the same woman from back then."

"Perhaps that should be addressed, but that's all in the past. There's no evidence of any wrongdoing in this present situation."

"Harassing phone calls, egg-smeared windows, and slashed tires don't happen without a reason, Tarynton. Somebody is lying. Either this woman is being led on, or she really is crazy."

"Then I should be talking to her. She's the one doing all these things."

"I don't care who you talk to, but you need to find out something from somebody. But haven't you always told me that the other woman or man is not the problem, that the blame should be placed on the one that the person is involved with? Then again, maybe *you're* the other woman. Have you ever given any thought to that? If you haven't, you should."

"That's cruel!"

"No, that's reality."

Tarynton shrank inside. "I hope that's not the case. And I think it's high time we change the subject. It's only making matters worse for me. In fact, it's making me ill."

"Suit yourself. I'm dropping in at the fitness center. Want to come along?"

"A workout might do me some good." Tarynton looked at the clock. "I have plenty of time before Drakkar is due to come over. I'll drive my car so you won't have to come all the way back here. It'll only take me a minute or two to gather my workout gear."

Tarynton felt drained of all energy as she let herself into the house. The after-workout shower had done little to revive her physically. But it was her spirit that was at its lowest point ever. Walking through to the kitchen, she sat down at the table to reread the newspaper articles. Reading the lies over again wasn't helping raise her spirits, so she retrieved her own *Los Angeles Times* to peruse the calendar section. She loved to read about the happenings in and around L.A. Travel was her second favorite section of the paper to read.

Having no desire to talk with anyone, Tarynton just looked at the phone when it rang. Once it stopped ringing, she checked her messages. After dialing the message center number, when prompted she punched in her pass code. Hearing that she had ten new messages caused apprehension to settle in.

Intently, she listened to each recorded message. The first three were hang-ups. All the rest were from Drakkar. Each one from him sounded more urgent than the last.

She decided not to call him back, though the decision came hard for her. She needed some space right now. Until she could sort everything out, she wasn't going to confront him with anything to do with his ex-girlfriend. *That's silly,* she thought. *You might never be able to sort it out, and you're certainly not going to do it without his help. He's the only one that has answers.* It might have been better to confront him now than to wait until matters get worse, if that was even possible. It didn't seem to her that it could get any worse than it was.

She saw that it was six-thirty when she looked at the clock. Drakkar was due in an hour. That would give her time to lie down for a short spell. Dragging herself into the bedroom, she took off her clothes and then put on a set of loose-flowing loungewear in basic black. Instead of her ordering takeout over the phone, Drakkar was going to order a couple of pizzas from home and pick them up on his way to her place.

As she positioned herself in the center of the bed, she thought about his phone calls. Maybe he wasn't coming over. The calls did sound somewhat urgent. He could've gone out of town at the last minute, but wouldn't he have just said that on one of the messages? Well, she mused, if he didn't show up within fifteen minutes of when he was due to arrive, she'd begin to worry then. Right now she was going to close her eyes and conjure up a peaceful place to rest.

At the light kiss that Drakkar had pressed onto her lips Tarynton opened her sable-brown eyes. Looking into his warm, beautiful golden brown gaze made her want to laugh and cry at the same time. She was glad to know that he hadn't gone out of town and that no physical harm had come to him. Even as she remembered that she had to ask for her keys back, her right hand stroked his handsome face. "Hey, you made it. I'm glad you're okay."

Stroking her chestnut-brown hair, he lay down next to her and brought her body flush with his. "Of course I'm okay. Why would you think that I wasn't?"

"Because of all the messages you left me. They sounded a little urgent. What was going on with you? Why all the calls?"

He blew out a ragged breath. "There's something I have to tell you and it's not good. Tamara has announced in the *Los Angeles Times* that she and I are engaged. When one of my coworkers congratulated me, I didn't know why. Then she showed me the paper. I was so embarrassed when she asked me if you and Tamara were the same person. She mentioned that the woman in the paper looked so different from the one I'd brought to the studio with me. You met Becky Souza that day. Also, a friend of mine that works at the station where I used to work called me when he saw the announcement in the Sunday newspaper in New Orleans. It seems that it ran in last week's paper, but he only read it today. He's been out of town for a while. I made all the calls to you because I wanted to tell you about the announcement before you read it in the *Times*. I wanted to be the one to share it with you before someone else did."

Her eyes filled with tears. "I've seen both papers, Drakkar. Denise brought them over here right after she got off work. It seems that I was supposed to find out, since the news is coming from everywhere. Denise's friend sent a New Orleans paper to her, but not because of this article. Putting it in the *Times* was a safe bet that you and I would definitely see it. *Are* you engaged to her, Drakkar?"

Drakkar's expression suddenly changed. He now looked like an angry thundercloud as he put some distance between them. "You really don't know the answer to that question?"

"I asked it, didn't I?"

Totally perplexed, he scratched his head. "If I were engaged to someone, I'd tell you in person." *Unlike your objectionable tactics,* he thought with rancor, the painful letter coming to mind. "I'm not engaged to anyone, T.C. Is that a good enough answer for you?"

Frustrated, she sighed hard, closing up the gap he'd put between them. "I don't know why I'm acting like this with you. I apologize for acting like a wretch. Denise posed some very hard questions to me earlier. She even suggested that I might be the *other* woman. I'm really on edge with all of this. I'm not scared, just seriously filled with tension. This is such an unpleasant ordeal for both of us." She looked up into his golden-brown eyes. "If you make love to me, the tension just might go away. In fact, I'm sure of it. Will you undress me and then ravish me?"

That was the type of question that she didn't have to ask him twice. He reached for her, enveloping her in his powerful but tender arms. His tongue found hers. The sensuous kiss melted her, heightening her physical desire for him. As his mouth worked its way down to the lower part of her body, she locked her fingers into his curly hair. Drakkar always left her breathless when his mouth made heated contact with her intimate treasures through her clothes. It didn't feel quite as good as it did on her naked flesh, but it was right up there at the top of the things she loved for him to do to her. After working his way back up to the top of her anatomy, his mouth eagerly wrapped around her left breast. Suckling her tenderly, he began to disrobe her.

While her hands slid inside his zipper, he gasped with wantonness. As she freed his majestic maleness, the feel of his hardened flesh made her tingle all over. Reaching around his back, she removed his wallet from his pants pocket and took out a condom. Pushing Drakkar onto his back, she worked feverishly to undress the lower part of him. Something she'd never done before, she put the condom in place with trembling hands, ignoring the heat rising in her cheeks.

The eroticism of her electrifying actions had them both nearly insane. Using the tips of her fingers, she manipulated his nipples, straddling him at the same time. As she filled herself up with his erection, she threw her head back, moaning from sheer pleasure. While gently working himself up into a sitting position, he tenderly gripped her buttocks. Their mouths collided in a wet passionate kiss as they began the thrilling ascent to ecstasy.

Tarynton awakened to find Drakkar staring down at her. "I crashed on you. I'm sorry."

He kissed the tip of nose. "That's okay, baby. We wore each other out. I just woke up myself. We've only been sleep about thirty minutes or so. Are you hungry?"

"The pizza! I forgot all about dinner while we feasted on each other. My sexual appetite has been deeply satisfied, so I guess I'd better replenish the fuel that my body needs to continue these amazing acts of erotica. I'll wash up before I warm the pizzas. Do you want to eat in here?"

He pulled her back into her arms as she started to get out of bed. "I have a better idea. Let's wash up together, in the shower. The pizza can wait another few minutes."

She looked concerned. "We can do that. But I have to ask this. Don't you think we should discuss this newspaper article further?"

"I don't know what else there is to discuss, T.C. Are

you in any doubt as to why she did it? Are you still doubting me, doubting that I'm not engaged to her?"

"No, to all three. Let's go take that shower."

Seated on the floor in front of the television in her bedroom, Tarynton and Drakkar were viewing the television series *Boston Public* while snacking on the pizza from paper plates. Plastic containers of Coke and Sprite had been placed on the table between the barrel chairs. Drakkar had also filled the ice bucket and put it next to the soda bottles.

"Did you know that Loretta Devine is one of my favorite actors?"

Drakkar looked over at her. "Actress, not actor."

"Actor! Women artists also consider themselves actors. It's one of the highest compliments you can pay to a female artist. Do you know the difference between an actor and a movie star?"

"There are a lot of differences between them. I classify an actor as a person who has studied his craft through and through and has paid his dues to the acting profession. It's one who loves live theater, and jumps at any chance to work at his profession. An actor lives in his profession and later dies in it. In my opinion, a movie star is somewhat of an overnight sensation, someone who's never paid his dues to the craft of acting. They're discovered one minute and end up on the big screen in the next one. A movie star doesn't seem to have the staying power of an actor. That's why a lot of child actors later fail in life. They've been thrust into a profession that they've not prepared themselves for."

She laughed. "That was some running commentary. But back to Loretta Devine. The girl can act her butt off. I loved her in *Funny Valentine,* a Showtime original. She and Alfre Woodard starred in it together. It was a wonderful story, emotionally jarring. Loretta was also the bomb in *Waiting To Exhale!* It seemed to me that she was the only one that kept her dress down."

"Do you have either one of those movies?"

"I have them both in VHS. I taped *Funny Valentine* from the television. I haven't had my DVD systems for very long. The one in the family room has both DVD and VHS. Do you want to go in there and watch one of them?"

"I think I'll save those two for the next time we set aside time to watch movies. Now that you've made me miss most of *Boston Public,* I'd like to at least see the ending."

"Sorry, but it seems to me that you were talking just as much as me."

He looked at her and then his gaze went back to the television. Not caring too much for being told to shut up, even if it wasn't verbalized, she stuck her tongue out at him when he turned his eyes back to the show.

"I saw that, T.C."

"Good!"

"You're such a little brat, Tarynton. Come here and lay your head in my lap. Pull your lip in and stop taking everything so seriously." He kissed her to smooth her ruffled feathers.

Tarynton closed her eyes as she rested her head in his lap. Although she denied having doubts, she couldn't help wondering if she was being a fool where Drakkar was concerned. Was she one of those people who saw the evidence of something amiss all around them but totally ignored it for fear of losing the one they loved, the one they didn't think they could live without?

Was it possible that Drakkar was playing her? Did she have love's blinders on? No matter what else he'd done, he had certainly played with Tamara's heart. Intentional or not, he had hurt her. This woman didn't develop these insidious ways because someone had been kind and gentle to her. Tamara Lyndon had been wounded deeply by love—and that pain had turned her darn near rabid. Drakkar was definitely guilty of being careless with Tamara's heart. Tarynton also suspected that Tamara had been deeply hurt repeatedly. A woman normally didn't snap after one bad relationship. Insanity usually came after a series of emotionally abusive ones.

Although she didn't agree with the vengeful tactics used by Tamara, Drakkar had brought all this drama on himself. When he decided to use Tamara, for whatever the reason, he'd set the beginning wheels of destruction in motion. It seemed to Tarynton that Tamara simply wasn't the type of woman who gave herself to a man and then rolled over and played dead when he decided that it was over between them. Tamara certainly had Drakkar taking notice.

Unfortunately Drakkar only had himself to blame. If nothing good came from this horrendous situation, Drakkar would probably never again devalue another woman. He would think twice before deciding to get involved with someone for the sole purpose of sex. Tarynton didn't know for sure that sex had been his only motivation for fooling around with Tamara, but the evidence certainly pointed in that direction. No one should ever use someone that way.

Drakkar ran his fingers through her hair. "Wake up, sleepyhead. You missed the rest of the show."

She stretched her arms. "That's okay. I'll catch it during the rerun season. And I wasn't asleep. I just had my eyes closed."

"Why don't you get back into bed? I'm about to leave anyway."

"I will, in just a few minutes." Looking for the right words to say to him, she paused a moment to give it some thought. "Since you've moved all of your things out, think I can get my house keys back? I keep forgetting to ask you for them."

He looked wounded. "Why do you want your keys back all of a sudden?"

"Because they belong to me. Besides, I tend to freak out when you appear in one of the rooms I'm in without my having heard you come in. It just makes me a little jumpy."

"Is that it? Or are you afraid I might walk in on something you don't want me to see?"

She clapped her hands. "Now that's the real reason. You hit the nail right on the head. If I'm in here getting my freak on with some good-looking brother, I don't want someone walking in on us, especially one of my other lovers. So there!"

Her snide remarks stunned him. "That's not what I was referring to, T.C."

"Then what did you mean?"

He shoved his hand through his hair. "I don't know what I meant. Satisfied?"

"Satisfied that you meant just what I thought you did. You'd asked me earlier if I doubted you, but it sounds like you might have some doubts about me. Is that feasible?"

Pushing her back onto the floor, he rolled on top of her and pinned her hands back over her head. "I have no doubt about what you feel for me. There are just times when I get caught up in thinking of whom you've been with while we were apart. It drives me crazy to think of you with someone other than me. I hate the images that I sometime see. When I do think about it, those types of insulting remarks are often the end result."

"Then don't think about it. You can't change it, or anything else to do with the past. So why stress over it?"

Drakkar had some nerve and no right to feel this way, she mused.

"I hear you. Just easier said than done. I'm sorry, baby." He rolled off of her and turned up on his side. "Still want your keys back?"

"Sure do. Nice try, though."

He grinned. "There are times when I'm too obvious, but that doesn't take away from your ability to see right through me." He got to his feet and then pulled her up. "You want me to tuck you in before I go?"

"That would be real nice, but since you can no longer lock the door behind you, I'll have to walk you out."

"See, there *are* benefits to me having a set of keys."

She smiled deviously. "I guess, but I'm still not giving them back to you." Sadness briefly touched her eyes. "I wish you didn't have to go. My spirits are at an all-time low."

"I'm sorry about that. It's nice to know you want me here with you. But I've got to run. I'm going to use the bathroom. Then you can walk me to the door. Can you get me a cold can of Sprite to take on the road with me?"

The minute Tarynton left the room, Drakkar undressed completely and slipped between the sheets. There was no way for him to deny her anything, especially seeing how disappointed she looked at him leaving. She had all but come right out and asked him to stay with her. And that's exactly what he planned to do, all night long.

Whatever Tarynton Batiste wanted and needed from him, Drakkar Lomax was going to be right there to give it to her.

Tarynton nearly dropped the can of soda when she saw the covered-up athletic form stretched out in her bed. Setting the can down on the table, she climbed into bed with Drakkar and lifted the cover. "Peekaboo," she sang out. "Someone is watching you."

Laughing, he dragged her under the covers with him. "Surprised?"

"No."

His gave her a skeptical look. "No! Why not?"

She gave him a riveting kiss. " 'Cause you've always had a hard time saying no to me." She kissed him again. "If you really have to go, you should, but not until after you've given me another sleeping pill. Fair enough?"

"There is nothing fair about your suggestion. If what you want from me is going to make you sleepy, what do you think is going to happen to me after you're finished working me over? It sounds as if you want me to risk driving while still under the influence of the drugging effects of your sweet body. How fair is that?"

"I see your point. So, are you saying that you're going to need to stay here tonight?"

He nodded. "If we're going to take another sleeping pill, I'm not driving while under the influence of your intoxicating loving. Agree?"

"Of course I do. This is the very outcome I wanted. I already mentioned that I didn't want you to go. I still don't. Do you want to talk awhile before we get it on again?"

"That sounds nice. First off, I'd like to hear more of what you've learned about Kwanzaa during your extensive research."

"Want me to name the seven principles? Keep in mind that the principles are different from the seven symbols."

"Sure, I'd love to hear them. It all sounds interesting enough."

"Okay, here we go. This is what I've learned: *umoja*—unity, *kujichagulia*—self-determination, *ujima*—collective work and responsibility, *ujamaa*—cooperative economics, *nia*—purpose, *kuumba*—creativity, *imani*—faith. Once I fully understand the concept of each principle, I'll explain them to you later."

"Wow! I'm impressed by your pronunciation of the foreign words. Was there a pronunciation key provided for you? Also, how was Kwanzaa started here in the U.S.?"

"There was a key inserted in parentheses after each word. Kwanzaa was established in 1966 by a Dr. Maulana Karenza. The doctor included an additional *a* to the end of the spelling of the word to reflect the difference between the African-American celebration and the motherland spelling, which is spelled *k-w-a-n-z-a*. Pretty interesting facts, huh?"

"Very interesting. I can't wait to learn more from you."

Twisting and turning her bottom lip between her thumb and forefinger, Tarynton pondered the next topic that she thought should be discussed. "Do you think it might do any good if you apologized to Tamara?"

He sat straight up in the bed. "Apologize for what?"

"For using her."

"Using her how?"

"Can you honestly say you were looking for a long-term relationship with her when you first slept with her?"

"Who said I slept with her?"

She looked baffled. "I guess I assumed that you did. Are you saying you didn't?"

He could lie to Tarynton, but that was not who he was. Though he thought it would hurt her, he had to be honest. "I did. But she knew that I didn't want a full-blown relationship in the beginning. That was a crazy time for me."

In the beginning, she mused. Did it mean that he'd

decided on a long-term relationship after he'd slept with Tamara? She still wasn't sure that Tamara was the woman who'd come between them. Perhaps he'd turned to Tamara after it was over with some other woman. She had to be careful in her questioning, had to obey her own rules about steering clear of the past.

"Do you think it was okay for you to have a physical relationship with her knowing you didn't want to be seriously involved with her?"

He looked exasperated. "Why are you asking these types of questions, T.C.? What point are you trying to make?"

"I'm trying to figure out why Tamara has to act in such a destructive manner. I think that she's been so hurt, so hurt that she can only purge this incredible pain by doing these horrible things. Don't you hold yourself responsible for any of her heartbreak?"

He was amazed by her question. "T.C., I don't get it. What are you trying to do here? Something tells me I should've gone home. You're in a weird mood."

"I can see that you don't get it. And that's pretty sad. Most people that use other people don't get it. You played with this woman's heart through casual treatment of it; therefore, you're responsible for what's happening as a result of it. The only problem is it's not happening to you. It's not your car that's she's screwing with. You're the one in part responsible for her pain, but I'm the one suffering."

"In part responsible? Who else do you hold accountable?"

"I also blame her. She's the one who gave you permission to treat her in a disrespectful manner. And whether you want to hear it or not, whether you like it or not, you disrespected her. By sleeping with her for the sole purpose of self-gratification, you also disrespected yourself."

"Tarynton, you sound like you feel sorry for Tamara, after all she's done to you. The question I have for you is why do you feel that way?"

"I'm a woman, Drakkar, in case you haven't noticed!"

He could see that she was angry now. Her passionate flame was red-hot. While he didn't quite understand her red rage, he wasn't going to discount it either.

"You don't have a sister, but if you did, would you want her treated so callously? To take that one step further, since you profess to love and respect me, would you want some other man to treat me in such a condescending manner? Would you want some man to use me just for sex?"

He was actually appalled by the thought of someone being used like that, but Tarynton had made her point of view crystal-clear for him. He had to admit that he was guilty of behaving in such a shameful manner. It wasn't a good feeling.

"You suddenly have the look of a guilty man. I'm sorry I lost my temper. Intentional or not, you hurt Tamara. She is acting like this out of her deep pain. That's why I think you owe her an apology."

He looked thoughtfully at Tarynton. "What good do you think an apology will do after all this time? The damage that I've caused her can't be undone."

"You're right, Drakkar. But a sincere apology from you could turn around this entire situation. Even if it doesn't stop her, apologizing to her is as much for your benefit as it is for hers. You'd be surprised at what a simple but heartfelt apology can do. I'm almost willing to bet that it will lessen the pain and help her get rid of the painful stinger that's probably still lodged in her heart. Saying I'm sorry is not only the right thing to do, it's also very healthy. All you're responsible for is what you do to make this right. Then it's up to her to choose how she wants to react to it. The ball will be in her court. I don't want to sound like a preacher here, but you need to acknowledge your guilt and ask for forgiveness. Then you have to forgive yourself for any wrong that you've done."

Was Tarynton speaking from experience, a broken engagement perhaps? He had to wonder. Had some guy hurt her the way she believed that Tamara had been hurt? Had she fallen in love only to find out that she'd been used just for sex? Her passion on the subject was darn near volatile. She had certainly articulated all of her points well, but that came as no surprise to him. Tarynton always did know how to get her point across. Often, she got it across in no uncertain terms. She had certainly gotten him to understand the different sides of this issue.

"How do you think I should go about making the apology?"

She shrugged. "I don't know. But I don't think it should be done over the phone."

"Are you suggesting that I go to New Orleans to talk with her?"

"Since you asked my opinion, that's how I'd want to receive an apology. Face-to-face is the only way I'd want it. Over the phone I'd never really know if the person was sincere. By looking into your eyes, Tamara will know if you're sincere or not."

"Will you come to New Orleans with me?"

"That would be an insult to her to have me there when you apologize to her for using her and then breaking her heart. That won't work for me either. This is a private matter between you and her, very private."

He hugged her tightly. "You've always been a generous person, but this is beyond anything I can grasp. I can't believe you don't have a problem with me going to New Orleans and being alone with someone I've slept with! I'm genuinely amazed, and I know that you're not fronting on this. I can easily see that this is how you really feel. I have to say that I'm extremely impressed. I never thought I could love and respect you any more than I do, but both my love and respect for you has been deepened."

"Okay, before you go blowing me up into a saint, let me break it down for you. I have no intentions of letting you go to New Orleans without me. I'm just not going to sit in on your meeting with her. You're going to put me up in a really nice hotel, where I'll be counting the seconds that you're gone, and maniacally biting my nails until you return."

He howled. "Okay! So you do have human frailties. I'm somewhat relieved."

"Good. And let me warn you, I'm going to want to know every little detail about the meeting. Is that clear?"

He kissed her gently on the mouth. "Clear. Can I count on you to make the airline and hotel reservations for our brief stay in the Big Easy?"

She grinned. "As soon as you get your work schedule, I can make the travel plans."

"I already know that I'm off next Thursday, Friday, and Saturday. I have to be back for the games on Sunday. Of course, I have to check Tamara's schedule. I can do that without her knowledge. I think it's safer for me to talk to her in one of the private offices at the studio versus going to her home. If I've hurt her as badly as you seem to think, it might not be a good idea for us to be totally alone. Can you work your schedule around mine?"

She gave him a smug look. "I set my own schedule. I'm an entrepreneur, remember?"

"Yeah, it seems that you got it like that, T.C.!" He pulled her close to him, kissing each of her eyelids. "Ready for that sleeping pill?"

She slid her hand under the cover and wrapped it

around his manhood. "I can feel that you are. Taking his hand, she placed it between her legs and pressed her thighs together. "Take me to dreamland. I have no objections to receiving an overdose."

Drakkar stayed awake long after Tarynton went out like a light. There were so many questions that both he and Tarynton needed the answers to. Both of them wanted to know about the years they'd spent apart, but Tarynton would never admit to that. He saw questions in her eyes, but it seemed that she might be afraid of his answers. He understood, because there were many questions about her that he feared the answers to. One day, he vowed, they'd get this all out in the open. It might hurt them, but in the long run it could only help them in moving on. Curling up behind her, he draped his arm across her abdomen and closed his eyes.

Thirteen

With a lot of things still to accomplish before the trip to New Orleans, Tarynton said a prayer before starting her workday. Pulling up her Kwanzaa article on the computer, she began adding more information. She first outlined the seven principles. While absorbing the information she'd gathered, Tarynton came to understand what each of them meant.

Umoja stressed the importance of togetherness for family and community. *Kujichagulia* defined common interests and decisions that were in the best interest of family and community. *Ujima* was a reminder of the obligation to the past, present, and future, and that each person had a role to play in the community, society, and world. *Ujamaa* stressed collective economic strength and encouraged meeting common needs through mutual support. *Nia* encouraged looking within self and setting personal goals beneficial to the community. *Kuumba* made use of creative energies to build and maintain a strong, vibrant community. *Imani* focused on honoring the best of the traditions, drawing upon the best of yourself, and helping to strive for a higher level of life for humankind.

The next bit of information she read caused her to look back to the items she'd already typed in. The new information mentioned that Kwanzaa could be jointly celebrated with the year-end happenings, but it wasn't to be used as an alternative for any of the other religious holidays. This was confusing to her. In another article she'd read that you couldn't celebrate Kwanzaa along with any other celebration. That was the reason the group had decided on two separate events. She also noted that the information before her cited red as being for the blood and the struggle of the people. The other information said that it was only for their struggle.

With so many different articles written on Kwanzaa, she didn't know how she was going to discern what was correct and what wasn't. Realizing that she needed more research, she closed the Kwanzaa file. It was probably best to leave their events the way they now were. It would be really confusing to change up again, especially since they'd already set the dates and times. Still, she wanted to know the correct way of doing things for future reference.

Tarynton picked up several travel brochures to study to come up with a few new ideas. It was the special touches that she loved to add to the dates that made them unique. Making up special baskets of goodies, paid for by the clients, was one of the things she enjoyed most. The baskets were optional items.

First Date baskets were always fun to do. She always inserted into the basket a special occasion card, with getting-to-know-you types of messages, signed by the one hiring her to arrange the date. She'd then fill it with several types of foil-wrapped candies, a scented candle, sparkling cider, and a little pink or black book. A black book would be inserted if the female was the client and the pink one was added if the client was male. Only one name and phone number would appear in the books, the name of the one giving the basket. Sometimes she would add a small stuffed animal. The baskets could be as simple or as sumptuous as the client decided.

In thinking of the baskets, she realized that she needed to check the supply cabinet where she kept all the items used in making the unique gifts. With the holidays just around the corner, she wanted to have adequate materials on hand. She tried to keep plenty of cellophane and ribbons, but she had run out a time or two around Valentine's Day and Christmas.

The phone ringing had her scurrying back to her desk. Before answering, she sat back down. Her greeting was polite and extremely pleasant. She listened to the caller give his name and then his request for services, writing down pertinent information at the same time.

"That's interesting, Mr. Jenkins. I'll also be in New Orleans on the same dates you're requesting. Can you give me an idea of what experiences you'd like to encounter on this special occasion?"

"Ma'am, I don't have a clue. I go numb just thinking about what to arrange on special occasions. I'd like to go on your recommendations. Design the time around the things you'd like to do. I do know that I want it to be very romantic. I also want us to visit one of the gambling casinos. My sweetheart is a hopeless romantic. She's very adventurous and she loves to take risks, so I think she'd like to take a chance or two with Lady Luck. Oh, a Jacuzzi tub is a must."

Tarynton laughed inwardly as Bob Jenkins's deep southern accent tickled her funny bone. "It sounds to me that you *do* have a clue, sir. You've actually given me a lot to work with. Without a seven days' advance purchase, airline tickets will be very pricey. Is that a concern for you?"

"I'll be using my frequent flier vouchers. Spare no expense on the hotel and the other events you think we might enjoy doing. I'm counting on you to make this trip real special."

"You got it! Mileage tickets will work great on this short notice. While I have you on the line, I need to fill out some paperwork. There are several questions I'll need to ask you. If you want to put these services on a credit card, I'm going to need to know the type of card you're using, the name and number as it appears on the card, and your billing information."

"What about a cashier's check? I can send the full payment by a courier service."

"You certainly can, but I'll still need a credit card to reserve the hotel. The room has to be guaranteed, but most hotels have simple twenty-four-hour-notice cancellation policies. If you only want to pay cash, you can still do that when you check out."

"I see what you mean. I don't have my credit card here at the office with me. Is it possible for you to take down all the other information and let me call you back with the card number? I could call you from home tonight, but I want to keep everything a secret from my sweetheart. You'll have the information first thing in the morning."

"We can do that. Sir, what airlines do you hold trip passes on? I will also need your mileage-plus number."

"I'll take care of the airline reservations. Sorry, I should've told you that up front."

"No harm done." Tarynton went on to explain her fees and the different methods of payment that she could accept. The client opted to send a cashier's check. After graciously thanking him for using her services, she rang off. No sooner had she hung up the phone than it rang again. Hearing Denise's voice caused her to grin broadly.

"I called to see if all was well. How did things go with you and Drakkar?"

"Everything is fine, we're fine. He told me about the newspaper articles before I even brought them up. He already knew about them. He's not engaged to her, Denise, and I never thought that he was. I know you mean well, but I don't want to doubt him on someone else's suspicions."

"That's understandable, T. I'm here for you. All you need do is call."

"Thanks. I appreciate that. I've talked Drakkar into apologizing to Tamara."

"For what?"

Tarynton propped her feet up on the desk. "He asked me the same question. For the wrong he did to her. Girl, you know how bad it hurts when you're under-appreciated. Drakkar used her, plain and simple. Losing at love hurts, and I think she fell in love with him. I sure did."

"You never cease to amaze me, T. I can't believe you're sending your man into the arms of someone he once slept with. Have you lost it, or what?"

"It's either that or have this woman continue to dis-rupt our lives. She's been hurt, deeply. Being a woman yourself, can't you understand what she's probably going through? It seems to me that Drakkar slept with her, took all that he wanted from her, and then he tossed her aside. If that's the case, he was dead wrong."

"How do you justify being with such a callous individ-ual if he's all that bad?"

Tarynton sighed. "This is not his normal method of operation. Drakkar was hurting, too, when he turned to Tamara. It wasn't his intention to use or hurt her. People get involved all the time, only to discover that it's not the right one to make a lifetime commitment to."

"Was that statement meant for me?" Denise asked dryly.

"No, but if the shoe fits, wear it."

"You should've been a dang psychologist. You got this relationship stuff all figured out, yet you ended up with a broken heart. But I think you're going to be okay this time around. You're going about all of this in a very mature, dignified way. By now I would've found this woman and have beaten her down for messing with my car. But you do practice what you preach. You're always fair. I admire that about you. But as your friend, I have to warn you. Don't be surprised if this woman shows you no gratitude or respect. You have what she wants. And you having Drakkar apologize to her does not necessarily mean that she'll be appeased. In fact, it may cause things to escalate further. Think about what I've said. Got to run. Love you!"

"Bye, Denise. Love you, too."

Tarynton looked at Drakkar as they entered the suite of the Canal Street Marriott located in front of the French Quarter. "Mr. Jenkins, this is a lovely hotel. I've chosen very well."

He cracked up. "How long have you known?"

"I didn't figure it out until you started telling me all the things you had planned for us to do while we're here in New Orleans. Your plans were an exact match to those I made for a Mr. Jenkins. Now I know why you couldn't give me a credit card to confirm the hotel. You would've had to give me your real name to use your credit card. But you did give me a credit card. So how did you handle that?"

"I had already used someone's name that I know very

well. So I had to go to them and ask them to let me use their credit card to confirm the room. Then, after I got a confirmation number, we just called and changed the name on the reservation and gave them the new billing information. It was actually a pretty simple task to accomplish."

She looked puzzled. "Why did you go through all the trouble of having me set things up if you planned to take care of them yourself?"

"I wanted for us to do the things you would love to do. This is your first trip to the Big Easy. I threw a few recommendations your way, but you knew that the client was relying on you to make it very interesting. As for the cashier's check to pay your fees, all I had to do is purchase it and reference the purchaser as Mr. Jenkins. Anyone can purchase a cashier's check for someone else. It's the payee that has to have proof of ID to cash it."

"You thought of everything. I loved that southern accent. Let me hear it again." He said a few words to her using the accent he'd used on the phone. Tarynton fell out laughing. "I can't believe you fooled me so easily. I thought I'd recognize your voice whenever I heard it."

"What are you talking about? You've always been easy to fool." His comment was made in jest, but he could see by the look on her face that she had taken it personally. "Hey, I didn't mean to hurt your feelings. I was only joking."

"If you say so."

"What, you don't believe me?"

"Let's not get any deeper into this. I admit that I took exception to being called a fool, but you said you were joking and I accept that."

"I didn't call you a fool, T.C. There's a big difference in the meaning of the word and in the way I used it."

He held up both his hands. "You're right, we don't need to get into this. What I have to do is stressful enough. I don't want to fight with you, period."

It was then that Tarynton began to realize that what he'd said had nothing to do with anything. Her short fuse was the direct result of why they were even in New Orleans. They were there for him to sit down with Tamara and offer a sincere apology for hurting her. He may've planned special things for them to do afterward, but until this mess with Tamara was settled she couldn't imagine them even thinking of having a good time.

He seated himself on the bed and then drew her down on his lap. "Are you going to be okay while I'm gone, T.C.? You seem pretty uptight."

She pressed her trembling lips to his forehead. "I'm just a little scared about all this."

"What scares you the most, baby? The possibility of things taking a turn for the worse?"

Her lower lip trembled violently. "Scared that she may try to seduce you, and that you may desire to fall back into her arms even if you don't. Afraid that I might lose you back to her."

With his thumb, he wiped away the tears fringing her lashes. "That's not going to happen, baby. I'm right where I've always had the desire to be, back in your life and back in your arms. You don't have a single thing to worry about." He looked at his watch. "I'd better get on over to the studio. We need to put this behind us so we can get on with our lives. I don't know how much good this face-to-face is going to do, if any, but I'm convinced that I need to at least give it a try. Why don't you lie down and rest while I'm gone? I promise not to be too long."

As Tarynton clung to him, he kissed her long and hard. If she had her way, they'd go right back to the airport and fly home—without him ever confronting this unpleasant situation. But in her heart she knew this was the right thing for him to do. The irony of the situation was that she wouldn't allow Drakkar to settle the past with her, but here she had all but forced him to resolve things with Tamara. A little contradictory, she told herself.

At the door of their suite, he kissed her again. "See you in a little while, baby. If you get too antsy, just call me on my cell phone. I'll have it on."

Reaching up, she pulled his head down and kissed him on the mouth. "Hurry back, baby love. Otherwise I may have no fingernails left to manicure."

Tarynton unpacked their suitcases to keep busy. Drakkar had already taken care of the clothes inside the hang-up bags. Both had packed very light. She fingered his silk boxers as she unpacked them and placed them in a drawer. Once everything was put away in the drawers and the closet she stripped out of her clothes and put on Drakkar's bathrobe. Wrapped up in the robe that had his scent on it made her feel closer to him. Lying down at the bottom of the bed, she picked up the hotel directory to peruse it. Reading in bed normally made her drowsy, the very thing she hoped for. She'd be better off if she could sleep through Drakkar's absence. Staying awake until he returned would only drive her crazier than she already felt.

Drakkar felt sweaty. His nerves were on edge. Before entering Tamara's office, he took several deep breaths. He gripped the doorknob, only to let go of it. This was harder than he had thought possible. Knowing Tamara as he did, he was sure she wasn't going to make it any easier for him. He had a good idea of what he could expect. None of his expectations were pleasant.

Tamara looked up as the door came open. Both shock

and surprise registered in her eyes at the same time. Then Drakkar thought he saw fear there. Several moments of silence passed before Tamara threw her pen down on the desk, which caused a loud thump.

"What do you want?"

"Good afternoon, Tamara. How are you?"

"As if you give a damn! But I'm fine. Now, why are you here in my office?"

He gestured toward a chair. "May I sit?"

Her steely gaze burned into him, making him uncomfortable. "Suit yourself."

"Thank you." He stroked his chin. "Think you can have your calls held for about twenty minutes or so? There are some things I'd like to say to you."

There seemed to be a bit of reluctance on her part, but she did as he asked. "With that out of the way, can we get on with this, Mr. Lomax? I have a job to do."

His gaze locked with hers. "Tamara, when we got together that first time, we both agreed that we weren't looking to get involved on an emotional level. The relationship went further than either of us planned, yet we never committed to becoming exclusive. What happened?"

"If you don't know, Drakkar, I can't tell you."

"What we had was never very comfortable in the short while we hung out. I never saw a future for us. There were too many issues of incompatibility. But there was an even bigger issue than that. I was in love with someone else. The same person I've been in love with since I was old enough to understand my feelings. You knew that from the start—"

She leaped out of her seat. "Save that love B.S. for somebody who gives a damn! If you were so in love, you would never have gotten into my bed." She spewed out a stream of obscenities at him. "I admit to making myself available to you at every turn, but you didn't have to take me up on it. You wanted me, there's nothing to dispute there. But now we both know you only wanted me for one thing. You're a weak man, Drakkar Lomax. You used me. And I let you use me. I didn't intend to fall in love with you. It wasn't in my plan. So sue the hell out of me."

He filled his jaws with air and then blew it out. This task was getting harder and harder for him, but it was what had to be done. "Tamara, I came here to apologize for hurting you, for using you, and then throwing you aside. I'm sorry. But, Tamara, I can't make my heart feel something that it doesn't. I just want this unpleasant ordeal over with."

"What you want is to ease your guilty conscience. You want me to go away so you can live happily ever after with Cinderella. It's not going to happen. There are consequences to every action, good or bad. When you decided to play me, you brought a heap of trouble on yourself. Your peace of mind is in my hands until the day you die, unless I die first. You will never know when I'm going to show up. I plan to star in your dreams and in your nightmares. I'm sure you already regret the day you met me, but you're going to regret it even more before this is over."

"It's threats like those that got us where we are today. You started threatening me the day I told you I couldn't continue seeing you—and you've made my life a living hell ever since then. With that stated, what would you have me do? Do you want me in your life knowing I love someone else? Do you want me to force myself into something when my heart is elsewhere?"

"As a matter of fact, I do want you back. If given another chance, I can make you happy. I can change whatever it is about me that you don't like. I'm the only woman that can satisfy your every need, Drakkar. And I think you know that. That's the real reason you're here. You want to come back, but you want me to beg you to do so. I can do that, too—"

"Tamara," he shouted, "stop the insanity. That's not why I'm here and you know it. What do I have to do to get through to you?" When she looked ready to burst into tears, he threw up his hands. "I only want a peaceful ending from you, so you tell me what you want from me. If you don't accept my apology, I don't know what else I can do to show you how sorry I am, deeply sorry. I mean that from the bottom of my heart. I never set out to hurt you."

A blank expression came across her face as she dropped back down in her seat. For several seconds she just sat there looking dumbfounded, as if it was hard to believe his apology.

He looked concerned. "What is it, Tamara?" His voice was soft and mellow. "Are you ill? Can I get you anything?"

There wasn't a readable expression in her eyes when she finally looked up at him. Then he saw tears forming again. His heart wrenched. That he actually felt sorry for this woman who'd made his life a living hell came as quite a shock to him. It even scared him.

"Do you have any idea of how much you've hurt me, Drakkar? Better yet, do you even care how much emotional damage you've done to me?"

"Yes, to both questions. I now recognize that all your insufferable anger against me is manifested from your emotional pain. I never really got a chance to see or hear your side of this. The moment I decided to end things, a campaign of threats and hostilities was waged against me. I was never able to sit down and talk with you rationally about anything like I wanted to."

She leveled a hard stare at him. "I tried to tell you how I felt, but you wouldn't listen. So how did you expect us to sit and talk?"

"Tamara, how does someone talk to a person who curses and carries on like a crazy person? That mouth of yours leaves a lot to be desired. You cursed me out every time you saw me. There was no possible way to get through to you. I tried talking to you after Tarynton's windows got smeared with eggs, then her tires, but—"

"Don't bring that little witch into this conversation! I don't want to hear her name or anything else about her. If given the chance, I would've slashed her throat, not her tires. I'll never admit to the tire incident, and you can't prove a damn thing. Are you clear on that?"

"You just proved my point for me. But that *little witch*, as you call her, what you call every other female in my life, is the reason I'm here. She's the one who pointed out to me what she thought I'd done to you. She came down hard on me for hurting you. But you wouldn't care about that, would you?" Drakkar was angry now. Her calling Tarynton out of her name and the threat on her life enraged him. Tamara was acting out the vulgar name she'd called Tarynton.

"If you expect me to believe that, you're crazier than hell. That might be what she wants you to think, but she doesn't fool me one bit. She's no Miss Goody Two-shoes. If she's all that, why did you ever turn to me? When you love someone, you don't screw over them or around on them. You did both."

"I turned to you out of my own pain. That wasn't an honorable thing for me to have done. But never once have you and I confessed to loving each other. Yes, I now admit to using you, but never consciously. You were all over me long before that. I wish I could change things but I can't. All I can do is ask for your forgiveness."

She began to sob. His first instinct was to comfort her, as a friend, but he feared she'd read more into it. With that thought, he remained rooted to his seat.

A little more in control of her emotions, she raised

her head. "Why do men hurt me? What is it about me that make you all play me so hard? I'm a beautiful woman. I'm smart and I have a great, good-paying job. Yet every guy that I've ever been with has used me and then discarded me like I was nothing. Why do you think that is?"

After thinking about her questions, he decided that candor and honesty were needed in this instance. The answers would hurt, but he didn't think they'd hurt any more than she was already hurting. "Do you really want the answers to your questions? I don't intend to pull any punches, Tamara."

"You never have. I'd really like to have the answers from a man's point of view, especially from one of the men who has hurt me."

He swallowed hard. "When I first came onto the Grambling campus, you made it clear to me that you were available for whatever I had in mind. That alone was a turn-off for me, as it is for most men if they're honest with themselves. The aggressiveness continued even after I didn't show any interest in the offers, nor did they stop once it was clear that I was seriously involved with someone else. Tarynton was on campus with me on many occasions, but that didn't stop the unattractive pursuits. The constant bold come-ons caused me to lose respect for you."

"Hold up! You lose respect for me; then you turn around and sleep with me?"

"We slept with each other. Your persistence eventually brought us to that end, but only after I was knee deep in pain. Even when I began to like you, I knew it wasn't a love connection. In the short time we saw each other, off and on, the road was never smooth for us. We agreed on very little, had next to nothing in common. To sum this all up, both men and women treat each other the way each of them treat themselves.

Respect has to be demanded. The disrespect you show for yourself is the biggest reason why you get played, Tamara. That is, if you've shown the other men in your life what you've shown me."

She was mortified at his assessment of her, but how could she argue with the truth? She had certainly acted shamelessly with him—and that had cost her the one man she'd fallen in love with, the only man she'd hoped to marry one day. "It hurts to hear how you see me."

"When you give off the impression that anything goes, with no strings attached, you leave yourself open to be disrespected. I affronted you and myself when I didn't walk away from something or someone I couldn't respect. You were right when you said I was weak. No one should ever get involved, especially sexually, with a person they don't respect or don't see some kind of future with. I'm sorry for that. Beyond an apology, I don't see what else I can do. It's up to you now. You do whatever is best for you. If continuing to harass me is your only way to get revenge, I'll have to live with those consequences. But I'm hoping that you will end this tirade of anger against me so that both of us can move on with our lives. This is destroying both of us, and for what? I can't offer you the outcome you may desire. That's the truth as I see it."

He got to his feet and walked over to her desk. Bending down, he kissed her on the cheek. "Good-bye, Tamara. I wish you only the best. I hope that you will one day forgive me for the way I've treated you. If I could take on all your hurt, I would. I am truly sorry."

Tamara stared after him as he made his way to the door. "Drakkar," she called out just as he turned the knob. "Thank you for coming. I do believe that you *are* sorry. The fact that you flew all the way here to tell me that very thing has me impressed. It takes a real man to admit to his wrongdoing. I've really listened to what you said about the disrespect I've shown to myself. I'm also sorry, sorry that we didn't have what it takes to share a lifetime together, sorry that I've disrupted your life on more than one occasion. I wish you the very best, too. Good-bye.''

Drakkar didn't know if she was calling a truce or not, but he wasn't going to weaken his position by asking. Time would tell. As he walked out the door, he felt emotionally full. Whether he got through to her or not would remain to be seen. But he sure hoped so, for the sake of everyone involved. Tarynton's state of mind was what concerned him the most as he hurried back to her. She was probably beside herself with worry by now.

At the sound of the key in the door, Tarynton jumped off the bed and ran up to the front of the suite. She flew into Drakkar's arms the minute he stepped inside. Lifting her off the floor, he carried her over to the sofa, sat her down, and then seated himself. She studied his expression and his eyes for any signs of pain. Wanting so badly to feel an even deeper connection with him, she pressed her lips against his. The urgency in her kiss and the slight trembling of her body were not lost on him. He felt every ounce of her anxiety.

He held her away from him. The sad look in her eyes caused him to wince. "It's okay, baby. It was rough, but it didn't get too far out of control." He took both of her hands. "Sit back and relax while I tell you everything that transpired between Tamara and me." He started out by telling her how angry Tamara was at first. Then he told her all of the different topics that were discussed and how Tamara handled the answers to the questions she'd asked him. "I don't know if the harassment is over or not, but I left her on what seemed to me an amicable note. You were right. She got hurt pretty badly, and not only by me. There've been other men that haven't treated her very well."

"She actually told you that?"

"Oh, yeah. That was what opened the door for me to tell her that men disrespected her because she didn't show any respect for herself."

Tarynton looked horrified. "Oh, no, you didn't?"

"What else could I do but be honest when she asked me why men seemed to play her? And I asked her if she really wanted the answers, because I wasn't going to pull any punches. She wanted the answers and I gave them to her. But I think I learned a valuable lesson from talking this over. I need to be more careful of others' feelings. I'm not the type that just goes around hurting women, but I don't like the fact that I was actually capable of using someone like that, unwittingly or not. Thank you for helping me to see the part I played in this nightmare. I'm grateful to you for that. It looks like we'll have to wait to see what Tamara's going to do next."

"We'll have to keep it in prayer, as well as her. Hopefully she'll do some soul searching. She's certainly a beautiful woman. She should be able to get any man that she wants, but she has to elevate her self-esteem. Then she has to set boundaries in her future relationships. Otherwise she's going to repeat the same destructive patterns of self-abuse." She kissed him on the cheek. "I'm proud of you. You should give yourself a pat on the back for being a man about this. You deserve it."

"Not really. It should never have happened in the first place. I still feel bad about it. Now that we've jumped that hurdle, are you ready to get out of this hotel suite and charm New Orleans the way you've charmed me?" He pulled out the itinerary she'd sent to his friend's home. "Let's see what's first on the agenda for us. Ah, yes, a sensuous, candlelit bath in the Jacuzzi tub for the weary travelers. Come here and let me help you out of these pajamas and into a tub of swirling hot water. You can help undress me when we get into the bathroom.''

"You seem pleased with the delicious plans I made for us, Drakkar.''

"Extremely pleased. I'm especially pleased with the plans I have for us at the end of each evening, when we're back in this room and all alone.''

"I can hardly wait!''

As the dollar coins poured out of the slot machine at Harrod's Casino, Tarynton was beside herself with excitement. As the coins continued to pour, Drakkar watched her jumping up and down, amused by her reactions to winning two hundred and fifty dollars. He couldn't even begin to imagine what she'd do if it had been a thousand.

"Can you believe I only put one dollar in and got all this back?''

"I can believe it. Aren't you glad I talked you into playing the dollar slots versus the quarter machines?''

"Yeah, but it sounds like you want half of the kitty. Am I right?''

He grinned mischievously. "I want all of the kitty! But you can keep the money.''

She blushed. "You're so awful, talking about making love when I'm on a winning streak.'' She gathered up the coins and put them in the plastic bucket. "You can have the honor of cashing these in for me.''

"You mean you're not going to play anymore?''

"Not a single coin. I know how to go out a winner. I already told you how quick I am to cash in. And you already know how cheap I am.''

Pulling her to him, he kissed her on the mouth. "How

cheap are you? Think I can afford about an hour of your time in my hotel room?"

She threw her head back and laughed. "Not *that* cheap. It took you a whole year to save up for our first time in a hotel room. I'm older and wiser now, so an hour in my company in your hotel suite is going to cost you way more than it did ten years ago. In fact, it may cost more than you can save in a lifetime." She wrinkled her nose. "But I guess I can have mercy on you. The hour won't cost you anything but a kiss and a smile since you've been so sweet to me."

"I can give you more than that, but you'll have to wait until we get back to the hotel to see how much more. Think you can wait?"

"It'll be hard, but I can manage."

"Good. Let's go cash these coins in so we get on with the rest of our evening. You're going to love all the exciting happenings in the heart of the French Quarter."

Fourteen

Tarynton checked her telephone messages before starting her first day back to work. The few days away had been loads of fun, but now it was back to business as usual. In a couple of weeks she'd be taking off again for the Thanksgiving holiday. Much to her joy, there were no hang-ups on the message center. She hoped that Drakkar had gotten through to Tamara and that she had decided to stop the harassment. That would certainly make life easier to bear.

Thoughts of Drakkar had her taking a minute to reflect back on the days in New Orleans. He'd been right about her loving the French Quarter. Drakkar knew every jazz place that there was in the area. He also knew most of the musicians on a first-name basis. Some of the Cajun food was a tad spicy for her, but she thoroughly enjoyed most of the delectable dishes that Drakkar had recommended. She'd never eaten a crawfish before, and now that she'd sampled one, she'd never eat another one. Drakkar had practically forced her to eat the one that she did.

A smile played at the corners of her generous mouth when she thought of the riverboat cruise down the Mississippi. It was romantic even though it was broad daylight. Later in the afternoon they'd hired a cab to take them out to Lake Ponchatrain. Their visits to a couple of plantation homes had been adventurous. She didn't dare think about the hot, romantic nights they'd spent in the hotel suite, not if she wanted to get some work done. The trip had turned out just as she'd planned. Both her and Drakkar's dreams for their stay in the Big Easy had been fulfilled. The only thing they regretted is that the vacation had been far too short.

Putting aside the fact that it didn't last long enough, it had been exciting, romantic, and adventurous—they'd done all the things that Mr. Jenkins thought his sweetheart would love to do, including taking a chance or two with Lady Luck.

In looking at the calendar, Tarynton saw that she and her friends were scheduled for a fitting at Madame Julia's shop at the end of the workday. They also had a meeting scheduled for early in the evening to go over the celebration plans. Everyone was coming to her house.

After taking a minute to think about what she could serve that was fast and easy, she decided to make a large tossed salad and several turkey sandwiches. When she thought of the tomatoes, cucumbers, and white onions that she had marinating in seasoned oil and vinegar, she made up her mind to serve them as well. Chips, dip, and pretzels would make great snack items or maybe she'd even fix some popcorn. Chunks of fresh fruit with whipped topping would be nice for dessert and easy on the hips and thighs. Since she didn't have any fruit on hand, she'd have to run down to the grocery store and pick some up. She made sure to keep the refrigerator stocked with Cool Whip. Drakkar loved to do amazing things with it, especially on her body.

Retrieving her purse from under the desk, Tarynton pressed the inside button to the garage opener. Before she could walk outside to her car, the phone rang. Running back to her desk, she picked up the receiver.

"What about dinner at my place this evening?" Drakkar asked.

"Hey, baby love, how's it going?"

"Pretty good. You sound rushed. Are you in a hurry?"

"I was on my way out to the grocery store. The girls are coming over tonight for a meeting. I'm going to fix a light meal for us, but I'm out of fruit. I plan to have it for dessert."

"I guess I have the answer to my dinner question. How long do you think your meeting will run? If it's not too late, maybe I can come over when you're finished."

"When the six of us get together, time has a tendency to get away from us, so I really can't even give you a rough estimate. But you don't have to wait until the meeting is through to come over. I'm sure the girls would love to see you. In case you haven't noticed, they all have a secret crush on you."

"I'm extremely flattered. What time is dinner?"

"Sandwiches and salad, not a full dinner. Think you can hang with that?"

"I have every confidence that I'm going to be happy with whatever you serve, T.C. Would it help you out if I bring the fruit when I come? I'll even fix it up real nice for you."

"That would be a tremendous help since I also have a fitting scheduled, before the meeting. Oh, Drakkar, I forgot to tell you about the fitting. You're going to need to be there too."

"I just finished with mine. Madame Julia's assistant

called me yesterday as a reminder. Because I wasn't sure how my schedule was going to run, I asked if I could come in earlier than the scheduled time. Her assistant called me back and said it was okay. So I did it already.''

"I'm glad she called, because I sure forgot to tell you about it. You do the fruit, I'll get over to the fitting, and we'll all meet back here around seven o'clock. Does that work for you?''

"Not a problem, baby. I'll see you at seven. Tarynton, I love you.''

"I love you more." Her heart skipped a beat at the words they didn't say often enough.

"That's not possible, but okay. We could debate that issue all night.''

"Hmm, I like that possibility.''

"In that case, shall I bring my jammies and my toothbrush?''

"Only the toothbrush. For what I have in mind, you won't need the jammies." She heard the call-waiting feature click in. "Can you hold for a second?''

"Sure.''

"Tarynton, Denise. Would it be okay if I bought Wilson along with me this evening? He wanted us to get together tonight, but I told him of our meeting plans.''

"I don't see why not. Drakkar is coming by, too. I'll see you at Madame Julia's.''

Tarynton clicked back to Drakkar once Denise rang off. "That was Denise. She's bringing her new beau with her this evening. Things are already starting to get very interesting. I'm going to run now. I'd like to toss the salad before I leave for the fitting. Don't forget the fruit.''

"As long as you don't forget how much I adore you.''

"Never! Good-bye, baby love. Can't wait to feel your arms around me.''

* * *

Drakkar was busy cutting up a variety of fresh apples when the phone rang. After wiping off his hands on a paper towel, he answered the call. Hearing Tamara's voice caused him to tense up. He had to will himself to remain calm. "How are you, Tamara?"

"I'm good, how about you?"

"Fine. What can I do for you?"

"I'm coming to Los Angeles for two weeks right after Thanksgiving. I'll be on assignment and I was wondering if you and I might get together for dinner while I'm there."

He frowned. "I'm not sure that's such a good idea, Tamara. We're supposed to be moving on with our lives."

"No, you're moving on with yours. But I'm only asking you to get together with me for old time's sake. I was willing to see you when you came here."

He noticed how her sweet voice had changed so suddenly to the angry, sour one that he'd become accustomed to. Then the latter part of her sentence had softened considerably. Her two very different personalities bothered him more than anything. "Tamara, you didn't even know that I was coming there to see you. So you can't use that one to gain leverage."

"Are you sure about that?"

"About what?'

"That I didn't know you were coming. Have you forgotten that I make it my business to know everything there is to know about you?"

No, he hadn't forgotten. He sighed hard. "So we're back to that, huh? I thought we had come to an amicable understanding on the issues of our past relationship. When you stopped the harassment, I thought everything was cool between us."

"So much for what you thought. But everything is cool between us. It will be even cooler if we have one last evening together. I promise to be on my best behavior. I won't try to seduce you even though I think you can be. I'm sure you haven't forgotten how good I am in bed."

"Tamara, don't! I'm in a committed relationship and I don't want to do anything to upset that. I think we should just nix this whole idea. One last evening is not going to change anything between us. I'm going to ask Tarynton to marry me when we go to her parents' home in Atlanta over the Thanksgiving holiday." He cursed himself for giving up that type of crucial information.

"Marry you? That's a joke. Have you forgotten that you weren't her first choice as a husband? Better read that letter again. At any rate, I still think we should do this. In the light of this new information you've sprung on me, I think it's imperative that we get together one last time. It might be a good idea to wait until after Thanksgiving to make the proposal. Once you hear what I have to say, you may not want to propose at all. The lady is not all that you think she is."

Tamara's remarks puzzled him, but he wasn't going to ask her to clarify her statement about Tarynton. He wanted this conversation over with even though he was curious as hell about her mention of the letter. "When are you going to be in Los Angeles?" After she gave him the dates, he let several moments of silence pass between them to make her think he was at least checking his calendar. "Sorry, but my schedule is completely full for both of those weeks."

"Change it!"

He looked totally bewildered. Before he could respond, the phone receiver was slammed down loudly in his ear. So much for peace in the valley. Tamara wasn't through with him yet. It looked as if she'd only given him a brief respite. Even though he knew it wasn't the answer, he briefly considered her request. Tamara would be all over him like a cheap suit if he were to give in to her demands. There was no doubt that her last remark was a demand. She certainly hadn't said *will* you change it. This woman had more nerve than anyone he'd ever met.

In debating whether to tell Tarynton of this latest development in the dramatic episode of Tamara Lyndon, he decided not to mention it unless Tamara started harassing her again. For sure, he wasn't going to have one last evening with this woman who constantly kept him on edge. But he couldn't rule out the possibility that she'd show up at his place to try and force a meeting between them. Suddenly his future with Tarynton wasn't looking as bright as he'd once thought.

At the front door of her house Tarynton greeted Drakkar with an awe-inspiring kiss. "Did you remember to bring your toothbrush?"

He first handed her the wrapped package containing the fresh fruit tray. He then held up his shaving kit for her to see. "And I also remembered *not* to bring my PJs." He brought her to him for another kiss. "I have a change of clothes, but I left them in the car. Didn't think you wanted everyone to know I had no intentions of leaving your house tonight."

While playfully tweaking his ear, she laughed. "There are times when you are so sweetly incorrigible. But I love that about you. Come on in. Everyone else is here. We were waiting on you so we can all eat together."

He swatted her on the rear end. "I'm right behind you, baby. Lead the way."

"Drakkar is here," Tarynton announced as she swept into the room. Tarynton was amused by all of her friends looking so eager to get just a glimpse of him. "Don't rush the table all at once, divas. You've been whining about eating since you got here, so let's get on with it. Sorry, ladies, my delicious-looking man is not on the dinner menu." Everyone had a good laugh at that.

"Can't we just eat in here for a more informal setting?" Roxanne asked. "We can conduct our meeting between bites. That's what we normally do."

Tarynton shrugged. "Not a problem. Let's all go into the kitchen and grab the food and bring it in here. Drakkar, you and Wilson can relax. You're our special guests this evening."

"Not me," Drakkar said. "It usually costs me something when you girls wait on me. I'm helping. How about you, Wilson? Want to help us bring the meal out?"

"No, Drakkar," Tarynton protested. "There aren't that many dishes to bring in here."

Drakkar looked at her out of one eye. "Are you sure you don't have something up your sleeve? You're acting weird."

She pulled a face at him. "I am weird. Take a load off, lover. You're holding up progress. Let me warn you. We women are like bears with sore tails when we get too hungry."

"Okay, okay, I get the message." Smiling, Drakkar looked after Tarynton as she left the room. Once she disappeared, he turned to Wilson. "How are things going for you?"

"They couldn't be better. Getting ready to go on the road for a couple of weeks."

"Where you off to?"

"We're going to play the New England states. Then we'll head down South for a few days. We'll be home just in time for Thanksgiving. I'm anxious to play Atlanta."

"Did Denise tell you that Tarynton's parents live in Atlanta?"

"She did mention that. She also talked about having Tarynton call her parents and have them come out and support us."

"I heard my name. What are you two saying about me?" Tarynton looked at Drakkar as she placed the tray of turkey sandwiches on the coffee table. "Are you telling my secrets?"

Drakkar grinned. "Which secrets?"

"If I told you, they would no longer be secrets."

He raised an eyebrow. "Acting weird is starting to seem like an understatement. I'm going to leave that one alone."

Wilson laughed. "I can sure tell that Tarynton is Denise's friend."

"And what do you mean by that?" Denise asked while setting the chips and dip down.

"Yeah, we'd all like to hear the answer to that, Wilson," Roxanne chimed in. Narita, Chariese, and Rayna also looked interested in the answer.

"I think I need to plead the Fifth on this one. You ladies look ready to beat me down if I say the wrong thing. No malice was intended." The expression on his face was one of uncertainty. He didn't seem to know what he'd just stepped into.

"At ease, ladies," Drakkar commanded, laughing. "Give the brother a break. Tarynton, since I'm your special guest, what about fixing me a plate?"

"It sounds to me like you're trying to change the subject and weasel Wilson a way out of this. But I'm too hungry to care what he meant by that questionable remark. Let's leave the interrogation for Denise to conduct later. Mr. Lomax, will you please lead us in prayer?"

"By all means, Miss Batiste. Please bow your heads."

Once all the smoked turkey sandwiches were passed

around, each person took a turn getting the salad. After Tarynton put two sandwiches on Drakkar's plate, she filled the salad bowl with the tossed greens. Knowing his choice in salad dressing, she doused it with a reasonable amount of ranch. Drakkar didn't like his salad soggy. Using a paper plate, she piled it with Ruffles potato chips and plopped several spoonfuls of avocado dip on the side. She then took the plate over to Drakkar and handed it to him.

"Where's yours?" Drakkar asked Tarynton.

"I'm going to fix it now, but you go ahead and eat. It's only going to take me a minute."

Once everyone was settled down, and had taken a few bites of their food, Denise began the discussion on how things were shaping up for the Kwanzaa/New Year's Eve celebration. "The Kwanzaa portion will begin at three o'clock and end at five-thirty P.M. The New Year's Eve event would begin at seven that same evening. There'll be about a forty-five-minute reception and then dinner will be served at seven forty-five sharp."

"I don't know if that gives me enough time between events to make myself even more beautiful for the next one," Roxanne interjected. Everyone gave Roxanne looks of intolerance. "What? You all know it takes me lots of time to prepare myself."

"Well, if you can't do it in an hour and a half, I guess you'll just have to miss the reception. That's your call," Rayna remarked.

"Roxy is just running her mouth. The way she loves to flaunt her beautiful self, especially when she's all dressed up, she'll be there on time. When have we not known her to throw a monkey wrench into most of our plans? That's just her nature," Chariese added.

Tarynton laughed along with the others. "I feel Roxy. I remember when I was upset about having to purchase two separate outfits. But the other day when I was cleaning out my closet, I found the cutest outfit hung way in the back. The colorful print of the fabric will fit in perfectly for the Kwanzaa event. So I can save my royal attire for the other celebration."

"You two are so vain," Denise accused Tarynton and Roxanne. "I don't know why you can't wear the same outfit to both events."

Laughing, Drakkar and Wilson exchanged amused glances. When all the female eyes turned on them, they got quiet.

"We're sorry," Denise said to both guys. "We don't normally act this way in front of company. But this is mild compared to what we do when it's just us, though we're always very respectful to each other. We just like to needle each other for fun." Smiling beautifully at Wilson, Denise cleared her throat. "Wilson and I have a surprise announcement to make, a very big one. We hope you're going to be excited about it."

The other women exchanged worried glances. Some of Denise's other surprises had been rather scary ones. Tarynton thought about the time Denise announced that she was going on a Safari to Africa with an African male exchange student she'd only known for a couple of weeks.

"Well, here goes! Wilson and I are going to be married." Everyone looked shocked, even Wilson. Denise couldn't help laughing at the expressions on everyone's faces.

"No, that's not the surprise. I thought I'd shock you all first, since that's what you're used to from me. Wilson and his band have agreed to play for us on New Year's Eve. The best is yet to come. They're not going to charge us. We're going to have the extremely talented Mystic Jazz Troupe play at our event!" Everyone clapped to show excitement and approval of the surprise.

Wilson wiped the nonexistent sweat from his brow,

smiling at Denise. "Girl, you had me worried there for a minute. You had me wondering if I'd proposed to you under the influence of an overdose of Seven-Up, since that's all I drink." Everyone laughed again.

Denise kissed her new man softly on the mouth. "Would that have been so bad if you had proposed?" she asked boldly. The other women held their breath in anticipation of his response.

"Take my advice and plead the Fifth on that one, too, my man. That's a loaded question. And you're in a no-win position," Drakkar advised Wilson.

"Okay, enough of this already," Tarynton gently chided her friends. "We need to get on with this meeting and get it over with. Drakkar and I have some serious business to attend to."

Inquiring eyes all turned on Drakkar.

"Don't look at me! She's the one that made the announcement," Drakkar charged.

"Can we stay and watch?" Roxanne playfully inquired of Tarynton and Drakkar.

"You need Jesus, Roxy, 'cause you're sick!" Tarynton turned to Chariese. "Were you able to pick up the items for the Kwanzaa table to be used at the *karamu*, which is the feast?"

"I have some of them. I'll run down for you what I have." Chariese pulled a white sheet of paper from her purse. "Here we go. I have the *kinara*, candleholder; the *mkeka*, a straw place mat; *kikombe cha umoja*, communal unity cup; and the *mishumaa saba*, the seven candles, one black, three red, and three green. I will wait until the day before the event to gather the *mazao*, the fruits and vegetables. Since none of us have children, I'm not sure if we'll need the *vibunzi*, ears of corn to reflect the number of children in the household. I also have a straw basket to place the crops in when I get them. And I purchased a *bendera*, the Kwanzaa flag."

"We don't have kids, but there will be other guests that do. Two ears of corn should be placed on the mat regardless. In keeping with the seven principles, the children of the community belong to all of us. *Ujima*, collective work and responsibility, reminds us of obligation to the past, present, and future. It also reminds us that we have a role to play in the community, in society, and in the world," Denise offered. "Children are a part of every community."

Drakkar held up his hand. "Isn't Kwanzaa celebrated over seven days? But you all seem to be focusing on just the sixth day. What are you going to do on the other six days?"

Tarnyton's adoration for Drakkar blazed up in her eyes. "Kwanzaa is based on the seven guiding principles. We observe one of the seven principles for each day. The observance can be done separately or collectively. One candle is lit for each day. For example: The first day is *Umoja*, unity, and then you observe another principle the next day, and go on from there. *Karamu* feast, which is what we're having, is celebrated on the sixth day. The last day of Kwanzaa is the first day of the New Year, a day of assessment of things done, things to do, self-reflection, and recommitment. Creative gifts traditionally are opened on the last day."

Drakkar grinned with satisfaction. "I can see that you're continuing to do your research. As I said before, you should be proud of yourself. I'm certainly proud of you."

"We're all proud of you, Tarynton," Denise chimed in. "I can't wait to read your article. When is it due?"

"Though it's not due until the first week of December, I'm turning it in before I leave for the Thanksgiving holidays. It'll run in the January issue of the magazine *Black Unity*. It's a very appropriate article. At first, I didn't know if I could do it justice, but I think my avarice appetite in gaining information on something I knew next to nothing about will make it a success."

"I'm sure," Narita said. "Speaking of Thanksgiving, where's everyone going to be?"

"Atlanta for me," Tarynton responded, "in less than two weeks."

"Home to San Francisco," Rayna remarked. "Cheriese is going home with me."

Roxanne didn't look too happy about the question. "I tend to isolate during the holidays since they weren't a very pleasant time in our home. My dad always got drunk and messed up everything for the family. Somebody should've taught him the seven principles of Kwanzaa. I'll probably be alone in my apartment with Mr. Tom."

"Mr. Tom? Who the heck is that?" Tarynton asked.

Freeing herself of the sudden dark mood, Roxanne laughed heartily. "Mr. Tom Turkey!" Everyone burst into laughter.

"You're not going to be alone, Roxy. I'm going to cook the meats, just like I've done for the past couple of years," Denise said. "The rest of the dinner is supplied through potluck. All of you that don't have plans can come to my house for dinner. You can bring along your favorite holiday dish. I usually have a large crowd and we have a blast. It normally lasts until the late evening."

Wilson nudged Denise. "Does that invitation include me?"

Denise flirted with him using her eyes. "Especially you!"

Tarynton looked at Narita. "You asked the question, but I didn't hear you state your plans. What are you going to do?"

"I really didn't know until this very moment. That's why I asked. Denise, you can count me in as a guest at your house. I'll bring a vegetable dish and several sweet potato pies."

"You got it," Denise sang out. "Your macaroni and cheese is to die for. Hint, hint."

Wilson turned to Drakkar. "We haven't heard your plans either, man."

"Tarynton and I are joined together at the hip. I'm heading to Atlanta with my baby. In case you haven't heard, she and I grew up together. We fell in love not long out of the cradle. Her family is my family and vice versa. She and I have been apart for a few years, but we couldn't find anyone that we liked better than we liked each other. Destiny brought us back from the unknown to the very familiar."

"That's real nice, man," Wilson said to Drakkar. "I wish you both the best of luck."

Tarynton felt uncomfortable during Drakkar and Wilson's exchange of personal information. She didn't like Drakkar's assessment of their time apart. He obviously had found someone he liked very much, enough to keep him away for six long years.

Tarynton turned her attention back to her guests. "Is there anything else we need to discuss regarding the events?"

Denise raised her hand. "I want to report that the tickets will be ready in a couple of days. I've already approved the final draft of the layout that we chose as a group. The gold ink was really expensive so I went with the black. I hope that's okay with everyone. If not, it's too late now. The printer has already gotten started."

"We had already talked about that. We left it up to you to decide, so no one should have a problem with it," Tarynton mentioned. The other women nodded their approval. "Well, with that said, I think we can adjourn this meeting. It looks like everything is right on schedule."

* * *

The phone rang just as Tarynton snuggled herself into Drakkar's arms. Her first thought was to let the answering service pick up the call, but something told her it might be important. Drakkar groaned as she moved away from him to respond to the ring. Tarynton froze at the sweet voice on the end. Although she'd only heard this voice calling her a vulgar name out of anger, she instinctively knew that it was Tamara. It was confirmed for her when Tamara identified herself as the caller.

"I called to see if it's possible for us to get together while I'm in Los Angeles. I'll be there for two weeks on a special assignment." Tamara then told Tarynton the dates she'd be in town. "Drakkar and I will be having dinner also, but we haven't decided on the date. I would really like to meet you. I think we have some interesting things to discuss."

Tarynton looked at Drakkar. The look on his face made her think that he knew who was on the other end of the phone line. When Tarynton silently mouthed Tamara's name, he sat straight up in the bed.

"Are you still there?" Tamara asked.

"I'm here. I was pondering your request, but I can't think of a thing for us to discuss."

"In a single word, Drakkar."

"What would you like to discuss about Drakkar? I know everything there is to know about him. We've only known each other all of our lives, twenty-eight years."

"That may be true, but I know there were at least six years missing out of that equation. If I'm correct in saying this, it's those six years of what you don't know about his life that's probably killing you. I'd be happy to fill in the gaps."

"I'm sure you would. If I ever have the desire for

such, Drakkar will be the one to clue me in. In fact, he's already tried. Sorry to disappoint you, but I have no burning desire to know anything about Drakkar's life when I wasn't a part of it. The past belongs in the past."

"That's very gallant of you. However, I still think you might want to hear what I have to say. Personally, I don't think you can have a future until you've cleared the dust from the past."

"I don't agree with that. If whatever you have to tell me is so important, maybe you should tell me while you have me on the phone."

"I didn't say it was important. I said that there are some things that you might want to know. And you won't know what they are unless you take the opportunity to hear me out."

"I guess I won't know then." Drakkar was going crazy trying to figure things out.

"You'll be sorry. But suit yourself. There are many surprises yet to come."

Tarynton could no longer deny that she was getting more curious by the second. But this was one curiosity she wasn't going to allow herself the satisfaction that knowing might bring. It could turn out to be something that she'd be better off not knowing. She couldn't help wondering what Tamara meant by more surprises to come. Tamara's last statement needed clarification.

"Surprises or more criminal acts against me?"

Drakkar finally put his ear to the phone.

"Why, sweetie, I see that Drakkar has you believing all sorts of bad things about me. I'm innocent of all charges, and no one can prove otherwise. If you'll meet with me, you'll learn all sorts of things about Drakkar, things that you can't begin to imagine."

"You know what? Maybe I will meet with you. Give me a call when you get into town. We can finalize the plans then. Keep in mind that lunchtime works best for me."

"Glad to hear that you've come to your senses. You won't be sorry."

"Is that all?"

Disgusted, Drakkar lay back and covered his eyes with his arms.

"For now. Tell Drakkar I said good night!" Tamara said.

Chills ran up and down Tarynton's back as she cradled the receiver. Tarynton was in no doubt that Tamara knew Drakkar was there with her. Visibly shaken, she went into Drakkar's arms. With his thought process in utter turmoil, he held her close to him. They lay there in total silence for several minutes.

Drakkar rolled up on his side and looked down at Tarynton. "I'm really concerned that you agreed to meet with her. I'm even more fearful of what she's capable of. I thought that I'd gotten through to her when we met, but that theory has been blown right out the window. I'm now back to trying to guess her next move."

"Fearful for me or fearful of what she might tell me about you?"

"I guess you think that your comment was fair?"

Tarynton shook her head. "I don't know what's fair anymore. I'm tired of all of it. Maybe I should've let you call it off between us when you suggested it before. This broad is not going to let us have any peace. I can see that clearly now. She's not going to stop until she gets what she's after. And she's after you. By the way, she told me to tell you good night."

He had no intention of responding to Tamara's message. "I never said I wanted to call it off. I only suggested putting our relationship on hold. I'm going to tell you the same thing you told me when I made that stupid suggestion. We are not going to do anything to disrupt our relationship. You also said that we couldn't give her our power and that we shouldn't break up just to satisfy her. Did those words not come out of your mouth, T.C.?"

"I admit to saying all of that. I also believed it at the time."

"So what's changed? Why are you considering us ending our relationship?"

"Can we sleep on this whole matter? I'm afraid I'm not thinking very clearly right now."

"I think that's a great idea. But I have to ask you this. Do you think it's in your best interest to have a meeting with her? No good can come of it."

Tarynton blew out a ragged breath. "I'm not going to meet with her. I just did that to buy time. If she thinks she and I are getting together, she may not do anything else drastic. She won't want to risk doing something that would cause me to change my mind. I have no intentions of meeting with this crazy sister. If you couldn't get through to her, I sure as hell can't."

Drakkar shuddered as he thought about Tamara saying she would've slashed Tarynton's throat instead of her tires if she'd been given the chance. If Tarynton had decided to meet with her, he would've had to tell her. Because Tarynton looked so worn down, he decided he would wait and tell her over breakfast in the morning. But she had to be told. It then dawned on him that he hadn't told Tarynton about Tamara's phone call to him.

"One more thing before we go to sleep. I also got a call from Tamara. It came before I left to come over here. It has suddenly occurred to me that she's trying to play us against each other. She tells each of us that she has something secretlike to reveal about the other. This is just another blatant attempt to pull us apart."

He grew silent for a couple of seconds. "I was going to wait until morning to tell you this, but I guess it's best to get it all out now. When I met with Tamara in New Orleans, the damage to your tires came up. She claims she's innocent, but she said something that really disturbed me. She told me that she would've slashed your throat, not your tires, if given the chance. Please, whatever else you do regarding this situation, don't change your mind about seeing her. You'd be placing yourself directly in harm's way."

Tarynton curled her body up against his. "I wish you had waited until morning. I'm probably going to have nightmares of Tamara holding a razor against my neck. I'm glad you're here. Promise to hold me all night?"

"I promise. And I want you to promise me that we're not going to let this ruin our upcoming holidays and that we're going forward with all our plans. Can you do that for me?"

She kissed him on the mouth tenderly. "I can do it for us. I promise."

The next couple of weeks for Tarynton seemed to drag on and on. She hadn't realized how many loose ends she had to tie up until she started working toward completing her tasks. Keeping busy helped her to take her mind off of the recent unpleasantness with Tamara.

While sitting her desk, she rechecked her list of things to do to make sure she had in fact accomplished everything on it. With that done, she went on the Web and programmed an away message for all her incoming e-mail. Since her parents were also on-line, she could check her messages from Atlanta. She also had Internet access on her laptop.

She checked the time. Drakkar was scheduled to pick her up in less than forty-five minutes. Satisfied that all her tasks were updated and completed, she shut the computer down. After reaching her bedroom, she looked around the room to make sure that she didn't forget anything important. As she ventured into the bathroom, she saw that her toiletry bag was still on the counter. She remembered that she'd left it out until she finished with her toothbrush and makeup. Glad that she'd done a second last-minute check, she retrieved the bag and packed it in her overnighter for easy access.

Excited about seeing her family, she made sure all her bags were closed securely before going into the living room where she'd wait for Drakkar to arrive. When he'd phoned earlier, he had told her to leave the bags for him to take care of. She was only too happy to obey.

A smile lit up her eyes as she thought of the four days that she'd spend in Atlanta. She couldn't wait to see her parents and her brother. Surprising them with Drakkar would be the icing on the cake. In her mind, this was going to be the most exciting holiday yet in the Batiste home. It was truly going to be like old times.

Fifteen

Tarynton could barely wait for Drakkar to stop the rental car in the driveway of the Batiste home in an upscale Atlanta suburb. At the same moment he put the gear in park, she was out of the car. Before reaching the front porch, she ran back to the car and opened the passenger door. "Only give us a couple of minutes before you come in. You might want to drive up the block and come back. I want this to be a total surprise. I'll leave the front door open for you."

"I got my end covered. Get on in there and see your parents before your heart gives out."

She blew him a kiss and then took off. Before entering the house, she waited for him to back out of the driveway and get halfway up the street. Taking a few deep breaths to calm her overexcited heart, she opened the storm door. Using the house keys her parents had given her on her first visit to them in their new home, she opened the front door and went inside.

"Mom," she called out as she started down the hall-way. "I'm home. Where are you?"

Pamela Batiste seemed to appear out of nowhere. "Oh, baby, Mommy's so happy to see her little girl." Pamela gathered her daughter into her arms and hugged her tightly. "You feel so good." Pamela held Tarynton at arm's length. "Let me look at my baby girl. Tarynton, you're still as pretty as ever. You look more rested than you did on your last visit." Pamela's large brown eyes shone with pleasure at seeing her daughter looking so well.

"Mom, you still have that great figure. You have a tad more gray in your beautiful mahogany-brown hair, but it's striking against your dark caramel complexion. You're looking so hot, lady." Tarynton warmly embraced Pamela for a brief moment. "Where's Daddy?"

Pamela put her arm around her daughter's shoulder and guided her into the beautifully appointed family room. All the seating was done in a mixture of fine gray and burgundy leather. Mahogany bookshelves took up an entire wall. A big-screen television and entertainment center took up another one. Gray and black throw rugs covered a portion of the shiny ceramic tile floor. It was warm and welcoming for such a large amount of space.

"He just stepped out, but he'll be right back. He went down to the corner store." Pamela snapped her fingers. "Where's your young man? You didn't leave him outside, did you?"

"He's getting the bags out of the rental car." Just as they'd planned, Drakkar entered the room. He was to come in when he heard Pamela ask about Tarynton's houseguest.

Tarynton smiled brilliantly. "Mom, my old boyfriend, my best friend, and my new love interest are one in the same. It's time to reacquaint yourself with the young man you've known since he was a baby."

Pamela nearly fainted when she saw Drakkar step into her vision. Then tears sprang to her eyes. "Oh, my God, I would never have guessed that Tarynton was talking about you. She gave nothing away when she was telling me about the new man in here life. Come here and give me a big hug, Drakkar. I'm so happy to see you. And you're still so very handsome."

Drakkar hugged Pamela and kissed her on both cheeks. "It's good to see you, too. Thanks for welcoming me into your home as a guest. I'm thrilled to be here. I wish my parents could be here also. We were all so close at one time."

"Guest? Boy, this is your home. Steven and I have always thought of you as a son." Pamela slapped her hands on both sides of her face. "Steven is going to lose his grip when he sees you two here together. He's been having a hard time preparing himself to meet your new boyfriend. Drakkar has always been his choice for you. This is such a wonderful surprise. Our Cinderella has pulled it off again. Come on in here and sit down. We've got a lot of catching up to do. Six years' worth."

Tarynton dropped down on the sofa and Drakkar sat down beside her. "When is Camden getting in, Mom?"

"He should be here at any minute. He left Raleigh long before the sun came up. He's called a couple of times to keep me posted on his whereabouts. I can't wait to see his girlfriend. Since he didn't have any special girls in his life, I'm sure it won't be someone we already know. All I know about her is that her name is Tiara."

"Tiara," Tarynton reiterated, "that's a nice name . . ."

Pamela put her finger up to his lips to quiet her daughter. "I think I hear your Dad," she whispered. "We should surprise him, too. Drakkar, go into the hall bathroom and wait until he comes in here to greet Tarynton. He'll know she's here when he sees the rental car. I just hope he doesn't have a heart attack when he sees you."

"I hope not, too." Smiling, Drakkar left the room.

Pamela squeezed her daughter's hand. "This is almost too much excitement for me. But it's the best surprise I've ever had. Thanks for keeping me in suspense. It's all been worth it."

Tarynton's father called out to his wife as soon as he came in from the garage.

"I'm in here," Pamela responded to his shout.

Steven Batiste appeared in a matter of seconds. His light brown eyes lit up the moment they settled on Tarynton. Standing well over six feet, he was a good-looking man. His wavy russet-brown hair was gray on the sides and at the temples. "There she is! Hello, beautiful." Tarynton flew into her father's arms, kissing him all over his face. "How was your flight, baby?"

"Great, Dad. I was disappointed that you were out when I got here. But I'm happy that you're here now. Can I get another hug?"

He brought her back into his warm embrace. "You can have as many hugs as you can stand. There's no shortage of them in this house." He looked around the room. "I thought you were bringing a guest home."

Just as before, Drakkar appeared in front of Steven, which caused Steven to step back.

Unable to believe his eyes, Steven stretched them to make sure he was seeing right. Then he began laughing uncontrollably. As he hugged Drakkar, he pounded him hard on the back. "Son, I can't believe it's really you. It's been a long time." Steven then looked at his daughter. "Is this just a coincidence or is Drakkar the guest you've been talking with your mother about?"

Tarynton grinned. "No coincidence. He's the man!"

"Well, I'll be doggoned! This reunion is wonderful

for all of us in so many ways. I can't wait to see Camden's face. Or does he already know about this?"

Tarynton shook her head. "Nope. I kept this from everyone. If Camden had known, Mom would've known. She can get anything she wants out of him."

"Is that so?" Camden asked as he came into the room.

"Cam!" Tarynton squealed. "You're here." She leaped into her brother's arms. Tarynton could see how much Camden was starting to look like their father. The older Camden got, the more he looked like Steven. They were the same height and had the same light-colored eyes. Camden also had the same color hair as his Dad before shaving it off. He was sporting the ever-growing popular bald look. And Tarynton thought it looked darn good on her gorgeous brother.

Drakkar couldn't take his eyes off the woman that came into the room with Camden. It was obvious to him that Tarynton hadn't seen the female newcomer yet. Knowing that her reaction wasn't going to be a good one, he hated to have her go through this. Before he could latch on to his next thought, Tarynton turned around and saw the woman with Camden.

Nearly choking on her own saliva, Tarynton began to cough uncontrollably, which sent Pamela fleeing into the kitchen to get her daughter a glass of water. Looking concerned for his sister, Camden took her arms and lifted them over her head to try and stop her choking spell. Pamela rushed back into the room with the water and handed the glass to Tarynton. After several sips of the cool liquid, Tarynton's coughing spell was eventually brought under control.

Camden made sure his sister was okay before he formally introduced his guest to the entire group. Tamara Lyndon looped her arm through Camden's as he looked down at her as if he were looking into the eyes of an angel in heaven. Tarynton and Drakkar stared on in disbelief as Camden simply introduced his friend as Tiara. No last name was given. Tarynton cringed inwardly when her mother embraced the beautiful but very evil woman.

While Camden started introducing the woman he called Tiara to each person in the room, she smiled so beautifully, making Tarynton want to throw up. When Camden got to Tarynton and Drakkar, Tiara didn't blink an eye. Not so much as a flicker of recognition for either of them flashed in Tiara's eyes. As though he needed to protect her from an evil spirit, Drakkar moved up behind Tarynton and put his hands on each side of her waist. *She's damn good at dark deception,* Drakkar mused, squeezing Tarynton's waist. Drakkar's hands on her helped to calm her down.

Tarynton noticed that Drakkar had paled considerably. She felt sorrier for him than she did for herself. She knew that he felt responsible for everything this phony woman did. Her concern was for how they were going to get through this latest nightmarish episode. An even bigger concern for her was how to protect her brother and keep him from getting hurt by the she-devil on his arm. Camden was just seriously trying his hand at love and it would be devastating to him to have his heart broken the first time out.

Camden leaned forward and kissed Tarynton on the nose. "This is my sister, Tarynton, the radiant beauty that I go on and on about all the time. Isn't she lovely, Tiara?"

Tiara nodded. "Very much so. She's as beautiful as you are handsome."

As hard as it was for her to do, Tarynton smiled. "Thank you, Tiara."

Chills raced up and down Drakkar's spine. There wasn't even a hint of a southern accent in the woman's voice. The conversation he and Tarynton had had about actors and actresses came to mind. Tamara was better than damn good. She was a master of poignant deception.

Pamela came over and embraced both her daughter and her son. "These are two of the brightest stars in my universe. Steven and I are so happy to have all our family home together. Thank you for being here with us for the holidays." She then brought Drakkar into her circle. "Tiara, Drakkar is our surrogate son. He's been in our lives since he was a little baby. He grew up with Camden and Tarynton. We love him as if he were one of our own."

"I second that," Steven announced with pride. "He has always been our boy."

Camden smiled at Drakkar. "Welcome back, my brother. We've missed having you around. Am I right in assuming that you and my sister have recharged that special glow you two always wore when you were together? If so, I hope everything works out between you."

"You have assumed right, and it will work out," Drakkar said emphatically. His message was meant more for Tamara than anyone else. "We've never stopped loving each other."

"Any wedding plans being discussed between you two?" Camden inquired.

Drakkar looked at Tarynton with adoration in his eyes. "We haven't discussed it yet, but we both know it's inevitable. Tarynton and I are meant to be together." Although he'd told Tamara that he was going to propose to Tarynton while in Atlanta, he didn't want to say anything about it to the others until he'd actually done so in private. This was definitely not the right moment.

Tarynton could barely breathe. First of all, she couldn't believe Camden had been so bold as to ask that question of Drakkar. The look Tarynton gave her brother let him know that he was out of line. Secondly, Drakkar's comments regarding marriage had also stunned her.

Tarynton watched Tamara for any signs of anger or distress over Drakkar's remarks, but all she saw was a beautiful smile. She seemed to have eyes only for Camden, but Tarynton wasn't fooled one bit by her premier performance. *Well, you better get a good, long look at him, Tamara/Tiara, whoever the hell you are, because your days are numbered. After this long holiday weekend, you are history in my brother's life.* Tarynton didn't know how she and Drakkar were going to pull this thing off, but she wouldn't think of upsetting her family's holiday. And she was sure that Tamara was banking on that. This woman was a very clever one.

Tarynton looped her arm through Drakkar's. "Now that everyone has been introduced, Drakkar and I are going to bring our bags in and get settled down. We've had a long flight. I'm sure we could both use a shower. Separately, of course," she joked, eyeing her father for his reaction. He only smiled and winked his eye at the daughter he absolutely adored.

"Tiara and I should get comfortable as well. Mom, can you show us where you want everyone to bunk for the next four days?"

"You and Tarynton can sleep where you always sleep when you're home. I'll let you guys decide which of the guest rooms you want to use for your guests. Aunt Cleo is going to take the sofa bed in the den when she gets here." Pamela looked at her watch. "I'm going to serve the evening meal around six-thirty. Aunt Cleo should be here by then. Is everyone going to eat here or have you made other plans for the evening?"

Camden frowned. "Mom, you've got enough to do in cooking for Thanksgiving. Why don't we just order food and have it delivered in? Is that idea okay with you guys?" Everyone nodded in agreement.

Shrugging her shoulders, Pamela turned up her palms and held them out. "Whatever you all want to do is okay with me. But I can't stand the thought of having to freeze that beautiful lasagna I prepared in your honor."

Lasagna was the magical word for Camden. It was his favorite dish and he didn't think anyone in the world could prepare it like his mother. "Let's trash the take-out idea since there isn't a one of us who doesn't love Mom's lasagna. Tiara, you're in for a real treat. My mother is black, but she has an Italian thumb. The lady can throw down on Italian dishes, but her soul food dishes are her specialty." Camden beamed at his mother. It was obvious that mother and son had a special relationship, the same as what Tarynton shared with her father.

"Mom, Drakkar and I will be here for dinner. We're all here to spend time with you and Dad. Even if we do other things, we'll be taking all of our meals here. Drakkar wants to visit the Martin Luther King Center, but we'll do that during the day. And I never come to Atlanta without checking out the underground shopping facilities. Both of those are something we can all do together." She winced at just the thought of having to spend all of her vacation time in Tamara's presence, but it was too late now. She'd already opened her big mouth. Hopefully Camden would have something else in mind for himself and the she-devil.

As everyone parted to get settled in, Tarynton and Drakkar headed out to the car to retrieve their bags. Steven followed them out to help so they'd only have to make one trip. Once their belongings were stored in separate rooms, Steven went back downstairs, and

Tarynton and Drakkar went down the hall to the audio-visual room/den.

This extremely large room was also filled with fine leather furnishings done in navy blue. The sectional sofa was equipped with reclining seats on both ends and the big screen stationed on one wall was even bigger than the one in the family room. The oak bookshelves were filled with hundreds of albums and the entertainment center housed state-of-the art audio equipment. Stacks of CDs were stored in several metal racks.

As soon as Drakkar closed the door to insure their privacy, Tarynton burst into tears. He immediately gathered her into his arms. "I know, baby. This is an unbelievable situation. How does she do it—and with such calm?" He led Tarynton over to the sofa and they both sat down.

Tarynton sniffled. "Did you mean what you said to Camden?"

"About wedding plans being inevitable?" She nodded, fighting back her tears. "With all of my heart. I meant every single word of it."

She began to cry again. "I want that, too, so very much. I love you, Drakkar. But I think we should wait before we decide on marriage. There are too many issues that have to be settled."

"Baby, I love you more than I can say. I can only show you how much. I will do my very best never to let you down. As soon as we get everything straightened out with Tamara, we'll sit down and talk about it then."

"I thought maybe you were just sending a message to Tamara when you answered Camden's question the way you did."

"That, too. Tarynton, I know you don't want to hear this, but I've got to say it anyway. When you wrote that letter telling me you'd found someone new, that you were engaged, I nearly died inside. The thought of you marrying someone other than me broke me up pretty badly. It was then that I turned to Tamara, for no other reason than that. My heart was fragmented beyond repair. She had been after me since the day I started school at Grambling, and in my pain I did the unthinkable. I slept with a woman I had no respect for."

The look on Tarynton's face made him regret that he'd gone against her wishes regarding talking about the past. She looked as if he'd stuck a dagger deep into her heart. Since he had dared to speak on it, she could no longer remain in denial over what had occurred between them six years ago. The facts were right in front of her face. It was time for her to deal with the truth.

He cupped her face in his hands. "I'm sorry I brought up the past. But talking about marriage gets me all worked up. I do want to marry you, Tarynton, but I refuse to go into the future with the shadow of the past hanging over our heads."

Tears poured from her eyes. "You bastard! How could you turn the truth of what happened around on me? How can you sit there and lie like that? And right to my face." She began to get hysterical.

Her reaction was scaring the daylights out of Drakkar. He shook her hard to bring her around. "What are you talking about? I can't believe how much in denial that you are. Listen to yourself, T.C."

Tarynton jumped up and stormed out of the room in a red rage. He followed after her. When she went into her bedroom, he stopped short of the doorway. Thinking that he should let her have some space, he started to go back into the den. She was in his face before he could turn around. She darn near pushed him into her bedroom and shut the door. She then thrust a worn typewritten letter into his hand.

Standing with her back to the door, as if she were barring his escape route, she glared at him with undisguised hostility. "You were the one who wrote the letter saying you were going to marry someone else, not me. I carry that letter with me everywhere I go. Read it for yourself, though I can't imagine that you haven't read it a thousand times from inside your head. I know that letter word for word, even the misspelled ones. I'm sure you do, too."

It was Drakkar's turn to look stunned. As he read the letter, tears filled his eyes. After reading the letter several times, he finally looked up at Tarynton. "I didn't write this letter to you. In fact, this letter says the same exact thing as the one I supposedly received from you. You were right when you said that I've gone over every word in this letter in my head a thousand times. These words are burned into my brain. I also kept the letter I received. I can't count the number of times I read it. It wasn't signed. It really made me angry that you didn't even bother to take the time to endorse your Dear John. I see that this one isn't signed either."

"Tamara?" they said in unison.

Trembling all over, Tarynton walked over to the queen-size bed and sat down. She then reached her hand out to Drakkar and he sat down beside her. "Could it have been her, Drakkar? But you said you only turned to her after you received the letter. So shouldn't that exclude her as the culprit?"

"That's true enough, but that doesn't necessarily rule her out. Like I told you, she was all over me from the start. She was also a very good friend to Charles Dody."

"Your college roommate, right?"

"Right. Tamara seemed to spend a good deal of time in our room. Charles was gone on her, but she never paid him any mind. She even told me that she'd gotten real chummy with him just to get next to me. Amazing, huh?"

"Truly amazing! Was Charles jealous of the attention she paid to you?"

"Very much so. He'd make crude comments to me. Then he'd wave it off as if he were just joking."

"Do you think Charles could've written the letters?"

"That's possible, but why would he? If he wanted Tamara, he wouldn't want to break us up. Us staying together would make me unavailable to her. I would think he would want to keep you and me together, not break us apart."

"That makes sense," Tarynton conceded.

"Anything is possible, but I don't think it was Charles. But whoever it was had to have access to my personal belongings. Charles had that, being that he was my roommate. Being Charles's good buddy, Tamara also had access to them when she was in our room. I recall Charles leaving her in there alone on several occasions." A thoughtful look came into his eyes. "Do you still have the envelope this came in?"

She only had to reach over to the nightstand to retrieve the envelope. She'd laid it there after taking the letter out of it for Drakkar to read.

Drakkar took the envelope and looked at the postmark. Though it was very faint from age, he could see that it had been mailed from Los Angeles, where Tarynton had gone to school. "Whoever sent it was in California at the time. I don't think she could've been there when this letter was written. I saw her around campus practically every day. But then again, I really don't know very much of anything about her background. Could someone from your school have been involved in this?"

Tarynton had to think hard about that question. There had been a few girls at school that hadn't liked her, the kind of girls that didn't like anyone who was attractive, smart, and popular. But that wasn't anything so unusual. Tarynton had been considered by her peers to have all of those qualities. She had also been quite active in several campus activities and had held office in many different social clubs.

She shook her head. "No real enemies that I can think of. Someone would have to have a real serious interest or hate for one of us to do something this cruel." Her eyes lit up. "What about Regina Webster? She was in love with you all through high school. She also went to UCLA. I saw her a couple of times when I visited Denise at her campus, but Denise didn't even know Regina before I introduced them. Regina hated me for being with you. I remember that she tried to bribe you into taking her to the prom. Do you recall that?"

Drakkar laughed with cynicism. "Who could forget that episode? She only offered me three hundred dollars to be her escort. Talk about desperation!"

"Exactly my point. The girl was desperate over you, in the same way Tamara is."

He stroked his chin thoughtfully. "Yeah, but Regina is a stretch. We were only teenagers then, and how would she have gotten my address at school?"

"Her brother, Randall, went to Grambling. You and he were good friends in high school and you both ended up at Grambling."

He shrugged. "I guess. But we may never figure it out." Just as the words left his mouth, Tamara's mentioning of the letter suddenly popped into his head. He snapped his fingers. "Tamara sent out those letters. I'm sure of it now." He relayed Tamara's earlier comments regarding the letter to Tarynton. "I never told a single soul about the letter. If she didn't write it, how would she know about it?"

"That's a good point, but you said she had access to your things. It could be that she only read it on one of the occasions she was in your room."

"I hadn't thought about that. But the most important thing for me to know is that neither one of us wrote the letters." He grimaced. "Do you know what this means? We've been had!"

"I know what it means for me. We didn't have to be apart all this time. I feel responsible for that, Drakkar. My ego was even larger than my pain. I was positively destroyed by that letter. There were times when I even thought I hated you. I think I made myself believe that I hated you in order to get through the excruciating pain of losing you. There were so many tears shed."

He put his arm around her. "You're not the only one to blame. I wrote you at least two hundred letters over the years, but I never mailed a single one." He brought her closer to him. "We've been had, T.C., big time. But we did more damage to ourselves than anyone else, when we decided not to communicate with each other. This could've been cleared up so easily had we just talked. Wow! This is an incredible revelation."

Tarynton looked into Drakkar's eyes. "I remember that day so clearly. I cried every day for nearly a year. And I've continued to cry regularly over it for the past six years. I was still crying about us when I first saw you again at Choices. I can't explain the hurt. There are no words to express what I felt. Knowing you experienced the same kind of hurt saddens me deeply, but it also makes me happy that we went through it together though separated. That we have managed to stay spiritually connected is awesome. I've never loved anyone but you." She lowered her lashes. "I have a confession to make."

"Only if you think you want to. You don't have to confess anything to me but your love for me. I love you regardless."

She laughed softly. "I didn't have a boyfriend when we ran into each other again. I was talking about you when I said was crazy about the man and that he was worth fighting for. It was only you all the time."

He couldn't blink back the tears. "Oh, Tarynton, we've been such fools. Promise me that we'll always talk, talk, and talk until there's really nothing else left to say."

She giggled nervously. "I promise. Now I want a promise from you. Will you promise to marry me, Drakkar Lomax?"

His body trembled from the force of his bursting emotions. "Yes, Tarynton Cameron Batiste, I'll marry you if you promise to marry me before the year is out. I'm yours for life."

She engaged him in a lingering kiss. "There's not much time left in the year, but I promise to do my best to make it happen. Is that good enough for you?"

"It is. Now I have a proposition for you. As soon as dinner is over, we're going to escape to a pay-by-the-hour motel to celebrate in private, but it won't be a cheap one. We can announce our engagement during Thanksgiving dinner."

She bit down on her lower lip. "We still have Tamara to contend with. She's feeding off my brother now and I won't allow that to continue. We can't forget that."

"We won't forget it, but we're going to put it aside for tonight while we celebrate our love for each other. I realize that the next several days and nights are going to be hard to get through, but we'll manage. But I want this to be a night that we'll never forget."

Tarynton and Drakkar saw their chance of getting away after dinner slowly slipping through their fingers. Aunt Cleo had brought up the idea of playing Monopoly, looking through old family pictures, and then later watching a video movie. Since everyone else seemed so eager to comply with her wishes, Tarynton didn't have the heart to go against the grain. As she exchanged wistful glances with Drakkar, the look in his eyes told her that he understood.

Just as Tarynton had thought, Aunt Cleo had a fit when she saw Drakkar. It had taken several minutes for her to pull herself together after a bout of screaming to show how happy she was to see her niece back with the man she loved. Although Tarynton thought it was a bit dramatic, it was a touching scene, one that had brought on tears. Aunt Cleo was five years younger than Pamela, but they looked to be the same age, and they also looked a lot alike. Cleo was a head shorter than Pamela, but they shared the same hair and eye color. What really surprised her is that neither one of them had picked up on Tamara's insincerity. They could normally spot a phony right off, but they both seemed taken with Camden's so-called girlfriend.

Every time Tamara touched Camden, Tarynton flinched inwardly. She couldn't get over how easily this woman was acting out the deceitful role she was playing. No one would've guessed that she even knew Drakkar, let alone in the biblical sense. From what Tarynton could see, Tamara didn't even try to avoid eye contact with either herself or Drakkar. And there didn't seem to be anything to suggest to Tarynton that Tamara was gloating outwardly or inwardly. Tarynton was beginning to believe that one personality had actually split between Tamara and Tiara. That revelation had her wanting to protect her brother with everything in her from this very scary woman. She had to start thinking of her as Tiara, so as not to slip up on the names.

When Camden invited Tarynton to come up to his room with him to help bring some gifts down, she jumped at the chance. She saw it as the perfect opportunity to carefully grill her brother about how much he knew about his strange houseguest.

Tarynton entered Camden's bedroom and dropped down on the bed. Fearing that her brother could be badly hurt, she watched him closely as he rummaged through his suitcase.

Retrieving several small packages, he held them up for Tarynton to see. "Got them, sis. We can go back downstairs now." As Camden started for the door, he turned back around, having sensed that Tarynton had something serious on her mind. "Hey, sis, why the long face? What's up?" He sat down on the bed and took her hand. "You look like you need to talk. Does it have anything to do with your relationship with Drakkar?"

She formed a steeple with her hands and blew a shaky breath of air into it. "It in fact has something to do with your relationship. I'm curious about Tiara. You haven't said where you met her. Other than her name, you haven't told us anything about her."

He grew relaxed. "If that's all that's on your mind, sis, I can help you out. I met Tiara when I was at a medical conference in New Orleans several months ago."

New Orleans! That certainly fit. Tarynton moaned inwardly. That was about the same time when she and Drakkar had gotten back together. "What does she do professionally?"

"She's a nurse practitioner for a school district in North Carolina."

"North Carolina? I thought you said she was from New Orleans."

"I said I met her at a conference in New Orleans. She lives in Charlotte, North Carolina."

Tarynton thought that Tamara had to be the biggest liar she'd ever run across. North Carolina and New Orleans were a far cry from each other. The situation seemed to get crazier by the minute. *Tiara,* she reminded herself. *You have to call her Tiara.*

"Have you been to her home in North Carolina?"

"No, I haven't. Our schedules just never seem to match up when I'm free to go there. She's been to my place in Raleigh a few times. In order for us to come here together, she drove up to my place. Her car is parked in my garage at home."

"Are you sleeping with this woman already, Camden?"

He looked embarrassed by the question. "Don't you think that's too personal a question for a little sister to ask her big brother?"

Tarynton blinked hard. "Maybe so. But, Camden, this is your first experience with a woman and I don't want to see you get all worked up over this relationship. You've been studying hard all your life. I'd like to see you live a little before you settle down."

He raised an eyebrow. "Who says this is my first experience with a woman?"

"Isn't it?"

"No, Tarynton, it isn't. Just 'cause I don't ring everybody up and clue them in on my personal life doesn't mean I don't have one. I've had a few female friends. There just wasn't enough time to develop things into anything serious. I have a little more time now to pursue a long-term relationship. The distance in miles between Tiara and me makes it difficult for us to see each other as often as we would like, but we're both comfortable with our arrangement. And to go ahead and answer your very personal question, not that it's any of your business, we haven't slept together. This one might be a keeper. I don't want to rush into anything with her."

"What's her last name?"

"Lyle. A nice but simple name."

Remove the *l* and the *e* and add *n-d-o-n* added up

to Lyndon in Tarynton's assessment. She'd never seen Tamara in person, but Tiara was a dead ringer for the woman Tarynton had seen in the newspaper article. Drakkar had no doubts about it being her—and he was the one that should know since he had once shared a bed with her. The thought of him in bed with Tamara really hurt Tarynton, but knowing now how Tamara had gotten him there had eased the pain a bit. If Tamara was the one who had written the letters, she had planned the whole thing out. She then saw to it that a broken-hearted Drakkar ran right into her open arms.

"Tarynton, are you okay? You're looking like a space cadet over there."

A light knock on the door thwarted Tarynton's response. Pamela poked her head in the doorway. "Sorry to interrupt you, but have you two forgotten that you have guests downstairs?"

Both Tarynton and Camden got to their feet at the same time.

"Sorry, Mom," Camden said. "We were catching up on the happenings in each other's lives and we lost track of time." He gathered up the gifts he'd come upstairs for. "We'll come back down right now."

Pamela smiled adorably at her two offspring. "Tiara looks scared to death to be alone with the family without you, Camden, and Drakkar looks extremely nervous. He seems to be on pins and needles. Is everything okay between you two, Tarynton?"

"We're fine, Mom. Before Aunt Cleo came up with her brilliant ideas for how the family should spend the evening, Drakkar and I had planned to slip away for an hour or two."

Pamela rubbed Tarynton's shoulders. "Oh, really. I wouldn't think of asking where you two had planned to slip off to. Needing a little space already, huh?"

Tarynton slipped her hand into her mother's soft one

as they started down the steps. "Not from you and Dad. Drakkar and I are like newlyweds since we got back together. We're still into lots of kissing and hugging. Having Aunt Cleo sitting right in between us makes it impossible for us to merely hold hands."

Pamela laughed. "I know what you mean. She loves her some Drakkar. If she didn't love you so much, and if she was a little bit younger, you might have to check her about your man," Pamela joked.

Tarynton saw what her mother was talking about when she walked into the room and saw Drakkar's face. He didn't look a bit nervous to her. He looked like he wanted to annihilate something or someone. Someone was more like it. His tension reached out to her from across the room. She had to rescue him before he blew a gasket.

"Drakkar, can I see you for a moment in private?"

He practically leaped out of his seat. "Sure thing." He rushed across the room and took Tarynton's hand.

Pamela sensed that something was terribly wrong, but she had no idea what. "Tarynton, do you think you and Drakkar can go and pick up a few last-minute things for me from the grocery store?"

"Sure, Mom. What do you need?"

"Come on into the kitchen. I'll make you a list."

Tarynton and Drakkar followed Pamela into her lovely gourmet kitchen. Pamela took a piece of paper from a pad on the counter and wrote a few things down and handed it to Tarynton.

Tarynton read the writing on the paper: *Go on and get out of here for a while. You both look like you need a few hugs and kisses from each other. I've got your back.* Tarynton reached for Pamela to give her a big hug. "Thanks, Mom. We won't be too long."

Pamela smiled as she pushed her daughter toward the doorway.

Tarynton and Drakkar wasted no time in grabbing their jackets and heading out the front door. Out on the porch Drakkar drew Tarynton to him, kissing her until she was breathless. He then guided her over to the rental car. "Do you even know the way to the store?"

"We're not going to the store. We're going to find somewhere to park so we can make out for the next hour or so. Mom saw how much we wanted to get out of there. She didn't need anything from the store. She just provided an escape route for us."

Drakkar kissed Tarynton thoroughly again. "Yes!"

Sixteen

While Tarynton, Pamela, and Aunt Cleo worked side by side in the kitchen, Drakkar was in the family room watching television with Steven, Camden, and Tiara. He would've been happier hanging out in the kitchen with the women, but Pamela wouldn't hear of him helping out. She wanted him to relax and chill out with the fellows. Had Pamela known the real situation, Tarynton knew that she would never have thrown Drakkar into the same room with the she-devil.

Tarynton was quite miffed that Tiara hadn't offered to help out in the kitchen even though she was glad that the evil woman wasn't anywhere near her. Still, she thought she could've at least offered to assist with the meal preparations. Her big feet were going to be under the dinner table just like everyone else's.

In preparing the yams for baking, Tarynton had stirred brown sugar, butter, cinnamon, and nutmeg into the boiling juices from the yams. Aunt Cleo had already mixed up the sweet potato pie filling, but she hadn't yet poured the mixture into the made-from-scratch pie shells. Pamela had just finishing making the macaroni and cheese and she was now working on the corn bread stuffing for the turkey. She always made an extra pan of herb dressing because there was never enough stuffing in the turkey to go around and to have later for leftovers.

Thanksgiving dinner in the Batiste house was served early in the afternoon. Second helpings were usually consumed in the early evening. The first dinner was more formal than the later one. The family had made a tradition of eating together during the early and later meal. It was also traditional for all the family members to cite aloud those things they were thankful for.

"Are you going to bake a chocolate cake, Mom?"

"Did you really have to ask? I'd never deny my daughter one of her favorite desserts. I live to make you and Camden happy campers when you come home to visit. But I know better than to make it tonight. It won't last until dinnertime tomorrow."

Noticing that it was after eleven P.M., Aunt Cleo grinned at Tarynton. "Does my lovely niece still have those late night cravings? Is that why you asked about the chocolate cake?"

"I guess that was easy enough to figure out. Mom, do you have any canned double fudge chocolate icing? I could eat some of that and a few dozen of those tiny marshmallows that are left over from the topping for the baked yams."

Pamela eyed Tarynton with concern. "Please tell me you're not with child."

Tarynton sucked her teeth. "Mom, you know better than that. I've had these types of late night cravings since I was a small child. If I were pregnant, you'd be the first to know."

"Sorry. And you're right. I do know better than that.

You've taken good care of yourself thus far. Not that I wouldn't mind having a grandchild or two to spoil rotten. Your Dad and I are going to be too old to enjoy them if you and Camden don't get married pretty soon and start your families. Your biological clocks' ticks are going to tock down shortly.''

Tiara suddenly popped into the room. "Is there something I can do to help, Mrs. Batiste? I'm sorry I didn't ask earlier."

Tarynton sighed hard. "Yeah, that would've been nice instead of waiting until everything is practically done before you offer to help." Her sarcasm couldn't have come across any plainer.

Pamela was shocked by her daughter's rudeness. "Tarynton, mind your manners! I know you're tired, but don't take it out on Tiara. You need to apologize."

Tarynton was sorry that she'd upset her mother. Aunt Cleo wasn't looking too proud of her either. When Tarynton saw that Tiara looked ready to burst into tears, she only wished the little phony witch would cry enough of them to drown herself in. The look she was getting from her mother told her that she'd better apologize to Tiara in a hurry.

"I'm sorry, Tiara. I didn't mean to be so rude. And I am tired, so I'm going to go to bed. Mom, I promise to get up with the sun to help you get everything finished. Please forgive me for upsetting you." Tarynton kissed her mom on the cheek.

Unable to be angry with her daughter, Pamela gave her a gentle hug. After hugging her Aunt Cleo, Tarynton left the kitchen, wishing she could reveal this treacherous game Tiara was playing with her entire family.

If it weren't for her undying love for Camden and her parents, she would've demanded that Tiara leave the Batiste home the moment she laid eyes on her. Drakkar's situation was tougher than her own. He was keeping quiet for the same reasons that Tarynton was doing so. His nerves had already been stretched to the absolute limit. While they'd sat in the car at the lake near her parents' home, Drakkar had told Tarynton of how helpless he felt. After talking the situation over for a few minutes, they both decided that this wasn't why they'd wanted to be alone. Their desire to be intimate with each other is why'd they'd flown the coop. While they didn't have enough time for the original plan of getting a motel, they had time to cuddle and be affectionate. If it weren't an arresting offense, they would've made love in the car's backseat.

The soft music from the car radio had allowed them to relax a little and indulge themselves in a short time of passionate foreplay and lots of kissing and hugging. Tarynton smiled at the delicious memories.

As Tarynton climbed the stairs, she thought of telling her mother what was going on in this love triangle between her, Drakkar, and Tiara. It was only on the holidays that the Batiste family was able to get together in one spot. Both Tarynton and Camden came home on times other than on holidays, but their schedules didn't always permit them to be there at the same time. Thanksgiving and Christmas were extra-special occasions in the Batiste household.

In really thinking it through, Tarynton decided that telling her mom would only ruin the holidays for everyone. Pamela wasn't the type just to sit back and let someone play a game of charades with her family. She would have no compunction in calling Tiara out for tampering with her son's precious heart.

Camden was Pamela's firstborn. That alone tied them in a very special bond. Camden had been around four years when Tarynton came along. It wasn't that Pamela loved Camden more than she loved Tarynton; she'd just loved him longer.

Removing a warm flannel gown from the dresser drawer, Tarynton stripped out of her clothes and went into the bathroom to take a brief shower. The bathroom, sandwiched between two of the upstairs guest rooms, was accessible from both rooms. Whoever was using the bathroom locked the door that led into the other guest room. When Tarynton tried the door it was unlocked, but as she stepped into the room, Tiara was already in there. She looked as if she'd been crying. Tarynton had only a fleeting moment of compassion for her.

Without making any comment, Tarynton turned around and went back into her bedroom. Then it dawned on her that Drakkar had been assigned that particular guest room. That made her wonder what the hell Tiara was doing in there. It also made her super angry. If this woman thought she was going to physically pursue Drakkar right under her and her brother's noses, she had better think again. Just as she thought about opening the door to put Tiara on notice in no uncertain terms, a soft knock came from the other side.

Tarynton braced herself knowing that only one person could be standing on the other side of her door. Then she said a silent prayer asking God to keep her from physically battering this intruder that had dared to bring her madness into her parents' home.

Trembling within, Tarynton sat down on the edge of the bed. "Come in."

Tiara popped through the door looking like a scared rabbit. Because Tarynton had expected her to come through the door with her claws unsheathed, and to show her true self behind Camden's back, the timid look on Tiara's face put Tarynton on an even higher alert. This woman was beginning to terrify her. She obviously had two very different sides, which lent more credence to her theory of Tamara possibly having a split personality. Tarynton made a mental note to keep her bedroom door locked at all times—and to tell Drakkar to do the same.

"Can I talk to you for a minute?" Tiara asked.

"I can't imagine what in the world we'd have to talk about."

Tiara outwardly flinched at Tarynton's sarcastic remark. "It seems that you don't like me. Since we've never met before, I'm having a hard time trying to figure out why you feel that way about me. It's puzzling, to say the least."

"Puzzling!" Tarynton threw her head back and laughed with derision. In taking a minute to think about the things Tiara had said, she realized Tiara was right about their having never met. But did she really think that because they hadn't met, Tarynton didn't know who she was, or that Drakkar wouldn't have told her if she hadn't known? Something told Tarynton not to reveal her hole cards, to sit tight long enough to hear out this strange piece of feminine work.

"So you want to talk? Okay. Why don't you pull out the desk chair and have a seat? Then you can tell me what you have on your mind." *But if you make one false move toward me, your butt is mine.*

Tiara folded her hands together to keep them from shaking. "I know that a lot of sisters are protective of their brothers, and vice versa, especially when they get involved in a serious personal relationship. But I want to assure you that I care a lot about Camden. I would never do anything to hurt him. I'm not the type of woman that plays a man's heart."

Tarynton swallowed hard. "Really? So, tell me, what type of a woman are you?"

Stunned by such a direct question, Tiara blinked hard. "I'm a decent, hardworking woman, no different from yourself. I don't know what I can say to convince you that I'm sincere in my feelings for your brother. I was thrilled when he asked me to come home with him to meet his family. Now that I'm here, I feel very unwelcome by the sister he adores. Your boyfriend also seems hostile toward me. Instead of sharing my feelings with Camden, which would no doubt hurt him, I decided to talk with you to see if we could clear the air if only for his sake.''

Tarynton was so confused that she felt like screaming at the top of her lungs. Frustration battled with the good and evil spirits within her. This woman sitting before her was nothing like the woman she'd come to know through harassing phone calls, egg-smeared windows, and slashed tires, nothing at all like the woman Drakkar had painted a portrait of using the broad strokes of different brushes to recreate the evil deeds she'd visited on him. But how could she deny that they were one and the same? She'd seen a picture of Tamara, a large one done in color. Mistaken identity as a reason for all this was far-fetched by any standards. She'd often heard that everyone had a double in the world, but she didn't think that it in any way applied in this case.

Tarynton understood how helpless Drakkar felt. She felt the same exact way. The sanity of the man she loved was hanging on by a mere thread. This situation was slowly driving him crazy. Her own mental state seemed to be in no less jeopardy since it was beginning to drive her crazy, too. But it was imperative that both of them kept their heads screwed on straight.

If Tamara and Tiara were indeed one and the same person, and Tarynton strongly believed that they were, she and Drakkar were dealing with a very sick woman. For that, she could show nothing less than the deepest of compassion for this conflicted person. Tarynton took a couple of minutes to plan out a reasonable way to handle this until she was sure of what was happening.

Tarynton looked Tiara in the eye. ''Maybe you're

right about me being overprotective of my brother. I'm sorry for being so rude. I love my brother like crazy. I think I should get to know you a little better before I make any more snap judgments. Is that okay with you?''

Keep your enemy close to you was a phrase that Tarynton had heard often enough. *Better to have them in your camp where you can keep a close eye on them.* As Tamara, this woman was definitely the enemy. As for the possibility of her also being Tiara, Tarynton couldn't possibly show malice toward a sick person. But it was to her advantage to have both personalities in one camp for the time being. She just hoped that Tamara wouldn't surface at any time during the weekend. Drakkar was going to flip out when she told him about her meeting with possible multiples.

"I'd like that, Tarynton. I want Camden to have a perfect holiday visit with his family." As Tiara came over to her to give her a hug, Tarynton momentarily stiffened, finding it difficult, at best, to embrace someone that frightened her as much as this person did.

When Camden popped his head in the doorway, Tarynton felt a torrent of relief rush from her body. He hadn't come a minute too soon. It was hard enough to get through this first one-on-one conversation with Tiara, and she didn't relish the thought of any more heart-to-hearts with her. Even though she knew that more conversations with her might possibly help uncover Tiara's agenda, Tarynton wasn't looking forward to them by any stretch of the imagination.

Tarynton's mind went straight to Drakkar as Camden and Tiara left her room. He must've lost his will to live by now, she thought. Knowing that she might be alone with Tiara more than likely had him worried sick. It surprised her that he hadn't come to check on her. Then she thought about Aunt Cleo, who'd been monop- olizing his time ever since she hit the front door and learned that he was there. With Aunt Cleo sticking to him like glue, he probably hadn't had a chance to go to the bathroom. She laughed at that thought. Aunt Cleo meant well, but that didn't diminish the fact that she could be one big pain in the butt.

Wishing he could wake up from this nightmare, Drakkar, already dressed for bed in silk pajamas and a matching robe, stood outside Tarynton's bedroom door. Before knocking, he prayed for enough strength for both himself and Tarynton. He knew that she had to be beside herself with anguish. Their relationship was no longer about them or what they wanted and needed to have with each other. It seemed to be all about a woman that would do anything, one that would go to any lengths to get what she wanted. Discomfort had taken him over the minute Tamara had left the room. When he saw her go upstairs, knowing she had been assigned to the downstairs guest room, he started worrying about Tarynton's safety. Getting away from Aunt Cleo had been a darn near impossible feat. But more than that, he hadn't wanted to arouse any suspicions by following her upstairs. He had given much thought to trying to talk to Tamara in private, but he realized that it wouldn't turn out any different than the outcome of his conversations with her in New Orleans and the one they'd had after he'd returned to California.

The woman was determined to keep his life in constant turmoil. The fact that she hadn't goaded him in any way had him stumped. He thought she would've covertly showed some sign of triumphant jubilee of how she had single-handedly orchestrated a plan to ruin their holidays. Drakkar could never even have imagined that Tamara would do something this drastic. He had already cursed himself a thousand times for telling her that he planned to ask Tarynton to marry him while they were in Atlanta for the holidays. That was the dumbest thing he'd done yet, even dumber than getting involved with Tamara in the first place.

The only time Tamara might possibly have seen Camden was when he'd visited Grambling a couple of times with Tarynton. She also could've learned who he was through Charles. That Camden had said that he'd met Tiara in New Orleans made sense, but he was sure it was no coincidence. And for Camden to bring her to meet his parents meant that Tamara had known him for longer than she knew that Drakkar and Tarynton were coming to Atlanta for the holidays. Complicated couldn't even begin to describe this situation.

Tarynton was sitting up in bed when he entered the room. "Mind if I keep you awake a few minutes longer?"

She patted the side of the bed. "I doubt that I'm going to get to sleep period. If you hadn't come to see me, I was coming to your room. I couldn't wait until morning to share with you the strange conversation I had with this Tiara person. What I have to tell you is so freaking bizarre."

Instead of sitting on the side of the bed, he stretched himself across the bottom of it. "I can't imagine things getting any more bizarre than what they are already."

"Then you'd better brace yourself. I'm starting to believe that Tamara and Tiara are the same person. It seems to me that there are multiple personalities housed in that one brain. I think Tamara has a split personality. That's the one thing that would explain all of this."

Drakkar looked skeptical. "Are you serious?"

"I couldn't be more serious. In talking with her, she showed no signs whatsoever that she was playing games with this family. She told me that she cared about Camden. She was very convincing. I actually felt that she was sincere. I think she would've gloatingly revealed her motives to us by now. The Tamara I've come to know through her undesirable machinations wouldn't be able to hide such a victory as this. She would've created an opportunity to get one of us alone so that she could gloat. You know her better than any of us. Do you really think Tamara is that good of an actress, that she could actually knowingly pull off this malicious scheme in such a convincing manner?"

He shoved a hand through his hair. "You know what? I don't have a clue what to think of her and this scheme. Whether it's multiple personalities or not, I don't know. Either way, we're dealing with a sick person. Only a sick person could do something like this."

"You're right. But the question is this: does she really know what she's doing? How can we hold her accountable if she is suffering with a split personality? I don't think we can. Are the two personalities even aware of each other? With Camden being a doctor, wouldn't he know he's dealing with a multiple?"

"Not if he hasn't seen both personalities. He's a neurologist, not a psychiatrist."

"A neurologist deals with diseases of the brain."

"Organic diseases, not psychological ones."

Tarynton threw up her hands out of agitation. "Whatever. If this woman has multiple personalities, she needs help. Camden would know where and how to get her what she needs. Since Tamara has mentioned slashing my throat, we need to be seriously concerned. One of these personalities is criminally evil. This is no longer something we can handle on our own."

"Are you suggesting that we clue Camden in on your theory?"

"Not necessarily. But I think we should ask him questions about the disease. We also need to carefully observe the woman's interaction with everyone. Until we're sure of what's going on, we have no choice but to let this bizarre scenario play out. I was praying that if a multiple thing was happening, Tamara's personality wouldn't show up during her visit in my parents' home. I feel differently now. The only way we can know for sure is that if both personalities are revealed to us.''

Drakkar looked horrified. "Oh, T.C., I don't think you want that to happen. I know that I don't want to see it occur. If your theory is correct, and if Tamara were to show up, we don't want it to happen here. I'm positive that the woman calling herself Tiara is Tamara. But if it turns out that they're one and the same through a psychological disease, this nightmare may only get worse. I don't think we should put off talking to Camden about this. If there is more than one personality, he's romantically involved with one of them. We owe the truth to him.''

Tarynton considered Drakkar's comments. "We'll do it, but can we wait until after Thanksgiving dinner? We don't leave until Sunday. An opportunity for us to talk to him alone should arise before then.''

"That's all well and good. However, I think you should tell Camden without me being present. This is a sensitive situation. He's going to be hurt as it is. But when he learns that I've been involved with the woman he's currently pursuing . . . well, I think you can figure out what I'm trying to say.''

"I'm feeling you. I'll talk to him alone. But Camden is not going to hold that against you. He didn't know this woman at the time you were involved with her. I'm the one with the problem. If my brother decides to stay with this woman despite what I have to tell him, I don't think I can handle that. Check this out. Tiara/Tamara as the woman who once slept with my man; Tiara/Tamara as my sister-in-law. Pretty screwed-up stuff, huh?''

Drakkar nodded. "I know what you mean and I'm

sorry that I brought this drama to you. You shouldn't have to deal with any of this." He got up from the bottom of the bed, sat down on the side, and took Tarynton's hand. "Are we going to survive this, T.C.?"

She leaned forward and put her head on his shoulder. "Our love is strong enough, but I'm not so sure that our nerves can take much more of this." She lifted her head and looked into his eyes. "I love you, Drakkar, through the good times and the bad. We can survive this."

"Thanks. I needed to be reassured that you're with me on this. Now that I'm sure we're still working together, I know we can survive." His passionate kiss made her weak with wantonness. "You'd better get some sleep so you'll have enough strength to get up early and help out in the kitchen. Your mom and Aunt Cleo are counting on you." He got up from the bed and leaned over her. "I love you. Sleep tight, baby."

"Love you, too, Drakkar." She opened her mouth to receive his next kiss.

At the door, before opening it, he looked back at Tarynton and grinned. "If we weren't in your parents' home, I wouldn't be leaving this room. Dream about what we're going to do to each other when we get back home. Make it a wet and wild one."

She blushed. "I'm all for the dream, but we still may find time to get that motel room."

"Let's keep looking for that opportunity." Smiling, he winked at her before closing the door behind him.

Tarynton's heart skipped a few beats at the smile Drakkar had bestowed upon her. Her life was finally complete with him back in it, but with all of his unfinished business, she had to wonder if they'd ever get back to where things were just about them and the love they felt for each other. She couldn't help thinking about what would have happened between them earlier if they'd had the time to check into a local motel. No doubt it would've been hotter than hot. In a way she was almost glad that it hadn't happened. Their lovemaking might have been too rushed, which would've only added to their mountain of frustrations. Before they'd gotten back together, they hadn't made love to each other for six years so four more days should be a breeze for them.

After saying her prayers, Tarynton snuggled herself under the soft white down comforter. Thoughts of Camden immediately came to her mind. How to tell him what was going on with her and the woman he was involved with was a big concern for her. Camden was a sensitive man and she didn't want to see her brother get hurt a little or a lot. He would no doubt believe her when she told him the story, but she was confused as to how much to tell him. If she didn't tell all of it, the dramatic saga would sound even crazier than it was, if that was possible. Crazy was the only way to define it no matter how you looked at it.

Tomorrow was another day, she told herself. Thanksgiving was a family holiday that everyone relished. She prayed that it would turn out to be as wonderful as all the others had.

Looking extremely handsome in a dark blue blazer and a crisp white shirt, Steven Batiste stood at the head of his dining room table holding the hand of his wife, Pamela, as he passed the Thanksgiving dinner blessing. Everyone seated at the Batiste table also held hands. Amen was simultaneously voiced by the other family members and guests once the prayer was finished. Pamela took the seat to the right of her husband but Steven remained standing.

"It is a tradition in the Batiste house that before we eat Thanksgiving dinner we go around the table and give each person a chance to voice what they're thankful for. We'll start with the ladies. Once Camden and Drakkar have spoken, I'll be the last one to speak. You can either stand or remain seated."

Pamela smiled as she folded her hands together. "Since I believe in letting my guests go first, I'll be the last of the ladies to speak. Tiara, since you're a newcomer to our family tradition, we'd love for you to go first."

Tiara looked nervous as she got to her feet. It appeared that the smile from Camden calmed her jitters. "I first want to thank Mr. and Mrs. Batiste for having me as a guest in their lovely home." She smiled sweetly at Steven and Pamela. "It is also a pleasure for me to meet the rest of Camden's family. I'm grateful to be able to share in this loving family gathering. My parents are no longer alive, so family holidays are nonexistent for me. I have a sister, but unfortunately we are estranged. Through no fault of my own, we haven't spoken to each other for many, many years. I'm extremely thankful for the opportunity to see how a real family spends the holiday season. Seeing how you all interact with one another has made me want to try to reconcile with my sister once again. I pray that she will let me back in her heart. Thank you."

Aunt Cleo got to her feet. "I'm thankful for my big sister and her loving family for allowing me to hang out with them every holiday. Since I have never married and don't have any children, I've come to love my sister's family as my own. I'm thankful for life, for the very air I breathe. I have food to eat, a warm shelter where I can lay my head, and I've been blessed with adequate finances. I'm grateful to God for all things great and small. Without Him, nothing in this life is possible."

Tarynton was slow to get out of her seat. When she did, she went over to her parents and gave them a warm hug. "I'm most grateful to God for giving me these two wonderful people as parents." She then moved to where Camden sat, hugging him also. "I'm so thankful to have such a great brother. He has always been so supportive of me. Each of these three people has never failed to be there for me when I needed them. I'm truly thankful for this loving family."

Tarynton put her arm around Aunt Cleo's shoulder. "I'm thankful for such a sweet, loving aunt. I love her despite the fact that I've had to wrestle my man away from her a time or two on this visit." Everyone laughed. "Last but not least, I'm thankful to God for bringing Drakkar Lomax and me back together before we got too old and gray to enjoy our happy reunion. I'm thankful for the blessings that God has given me in such abundance."

Pamela had tears in her eyes when she stood up. "I'm thankful for the loving husband and the adorable children that God has seen fit to bestow upon me. I'm grateful for each of my guests who have delighted us with their presence over this holiday weekend. I'm so thankful that everyone arrived safely. I'm most thankful for the gift of life."

Camden looked around the table before he began his remarks. "This is such an awesome time for the Batiste family. I'm grateful to God for every moment that I get to spend with my mom and dad and my sister. These three wonderful people are my lifeline. I'm thankful to God for choosing to work through me as one of His healers. Aunt Cleo, I'm grateful to you for all the baked goodies you sent me at college over the past eight years, and for all the support you've always given me." He looked down on Tiara. "I'm thankful that I was blessed to meet Tiara, that we occupied the same space at the same time. Like my mother, I am most thankful for the gift of life, in all forms."

Drakkar stood up. He took a couple of seconds more to gather his thoughts. "There are so many things that I'm grateful for, too many to name in one standing. I have a great job and I'm now living in a fabulous city, the same city where the woman I love is living. I'm so grateful that I went out to the nightclub Choices one evening, the very same evening I was reunited with the incomparable Tarynton Cameron Batiste. I'm extremely thankful that our reunion was orchestrated by divine intervention. I'm thankful for sharing the holiday season with the Batiste family and Aunt Cleo. I'm most thankful for the God I serve, for a Father who is all-knowing and so very merciful. I'm thankful to my Father in heaven who sent His only begotten Son so that we might have life everlasting."

Tarynton's eyes filled with moisture at Drakkar's statements.

Steven remained seated as he looked at each person at the table. He then got to his feet. "I'm grateful that I've learned to live in the moment, to savor each and every second that I spend with my family. I'm thankful to my sister-in-law, Cleo, for being here for my family, especially on those times when I was out of town. I'm also thankful to Cleo for her loyalty to Pamela. I'm grateful for the extraordinary senses of tasting, hearing, smelling, seeing, and feeling, thankful that they're all still intact in a man my age. I'm thankful for the gifts of two beautiful children that my lovely wife has given to me. I'm thankful that we're all here together to share in one more family holiday. As the events of September eleven have given most of us the opportunity to see life with renewed vision, I am thankful to those who risked and lost their lives to save the lives of so many others. I, too, am thankful to God for the gift of life and for the understanding that some must die for the greater cause of good versus evil. As we are all thankful for the wonderful meal we're about to partake of, we must also be thankful for the many hands that prepared it. I am so grateful for my wife, the mother of my children. With that said, please pass the turkey.''

Looking eager to dig into all the great-smelling food and delicious-looking desserts, everyone clapped and shouted amen. Once all the different foods were passed around, everyone began eating. Moans and groans of pleasure came soon after the first bites of food.

After helping clear the table and putting the leftover food away, Tarynton had gone upstairs to the audio-visual room to retrieve the movie *Soul Food* for her father. As it was one of his favorites, he liked to watch it when the family was together. Tarynton thought they'd already seen it several times too many, but she went along with the plan to watch it because it brought her father pleasure. *Down In the Delta* was another of his favorites so she pulled it out as well.

As she turned to leave the room, Tiara entered. Not wanting to be alone with Tiara, Tarynton became some-what anxious about it. When Tiara closed the door behind her, Tarynton's tension mounted.

"Do you have a couple of minutes, Tarynton?"

"Only a couple of minutes since Dad is waiting for me to bring him this movie."

Tiara sat on the sofa. "I just want to thank you for making things more pleasant for me. Before coming here, Camden seemed to think that you and I would get along well. I'm happy that he hasn't been disap-pointed. I hope that you and I can one day develop a good relationship."

Tarynton sat down on the arm of the sofa. "Speaking of relationships, I'm sorry that you and your sister aren't speaking. I guess that must be very tough. I can't even imagine Camden and me not talking. We are so close to each other. In fact, Camden is my other hero. My Dad holds the number-one hero spot in my life. You mentioned trying to reach your sister again. I hope that it will all work out for the both of you. Sisters should also be best friends. Who's the oldest?"

Tiara laughed. "We're almost the exact same age."

Tarynton looked puzzled. "How can that be, unless . . ."

"Unless we're twins? You're right. We are twins. Tamara is a couple of minutes older than me, but I've always been the most responsible one."

Tarynton's eyes widened with disbelief. Had she said Tamara? This couldn't possibly be happening, she thought, shaking her head from side to side. But then again, if it were true, it made perfect sense. If Tamara Lyndon was Tiara's twin, there was no split personality involved. But Tiara's last name was Lyle, so that piece of information didn't exactly fit into the puzzle. Still, Tarynton was amazed by what she'd just heard. Her heart was beating faster than normal and the sound of it seemed to thump wildly inside her head.

"Are you okay, Tarynton? You suddenly look so pale."

"Did I hear you say that your twin's name is Tamara? If so, what's her last name?"

"You heard right. Her last name is Lyndon. Tamara was married the same month she graduated from high school, but it was annulled before she went off to college in the fall. That's why our last names are different. I don't know why Tamara continued to use that name, but there's a lot of things about Tamara that I'm clueless on. And I don't understand half the things I do know about her."

Tarynton got up from the sofa and began pacing the floor. "This is so complicated, but it's all starting to make sense now. I don't know how to tell you this other than to come right out with it. I know of your sister and she's not a very nice person. In fact, I thought you and she were one in the same. I've never met Tamara, but she used to be involved with Drakkar for a brief spell. Ever since he's been back in my life she's seen to it that we don't have a moment of peace. She has done horrible things to my car and has made constant threats against Drakkar and me."

Tiara looked at Tarynton as if she'd lost her mind. Tarynton watched in horror as Tiara's color drained from her face. Tiara's reaction made Tarynton wonder if she'd made the wrong connection. Or could it be that she was she right on the money? Tiara was obviously stunned.

Tarynton hit her forehead with an open palm. "I'm sorry. This person I'm talking about may not even be your sister, but you and she are identical in looks and her name is Tamara Lyndon. Did Tamara go to Grambling?" Tarynton changed her tactics in case she was wrong.

"Everything you've said makes me know that the Tamara you're talking about is my twin sister. This is just too incredible for me to take in all at once. Tamara has a very obsessive-compulsive personality. I'm sorry that you've been directly affected by her viciousness. My sister came after me in pretty much the same way she has done you. It was also over a guy. She went after a guy that I had been dating for months. When he didn't fall under her charming spell, and right into bed with her, she did everything in her power to make our lives a living hell."

"Your own flesh-and-blood sister went after someone you were romantically linked to?"

"So much so that he ended the relationship with me. I'm afraid that her brief marriage has left her a very bitter woman. Her husband is the one that sought the annulment after Tamara nearly drove him insane with her obsessive behaviors. I was hoping that she had gotten better, but it seems that my sister is still very sick. I wish I could help Tamara overcome her rage."

Tarynton surprised herself when she grabbed Tiara and hugged her. With tears in her eyes, Tarynton once again apologized for her rude treatment of Tiara. "I've been so stumped by you and how different a person you seemed to be than the person we thought you were, which was Tamara. Drakkar and I thought that you had purposely connected with Camden to bring us further grief. Just before we came here, she called both Drakkar and me to see if we could meet with her, separately of course, when she comes to Los Angeles right after we get back. I told her I'd meet with her just to buy us some time. Then, when we saw you, we were so sure that you were Tamara. I'm glad that you're not, but this is still a very complicated mess. When Tamara learns that you're somehow involved with my family, I think there's going to be even more hell to pay. She may see it as a double betrayal."

Drakkar and Camden walked into the room at the same moment Tiara warmly embraced Tarynton. Drakkar looked confused by what he saw. He couldn't imagine what prompted Tarynton to allow such a show of warmth from the woman who scared her half to death.

On the other hand, Camden was deeply touched by the scene before him. "Isn't this sweet? We came up here because we were worried about you two, but it looks as if we have nothing to worry about. Glad to see you two getting along so well."

Tarynton smiled weakly. "Tiara and I have been getting to know each other a little better. I have discovered some incredible facts about her. Camden, you never told me Tiara was a twin."

Camden looked shocked. "A twin? I'm just hearing it for the first time myself. Tiara, I couldn't believe it when you mentioned at dinner that you had a sister, let alone a twin sibling. You mean to tell me that there's another woman out there that looks similar to you?''

"Similar is an understatement. Tamara and I are identical twins. I'm sorry, Camden, for not being more forthcoming about my family history. I thought I'd wait until I saw where our relationship was going before I told you too much. I didn't want to scare you off by giving you too many details all at once. There are lots of problems between my sister and me.''

Drakkar looked from Tarynton to Tiara as if they both had invaded his planet. His heart raced at top speed inside his chest as he tried to swallow the huge lump in his throat. "You have an identical twin—and her name is Tamara? Tamara what?''

Tarynton took a firm hold of Drakkar's arm. "Lyndon, Drakkar. Her last name is Lyndon. The Tamara we know is Tiara's twin sister. Tamara was married for a short time and that's why they have different last names. Is this too bizarre for a simple explanation or what?''

Camden looked around at everyone. "Is there something else I need to know? You all are acting very, very strange. Tiara, what's up with this story regarding your twin sister?''

Tarynton asked everyone to have a seat. She then began to clue Drakkar and Camden in on her and Tiara's unbelievable discoveries. As he listened intently to Tarynton laying everything out for him and Camden, Drakkar suddenly found it hard to breathe. The air had grown thin. The new revelations made him sick even if it did make everything else crystal-clear for him. He felt relieved to know that Tamara didn't have a split personality. But like Tarynton, he saw Tamara making things even tougher for them once she found out that her twin sister was romantically involved with Tarynton's brother, a sister that she had been estranged from for many years.

With Tarynton attempting to pen her first full-length novel, Drakkar didn't know if she could've come up with such an extremely unusual plot. The evil twin versus the good twin was a common enough storyline. But it was the other strange twists and turns that further heated up the already boiling pot, a pot threatening to boil over with red-hot intrigue.

Steven walked into the room to find practically everyone talking at the same time. Their loud chatter was what brought him upstairs in the first place. They all seemed excited about something, but their animated discussion was coming across to him in a troubled way. Nobody looked too happy about whatever the chosen topic was.

Steven looked at Camden. "Is everything okay up here? We can hear you guys all the way downstairs." He then eyed his daughter. "What happened to the video I asked you to get for me? Weren't you able to find it?"

Tarynton picked up the two video movies from the coffee table. "Here they are, Dad. I'm sorry for the delay. The four of us got involved in a very passionate discussion. But we're okay."

Steven eyed his son and daughter with slight wariness. Tarynton knew that look of his. It seemed to her that Steven had guessed that they were covering up something. She also knew that he wouldn't try and pry any information out of them. He respected them as adults.

Smiling gently, Steven took the videos from Tarynton's hand. "I'm going back downstairs now. If you want to watch the movie, come down when you're ready." He looked at both Camden and Tarynton with mild concern before leaving the room.

Camden got to his feet. "I think we should let this go for now. We'll all have to figure out what we can do to ease this situation. I think Tarynton's idea of trying to get Tamara professional help was a good one. But unless Tamara decides that she wants it, it's not going to do any of us any good, especially her. We should try and enjoy the rest of the holiday weekend. We don't want to ruin things for Mom and Dad. They live for the times that we come home to visit.''

"Though Dad didn't voice it, he was concerned about our loud discussion. I agree with what Camden said. We have to let go of this for now. Drakkar and I are relieved that Tamara isn't suffering from multiple personalities, but we're still worried about her mental stability. Tiara, if it weren't for you being so open about your problems with your sister, we might never have figured this out. Thanks for the light you've shed on this for us.''

Tiara hugged Tarynton. "You're welcome. And I think it's very generous of you to want to help my sister in the light of all that she's done to inconvenience you. Not many women would see it the way that you do. You have a pure heart, just like your brother has said.''

Camden hugged Tarynton and Tiara. "Let's get downstairs and see this movie we've watched countless times. This weekend is all about family!''

"I second that," Tarynton said, looping her arm through Drakkar's. As they exited the room, Tarynton stopped and looked up at Drakkar. "I love you, baby love. It's going to be okay for us. I can feel it. Everything is going to work itself out.''

He kissed her softly on the mouth. "I hope you're right. I love you, too, baby. I would move mountains for you and me to be together. Since we didn't announce our plans to marry over dinner, when do you want to do it?''

She smiled. "We'll save it until everything is worked out. When we do announce it, I don't want any unpleasantness hanging over our heads to dampen the joy everyone is bound to feel. Is that okay with you?"

He nodded. "Anything you do is okay with me, as long as you don't change your mind about marrying me. We've got so much to look forward to."

"Yeah, it's starting to look like we're going to have our forever one moment in time."

Seventeen

Tarynton hadn't had time to reflect over the long holiday weekend spent in her parents' home since her return to California over a week ago. Her answering machine was crammed with calls from old clients and many messages from potential clients seeking information about the special services she provided.

Upon returning the calls, she had landed five new contracts for creating special events for several return customers and she had also gotten seven new clients. Less than half of the requests were from female callers. All of the arrangements were needed for the upcoming Christmas holidays. Last-minute bookings always made for a hectic schedule since most people made holiday plans well in advance. Most of the clients had asked for local arrangements as opposed to leaving town for the holidays.

A few of the male customers were interested in California snow resorts such as Big Bear and Mammoth. One fifty-eight-year-old gentleman wanted to take his twenty-one-year-old girlfriend to Disneyland because she loved theme parks. He was so eager to please his lady friend, whom he'd referred to as his pretty, young maiden. The female clients had inquired about first-class accommodations in places like Big Sur, Palm Springs, and even Temecula; a lesser-known wine country offering all the charm, vistas, and wine that the Napa Valley offered and only an hour-and-a-half drive from Los Angeles. Clients requesting specific cities allowed Tarynton to concentrate only on the hotels and activities in that particular area. Tarynton welcomed the suggestion. She certainly had her work cut out for her. As always, she felt confident in her ability to deliver to her clients the very best for their money.

As she looked at the clock, Tarynton's nervousness increased. She was to meet Tamara Lyndon in less than an hour. They were going to have lunch in one of the restaurants in Tamara's Van Nuys hotel. Drakkar had tried to persuade her not to meet with Tamara alone, but as a woman of her word, Tarynton could not be dissuaded. After she told him where the meeting would take place, he felt a little better about it. If he'd had his way, the meeting wouldn't take place at all. He was to meet with Tamara over dinner in the evening near the studio where he worked—and he thought his meeting with her should be enough. It bothered him that she'd insisted on meeting with Tarynton as well. Her intended agenda worried him even more.

Once Tarynton put away her work materials, she went into the house to dress for her meeting with Tamara. This was one meeting that she wanted to look her very best for. Knowing how very beautiful Tamara was only added to her desire to dress to impress. She wasn't in competition with Tamara, but she wanted her to know that she could compete—and not just in looks and dress. Tarynton knew that she had much more than looks and great clothes going for her. She had a heart, which Tamara had obviously lost sometime during her twenty-eight years of life. While Tarynton felt sorry for Tamara's unfortunate love affairs, she couldn't allow her compassion for this woman's plight to cause her to let her guard down in Tamara's presence.

Tarynton never did like waiting for anything, but she hated it when someone was late for a scheduled meeting. Tamara was already fifteen minutes overdue. The most time Tarynton was prepared to give her was another ten minutes, which she thought was more than generous.

The wait had given her time to reflect on her heart-to-heart talks with Tiara during their time in Atlanta. Since her return home, she and Tiara had talked on the phone every night. The main topic of their conversation had been Tamara. Tiara had wanted to come to Los Angeles for Tarynton's meeting with Tamara, but Tarynton convinced her that it wasn't a good idea and wasn't in Tiara's best interest. If and when the twins were going to reconcile their relationship, Tarynton wanted to keep her, Drakkar, and Tamara's issues separate from those plaguing the two siblings.

Although Tarynton had seen a picture of Tamara, she wasn't prepared for the beauty of this woman up close and personal. Even though the sisters were identical, Tamara had somewhat of a more worldly, sophisticated look going for her. Tiara had the girl-next-door look, more wholesome and fresh. Tamara's perfume was so overpowering that Tarynton had to cough to clear her lungs of the strong flowery scent.

"You don't have to be nervous, dear. I'm not here to hurt you." Tamara swept into the booth with one graceful movement. "Sorry for being late. My last appointment lasted longer than I had anticipated. I'm a known hell-raiser, but I do have some scruples."

Tamara picked up the menu and looked it over. She then summoned the waitress. Tarynton looked on in utter confusion as Tamara ordered a large amount of food. For someone who had such a beautiful figure, Tarynton wondered how she kept it with all the fried food she'd ordered. When the waitress turned her attention to Tarynton, she didn't have a clue what was on the menu since she hadn't looked at it. Guessing that salads were more than likely a featured menu item, she ordered a Caesar with grilled chicken. As soon as the waitress left the booth, Tamara fixed her eyes on Tarynton. The look Tamara was giving her made Tarynton's nervousness grow tenfold.

"You look a lot different from what I remember," Tamara began. "To tell you the truth, I didn't see what Drakkar saw in you back then. I thought he could do much better for himself. For a man that is as fine as he is, he could've had his pick out of the most beautiful women on the campus."

Tarynton looked Tamara straight in the eye. "Did you ask me here to insult me? If that's your intention, I can tell you now that I'm not going to sit here and listen to you put me down. If you have something on your mind other than hurling insults at me, I think you should get right down to it. Otherwise I'm out of here."

"Calm down. Ruffled feathers aren't very attractive, especially on a lady. I asked you here because I wanted to tell you what I think about you and your unfaithful man. I thought you should know that I had decided that I would never give Drakkar any peace. As I told him, I was going to be in his every dream and become a star in his every nightmare." Tamara slowly sipped on a glass of water through a straw. "But my agenda has changed drastically since we set up this little no-holds-barred meeting."

Too overwhelmed to speak, Tarynton just stared at Tamara.

"Aren't you interested in knowing how my agenda has changed?"

Tarynton did her best to will her voice into play. "I'm ~~not~~ so sure *interested* is the correct wording, but I have a feeling that you're going to say whatever you feel whether I'm interested or not." Tarynton looked at her wristwatch. "You have exactly two minutes to get on with it. I have a business to run."

Tarynton saw that Tamara looked totally disinterested in her last statement. Because the waitress had just come to the table with the orders, Tarynton thought she'd suffer through this indignation long enough to eat her salad. No doubt that she had to pay for it since she'd ordered it. The thought of jumping up and leaving the bill for Tamara to settle put a slight smile on her lips. But seeing how formidable a woman Tamara was, Tarynton figured that she would never allow the restaurant to stick her for the charge.

Tamara picked up her fork. After eating two french fries drenched in ketchup, she set her fork in the middle of her plate. She then eyed Tarynton's right hand. "I don't see a large rock on your hand. Does that mean you and Drakkar didn't get engaged as planned?"

Tarynton finished eating the forkful of salad she'd placed in her mouth. "Drakkar and I *are* very much engaged. We don't need a ring to seal our commitment to each other. But knowing Drakkar as I do, I'm sure the ring will come later. I see that you're bent on talking about everything but why I'm here. I'm beginning to think you have nothing worthwhile to say."

Tamara gave Tarynton a chilling look. "I see that you're not above trading insults either. Don't dish it out if you can't take it. I'm positive that you're not as good at it as I am. At any rate, I'm no longer interested in your man or you. I've found someone who can see straight through all my bull. This man has somehow unearthed my heart. I've known him for a long time, but I've only realized recently that he's different from any other man I've ever met. Perhaps in taking Drakkar's advice, I've finally been able to recognize one of the good guys."

"Drakkar's advice about what?"

"How a woman should handle herself with a man. He told me some things about myself that I really had to stand up and take notice of. When I stumbled on this old friend of mine over the holiday weekend, I used a totally different approach with him as I discovered that I was intrigued with him. He was better looking than I remembered—and he's now a very successful entrepreneur. But it wasn't either of those things that attracted me to him. When I knew him before, I was so busy trying to land someone who only had eyes for another woman that I failed to see his inner glow. It's possible that I have you to thank."

Tarynton looked puzzled. "Me? What did I do that you need to thank me for?"

"Drakkar told me that you were instrumental in getting him to see how he may've used me. He apologized for his part in it. But he didn't hold back on telling me the part I played in what happened between us. He spelled my unsavory behavior out for me in no uncertain terms. He left me with no choice but to do self-examination. Once I put myself and my past behavior under the microscope, I didn't like one bit of what I saw. Now that Charles and I are interested in developing a serious relationship, I made the decision to settle the past and move on. That's the same thing that Drakkar was interested in when he came to see me. Charles hadn't happened to me when I decided not to accept Drakkar's apology. Being vindictive was much easier for me."

"So, did you do a reality check on yourself before Charles or after him?"

"I had already started looking into myself, but I did a more in-depth study after running into him again. I have to tell you that I thoroughly enjoyed keeping Drakkar on edge. I loved having the upper hand. When he asked me if I wanted him to be with me knowing he loved someone else, I was all for whatever would bring him the most misery. But then I came to realize that I'd like one day to have exactly what he had. In fact, there was a time when I thought I already had it. He was madly in love with his childhood sweetheart, and mine had dumped me within a couple of months of us getting married."

Tarynton raised an eyebrow. "You married your childhood sweetheart?"

"I not only married him, I was carrying his child. When he walked out on our marriage, leaving me pregnant, I was mortified. Then I became a raving lunatic, right after I lost the child. It was then that I made a vow to make every man on this planet pay for what Bobby Lyndon did to me. Lest I should dare to forget, I kept his name as a constant reminder of the horrific pain he'd caused me. Had Drakkar stayed with me, I would've eventually chewed him up and spat him out all over the place. I'm a classic man-hater. Even more than that, I doubly hated men who were strong enough to resist my charms. Drakkar definitely fell into that category."

What Tamara was saying didn't exactly match up with what Tiara had told her, but it was possible that Tiara wasn't fully aware of Tamara's situation. Tiara had said that Tamara's husband had left her because of her possessive, obsessive behavior. That was easy enough for

Tarynton to believe because of Tamara's history with Drakkar. That she actually hated Drakkar came as quite a shock to Tarynton.

Tarynton was nonplussed. "Tamara, I have to ask. Why are you telling me all of this?"

Tamara studied Tarynton for several seconds. "Would you believe me if I told you it was because of your compassion?"

"I have no reason to dispute you. But according to you, you were ready to continue the harassment until you met Charles. When did compassion come into play?"

"Oh, I was deeply moved by what Drakkar had said about the part you had in him coming to see me, but there's no way that I would've let him know it. Not only that, I didn't think any black woman was that stupid. In other words, I thought he was tripping about you telling him he should apologize to me before I realized otherwise. Also, I'd long ago convinced myself that he was just another man that I needed to bring down to his knees. As for women, I put all females in the same category with the woman who took Bobby from me. In looking back on everything that has occurred, I began to realize that I'm the one with the serious problem. Bobby has been happily married for several years now and all I've ever let myself know is misery. I simply saw a need for change."

"Drastic changes! I'm sorry that you got hurt and I'm happy you've found someone that you can be happy with. I wish you only the best. But don't fault me if I'm a little skeptical over here. How do I know that you're not going to change your mind and start harassing Drakkar and me again? Can you guarantee that there'll be no more damage to my car and malicious phone calls? Since you brought up the subject of believing you, why should I believe all this, Tamara?"

"You shouldn't. All I can say is that time will tell. I have a lot of amends to make to many people. I have a twin sister that I've treated worse than anyone. It's past time for me to try and heal that relationship. I've already put a call in to her. I can only pray that she returns it."

"Why did you want to hurt your sister?"

"I couldn't have answered that question a few days ago. I can only answer it now because I dared to look within. Tiara is everything that I'm not, everything that I wish I could be. She's sweet and caring and she couldn't hurt a fly. People are drawn to her because of her sincerity and compassion. Her angelic spirit is revealed in everything that she does. Guys love to be around her and they simply tolerate me. We are as different as night and day despite the fact that we're identical twins. Tiara is as close to perfection as anyone can get. I'm the evil twin, through and through. I understand your skepticism, but I'm in a different place in my life. I want something good and right for a change. I want a man that loves me as much as Drakkar obviously loves you. I won't apologize for things that I intentionally did. That would make me a hypocrite. I did them because I wanted to make people like you and Drakkar suffer. Just know that I'm not the same person that did those things or had them done."

"Are you admitting to slashing my tires, Tamara?"

"That would make me a fool. I'm afraid I'm not that reformed yet. If I confess to anything, it won't be to a mere mortal. I'll just say this. I wouldn't worry about anything like that happening again if I were you."

Tarynton realized that she hadn't touched her food since the first bite. It no longer looked appetizing. Besides, Tamara had certainly given her a heaping helping of food for thought. But did she even dare to try and digest it? Was she being gullible in thinking this woman was the least bit sincere? Tarynton had to admit to herself that she didn't know what to think. Like Tamara said, only the passing of time would tell.

Tarynton folded her hands and placed them on the table. "I have one more question and I hope you will see fit to answer it for me. It's really an important one. Are you responsible for the letter that I received from Drakkar saying that he'd fallen in love with someone else—and that he intended to marry her?"

Tamara didn't so much as bat an eyelash. "Ah, the infamous letters! The same answer I gave to your other question applies to this one. But I have some good advice for you. Nothing I could ever have said or done would've kept you two apart. No one can foil destiny."

Whether it was intended or not, Tamara had admitted guilt regarding the letters. A person who had no knowledge of the letter would more than likely have asked questions about it. Drakkar hadn't told a soul about the letter he'd received from Tarynton, but Tamara had recently mentioned something about the letter to him. The fact that Tamara had called them the *infamous letters* was more than enough evidence of her guilt for Tarynton, especially since she'd only questioned her about one letter, not two.

Tamara summoned the waitress who immediately came to the table. "Check please."

"Can I have a separate check?" Tarynton asked. "I'm using a credit card."

Tamara smiled. "I've got it covered. I can't undo the damage I've caused, but I can pay the tab for lunch. Thanks for coming. Tell Drakkar hello for me. I wish you both the very best."

"Aren't you seeing him later for dinner?"

"I can see that you didn't talk to him before coming here. I had to cancel. Charles is flying in this evening. We're going to spend a couple of days hanging out in

L.A. I've got lots of friends here, crazy friends. The kind that'll do anything for a buck.''

Tarynton couldn't help wondering if there was a hidden message in that last statement. Had that been Tamara's way of telling her that she'd paid to have her car worked over? Knowing Tamara wasn't going to answer that question either kept Tarynton from asking it. She was beginning to see why Drakkar got so frustrated with her when she refused to answer a direct question. Tamara probably frustrated Charles in the same way. It suddenly dawned on Tarynton that the Charles Tamara was talking about might be Drakkar's old friend.

"Is the Charles you're talking about Drakkar's old college roommate?"

"That's a question I can answer without the fear of incriminating myself. They are one and the same. You better have an oxygen tank around when you tell Drakkar. But then again, he might not be a bit surprised. Drakkar has always known that Charles had a thing for me. But tell him not to worry about his old friend. The new Tamara who's now in therapy wouldn't think of hurting Charles. I've got to run now. Have a great life.''

Before Tarynton could get up from her seat, Tamara was back at the table.

"By the way, if you're wondering if I'm going to be upset because my sister is dating your brother, you shouldn't worry about that either. Tiara is a good woman. She'll be good for him and good to him.'' Tamara winked knowingly at Tarynton as she took off again.

Stretched out in her bed, lying perfectly still in Drakkar's arms, Tarynton hadn't quite come to grips with all the things that Tamara had said to her over lunch. While she hadn't outright admitted to any wrongdoing against Tarynton, Tamara had surely made certain implications. With Tamara having mentioned that her sister was dating Tarynton's brother, Tarynton was still having a hard time taking that one in. Tamara seemed to know so much about all of their lives. It seemed that she had eyes and ears all over the place. It also looked as if she kept herself abreast of her sister's comings and goings despite their estranged relationship.

Drakkar rolled up on his side and brought Tarynton's body flush with his own. "Why are you so quiet? You haven't had much to say all evening. Are you feeling okay physically?"

She kissed Drakkar's chin. "Physically, I'm fine. Emotionally, I can't seem to pull it together. I'm still quite unnerved over my lunch date with Tamara. I'm very concerned over what impact Tiara's involvement with Camden is going to have on our relationship. I can't imagine us all sitting down to dinner as a family knowing what I know about you and Tamara. Tiara is going to want her sister around should they reconcile. That's a difficult one to stomach."

"I know, baby. I share in your concern. But there are worse scenarios."

"What could be any worse than Camden marrying into a family of someone you used to be romantically involved with? Someone who has caused us so much turmoil."

"Us not being together at all is the worst-case scenario for me. Baby, I couldn't stand living separate from you again. My involvement with Tamara was the biggest mistake I've ever made—and it looks like I'm going to pay for it for some time to come. Now you're paying for it, too. Our future is in serious jeopardy if you don't think you can get past this. You're going to have to tell me what you want me to do because I don't know what can be done to ease your anguish. I certainly can't erase the past and neither do I want to carry it into our future. Tell me what you need from me, Tarynton."

"I need your love, Drakkar."

"You have all of that. But is my love going to be enough to get us through this?"

She ran the back of her hand across his cheek. "It's going to have to be, because I'm not giving you up. It may take time, but I know I can overcome this. It's not like Camden and Tiara are getting married tomorrow, if ever. We also live in different parts of the country. I don't know about Tiara, but Camden would certainly understand us not wanting to get together with them when Tamara is also expected to be there. We'll just have to make that clear from the start. However, if they do get married and have a big wedding, I won't have a choice in that instance. Nothing would keep me away from Camden's wedding. As for Tamara being with Charles, you've never said how you feel about that."

"That's because I don't feel anything. If Charles is as sappy around her as he was in college, she's going to walk all over him. But maybe he's grown some backbone by now. Any man involved with Tamara will have to possess a firm hand. But I think we've given more than too much time to the subject of Tamara Lyndon and her unpredictability. She has occupied way too much of our time since we've been back together. It's time for us to start concentrating on us and on our future. Think we can do that?"

"Yes, Mr. Lomax, we can do that. What would you like to concentrate on first?"

He grinned devilishly as his fingers began to unbutton her silk pajama top. "You'll soon have the answer to your question. Lie still while I whisper it all over your sweet body."

Drakkar's lust-filled voice went straight through her. As his lips whispered promising kisses onto her naked breast, she filled her hands with his hardened flesh. Using his teeth, he inched her pajama bottoms down her hips and over her legs. His warm hands roved her naked flesh until he felt her need for him increase greatly. Before she had a chance to cool down, he quickly sheathed himself in anticipation of things to come.

Once his hands took complete charge of her again, Tarynton's body melted under his heated caresses and passionate kisses. His tongue sought out hers over and over again, nearly driving her insane with the desire to have him deep inside her.

As his mouth slowly worked its way down to her core of inner secrets, her body throbbed with eager anticipation. As his warm, moist tongue finally united with the most sensitive area on her anatomy, her legs immediately spread apart in a most inviting way. Then her fingers entwined in his curly hair, tugging on it gently. It was all she could do to keep from screaming out for him to take her. His tongue continued to lather her up until she became a near babbling idiot. Just as she didn't think she could stand another minute of him being outside her, she felt his throbbing manhood thrust deeply into her inner core.

As he hovered above her, gently plunging in and out of her moist flower, she raised up to meet his sweetly torturing thrusts. His wildly gyrating body sang a sensuous love song to hers as it swept her into another realm. With nowhere to go but way up on high, she lay back and allowed him to navigate to their final destiny. Her body rocked from side to side beneath him, swaying wildly to the deeply moving rhythms of the sweet, tantalizing force of the provocative dance recital his manhood was staging inside her.

Unable to hold back another minute the release of his desire for completion, Drakkar made sure that he first brought her to the very edge of fulfillment. Then, with several deep, soul-stirring thrusts, he lifted her buttocks up and soared them both over the top.

After a safe landing back to earth, Drakkar continued to kiss Tarynton until she was breathless. Having her in his arms like this was what he'd lived for every day over the past six years. Believing that she could now handle the past, he dared to dream about the day when she would become his forever. Their time had finally come.

He smiled down at her. "What about a hot shower?"

"Make that a cold one and you've got yourself a shower partner."

He shivered in jest. "Sounds a little chilly to me. But if that's the only way for you to cool down, a cold shower it is."

"That's not the only way I can be cooled down, but I don't think I can handle another wildly passionate session like we just had. At least, not right now."

"I love your honesty. Let's hit the water, T.C."

In the bathroom, Drakkar turned on the cold water. Once Tarynton was installed under the brisk flow of clear liquid, he returned to the bedroom for a brief moment. Joining her in the shower, he immediately began to lather her sponge with foaming gel. As he scrubbed her back, she jumped when something sharp grazed her flesh.

She took the sponge from his hand. "There's something sharp in the sponge. It scratched my back. I hope it isn't a piece of glass." As she examined the sponge, she found the large piece of glass. Only it wasn't glass. It was a princess cut-diamond solitaire.

Her heart leaped into her mouth as tears filled her eyes. Before she could utter a word, he took possession of her mouth, kissing her until he ran out of breath. Not ready for this dreamlike moment to end, she recaptured his lips in another passionate kiss.

He gently pushed her hair back from her face. "Do you remember asking me to marry you at your parent's home?" She nodded. "My answer is sparkling right before your eyes. What do you think the answer to your question is?"

"Yes!" Screaming, she jumped up into his arms and wrapped her legs around his waist. "We're finally making good on our promise of long ago to only marry each other."

"A promise that will soon be fulfilled. I love you, Tarynton."

"And I love you more. Care to debate the issue?"

"Yeah, for the rest of our lives."

Only moments before, Tarynton hadn't thought she could withstand another passionate coupling with Drakkar. But she had been wrong. As she wantonly seduced him, she prayed that it would always be like this for them. In realizing she could never get enough of him, she was sure that she could now deal with anything that came their way. Nothing or no one was ever going to separate them again. Their love had always been for keeps and their hearts had reunited.

After all, this very moment was the rebirth of their one moment in time. . . .

It saddened Tarynton that she wouldn't be able to go home with Drakkar for Christmas. Her workload had doubled in the past two weeks and all of her spare time was committed to the Kwanzaa celebration. He had told her that he understood her plight, but she knew that he was bitterly disappointed. She should've thought it all through before she'd ever agreed to go home with him. But he had known that she had to be back in Los Angeles by the day after Christmas.

Even though the big celebration wasn't going to take

place until New Year's Eve, there were a lot of things that had yet to be accomplished. It looked as if the group was going to be busy up until the last second ticked off the clock. A couple of the other girls who had planned to go out of town had also put their Christmas holidays on hold.

Drakkar had been out of town for the last three days and he was due back this evening. She couldn't wait to see him. They had talked several times each day on the phone, but it wasn't the same as him being there with her. The phone rang and she hoped it was Drakkar calling. Although it wasn't her man, she wasn't disappointed when she heard Camden's voice.

"Hey, big brother! How's it going?"

"I have some great news!"

Her heart sank. She feared that he was going to tell her he was getting married. Being in the same family with Tamara still niggled at her even though she tried not to let it. She was only human, but that didn't mean she was going to let it interfere with her and Drakkar's happiness.

"Let's have it. I'm eagerly awaiting." She immediately felt guilty for lying.

"I'm going to be working in England for a year. This is an opportunity of a lifetime for me. I'll be working with quite a few prestigious names over there. It can only make me a better surgeon as I continue on in my neurosurgery residency."

"That is great news! I'm so happy for you. But how is Mom taking it? I know she's having a fit over her baby living in another country."

"Believe it or not, Mom is fine with it. Both she and Dad see it as a great opportunity. Of course, she's already making plans to visit me over there. Have you and Drakkar set a date yet?"

She chewed on her lower lip. "We haven't. He made

me promise that we'd get married before the year was out, but I don't think that's going to happen. In fact, he hasn't even brought it up again. But we both have been extremely busy since we were in Atlanta. My business is growing at an alarming rate and he's doing a lot of traveling. He's also trying to land a daytime news anchor position so he won't have to travel as much. He loves doing sports, but he thinks he can be happy working at the news desk. Drakkar has already survived the first interview cuts. When are you leaving for your new assignment?"

"Not until the end of January. I've got a lot of things to wrap up here in North Carolina before I can move on. Tell Drakkar I'm pulling for him. And you know that I'm pulling for you guys. You've always belonged together."

"Yeah, I know. What about Tiara? How's that going to work out with you in England?"

"You know, Tiara and I get along very well, but we're not into anything hot and heavy. I somehow feel that we'd be better off as best friends as opposed to lovers. She has lofty career goals as well. We're both too wrapped up in our perspective careers for us to get into anything serious. And I'm really not ready for an intense relationship. That's why I haven't pursued an exclusive relationship with Tiara. We're both very comfortable with things the way they are."

Tarynton breathed a huge sigh of relief, hating herself for doing so. But she was glad to know that her brother hadn't involved himself in a physical relationship with Tiara since he wasn't ready for that kind of a commitment. He was being responsible as well as being careful with Tiara's heart. If he wasn't ready to trust his own heart to anyone, he was playing it smart.

"I hear that you're not coming home for Christmas. I'm sure you know the folks are very disappointed, but they do understand. This will be the first Christmas spent without you. That's going to feel really weird."

"I know what you mean. But my plans with Drakkar have also changed. I'm not going to Pennsylvania with him for the holidays. I'm afraid I've bitten off more than I can chew, especially if I take any days off. I can't afford to get behind. And I can't abandon this project I've started with my good friends. Denise would have a fit if I walked out on this now."

In thinking of the mad crush he once had on Denise, he laughed softly. "How is Denise? Has she found what she's looking for in a man yet?"

"You know Denise, forever the bridesmaid but never the bride. Everyone is not cut out for marriage. I'm not sure she'll ever find Mr. Right. As one of the other girls said, Denise just may be Miss Wrong."

"Wow! That's a bad rap to put on her. You never knew that I had a crush on her, but I did go there for a short while."

"You've got to be kidding, Cam!"

"Why is that so hard to believe? Denise is a gorgeous woman."

"I didn't mean it like that. You just never seemed interested in any woman. I would never have guessed that you had the hots for Denise. Boy, I can't wait to tell her."

"You better not! Girl, Denise would never let me live that one down. It would only bring her sick pleasure to know that I had once been pining away for her. Don't betray me now."

"Why do I get the feeling that you actually want her to know about your feelings for her despite what you're saying? Could I be right?"

"Don't be silly, Tarynton. I'm not sophisticated enough for Denise. She seems to like worldly men. I'm a far cry from that description."

"Camden Batiste, you still have a serious crush on her, don't you? Go ahead and admit it. You can rest assured that your secret is safe with me."

"The only thing that I'm going to admit to you is that I have to run. I've got hospital rounds before I can call it a day. Love you, baby sister. Talk to you soon."

"I love you, too. Good-bye, Camden."

Tarynton was grinning like a Cheshire Cat as she hung up the phone. Camden having a crush on Denise was so adorable. What was even more endearing was his trying to hide it after admitting to it in the first place. What an unlikely couple but such an attractive pair would those two be, she thought. It wasn't something that was likely to happen, but she couldn't help smiling at the possibility, especially since Denise had told her on more than one occasion that she thought Camden was as sweet as he was handsome.

Eighteen

Tarynton couldn't have been unhappier than she was on this dreary Christmas Eve morning. Her spirits had been taking a downward spiral over the past couple of weeks. She had grown more discontent as the holidays grew closer and closer. Although she knew it was very selfish of her, she had hoped Drakkar would decide to change his plans of going to Pennsylvania for Christmas and stay home with her.

All through the entire week that it took them to completely decorate the house, to put up the Christmas tree, and then trim it, she thought he would announce his attention to stay at home with her. They'd even set up a Kwanzaa table complete with a *kinara* and *mishumaa saba*, the candleholder and seven candles. When the announcement didn't come, she began moping about the house with a long face. Drakkar ignoring her childish antics made her disappointment grow.

His plane had taken off about an hour ago. She had offered to go to the airport to drop him off, but he hadn't seemed eager to take her up on it. He'd stated that he wanted his car to be there when he got back. That had reminded of her the time she'd told him it would be better if his car was there upon his return, after he'd asked her to drop him off at the terminal and come back for him.

The doorbell startled her. Looking down at her frumpy flannel attire made her scowl. She looked like an old bag lady. As she viewed the visitor through the peephole, her heart nearly leaped from her chest. After practically ripping the locks away and throwing the door open, she threw herself in Camden's arms. "What are you doing here? I thought you were going to Atlanta."

He kissed her gently on the lips. "I couldn't let my baby sister spend Christmas alone. Every time I talked to you on the phone over the past week you sounded like you were about to cry. I thought I was going to have to pay through the nose for a last-minute flight, but I got a pretty good deal. But you're worth every penny I might've had to spend. Give your big brother another hug." He opened his arms wide to receive her once again.

"Gladly!" She went back into his arms and hugged him tightly.

He looked at what she was wearing. "Girl, you're looking rough. If your style of dress is any indication of your mood, your spirits must be lower than low. While I bring my bags in, why don't you go and change into something cute so we can go out to breakfast?"

"Do you need me to help you out, Cam?"

"No, Tarynton. I've only got two bags." He kissed the tip of her nose. "Scoot. This brother of yours is starving. These airlines and these skimpy meals have got to go."

Tarynton was beside herself with joy as she took the quickest shower she'd ever taken in her life. "Thank you, God," she cried happily. "Thank you for such a loving brother."

Then she thought of what her parents must be feeling. Guilt came in to spoil her joy. This family split at Christmas time had never happened before. It was only now that she realized that Camden had sacrificed a lot to be there with her. She was aware of how wimpy she'd been sounding over the past couple of weeks, but she hadn't realized the affect it was having on others. Well, she thought with rancor, it hadn't bothered Drakkar in the least. He had left her anyway, knowing she was going to be alone. She scolded herself on her thinking.

If she kept dwelling on his leaving, it was going to drive a needless wedge between them. She had known of his plans for the holidays just as he'd known of hers. There was really no one to blame in this situation. He wanted to be with his family as much as she did—and she had been with hers for Thanksgiving. She shouldn't begrudge him for wanting to have the same pleasure. They had fought hard to put so much behind them and it would do no good to let petty issues bring dissension into their bright future. They had a lifetime of holidays ahead of them.

Dressed in denim jeans and a beautiful pink cashmere sweater, she started up the hallway whistling a happy tune. Nothing could have prepared her for what she saw as she practically skipped into the living room. Seated on the sofa were Pamela and Steven Batiste. Burning tears came to Tarynton's eyes and then excited screams and joyous laughter filled the air.

Wiping the tears from her eyes, she dropped down between her parents on the sofa. "Oh, gosh, I can't believe you guys are really here. Camden, you arranged this, didn't you? I can never repay you for this. I am so excited I could cry all day." Camden only chuckled.

Steven ruffled his daughter's hair. "Please don't do

that. We didn't come all the way here to make you cry. We're here to cheer you up."

Camden sat down in the chair opposite the sofa. "Mom couldn't stand the thought of you being here all alone after you told her Drakkar was going home and you couldn't go. After tossing it around for a couple of days, we decided to join in this special surprise for you."

Pamela hugged her daughter. "Christmas wouldn't have been the same without you, Tarynton. We were glad to come. I hate to fly, but your happiness always comes first with me."

"Thanks, Mom." Aunt Cleo came to Tarynton's mind. "Aunt Cleo must be upset since she always spends every single holiday with us."

Steven and Camden roared with laughter. Their reaction puzzled Tarynton. Laughter wasn't something she expected from them in considering that her aunt was home alone.

Pamela put her arm around her daughter's shoulders. "Honey, let me tell you the unbelievable news about your Aunt Cleo. Excuse my English, but my baby sister done gone out and found herself a living, breathing man, a real good man. So don't go worrying about her 'cause she's not spending a single moment thinking about us. We asked her about coming here, but she's not going anywhere without Mr. Jeremy Foster, her retired engineer. But she did say that if she could get him to come out here with her, she might be along a little later. Don't count on it."

"What? Aunt Cleo's in a real relationship? Tell me all about it."

"In the car," Camden piped in. "I wasn't kidding about being hungry even though I used it as an excuse to get you out of the room. I'm ready for a silver dollar stack at IHOP."

"Let's go," Tarynton said. "I'm so excited but never too wound up to eat. I'll drive, Camden, so you can start to unwind."

"Good! Coming here from the airport was enough L.A. driving for me. These drivers out here . . ." Camden's cell phone ringing kept him from finishing his statement.

Tarynton had a pretty good idea of what he was going to say. Everyone made crude remarks about L.A. drivers, including her.

Everyone was seated in the car, but Camden was still outside talking on the phone. When he knocked on the window, Tarynton rolled it down. "What IHOP are we going to?"

"Right around the corner, Cam. Why are you asking?"

"One of my old buddies is going to meet us there." Tarynton then gave Camden the exact cross streets where the restaurant was located. Camden relayed the information to his friend as he jumped into the front seat.

The moment Tarynton parked in front of the restaurant everyone filed out of the car. Much to her dismay there was going to be a wait for seating, but not a very long one. Tarynton gave her last name and the number in her party.

"Make the Batiste seating for three more," said a muffled voice behind Tarynton.

Thinking the deep voice belonged to Camden's expected friend, Tarynton turned around to take a look since she had forgotten to ask for an extra seat for him. For the second time in one morning, her heart leaped into her mouth. Since they were in a public place, she muffled her screams, but nothing could've kept her from flying into Drakkar's arms. Then she spotted his parents. Despite where they were Tarynton could no longer hold back the loud screeches of pure excitement fighting to escape her throat. This latest surprise had stolen away her self-control.

For the next several minutes joyous greetings were exchanged between the two families. Tarynton was the only family member that hadn't been clued in on the plans. Drakkar had begun to arrange the entire holiday family reunion once he'd learned that Tarynton couldn't get away. Camden apologized to Tarynton for being less than forthright about the arrangements, but he couldn't blow Drakkar's special surprise for her. She more than understood.

In less than ten minutes the hostess was directing the Batiste and Lomax clans to the large corner table set for seven.

As Drakkar and Tarynton walked hand in hand toward the table, she stopped abruptly and turned to face him. "I feel so guilty over my behavior during the last couple of days. I've been rather miffed at you for leaving me alone for the holidays. But I made a conscious decision to come to terms with it just a couple of hours ago. I realized I was being selfish. Now I know just how selfish. This is such a selfless act on your part. Thank you for the most wonderful Christmas present a girl could ever hope for. I should've known that you wouldn't fail me. You haven't failed me yet. May I kiss your sweet lips?"

He took her in his arms. "My lips are all yours, baby."

Standing on her tiptoes, Tarynton kissed Drakkar deeply and passionately. When all the members of the two families clapped loudly, only then did Tarynton and Drakkar pull apart. The blush in her cheeks was refreshing to Drakkar. Seeing that she was still as fresh as the first rose to bloom in spring made him very proud that she belonged to him.

Drakkar pulled out a chair for Tarynton before seating himself. Leaning into her, he brought his mouth close to her ear. "Have you already shown off your engagement ring?"

She shook her head. "I haven't done so yet, but I'm glad that I didn't. Having you here with me will give the moment even more meaning." She stood up. "Can I have everyone's attention for a minute?" The others looked up at her. "You all know that Drakkar and I are engaged to be married, but you haven't seen my beautiful ring yet." She held up her hand for everyone to see the fireworks bursting into fiery flames of sparking light on her finger. "Isn't it exquisite? I won't tell you how he presented it to me until after we're married."

"Uh-oh," Camden shouted. "Must be X-rated."

Tarynton winked at her brother. "How you'd guess?" Before sitting back down, she gave Drakkar another passionate kiss. The clapping started up all over again.

As her tea-brown eyes twinkled with love, Lace Lomax smiled at her future daughter-in-law. Lace was a fabulous-looking woman with wrinkle-free cocoa-brown skin. It was her beautiful smile that was her best feature. It could brighten the darkest room. Compared to her tall, burly husband, whose sienna skin and golden-brown eyes were the same colors as Drakkar's, Lace was a mere slip of a woman.

Tarynton couldn't help noticing how Eddington Lomax still looked so mesmerized by his wife after all their years together. It was the same kind of look that Steven always had in his eyes when he gazed at Pamela. Marriage suited them all, very well.

"Tarynton, when Drakkar called to ask us to come here for his wedding, we nearly flipped out. But when we found out that it was you he was going to marry, we did flip our lids. We couldn't be any happier than we are about your reunion. We've always loved you, sweetheart.

Welcome home to the family. Jordan and Ellison send you their love."

Tarynton looked as if a bolt of lightning had just hit her. Had Lace said Drakkar asked them to come to his wedding? While fighting off her inner turmoil, she smiled back at Lace. "Thank you for your kind, loving words. I'm thrilled to be back home where I belong, which has always been in Drakkar's arms, Momma Lomax. I'm so thrilled to see all of you."

Drakkar draped his arm around Tarynton's chair. "Mom, since you let the cat out of the bag, and I can see that it's affecting my lady love, I need to go ahead and clue Tarynton in right now as opposed to when we're alone later. Tarynton, I asked our families to be here because I want us to get married on New Year's Eve. It is my heart's desire that we be pronounced man and wife right on the dot of the magical hour of midnight. Is that something I can coax you into? Before you answer, remember that you promised to marry me before the year was out."

Tears fringed her lashes. "I never renege on a promise. It would be a blessing and an honor to become your wife on New Year's Eve. Midnight it is!"

Drakkar kissed his bride-to-be passionately and with longing as the others looked on with reverence and joy in their hearts. Once they came up for air, the happy couple's faces were beaming with the look of love. Even Tarynton's tears appeared to dance joyously down her face.

Tarynton lazed her finger down Drakkar's cheek. "I'm assuming that you've worked out all the details—and that all I have to do is show up for the wedding. Is that right?"

He nodded. "Your girl, Denise, helped me pulled it all together. The wedding will be in the same place as the Kwanzaa celebration. Pastor Lemoyne will preside over the nuptials. If he sticks to the time schedule, on the hour of midnight we'll become husband and wife. Camden has agreed to stand in for me since neither of my brothers could be here. Denise seems to think she owns the spot as your maid of honor, but she is waiting until you ask her just in case you want to choose one of the other four girls."

Tarynton smiled mischievously at Camden.

"I don't think we can find two better friends than Camden and Denise to stand in for us," Tarynton said. "They'll make a beautiful best man and maid of honor, not to mention a striking couple."

Camden's eyes warned Tarynton not to go there, but he couldn't help smiling.

Breakfast was consumed with the two families chatting happily while catching up with the things they'd missed out on over the years. Christmas cards had been exchanged the first few years after the Batistes moved, but it seemed that after Tarynton and Drakkar had broken their relationship off so had the communication between the two families.

With a warm fire crackling in the fireplace, the Batiste and Lomax families were comfortably seated in Tarynton's family room. Both Pamela and Lace had brought along with them numerous pictures that they'd taken of Drakkar and Tarynton during their different stages of growth. Much laughter was had at Tarynton and Drakkar's expense over some of the more embarrassing pictures, like the nude ones that most mothers loved to take of their babies.

While both sets of parents went into the kitchen to prepare some snack items for Tarynton's friends who were stopping by later, Camden went out to Tarynton's office to check his e-mail account. With everyone gone from the room, Drakkar and Tarynton stretched out on the carpeted floor in front of the fireplace.

Tarynton took Drakkar's hand. "This is the perfect Christmas Eve. I owe it all to you."

"Thanks for the sentiment, baby, but you don't owe me anything. I'm so happy with how things are going for us. In eight days you'll be my wife. Speaking of perfect, our wedding is going to be the most blissful event we've ever shared in." He kissed her gently on the mouth.

"Can't wait for that main event! Do you remember the Christmas you gave me two engraved pencils with the logos of the Steelers and the Eagles?"

He laughed. "I can't believe you remember that silly little gift. We weren't even in junior high school yet. What age were we, about twelve?"

"Eleven. We were both in the sixth grade. And the gift wasn't silly. I still have them—and they've never been sharpened."

He looked stunned. "You do?" She nodded. "It's amazing that you kept them all these years. But I also kept several of the things you gave me. I still have the mini football with the name of our high school on it. Then there's your graduation picture, the one I had blown up to poster size. The most important of the items I kept is your white gold senior class ring with the garnet setting. Do you still have mine?"

"Oh, my gosh! This is unbelievable. I must admit that I've never given any thought to my class ring for several years now, but I wore yours around my neck on a gold chain up until about a year ago. When I finally decided to take it off, I locked it away in the hidden drawer in my jewelry box. That means I still have it. Aren't you the lucky one?"

He kissed the tip of her nose. "If you ask me, we're both more than lucky. We've been greatly blessed by the Creator. Luck can't make these kinds of miracles happen, sunshine."

"I agree wholeheartedly. You and I are also His miracles."

Camden strolled into the room. "What time are your girlfriends coming over, Tarynton?"

"Girlfriends or Denise?"

"There you go again, Tarynton. Sounds like you're trying to play matchmaker. I am so not interested in having you embarrass me in front of your girlfriends, especially Denise. Are you feeling me, baby sister?"

Tarynton appeared surprised. "I'd never embarrass you in front of anyone, Cam. I love you. I have been laying the teasing on kind of thick. You trusted me with a confidence and I've been rubbing your nose it. I'm sorry. Can you forgive me?"

He grinned. "Only 'cause it's Christmas, the season of charitable spirits. Just give me a break about Denise. Okay?"

"Okay, I promise." Tarynton paused a minute. "There's the doorbell now. Since we're not expecting anyone else, it must be the girls. Camden, would you mind getting the door?"

"Not a problem. Just remember to keep your promise." Camden didn't wait for a response from his sister since she was good at keeping her word.

Deciding that she wanted to see Denise's reaction when Camden opened the door, Tarynton got up from the floor and quickly followed after her brother. She reached him just as he flung the door open. Tarynton was not disappointed when she saw the look on Denise's face as Camden embraced her as if she were a long-lost friend. The girl was blushing all over the place but Camden was as cool as a cucumber. The other four girls were meeting Camden for the first time and the expressions on their faces were as priceless as the one on Denise's.

Tarynton stepped forward and hugged each of her friends before formally introducing them to her handsome brother. Once the introductions were made Tarynton led the way into the family room where her parents, Drakkar, and his parents awaited the arriving guests. Tarynton once again did the introductions. It wasn't long before a level of easy comfort was attained by all of Tarynton's friends and family members as they enjoyed the snacks that had been prepared.

Tarynton had to take a quiet moment for herself to thank God for the mountain of blessings she'd received in just this one day, the day before the birth of His only begotten Son. Christmas Day, a holy day of reverence, glory to God in the highest.

The two families had observed Christmas Day in an extremely quiet manner. No expensive gifts were exchanged; only tokens of love and affection had been handed out. In the eyes of each family member, being together was more than anyone could've asked for. It seemed that the parents were preserving their energy for the biggest event that was yet to come, the much-anticipated wedding day between their two children. On the day after Christmas, Tarynton, Drakkar, and their families began the first day of the Kwanzaa celebration by lighting the first candle, the black one, which symbolized that the people come first. It was most appropriate for the two families to light them together since *umoja* stressed the importance of togetherness for family and community, reflecting the African saying; "I am We," or "I am because We are."

The past four days had been a whirlwind of activity in getting ready for the triple celebration on New Year's

Eve. Drakkar and Tarynton saw very little of each other
during the hours of daylight, but the two families came
together in the evenings to dine and also light the candle
in observance of that particular day's Kwanzaa principle.

Much to Tarynton's surprise, since she'd been led
astray as to whether her aunt would come to L.A. or
not, Aunt Cleo and her new beau arrived on Tarynton's
doorstep three days after Christmas. Aunt Cleo made it
very clear that she and Jeremy Foster had booked a
hotel near the airport and that they couldn't be swayed
to stay elsewhere. She also made it a point to let her
family know that she had requested a separate room.

Unable to believe the indescribable beauty they'd created in the garden room of a local community center,
Tarynton and her five girlfriends stood in the center of
the room with their mouths agape. The decorated
theme tables were absolutely gorgeous even without the
place settings. Professional decorators couldn't have
done a better job.

Although each one was absolutely exquisite, Tarynton
was especially proud of the golden anniversary table
she'd created with her own two hands. All she had to
add to it was the china she'd bought long ago in anticipation of her own wedding. The tables wouldn't be set
until the next morning, the day of the three important
events. Her wedding day, the most important event of
all for Tarynton, would take place just a short time
before the midnight hour.

The various symbols of Kwanzaa dominated another
spacious room of the community center. The huge
space was exquisitely decorated in the symbolic colors
of red, black, and green. The decorations included loads
of balloons and streamers. The cloths draped on the
dining tables had been fashioned from various African

prints. Beautiful donated works of African art and magnificent black sculptures were very much a part of the character of the room.

Roxanne inhaled a deep breath as she took in the beauty of the room. "Everything looks awesome. We should be proud of ourselves."

"Yeah, we have really put our heads together on this one," Rayna chimed on.

Narita waved her hand in the air. "Don't leave out the Tabahani Book Circle. None of this would've been possible without them. Those sisters came together for us in a big way. Just like all of their other events, this one will also be a golden memory."

Chariese clapped her hands. "Everyone involved in this effort deserves a round of applause. And we must pay tribute to the Tabahani Book Circle with a standing ovation after each club member is introduced. We must show our appreciation for all of their hard work."

Denise took a bow. "As a member of the book circle, I think that's a magnificent idea. There's no gesture that would be more appropriate than that. With that said, let's get started on the last-minute chores."

Denise put her arm around Tarynton and pulled her off to the side. "How are you dealing with all the surprises Drakkar has laid on you? The man has certainly taken control of things."

Tarynton's smile was dazzling. "I've loved every single one of them. He has always been a take-charge kind of a man. Drakkar really outdid himself this time. He had mentioned to me in Atlanta about getting married before the year was out, but since he hadn't brought it up again, I figured he'd changed his mind. I'm still amazed at how well he's pulled everything together in such a short amount of time. With your help, of course. Thanks for lending him your most capable hands."

Denise's mood grew somber. "What about that witch

of a woman? Do you really think everything is settled with her?''

"I'm inclined to believe that. We haven't heard a single peep from her since I had lunch with her. I still cry every time I think about the letters that kept Drakkar and me apart all these years. Although she wouldn't outright admit that she wrote them, both Drakkar and I believe that there's no one else that could have done it.''

"What makes you both believe that she's guilty of the letters?''

"The proof was in the fact that he never told her about receiving the Dear John letter period—and the fact that she knew there were two letters. That was something that neither Drakkar nor I was aware of until we discovered it in Atlanta. Maybe she'll find what she's been looking for in Charles since they go way back. Love is miraculous in changing people and circumstances. Drakkar and I wish her nothing but the best. There was a time when I didn't think that there was an ounce of redemption in her, but I'm still hoping that I was wrong. As usual, only the passing of time will tell.''

"About her twin sister? Is Camden heavily involved with her?''

"Why do you ask?''

Denise shrugged with nonchalance. "Just wondering. No particular reason.''

"According to him, they're not heavily involved. Besides, he's going to continue his residency in England for a year. At any rate, I don't think she's *the* one, if you know what I mean. Camden doesn't see wedding bells in their future.''

Denise nodded. "Got you. And what a relief that must be for you under the awkward circumstances. A trip to England in the very near future might be just what I need to get by." Wearing a knowing smile, Denise winked at Tarynton, nudging her playfully.

Tarynton raised an eyebrow. "Are we about to forsake Wilson?"

"Unfortunately he's not *the* one either. It's fortunate for me that I've arrived at the conclusion a lot sooner than I did with the others. I'm just glad that the revelation didn't come before we got the band to play for free." Both women laughed. "We'd better finish up what we came here to do, Tarynton, so we can move on into other things. I've never been in a wedding where there's been no rehearsal, but Drakkar insisted that he wants the ceremony to be spontaneous. That man is something special. And so is the sexy doctor that you have for a brother!"

In thinking of the two men she loved, Tarynton beamed from head to toe. "Oh, yeah, they're certainly that! And in less than twenty-four hours, the one that's not my brother will be all mine, physically, spiritually, and officially. Mr. and Mrs. Drakkar Lomax! What a perfect uniting of two hearts during a perfect time of celebration."

Tarynton had a hard time concentrating on the Kwanzaa program conducted by the members of the Tabahani Book Circle. As the president of the club gave the *kukaribsha*, the welcoming, including the recognition of distinguished guests and all elders, Tarynton had a hard time keeping her mind from straying to the later event, her wedding. Seated next to her, Drakkar held on to her hand, squeezing it gently when it appeared to him that her mind was drifting. But Tarynton listened intently to the brief lecture delivered by an African world-renowned female doctor. The dynamic speaker had captured her attention with ease.

Kukumbuka, candle-lighting ceremony, came right after the short lecture. Six of the candles were lit as the guests recited the importance that the principle had for them.

The *kuumba,* remembering, came next. Tarynton was all ears during the *kuchunguza tena na kuto ahadi,* reassessment and recommitment, similar to New Year's resolutions. Once recommitted, the *kushangilia,* rejoicing, began, followed by cultural expressions delivered through song, poetry, and dance.

Last but not least, *tamshi la tambiko,* libation statement, was realized. Recited like a prayer, the libation statement embodied the past, the present, and the future. Water, as it holds the essence of life, was placed in the unity cup and poured in the direction of the four winds: north, south, east, and west. The cup was then passed among the guests for them either to sip from or to make a sipping gesture. A small amount of liquid spilled on the floor to honor the dead marked the end.

Drakkar made a sipping gesture, then held the cup up to Tarynton's lips for her to do the same. Tarynton noticed that there were very few dry eyes in the room during *kutoa majina,* calling of the names of family ancestors and African-American heroes. The drum sounded once the last name was called. It was now time for the *karamu* feast to begin. Once the feast was over, *tamshi la tutaonana,* farewell statement, would be given. It was then customary for everyone to shout *"Harambee"* seven times to signal the end of the feast.

In order to prepare themselves for the later event, Tarynton, Drakkar, and other members of the wedding party slipped away from the Kwanzaa celebration the moment it was over.

* * *

At exactly eleven-fifteen on this thirty-first day of December, Tarynton Cameron Batiste flowed with angelic grace down the center of the aisles of tables and chairs on the arm of her handsome father, Steven Batiste, who was elegantly dressed in a dark suit, complemented by a tie and handkerchief designed from Kinte cloth.

Dressed in the stunning custom-designed African-print gown in deep royal colors of purple, red, and blue, Tarynton looked as proud as any African queen on her wedding day. Wrapped around her head to cover all of her hair, the striking headdress she wore matched the print of her dress.

Waiting for her at the bottom of the dais, Drakkar looked every bit the part of an African king and a strong warrior. Wearing his royal robes with pride, fashioned from the same material as his bride's attire, he was an extremely handsome groom. It was the glowing smile on his face that showed how very proud he was to be marrying the woman floating toward him.

Admiring the gentle beauty of the woman they both loved dearly, Denise and Camden stood on each side of Drakkar. Ellison and Jordan, Drakkar's brothers, had surprised him by showing up at his apartment only minutes after he'd arrived home from the first event. Although Camden was acting as his best man, Drakkar insisted that his brothers also stand with him on the most important day of his life, one of those spontaneous moments he'd spoken of.

The parents of the bride and the groom were seated at the wedding theme table along with Aunt Cleo and Jeremy Foster. Beaming with pride for their dear girlfriend, Narita, Rayna, Chariese, and Roxanne were seated at the New Year's theme table.

The distinguished-looking minister, Arthur Lemoyne, came to the podium. ''We are gathered together to join this man, Drakkar Lomax, and this woman, Tarynton Batiste, in holy matrimony. It is the desire of this couple to recommit themselves to each other and to the sanctity of marriage by using the seven principles of Kwanzaa as a basis for uniting their two hearts. A candle shall be lit in affirming each of their vows. You will now hear from the bride and the groom." Nodding, Pastor Lemoyne looked down on the couple from the podium.

Hand in hand, Drakkar and Tarynton walked the few steps to the table that the *kinara* had been placed upon. The couple then turned to face each other.

Drakkar took both of Tarynton's hands. "*Umoja* stresses the importance of togetherness for the family in the community. As your husband, I vow to honor this principle in standing steadfast by my family and our community." Together, they turned to the *kinara* and lit the first of seven candles.

Tarynton smiled brilliantly at Drakkar. "In honoring *kujichagulia,* I promise to always come together with you in defining our common interests and in making decisions that will best serve the interest of our family and community." The second candle was lit.

"*Ujima* reminds us of our obligation to the past, present, and future. As we enter into this obligation as a couple, I vow to take seriously my role in this marriage, as well as in the community, society, and world," Tarynton voiced softly. Their eyes locked in a warm embrace as the third candle was ignited.

"*Ujamaa* speaks of cooperative economics emphasizing our economic strength. As you are my soul mate and I am yours, I promise to give you mutual support in order to meet our common needs," Drakkar stated.

"In fulfilling *nia,* I promise to always look inside myself and to set personal goals that are beneficial to both us and the community."

"While using *kuumba* to build and maintain a strong

and vibrant community, I vow to use that same creativity to ensure that we maintain a strong and vibrant marriage," Drakkar promised.

"In keeping with *imani*, we promise to honor our marriage, draw upon the best in ourselves, and strive for a higher level of life for humankind. As marriage partners, we vow to always affirm our self-worth and assurance in our ability to succeed and triumph in virtuous struggle," Tarynton and Drakkar said in unison. After lighting the seventh and final candle, they turned their attention back to the minister.

"By the powers vested in me by the state of California, I hereby pronounce you man and wife. What God has joined together let no man put asunder. You may now kiss the bride!"

Just as the hand on the clock struck midnight, Tarynton's and Drakkar's lips came together in an earth-shattering kiss. While locked in a loving embrace, engulfed in their most precious one moment in time, melodious bells rang in the New Year. "Congratulations," "Happy New Year," and "Happy Kwanzaa" rang out from all around the room.

Their hearts rejoiced as Drakkar danced Tarynton around the room to soft music. "I'm glad I found you, Tarynton, happy we found love again in each other's arms. I promise to cherish you always. Happy New Year, Mrs. Lomax."

Satisfied with the magnificent outcome of their reunion, Tarynton now had the perfect ending for her novel, the fairy-tale finale that she had desired for most of her life.

"Happy Kwanzaa, my darling husband!"

Dear Readers,

I sincerely hope that you enjoyed reading *One Moment in Time* from cover to cover. I'm interested in hearing your comments and thoughts on the story of Tarynton Batiste and her love interest, Drakkar Lomax.

Please enclose a self-addressed, stamped envelope (SASE) with all your correspondence.

Please mail correspondence to:

Linda Hudson-Smith
2026C North Riverside Avenue
Box 109
Rialto, CA 92377

You can e-mail your comments to *LHS4romance@yahoo.com*

Web site http://www.lindahudsonsmith.com

ABOUT THE AUTHOR

Born in Canonsburg, Pennsylvania, and raised in the town of Washington, Pennsylvania, Linda Hudson-Smith has traveled the world as an enthusiastic witness to other cultures and lifestyles. Her husband's military career gave her the opportunity to live in Japan, Germany, and many cities across the United States. Hudson-Smith's extensive travel experience helps her craft stories set in a variety of beautiful and romantic locations. It was after illness forced her to leave a marketing and public relations administration career that she turned to writing.

Romance in Color chose her as Rising Star for the month of January 2000. *Ice Under Fire,* her debut Arabesque novel, has received rave reviews. Voted as Best New Author, A.A.O.W.G. presented Linda with the 2000 Gold Pen Award. Linda has also won two Shades of Romance awards in the category of Multi-Cultural New Romance Author of the Year and Multi-Cultural New Fiction Author of the Year 2001. *Soulful Serenade,* released August 2000, was selected by Romance In Color readers as the Best Cover for August 2000. She was also nominated as the Best New Romance Author, Romance Slam Jam 2001. Linda's novel covers have been featured in such major publications as *Publisher's Weekly, USA Today,* and *Essence Magazine.*

Linda Hudson-Smith is a member of Romance Writers of America and the Black Writer's Alliance. Though novel writing remains her first love, she is currently cultivating her screenwriting skills. She has also been contracted to pen several other novels for BET.

Dedicated to inspiring readers to overcome adversity against all odds, Hudson-Smith has accepted the challenge of becoming National Spokesperson for the Lupus Foundation of America. In making lupus awareness one of her top priorities, Linda travels around the country delivering inspirational messages of hope. She is also a supporter of the NAACP and the American Cancer Society. She enjoys poetry, entertaining, traveling, and attending sports events. The mother of two sons, Linda and her husband share residences in both California and Texas.

Linda Hudson-Smith
2026C North Riverside Avenue
Box 109
Rialto, CA 92377

Arabesque Romances
by *Roberta Gayle*